THE FAMILY BUSINESS

THE FAMILY BUSINESS

★

MIKE KUPARI

THE FAMILY BUSINESS

A Baen Books Original

Baen Publishing Enterprises
P.O. Box 1403
Riverdale, NY 10471
www.baen.com

ISBN: 978-1-9821-2502-8

Cover art by Sam R. Kennedy

First printing, July 2021

Distributed by Simon & Schuster
1230 Avenue of the Americas
New York, NY 10020

Library of Congress Cataloging-in-Publication Data:

Names: Kupari, Mike, author.
Title: The family business / by Mike Kupari.
Description: Riverdale, NY : Baen Books, [2021]
Identifiers: LCCN 2021016574 | ISBN 9781982125028 (trade paperback)
Classification: LCC PS3611.U6 F36 2021 | DDC 813/.6--dc23
LC record available at https://lccn.loc.gov/2021016574

Printed in the United States of America

10 9 8 7 6 5 4 3 2 1

This book is dedicated to Luna,
gone but not forgotten, and to good dogs everywhere.
They are truly man's best friend.

Las Vegas, Nevada

VEGAS, NATHAN FOSTER THOUGHT, taking in his surroundings. *What a town.* While still a far cry from the gleaming, expensive tourist trap it was before the war, Sin City had emerged from the conflict relatively unscathed. It was grittier and dirtier than it used to be, and there were several neighborhoods where the police only patrolled in pairs. As the postwar reconstruction efforts progressed, though, people increasingly had money to spend, and an entire city dedicated to gambling, booze, and sex was too lucrative of an idea to stay dormant.

The place was called The Desert Flower Cabaret, and it was nicer than he had expected it to be. Part bar and nightclub with a burlesque show, the Cabaret was raucous and crowded. An eclectic mix of rock and country music blasted over the sound system throughout the night. Armed bouncers watched the crowd like hawks, and everyone who came in was swept with a metal detector. Nathan had talked to management ahead of time, though, and had been allowed to bypass the door guards. He was armed with his Undercover Special, a hefty little five-shot, snub-nose .41 Magnum.

"Hey there, handsome."

He stopped scanning the crowd and looked up at the woman who had sauntered over, smiling at her as she sat next to him. "Roxanne."

"No luck so far?" Roxanne asked, crossing her legs as she settled next to him on the couch. Her brown curls hung tantalizingly over bare shoulders. She adjusted the red and black corset she wore so as to make her breasts look a little perkier. She caught Nathan looking and smiled. "It gets me better tips," she explained, without a hint of apology.

Nathan chuckled and took a sip of water. Between the smoke and the naturally dry air of Las Vegas, he was parched. "A club full of strippers and working girls, and guys still hit on the bartender. Men can be idiots sometimes."

"Men are idiots *all* the time, hon," Roxanne said. She had to have been in her forties, but she took care of herself and it showed. "They want what they can't have."

"You think he'll show tonight?" This was the third night in a row Nathan had been haunting this place, waiting for his mark to show up, and in spite of all the half-naked women he was getting tired of it.

"Oh, I think so," Roxanne said. "Destiny is singing tonight. He always comes around when she's on."

"Strippers, prostitutes, alcohol, singers . . . y'all have quite the variety show, I'll give you that."

"Lois didn't want to run some sleazy dive," Roxanne said. Lois was the owner of the Cabaret. "She told me she wanted it to be a modern old-west burlesque saloon, where anyone can have a good time no matter what they're into. If you're here tomorrow, it's karaoke night. That's always fun."

Listening to drunk people try to sing didn't sound fun to Nathan. "I gotta admit, I've been in a lot of strip clubs, dive bars, and whore houses in this line of work, and this is probably the nicest one I've seen." He sipped his water again and watched as a pair of gorgeous Mexican girls, twins he thought, spun gracefully around brass poles in perfect synchronization. They wore nothing but smiles and skyscraper heels.

He stopped talking as a voice came over his earbud. It was his nephew, Ben. "Uncle Nate," the boy said, excitedly, his voice cracking just a bit, "he's here!" Ben was out in the parking lot, in the truck, doing surveillance. Nathan didn't think he was the best guardian a kid could have, but even he had reservations about taking a fourteen-year-old into a titty bar.

"What's wrong?" Roxanne asked.

Nathan held up one finger while pressing the bud into his ear with the other. It was hard to hear over the background noise. "Are you sure?"

"Positive. The Identifier is ninety-plus percent confident." The Identifier was a godsend in Nathan's line of work: a combination camera and night-vision device with telescopic optical zoom and built-in facial recognition software. It had the bulk of an old analog camcorder but it worked well.

"What's he wearing?"

"Black long-sleeve shirt and blue jeans. He's a little fatter than in the file picture. Still bald."

"Got it. Good work, boy. Stay in the truck and monitor the radio." He looked up at Roxanne. "He's here."

The bartender quickly stood up. "I'll go tell Destiny."

"You sure she's good with this?"

"Oh yeah. Her parents died during the occupation of California. She's happy to help."

Nathan nodded. "Alright, then. Let's do this."

The twins cleared the main stage and the background music quieted in preparation for the evening's live music. Heavy velvet curtains drew closed as the stage crew set things up. After a few minutes, the DJ announced the next act. "Ladies and gentlemen, please put your hands together for Destiny!" Men in the crowd clapped, cheered, and wolf-whistled as the curtains drew back. A gorgeous young woman slinked into the spotlight, stopping in front of the microphone. Nathan could see why his target was so enamored with her: she was *beautiful*, tall and curvy, with long legs and ebony skin. The little red dress she wore was short, tight, and low-cut. Her singing voice was a sexy, dusky contralto, the kind that could get a man wrapped around her little finger.

She started to sing. "Been a fool, been a clown, lost my way from up and down, and I know . . . yes, I know."

Nathan spotted the man he was looking for, then. Heavyset, bald, black shirt and jeans, just like Ben had said. A table had been left open, right in front of the stage, and the mark found his way to it.

Destiny made eye contact with the man and serenaded him as she sang. Her singing was sultry and seductive, so much so that even the rowdy assholes in the crowd had stopped whistling to listen to her beautiful voice. "Don't care . . . for me. Don't cry, let's say goodbye, Adieu . . ."

Nathan watched the back of his target's head, silhouetted against the light on the stage. His name was Carter Reid, and the bounty on him was fifty thousand dollars. He looked like just another regular person, but Carter had been a very bad boy during the war. During the aliens' occupation of the West Coast, Mr. Reid had been an overseer of one of their detention and indoctrination camps for defiant humans, and he'd gone to ground when the Army retook California. Maybe he figured that after eight years it would be assumed that he was dead, and he could show his face again.

He was wrong about that.

Destiny reached the song's climax. She was looking directly at the target still, singing to him. "Lost in a memory . . . I seeeee . . . your faaaaace . . . aaaaaand smile." When she was done, the audience erupted into cheers and applause. Carter Reid stood up and clapped. The singer, smiling, thanked the crowd and disappeared backstage as the curtains closed. The background music started back up, and the DJ announced that shots were half price for the next hour.

One of the waitresses approached Carter Reid then. She bent down and said something in his ear. After a little back-and-forth, he stood up and followed as the waitress led him away. This was Nathan's cue. Moving quickly, he met Roxanne by the far wall of the club, next to a door marked EMPLOYEES ONLY. She opened it and let him in. He keyed the tiny transmit button for his radio, and pressed his earbud in with two fingers. "Ben, we're on. Bring the truck around to the back, get Shadow ready, and be waiting outside. There's a back door that I'll be bringing him out through."

"Roger!" the boy said, excitedly.

Nathan looked at Roxanne as she led him past dressing rooms and maintenance closets. "He'll be waiting out back for us." The club owner wanted everything done discretely, so as not to scare off her clientele. The plan was to roll up Carter Reid inside one of the private rooms and frog-march his traitor ass out the back, and nobody would be the wiser.

"This way," the bartender said, quietly unlocking another door. Through it was a small washroom, but she left the lights off. Inside was a door to another room. "That's the VIP lounge," she whispered. "Destiny is in there."

Nathan nodded, and with a jerk of his head told Roxanne to clear out. She very quietly closed the door, leaving him alone in the darkened washroom. There was enough residual noise from the club that there was little chance the target would hear him, but he was quiet nonetheless. He crept up to the door. It was one of those thin, hollow-core ones they use on cheap houses. He could hear Carter Reid and the singer talking through it.

"I've seen you every time I sing," Destiny purred. "I love a dedicated fan." She was laying it on thick.

Carter was taking the bait. "I just love listening to you sing. It helps me forget the world, forget everything."

"All of us want to forget something," Destiny said. "Would you mind pouring me a drink? Vodka, neat. I'm going to go wash up and maybe slip into something a bit more comfortable, if you don't mind."

"Not at all!" Carter said, in that unmistakable, excited tone of a man who was sure he was about to get laid. "It'll be waiting for you when you come back."

"Thank you, honey. I'll be just a moment." Nathan backed away from the door as Destiny approached, stepping aside so that Carter wouldn't see him when she opened it. Light filled the room briefly as the door swung open. The singer stepped inside, closed the door behind her, and turned on the light.

Damn, Nathan thought. She was even more beautiful up close. With her heels on she had to be six feet tall, and she was all legs. Her midnight-black hair had red streaks in it that matched her dress. Her eyes were big and brown. She could have been a model. She didn't say anything to him; she just looked into his eyes, pensively. He could tell she was unsure about this. Maybe she felt bad deceiving a guy like that, even if he was a traitor. It was understandable.

Nathan mouthed the words *thank you* and motioned toward the back door. Destiny left him alone in the washroom, turning out the light as she left. He keyed his microphone once again. "Ben, executing now," he said, his voice little more than a whisper. His throat mic would pick it up.

"Roger," Ben said. "I'm out back with Shadow. We're waiting."

He clicked the microphone twice in acknowledgment. He then reached into his shirt and pulled out his bronze Federal Recovery Agent badge. Agents were legally required to display it when executing an arrest. He left his gun holstered, instead opting for OC spray. The bounty hunter took a deep breath, shook off the nervousness, and opened the door.

The VIP lounge was dimly lit with blue light and neon accents. The floor was plushly carpeted, and there were cushy couches against the walls. Carter was by the liquor cabinet. His back was to Nathan, but the walls were covered in mirrors. He saw the bounty hunter's reflection, bronze badge glinting in blue light, and his eyes went wide.

"Carter Reid!" Nathan announced. "Federal Recovery Agent. You are—" He was cut off as the collaborator turned and whipped a full bottle of vodka at him. He barely had time to shield his face before it hit. Before Nathan could aim the OC spray, Carter charged. The fugitive slammed into him like a linebacker. He was a big boy, probably 300 pounds, and knocked Nathan flat on his ass as they collided. They both fell to the floor, the wanted man on top of the bounty hunter. Carter pushed himself up and stomped on Nathan's chest as he ran out the room, through the washroom, and into the back hallway. "Ben!" Nathan wheezed, keying his mic. "Target is not secure! He's running!"

"What?"

"He's running! Get ready!"

Nathan scrambled to his feet and ran to the back hallway. Terrified girls watched from dressing room doorways. Four bouncers were waiting in the hall, blocking Carter from getting to the dressing rooms or going back onto the club floor. He looked back at Nathan as the bounty hunter drew his gun, then at the emergency exit door along the wall. He slammed the door open and disappeared outside.

He didn't get far. "Holy shit!" he screamed.

Coming to the still-open back door, Nathan stepped outside. Breathing hard, Nathan watched with bemusement as Carter struggled with Shadow. The 120-pound, jet-black, military-grade enhanced working dog had latched onto him and pulled him to the ground. The fugitive screamed and pleaded as the dog made a chew toy out of his right arm.

"Shadow!" Nathan commanded. "Out!"

The dog looked at his master and, after a short pause, let go of Carter.

"Good," Nathan said. "Heel." Shadow sat, but kept a watchful eye on his prey. Nathan approached, gun drawn, but Carter didn't get back up. He just laid on the ground, clutching his now bleeding arm. The bounty hunter crouched next to him, holding his revolver where the wanted man could see it. "As I was about to say: *You are under arrest. In compliance with the Extraterrestrial and Collaborator Recovery Act, and by virtue of the authority vested in me as a licensed and bonded Federal Recovery Agent, I am taking you into custody. You have the right to remain silent, and to be given proper and humane care while in my charge. If you attempt to resist or flee, I have the legal authority to use lethal force without further warning. You will be transferred to federal custody for processing and adjudication. Do you understand?*"

"Fuck you, Bronze!" he snarled. "And fuck that bitch! She set me up!"

"Her family lived in California during the occupation," Nathan said, coldly. Carter still clutched his arm, but there was understanding in his eyes. He realized then, Nathan thought, how badly he'd fucked up. He continued, "Do you understand your rights under the Thirty-first Amendment? I hope so, because I'm not chasing you again. You run and I'm going to shoot your ass. I still get paid if I hand over a corpse."

"Yes, fine, I understand, whatever, just keep that fucking dog away from me."

Shadow was perched like a falcon, ready to swoop in and maul the bad man again if he tried anything. He licked his chops and didn't take his eyes off Carter.

Nathan stood up. "Ben, shackle his feet, then go grab the first-aid kit. We need to patch up his arm before we cuff him." He looked down at the prisoner. "Sit up."

"This is a mistake," Carter complained, but he did as he was told. Ben clamped the leg braces around his ankles. "Is this really necessary? You have the wrong guy."

"Then why'd you run?"

"What the fuck was I supposed to do? I turn around and some guy is in the room with me! I thought you were going to rob me!"

"Uh-huh. Roll up your sleeves."

Carter carefully rolled up his right sleeve. His forearm was still bleeding from where Shadow had bitten him. "This better not get infected."

"Roll up your other sleeve."

He hesitated. "What? Why? The bite is on this arm!"

"Roll up your other sleeve or you get round two with the dog."

"Alright! Alright, fine!" Doing as he was told, he rolled up his left sleeve. In the amber glow of the single light illuminating the back lot, an alien marking was clearly visible on his forearm. It was a row of script eight inches long, an identifier they used to track their humans. It looked like a tattoo but was something more. The marks were living organisms. If scraped off it would grow back. They were difficult to remove and nearly impossible to forge.

"Wrong guy, huh?" Nathan said, disdain in his voice. Ben had returned with the first-aid kit. "Patch up his arm, Ben, and let's get this piece of shit in the truck. I'm ready to call it a day."

A short while later, Nathan found himself in the office of Lois Lazar, the proprietor of The Desert Flower Cabaret. Her hair was long and blonde. She wore a corset, short-shorts, and thigh-high, high-heeled boots. The office was small and cluttered. Her desk was covered with documents, a computer with multiple screens, and a dirty ashtray. Pictures and newspaper clippings decorated one wall. There were photographs of somebody's former life, scenes from the war, and a shadow box with a folded American flag and Army insignia. Lois was a drag queen, everyone knew that, but that was all most people knew about her.

"Yeah, that's me, sugar," she said, lighting a cigarette. "I enlisted right after they dropped the rock on Phoenix. It was my hometown, but I was away on a trip. I lost everything. My family, my life, my business—everything. I wanted to do something, you know?"

"Believe me," Nathan said, "I understand. 1st Armored Division. I was a tanker. You?"

"4th Infantry," she said. "Just a truck driver, but I saw some things. Things I'll never forget. It changed me. I guess the whole world changed."

"Is that why you . . . you know?"

She chuckled. "Adopted this persona? Maybe. It helps me forget."

Nathan didn't really understand Lois's life choices, but he definitely understood wanting to forget. "I appreciate your assistance in this matter." She had initially wanted him to try and grab Carter Reid in the parking lot, before he even got into the place. Nathan had been concerned that he'd be armed, though, but knew his target would be checked for weapons before being allowed into the club.

"You were right. He deposited a gun at the property check. I heard he put up a fight."

"He chucked a bottle at me and then knocked me down. I'll be sore in the morning," Nathan said, even though he was already sore, "but I'm fine. I'm glad he didn't have a gun."

"About that," Lois said. She reached into her desk drawer and produced a break-top revolver. It had a short barrel, maybe three inches, and a rounded grip. "Will you take this? It's his gun. I don't want it."

"Sure," Nathan said, taking the weapon from her. It had a lever on the side of the frame that, when depressed, allowed the action to break open. The ejector snapped up and back down. The cylinder was empty.

"I threw the ammo away," Lois said.

"No problem," Nathan said, and stuffed the gun into his waistband. "I'll take this if you want. Anyway, as I was saying, I appreciate your help. Legally I can't share the bounty with you, but I can pay you a fee for your trouble. I'm not exactly sure how much it'll be. My partner, Stella, handles all that. It's based on a government schedule. We have to keep the books straight or we'll lose our license."

Lois shook her head. "Amazing. Half the world got blown up, we hardly have any federal agencies anymore, but they managed to keep the red tape."

"The more things change," Nathan said. "I gotta jet now."

"What will happen to him?"

"Carter? I'll be hauling him back to the office in Arizona. We've got a holding cell we'll keep him in while we process the claim. Homeland Security will be along to pick him up in a few days. After that, he'll get sent to a detention facility to await trial. He was a high-ranking officer in the United Earth Alliance and is suspected of having administrated an internment camp in Occupied California."

Lois's eyes narrowed. "Well then. I hope they hang the motherfucker."

"I hope so, too. My partner will contact you in a few days about your compensation. Thank you again, Lois."

"Be careful, Mr. Foster."

Prescott, Arizona
The next morning . . .

NATHAN AWOKE to Shadow panting in his face.

Shadow was a smart dog, a big Doberman-Shepherd mix, genetically enhanced and specifically bred to be a working dog. He always woke somebody if he had to go. Looking at his watch, Nathan realized it was barely six in the morning. "Can't you hold it?"

Shadow whined.

Guess not. "Ben!" he said, loudly. Ben's cot was on the other side of the room. "Ben, wake up!"

Ben stirred in the dim morning light. "What's wrong?"

"Shadow needs to go out."

He rubbed his eyes and sat up. "Seriously?"

Nathan looked at the dog. "Shadow, go get Ben. He'll take you out."

Shadow understood at least some of that. He skittered across the room and jumped on Ben's cot, trampling the boy while he licked his face. His tail was wagging.

"Okay, okay!" Ben said, sputtering. "Yuck. Get down, Lug, I'll take you outside!"

Shadow jumped down from Ben's cot and trotted to the door, pausing to make sure Ben was following him.

"That was a dirty trick," Ben said, shuffling toward the door.

"I'll get us some breakfast," Nathan said, sitting up. As the boy and the dog left, he took a deep breath, closed his eyes, and tried to get his heart to slow down. He had *that* dream again. He was dragging his gunner out of his tank. His driver was in pieces, his tank on fire. The sun was bloodred through the smoke. There was so

11

much smoke it was like a forest fire. The alien mech, the one that had killed his crew, was in a smoking heap a hundred meters away. Thick blue fluid poured out of where a 150mm APFSDS round had punched through it, going right through the meaty parts. The brain-shot usually killed them instantly, but it was a tough shot to make when they were moving.

Nathan thought he could smell the smoke, the acrid stink of burning metal, even in the dream. He had heard the strange, electronic hooting noises the biomechanical synths made. He could feel the pain from where he'd been burned even though the wounds had long since healed. The dream usually ended the moment he realized that his gunner, SP5 Cole Jackson, was dead.

It had been eight years and he still had the dream every so often. They eventually found enough of his driver, PFC Jake Guthrie, and his loader, SP4 Greg Rasmussen, to bury. Nathan still didn't know how in the hell he managed to survive a catastrophic kill to his tank that had claimed the lives of his crew. It had been luck, nothing but dumb luck. It seemed so unfair.

"Uncle Nate?"

Surprised, Nathan looked up. It was Ben. "Oh. Hey. I didn't hear you come back in."

"Everything okay? You were, like, zoned out there for a minute."

"Yeah," Nathan lied. "I just need some coffee." That part, at least, was true. "What do you want for breakfast?"

Nathan and Ben had spent the night at the shop. Carter Reid was locked up in the holding cell down in the basement, and technically someone had to be on the premises constantly while they had a prisoner in custody. Nathan's partner, Stella, had contacted Homeland Security immediately after receiving notification that the fugitive was in custody, but sometimes it took them a couple of days to show up. Eventually they'd come get him, but until then, he couldn't be left alone in the building, even though there was almost no chance he could escape.

"Stella's here," Ben said. "She brought food."

"She's here already?"

"Yeah, she got here while Shadow was pottying. I guess she went to Ranchero's on the way here."

Nathan's stomach growled. "That sounds pretty good. Go eat, tell her I'll be out there in a minute." He needed to take a leak and get dressed.

Stella Rickles was already at her desk when Nathan stepped into the main office. She was typing away on her computer, probably filling out the paperwork on Carter Reid. "Good morning, sunshine," she said, smiling at him. She was pretty, in a girl-next-door kind of way. Late thirties, auburn hair, and a curvy figure. Even though they didn't have a dress code, she always looked nice when she came into the office. Today she was wearing a business skirt and heels, which, when paired with her glasses, made her look like a librarian. "You sleep okay?"

Nathan was still sore. Between getting clocked the night before and sleeping on a surplus cot, he felt pretty rough. "Oh yeah. Slept like a baby."

She raised an eyebrow. "Liar. You know, we can get real beds in here instead of those god-awful cots."

"Hey! I like my cot!" He chuckled. "The boy said you brought food?"

She had a half-eaten breakfast burrito on her desk. "There's a steak-and-egg burrito for you. It's in the break room. I put a pot of coffee on, too."

"I could not do this job without you," Nathan said, smiling. "You're the best."

"And don't you forget it," she said, returning to her typing. "Don't forget to feed the prisoner. I didn't bring him a burrito."

Nathan nodded. "Oh, right. Yeah. I'll toss him a can of Spam or something after I eat." He turned and left the office, heading into the break room. He hadn't been joking when he told Stella that he couldn't do the job without her. There was a lot of administrative stuff that went along with bounty hunting. It wasn't so bad for the state jobs, but the federal stuff came with a lot of paperwork. The Department of Homeland Security was the agency that processed claims for alien collaborators, traitors, and war criminals. The rewards were usually bigger, but getting them processed was like filing your taxes or going to the VA. Stella handled all that for him.

He'd originally hired her to handle the admin work. After a year of keeping him from violating government regulations (which came with stiff fines), she asked for a raise. Instead he made her a full partner in the business and had never regretted it. Stella had been a counterintelligence agent for Homeland Security during the war. She'd once confided in Nathan that she could be making a lot more money back east, or working for the government still, but she'd gotten sick of that world. At first she thought of returning home to West Virginia, but her maternal grandmother had settled in Arizona before the war. After she passed away, she left her house in Prescott to Stella, giving her a paid-for place to live. There just wasn't much call for Stella's area of expertise there, except for recovery work.

Ben was in the break room, eating his own burrito. His laptop computer was set up in front of him, and he scrolled the internet as he ate. Shadow sat next to him, looking pitiful. It was kind of funny, Nathan thought, watching a huge, genetically engineered working dog beg for table scraps.

"Hey, Uncle Nate," Ben said, talking while chewing. "That guy we snagged last night? Stella told me the reward for him is fifty grand."

"That's right," Nathan said, before taking a bite from his burrito. He continued after swallowing. "A prison camp administrator like our boy downstairs has a lot to answer for."

Ben looked thoughtful for a moment. "How come we do this?"

"Huh? Because they're paying us fifty thousand dollars, that's why."

"No, I mean, how come the government pays us to do this? I read that before the war, the police or federal agents did this kind of stuff, not bounty hunters."

Nathan set his burrito down. "You're right, it was a different world back then. Sometimes I forget how young you are." Ben had been born during the war and was all of six years old when it had ended. He didn't remember the world as it had been before. "I guess I've never explained this to you, huh? Before the war, federal laws were enforced by dozens of alphabet agencies from several different government departments. They often had redundant and overlapping areas of responsibility, and didn't always work together well. Turf wars and battles for budget share were common. Being official apparatuses of the government, they had what they called qualified immunity. It meant that they usually couldn't be sued for misconduct or mistakes. The federal bureaucracy made it nearly impossible to fire people for cause, leaving agencies with little choice but to transfer poor performers or just learn to live with them. Oversight was lacking and there wasn't nearly enough accountability, at least not in my opinion."

Ben ate his burrito as he listened to his uncle.

"Millions of Americans had willingly sided with the Greys, too," Nate continued, using the derisive nickname for the extraterrestrial Visitors. "Hell, a bunch of people defected to their territory before the war started, and some even went over afterward. People were scared, thought there were traitors everywhere."

"There *were* traitors everywhere," Ben said, through a mouthful of his breakfast. He swallowed. "That's why we're so busy now."

"It was worse than that. People became paranoid. The government basically turned all those federal agencies loose, gave them free rein to do whatever they thought they needed to do. Before the war they tracked and monitored alien sympathizers, harassed troublemakers, shut down pro-alien propaganda outlets. They spied on people without warrants and arrested them without probable cause. All it did was drive people over to the Greys, make the aliens seem more sympathetic. People were fed up. They were about to revolt."

"What changed?" Ben asked.

"The Greys dropped the rock on Phoenix," Nathan said, staring off into the distance. He looked at his nephew. "A million or so people died in an instant. Then the nukes started flying, and..." He trailed off. "That part of the war only lasted a couple months. It got a lot more conventional after that...as conventional as a war with aliens can be, I guess. In any case they stopped the orbital bombardment and we quit launching nukes at them." He sighed. "Nobody cared much about their rights when they were worried about being exterminated. The Constitution was all but suspended during the war. All those federal agencies were used to police the population. People were rounded up and put in camps if they made trouble or protested. It was wrong, it was all wrong."

"But we won," Ben suggested. "We won the war."

"We did, against all odds. That doesn't make it right, though. The ends don't always justify the means, and besides, I'm not convinced shredding the Constitution helped us win. It damn near tore the country apart, though, and after the war, things got worse." Nathan paused to take another bite from his burrito. "When it was all over, after so much death and destruction, people were angry. They wanted revenge. They got it."

"What does that mean?"

Nathan hesitated. Ben was too young to remember most of this stuff, and some of it Nathan preferred not to think about. Even still, he needed to know why they did what they did. "A lot of the collaborators were just rounded up and shot. People turned against each other. People suspected of being collaborators were strung up by mobs. There were riots in some cities. The Feds still had tens of thousands of people in internment camps, and most of 'em had never gotten a trial or a lawyer or anything. The government had said that the extraordinary measures needed during the war were temporary, but after the war, they didn't give up their emergency powers. Not at first."

"But they did eventually."

"They did, but it took violence and the threat of an open revolt. A lot of vets came home from the war and didn't like being spied on and not being able to speak their minds. You couldn't travel on the freeway half the time without running into a Homeland Security checkpoint. That isn't what we fought for. Things got pretty tense for a few months there, especially after President Kirkpatrick was assassinated. A lot of us thought there'd be a civil war."

"That's when they called the Constitutional Convention," Ben said.

"That's right. It was a smart move. It brought everybody to the table and allowed us to work things out. They passed four or five amendments, I don't remember."

"It was six," Ben corrected.

Nathan grinned. "How come you're asking me all this? Seems like you know history better than I do."

"You were there. It's different from reading it."

"Fair enough. Anyway, things changed after that. They gutted federal law enforcement, and most of those agencies got disbanded. There was still the problem of all of the collaborators, though. When the war ended, the aliens left their human flunkies behind, and a whole bunch of their own kind as well. The aliens are easy enough to deal with, since the law treats them the same as enemy combatants. People wanted the collaborators brought to justice, though, and they didn't trust the Feds with the power to do it. That's where we come in." Nathan smiled, and spread his hands. "The grand compromise that saved the country."

Stella walked in then, her heels clicking on the cement floor. "The processing for Mr. Reid is done. The computer is ninety-plus percent confident, based on biometrics, that he is who we think he is. DHS will be sending a transport to pick him up today."

"Wow," Nathan said. "That was fast."

"Yeah. I guess he's got a bunch of indictments waiting for him—treason, conspiracy, aiding and abetting, war crimes. The usual."

"The usual," Nathan agreed. "Anything else on your radar?" The bounty on Carter Reid was $50,000. That was a pretty good chunk of change, but after taxes they'd only get $35,000 of that. The agency also had expenses to cover.

"I have a couple of leads," Stella said, "Department of Justice and Homeland Security both." She had built up an impressive network of contacts and informants in the time they'd been working together. She handed Nathan a few pieces of paper. Each was essentially a detailed wanted poster, with a photo of the wanted man, a description, a list of his crimes, and other pertinent information.

"Luis Santiago," Nathan read. "Wanted for the murder of a judge in El Paso. Thirty-five-thousand-dollar reward, dead or alive." *Texas doesn't fuck around*, he thought. He flipped to the next one. "Erik Landers . . . twenty-thousand-dollar reward . . . arms trafficking?"

Stella leaned on the wall by the door. "He's suspected of running guns to ex-UEA militant groups."

Nathan shook his head. "They just can't accept that their masters left them, can they?"

Stella shrugged. "There's about an even chance the part about the militants is bullshit. You know how it is. They convince a judge that the alleged crime is covered by the Thirty-first Amendment and boom, instant nationwide bounty."

"With federal preemption," Nathan added.

"Exactly. Anyway, a little birdie chirped in my ear that this guy is staying at a motel in Tuba City."

Nathan looked over at Ben. "He's in Tuba City. What do you think?"

His nephew looked thoughtful for a moment. "That's the Navajo Nation. It would be a good place to lay low until the heat's off."

"And why is that?"

The boy looked thoughtful for a moment. "Under the Treaty of Window Rock, Federal Recovery Agents are required to notify the tribal government that they will be operating under their territory, and the Navajo Nation can refuse them if they want."

Stella beamed. "Very good, Ben!" She was the one who educated Ben on the legal aspects of the business.

"What happens if they say no?"

"In that case," Stella replied, "we're supposed to notify the Department of Justice, and they can dispatch US Marshals to arrest the person we're looking for. In practice, they're not always willing to send out the Marshals based on the say-so of Recovery Agents. It depends on how convincing the information is."

"Take a look at the tasking sheet, Ben, and see what else you can tell from it."

Ben took the piece of paper and studied it for a moment, reading it carefully. "It says *wanted alive.* That means we don't get paid if he dies, right?"

Nathan shook his head. "Not exactly. For certain crimes they'll specify that the bounty is wanted dead or alive. That means he's just as valuable to us dead as he is if we bring him in breathing. Those are pretty rare, though, and are usually only issued for the most serious crimes. Like this," he said, showing Ben the wanted poster for Luis Santiago. "This asshole murdered a judge in Texas. They'll take him alive or as a corpse."

"Why do they do that?"

"It's a balancing act," Nathan explained. "Dead men can't stand trial, and even collaborators still have a right to presumption of innocence. They don't want to give Recovery Agents the financial incentive to just shoot their targets."

"On the other hand," Stella said, "for certain serious crimes, they want to incentivize dangerous criminals to surrender. Knowing that the Recovery Agent will get paid just as much if he brings you in dead might convince you to cooperate."

"But when we arrest a collaborator," Ben said, "we read them their Thirty-first Amendment rights, and we always say that we can use lethal force without further warning."

Stella nodded. "That's right. Thirty-first Amendment taskings are special. If your case is covered under the Thirty-first Amendment, it means that you're materially supporting a hostile power attempting to destroy the United States. Lethal force is always an option to protect the country, or so the logic goes. Remember, these amendments were passed right after the war."

Nathan leaned in a little. "Long story short, if I do have to shoot this asshole, we'll still get paid, but it'll take a lot longer and involve a lot more paperwork. If a Recovery Agent uses deadly force enough that he draws the attention of the Federal Recovery Bureau, they'll suspend his license and launch an audit."

"That's something you never want to happen," Stella said. "It can take weeks or months and we're not allowed to work while the audit is in progress. They'll send people down here to inspect our facilities and our records, and if every bit of paperwork isn't filled out correctly, we can face large fines, revocation of our operating license, even criminal prosecution."

"Holy crap," Ben said.

"Always remember," Nathan said, "a Recovery Agent is responsible, legally and morally, for everything he does. We operate under the color of law, but the law only gives us so much protection. We get into a gun battle with a wanted man, we are personally responsible for every bullet we send downrange. One of our shots misses a target and kills a bystander, we can end up in prison for it. One of those bullets damages someone's property, they can sue us for recompense, and the damages will come out of our pocket."

Ben looked bewildered. "Why does anyone do this?"

"Because it's good money," Nathan said. "Look at this Erik Landers guy. We drive a couple hours north and pick him up, we'll make twenty grand for a day's work. That's hard to beat these days."

"Does that mean you're going after Erik Landers?" Stella asked.

Nathan nodded. "He's close by and you have a good lead. It's too good to pass up. Does he have any known associates up there?"

"Not that I'm aware of, but my little birdie works at a motel there. I can send you to her for more information. I'll give John Yazzie a call and let him know you're coming."

John Yazzie was a lieutenant in the Navajo Nation Territorial Police. He'd served with Nathan during the war, and the two men were friends. "Thank you," Nathan said. "I'm gonna swing by Jesse's place to pick up some equipment, then we'll roll out."

Stella smiled. "Be safe. I'll see you boys later."

THE WEATHER IN PRESCOTT WAS NICE IN THE FALL. Being both farther south and at a lower elevation, it wasn't nearly so cold and windy as Flagstaff was in the winter, and in the summer, it didn't get as hot as it did in desert around the Phoenix Crater. It was a pleasant morning and Whiskey Row had its share of locals and travelers, even if the bars and brothels weren't open yet.

Traffic was light. Gasoline and diesel weren't rationed anymore but were still expensive. Many people walked or rode bicycles to get around, especially on such a nice day. There were even a few folks going about their business on horseback, just like they would have done a hundred years earlier.

Nathan and Ben, riding in their up-armored diesel truck, came to a stop at a traffic light near the old courthouse. "Give Jesse a call," Nathan said, pointing at his phone. "Tell him we're on our way over. I don't want to drop in unannounced."

"You got it!" Ben said. The phone was plugged into the truck's docking station and connected to its main screen. The screen was in a fixed position, but the camera could be pointed at either the driver or the passenger. Ben turned the camera toward himself, dialed Jesse's number, and waited. The screen was black for a few moments, with CONNECTING . . . appearing on it, until Jesse picked up.

Jesse was an affable-looking guy with a goatee and curly hair. "Larimer Technologies," he said, his voice sounding over the truck's speakers. He wasn't looking at the camera, and appeared to be soldering something. "What can I do for—ow! Damn it!"

"Hey, Jesse!" Ben said. "Is this a bad time?"

"What? Oh," he said, putting his finger between his lips where he'd burned it. "How're you doing, Ben? Hi, Nate! I can't see you, but I know you're there."

"Are you busy?" Nathan asked. "I'm gonna drop by in a little while."

"No, come on by. What do you need?"

Nathan reached over and pointed the camera at himself. "I'll talk to you when I get there."

"Okay. I've got some cool stuff I want to show you, too. See you in a bit." Without saying goodbye, he terminated the connection, and the screen went blank.

Nathan had known Jesse since high school. The Larimers had been a fixture in Prescott for over a hundred years. Jesse was the last scion of a long line of notable eccentrics, and he loved regaling people with tales of his family's colorful history. Jessup Beauregard Larimer settled in town in 1888 and got rich after discovering gold. He also claimed to be able to alter the weather; using smoke pots atop wooden towers, he was reportedly able to make it rain, though his formula was lost when he died in 1896 of wounds sustained in a duel (historians questioned the authenticity of the accounts).

Hamilton Larimer, Jessup's son, was an Army Air Service airship pilot in the years following the Great War. He was said to have been the first man to have ever shot and killed a bear from an aloft dirigible (though the Germans disputed the claim). His son, John Larimer, had a long and distinguished career as an Air Force pilot.

In as much as such an eccentric family could even have a black sheep, Jesse was the black sheep of the family. He had dropped out of Arizona Tech's College of Engineering after only two years, and instead took to rally racing and working as a handyman to make ends meet. Like many people, he'd been drafted during the war. He lost his parents in the destruction of Phoenix and his older sister, an Air Force fighter pilot, was killed in action a year later. Jesse became the sole inheritor of what was left of the family fortune. He lived with his son at his ancestral home on the outskirts of town.

It took Ben and Nathan about fifteen minutes to get to Jesse's residence. Nathan pulled his truck into the drive and parked next to Jesse's off-road 4x4 and motorcycle. Off to the side, under a tarp, was an old Potomac Motors Galaxy, a classic muscle car that Jesse was slowly rebuilding. There was a goat standing on top of the car, looking down at them smugly, as Nathan and Ben got out of the truck.

"Hey, get down from there, Duke!" Ben said, waving his arms at it. With an obnoxious bleat, the goat jumped down and approached the boy, thinking he had food. Daisy, the female, came running from behind the house, the bell on her collar clanging as she went.

"Ben, would you try and get the goats back in the pen, please? Let

Shadow out, he'll herd them for you. I'm gonna go inside and talk to Jesse."

"Sure thing, Uncle Nate," Ben said, opening the back of the truck. "Come on, buddy!" The huge black dog excitedly jumped from the back of the truck, his tail wagging enthusiastically. The goats, seeing their old nemesis, turned and ran, with Shadow in hot pursuit. Ben took off after them. Chuckling, Nathan made his way to the house's armored security door and rang the buzzer.

A small screen next to the door lit up, with Jesse's face appearing on it. "Hey, Nate." He hit a button on his desk, and the door loudly clicked. "It's open. C'mon in, I'm back in the shop."

"Your goats got out again. One of them was on your Galaxy."

"Damn it! They're little escape artists, I swear."

"Ben and Shadow are getting them back into the pen for you. Again."

Jesse grinned. "You know, this is a perfect opportunity to test out my new thing. Change of plan, meet me around back by the goat pen."

"Uh, sure, Jess," Nathan said. "See you in a minute."

Jesse was waiting for him behind the house, with Ben and Shadow. Over his shoulder was a stubby, tubular device with a pistol grip and a shoulder pad, like a sawn-off rocket launcher. Where the rocket would be, however, there were instead four padded prongs, each eight inches long, angling outward.

"You're not going to blow the goats up, are you?" Nathan asked.

"No, no," Jesse said, letting himself into the pen. "Watch this."

Shadow watched intently as Jesse entered the enclosure, daring the goats to try and escape again. Daisy hid in their little shelter while Duke defiantly stood on top of a barrel, warily looking down at the dog. They had played this game many times before.

"See," Jesse continued, "I got to thinking about your business. Sometimes you have to chase people, right?"

"Shadow does most of the chasing these days, but it does come up."

"Exactly. It's exhausting and a waste of energy. I thought to myself, there's got to be a better way." He shouldered his contraption and pointed at the goat, who was still haplessly perched atop the barrel. "Turns out there is."

BOOM! The device fired with a deep, hollow bang and a puff of smoke. In an instant, the barrel was lying on the ground, knocked over. Duke was lying next to it, ensnared in a net, bleating his unhappiness about the situation. Jesse looked up at Nathan, grinning ear to ear. "What do you think?"

Nathan had doubled over laughing.

Ben ran to the fence. "Duke! Is he okay?"

"He's fine," Jesse said, looking down the prostrate goat. "It's not electrified or anything. I'm still working on that part." After a few moments, Duke had given up struggling and just laid there, breathing heavily.

Ben walked over to the gate. "I'll get him out!"

"Put gloves on first," Nathan advised.

Jesse raised an eyebrow. "The wires aren't sharp or anything."

"No, I just don't want him smelling like goat piss."

Jesse stopped and sniffed his fingers. "Yeah, he is a little rank." He left the pen as Ben entered. The boy got to work trying to untangle the confused goat. "I got the idea from the net launchers they use to catch wildlife. They work okay for wild animals, but they're not designed for people. This one is. It's actuated by blank cartridges. The net has little hooks all over it."

Nathan raised an eyebrow. "To dig into the flesh? I might come under some scrutiny if I bring my customers in all tore up."

"No, not like that. The hooks aren't sharp enough to puncture the skin. They allow the net to hook to itself as it wraps around the target. Let me tell you, you're not going to be able to just pull it off. It takes forever to get out of. If you try to run it'll tangle around your legs and you'll trip."

"Huh. That's kind of clever."

"Out to about twenty feet, it's pretty much guaranteed to fully entangle a grown man. After that, you might only get a partial catch, but it could either trip them up or immobilize the arms. The net itself is a nylon composite weave. Each strand has over a hundred pounds of tensile strength, and multiple strands are braided together to make the net. I had to balance making it strong with making it light enough to get launched. I don't think even a big, strong guy will be able to tear his way out of it."

"This must have taken a lot of work."

"Yeah, I started playing around with it last year, but kind of forgot about it for a while. It took a lot of testing but I think I've got it down."

"Holy hell, how many times did you shoot that poor goat?"

"What?" Jesse seemed genuinely distressed that Nathan thought he was mistreating his goats. "It's not like that. I tested this thing on myself. I had Tycho shoot me with it a bunch of times. It's as safe as I can get it while still being effective."

Nathan chuckled. "I bet he thought that was a hoot. Say, where is your boy, anyway? He's usually real excited to see Ben."

"Huh? Tycho's in school. It's Tuesday morning."

"Oh, right. I guess I forgot."

"Hey, how's Ben doing, anyway?" he asked, quietly, so that the boy couldn't hear. "Does he have friends or anything?"

Nathan sighed. "Not really. Truth be told, he's really shy. I wish I could socialize him more, but I don't really hang out with a lot of other fourteen-year-olds, you know? He's got friends on the internet."

Jesse frowned. "Have you thought about putting him in school?"

"Can't. He tested out. Got his GED already."

"Really? Holy crap."

"Yeah, he's real smart. Takes after his mom."

"This life can't be good for him," Jesse said, delicately.

Nathan frowned. Jesse wasn't wrong; Ben had spent the night with him at the office, guarding Carson Reid. When other kids were in school, or hanging out with their friends, his nephew was chasing criminals and traitors. "It's the only life I've got," he said with a shrug. "He's got no other family. Even if I wanted to put him in foster care, the system is still overwhelmed with all the orphans from the war. If I gave him up, odds are he'd end up in some kind of government institution. Way I see it, this is better than that, even with the risks."

Jesse nodded solemnly. He was one of the few people who knew about what Ben had been through and what had happened to his mom. "It just seems so unfair to the kid."

"You ain't wrong. Hell, what happened to the whole goddamn world was unfair, but it is what it is. Now, what else did you want to show me?"

"Oh! Right! I forgot. Come on into the shop."

Jesse's shop looked cluttered and chaotic, but he seemed to know right where everything was. The centerpiece of it was a CNC mill and a lathe. Electronics projects cluttered one workbench, while firearms projects took up another. A faded Arizona flag hung on one wall, as did a prewar, fifty-star US flag. Next to them was a pair of posters. REMEMBER PHOENIX, one declared, while the other proclaimed KEEP WATCHING THE SKIES! Below those, framed, was his certificate of his completing the Arizona Ranger training course and a photo of his swearing-in ceremony. Leading Nathan to his gun-bench, Jesse picked up a large pistol and proudly handed it to his friend.

"What's this?" Nathan asked, examining the gun in his hand. It wasn't anything he'd seen before, and he knew his way around a gun. "Did you make this?"

"I did," Jesse said, beaming. "That's my third prototype. It's ready for field testing."

The gun was a hefty semiautomatic, but the magazine well was located in front of the trigger guard. Nathan locked back the slide, verifying that the weapon was unloaded, and looked at the markings. ".45 Win Mag?"

Jesse grinned. "Yup! The problem with most magnum semiautos is that they're huge, right? It's because they're trying to cram a revolver-length, rimmed cartridge into a pistol grip. You end up with a grip like a two-by-four. I solved that by moving the magazine well out of the grip."

"Like a Broomhandle Mauser," Nathan said.

"Only in overall layout. This gun is striker-fired. It's roller-delayed, recoil-operated, like the Kraut STG-88 assault rifle. Try the trigger!"

Nathan released the slide and squeezed the trigger. With only a little bit of take-up, it felt like a thin glass rod breaking. "Damn."

"Three and a half pounds' pull weight on that, and it doesn't feel mushy. I added a thumb safety because the trigger pull is so light, and to make it extra drop safe. I tossed my second prototype off the roof, onto the driveway, over and over again, trying to get it to discharge, and the safety held. Anyway, the barrel is fixed, so it's real accurate. For the next prototype, I'm working on a user-serviceable quick-change barrel system. You'll be able to swap from the five-inch service barrel, like on this one, to a longer, heavier target barrel, and even a short snub barrel. I figure I can machine a scope mount into the heavy barrel, so it'll be good for handgun hunters. I may be able to figure out a caliber conversion system, eventually, too."

"This is really nice, Jesse," Nathan said, aiming the pistol at an antelope head mounted on the wall.

"The magazine holds ten rounds. I'm working on a twenty-rounder, but I haven't put it together yet. Even still, that's four extra shots over a typical police revolver, it's more powerful, and it reloads quicker."

"I'm impressed, Jesse. Very nicely done. You gonna put these into production?"

"Eh, I really can't. I'm a one-man outfit. I don't have the capability to mass-produce a gun and making these as one-offs would make them too expensive. Once I get the design finalized, I'm going to try and sell the manufacturing rights."

"Yeah, I guess that makes sense." Nathan flipped the gun around in his hand and offered it to Jesse butt-first. "You gonna pack this beast on your next Ranger call-up?"

"You know, I might. We don't really have any formal requirements as to what sidearms we're supposed to carry. A lot of guys pack single-action revolvers just for the aesthetics." Jesse took the gun back. "I've taken a bunch of javelina with this. I even shot down a leatherwing with it."

"You shot down a leatherwing," Nathan repeated. "Bullshit." The alien creatures, superficially resembling pterosaurs, had been hybridized to flourish in the Earth's atmosphere. Having no natural predators, they were a menace to livestock and unwary people alike.

"No, I did! I was out by Thumb Butte. It wasn't a big one. He was circling overhead and decided to swoop down on me. I nailed him as he came in. The damned thing crashed into me, knocked me on my ass, and coughed up a bunch of slime on me. I had to burn those clothes, it stunk so bad."

Nathan laughed. It was just crazy enough to have actually happened. "That reminds me." He reached into his waistband and pulled the revolver he'd recovered off of Carson Reid. He handed it to his friend.

"What's this?" Jesse asked, taking the gun. Depressing the release lever with his thumb, he opened the top-break revolver and verified that it was unloaded.

"It belonged to my last bounty."

Jesse looked closely at the markings. "It's Canadian. See, it's got the little maple-leaf marking on the side of the frame. It's a Northstar Ordnance Mk.VI, .38 Special, made in Halifax, Nova Scotia." He looked up at Nathan. "Nova Scotia is a Canadian province."

"Man, I know where Nova Scotia is!"

"Right. Sorry. Anyway, a lot of Canadian cops used these until they started switching to 9mm semiautos. This one has the compact grip and the shorter, 83mm barrel." He paused for a moment. "That's about three and a quarter inches."

Nathan just glared at him.

Jesse didn't seem to notice. "This was probably an off-duty carry, or detective's gun. Bunch of these got imported as surplus after the war, when Canada's economy collapsed. They're good guns, though, well-made and reliable."

"I'm thinking about giving it to Ben. Is it in working condition?"

Jesse opened and closed the action a few times. He pulled the trigger, cycling the cylinder through all six chambers, and inspected the bore. "Yeah, I'd say so. The finish is a little worn, but I don't think it's been used much. I can clean it up for you if you want."

"I'd appreciate it. I'll need some .38 then, too. Target loads and some hollow-points."

"You guys going on a job?" Jesse asked. "Another collaborator?"

"Gun runner." Retrieving his PDA from his pocket, he flipped open the folding screen, pulled up the tasking info on Erik Landers, and showed it to Jesse.

Jesse whistled. "Damn. Twenty grand? You make some bucks doing this, hey?"

"The money's good but the work can be sporadic. Getting two bounties in a row like this is rare. Hell, we just got back from a job last night! Also, the government takes anywhere from a fifth to a third of your bounty earnings in taxes, so you have to take that into account. But," he said, before Jesse went into another rant about how taxation was government-sanctioned theft, "it can be lucrative if you don't mind the risk."

"Hmm," Jesse said, rubbing his chin. "Maybe I should get into this line of work."

"Really? You don't get enough excitement in the Rangers?" The

Arizona Rangers had been reconstituted during the war. Originally made up of old guys and others who couldn't pass the physical requirements for the military, the Rangers served as a volunteer civil reserve militia. Their funding was limited and individual members had to supply their own equipment, but they could be mustered faster than the National Guard.

"Not like that. These days we mostly get called up for search-and-rescue missions, controlling extraterrestrial wildlife, and helping fight wildfires."

"Well, I could use a hand sometimes. If you get yourself licensed I can hire you as a contractor. Getting licensed is a process, though. First you've got to apply, and just getting that processed can take a while. Once that's done, the FBI does a background check on you, and that takes a while, too. You can download the study materials for the written exam off the internet, but you have to actually go to a federal building to take the test. If you pass, you'll be interviewed by a board from the Federal Recovery Bureau, and they decide whether or not to certify you. If you're declined, you can appeal it, but with your background I don't see that being an issue. The process takes months sometimes, and there are a lot of fees up front. You also need to get liability insurance, and it's a mistake to go with the bare minimum on that. You want the full coverage, trust me. It's also a good idea to have an attorney on retainer, one who specializes in use-of-force cases."

"Holy crap. Has Ben done all that?"

"No, he's still a minor. I can't even claim him as an apprentice until he's sixteen. He's not officially on the job, and isn't allowed to apprehend people or anything."

Jesse snapped his fingers. "I forgot to ask! You said you needed some equipment?"

"Yeah, I wanted to get Ben fitted for body armor."

"I think I've got something that might work. I bought a big box of surplus police vests, and some of them are pretty small. Go get him and I'll dig them out for him to try on. You want the net launcher, too?"

"Sure, why not?"

"Great! Let me know how it does, and if you think of any way it can be improved. I don't have any .38 on hand, but I'll be able to get some by the time I get the gun cleaned up for you. You don't need it today, do you?"

"No, take your time. I'm not handing a teenager a firearm without teaching him how to use it first, and we're heading out as soon as we leave here."

"Got it. Okay, let's go see if I have a vest that'll fit him."

Federal Detention Facility
Gallup, New Mexico

SITTING ALONE, Emmogene Anderson looked down at the alien tattoo on her left forearm. It was a length of script and symbols, embedded into the flesh from just below the elbow to just above the wrist. The only way to remove them was through surgery and medications, she'd read once. It wasn't just a marking on the skin, it was part of the body. If you just tried to scrape it off it would grow back. It was the mark of the alien collaborator. It was how the Visitors had kept track of the humans who had served them.

Visitors, she thought bitterly. It was the name they had preferred. It sounded nonthreatening. They claimed to have hailed from a star in the constellation of Sagittarius, specifically the Sagittarius Dwarf Irregular Galaxy. Most people simply called them aliens, or the Greys, but they were more formally known as Sagittarians.

It was strange, she thought. The most momentous occurrence in all of human history happened, followed by the bloodiest and costliest war ever. She'd been right there in the middle of it all and yet she could scarcely remember it. Her memory had been wiped by the Visitors at the end of the war, some eight years earlier. She had only broken, fragmented memories of her life before that. Why did her mother take her to the Visitors? What had she done when under their influence? What did they do to her? Emmogene had few answers. Maybe when she got out, she could figure out who she used to be, and why she did the things she'd done.

Getting out was something she'd not thought of very much. She had almost no recollection of being "free"; being a prisoner in one way or another was all she knew. For the first three years after the war ended, she'd been on the run with United Earth Alliance holdouts,

31

people who refused to accept that the Visitors had abandoned them. They rarely stayed in one place for more than a few months, and she was never allowed to leave. After that, she'd been captured, shipped back to the United States, and put on trial.

She frowned and looked at the remains of the food on her tray. What was the point of worrying about all this now? It would be months before she was even eligible for early release. Until then, the only thing she could do was keep her head down and stay out of trouble. She spent most of her free time in the facility's small library. She expected that by the end of her sentence, she'd have read every single book there.

It was a goal, at least. Books helped fill in the gaps in her memories, let her know what transpired during the years she'd lost. They also provided her with a badly needed distraction from reality. In any case, it was a new month! They usually got a batch of new books in at the beginning of each month. She decided to head to the library and see if they'd gotten anything interesting in. Emmogene stood up, grabbed her tray, and turned to head to the trash cans... and immediately crashed into someone. She lost her grip on her tray, as did the woman she'd bumped into. Half-eaten chili-mac splashed up on the poor woman's face and chest.

"Oh my gosh, I'm so sorry!" Emmogene sputtered. The other woman was shorter than her, with a stocky, muscular build, short-cropped red hair. On one forearm she had a length of alien script similar to Emmogene's. On the other, she had a terrestrial tattoo of an inverted sword behind an eye.

Emmogene knew what that tattoo meant: this woman had been Internal Security. InSec.

"What the fuck!" the woman snarled, wiping her face on her sleeve. Undaunted by their height difference, she reached up, grabbed the collar of Emmogene's coverall, and pulled her down to eye level. "You need to watch where you're going, bitch, or ..." She paused, and looked down at the Sagittarian script on Emmogene's arm. "You were Section 37."

"What?" Emmogene asked.

Before the woman could answer, a pair of the guards approached, shouting at the woman to let her go.

"Yeah, yeah," the woman said, releasing Emmogene. "It was just an accident."

The female guards weren't impressed. "Second warning, Red," one of them said, baton held at the ready. "One more incident out of you and it's a month in the cooler."

The woman, Red, glared up at Emmogene before picking up her tray and walking off.

Emmogene, for her part, exhaled heavily as the guards intervened. They wore blue uniforms, with body armor, helmets, and face shields. Each carried a long metal baton and a big canister of OC spray.

"You're the new girl, right?" the taller one asked. "Just got transferred over from Barstow?" Her voice was rough.

"Y-yes, ma'am," Emmogene replied. "Anderson, Emmogene, Prisoner ID 21645899."

"That's what I thought," the woman said, with a smirk. "You been here a month and you're already getting into trouble."

"I didn't mean to cause any trouble!"

"You should be more careful. Red's a vindictive bitch."

"What?"

"I'd stay away from the places the cameras don't cover if I were you."

Emmogene's eyes were wide. She was trying not to shake. The facility in Barstow, California, had been made up mostly of low-level offenders like her, and there was rarely any trouble. "Okay. Thank you."

The shorter guard flipped up her visor and glared at Emmogene. "Don't ever thank us, you fucking traitor."

"What?"

The guard looked down at the mess on the floor. "Clean that up."

Without another word, the two guards left Emmogene standing there. Her tray was still on the floor. She'd never felt more alone.

The Navajo Nation
Tuba City, Arizona

"I WAS YOUNGER than you the first time I came here," Nathan said, as they waited at a traffic light. "Your grandparents took me on a trip to the Four Corners. We stopped here in Tuba City for lunch." The light turned green, and he started to accelerate. "Things have changed so much in some ways but not at all in others."

"The American Indians have a gene which made many of them naturally resistant to the Sagittarians' weaponized hemorrhagic fever," Ben said.

"Is that right? They were lucky, then. Those were some bad years." Millions of people died as a result of the alien-engineered biological weapon. It was finally stopped when defectors from the United Earth Alliance released information on how to produce a vaccine. "We called it the Red Death." Nathan was quiet for a few moments. "Honestly, boy, I'm glad you're too young to remember the war."

They rode in silence for a while before Ben pointed at the dashboard screen, on which was displayed GPS routing. "We're almost there. Sunset Motel."

"So we are," Nathan said, hitting his turn signal. "You remember who we're supposed to talk to?" Nathan wanted to see if Ben had retained the information Stella had given them.

"Her name is Mary," Ben said. "Daughter of the owners. Five foot two, long black hair, twenty-four years old. She works at the front desk." He held up an envelope full of cash. "We hand this to her, and she tells us which room he's staying in. Oh! I mean, we show her the money, and give it to her once she gives us the room number. Hey, why don't we just get a key from her?"

"We can, but if he's in the room it'll likely be deadbolted. We're still going to have to try and get him to open the door. You remember what to do?"

"Yeah!" Ben said, excitedly. He was thrilled to be part of the plan this time, not just waiting in the truck. He was wearing, under his jacket, the body armor vest that Jesse had given him. "Don't worry, I can handle this."

Nathan parked his truck on the street near of the Sunset Motel, out of the view of anyone in its rooms. It was one of those places where each room had its own door to the parking lot, and shared a wall with the room on either side of it. "This place has seen better days," he muttered, as they made their way up the sidewalk. It looked like it had been *vintage* even before the war. The paint was faded from the sun, and there were only a couple of cars in the lot. The neon sign had a letter burned out, and read *SUNSET M TEL*. It was the kind of place where you could pay cash and nobody would ask for an ID. "Stay here," he told Ben. "Get your stuff ready. I'll get Shadow."

The office was at one end of the U-shaped structure. Mary, the girl at the desk, went wide-eyed as Nathan walked in with Shadow. He was a big dog and he struck an imposing figure. The transaction went exactly as planned; only a few words were spoken, though Mary did come around the desk to pet Shadow. Erik Landers was in Room 2, at the far end of the building. The nondescript black Town Car parked in front of the room was the vehicle he'd arrived in. She hadn't seen him leave, but admitted she hadn't been able to watch the whole time. She also said that other people had come and gone from the room over the past few days, but none of them had checked in at the desk.

That was enough for Nathan. He thanked the woman as he handed her the envelope full of money. He led Shadow out of the office, and signaled Ben on his radio. Nathan and the dog made their way along the front of the building, staying in the shade of the overhang. In the chance their target was watching them out the window, it would look like they were just going to one of the other rooms, and he wouldn't be able to see them approach after they turned the corner. Each room had a window that faced the parking lot, but coming from the direction they were, they wouldn't have to walk past the window for Room 2 before they got to the door.

Meanwhile, Ben exited the truck with an empty pizza box in his hands. He was wearing a red ball cap with a slice of pizza embroidered upon it. They had done this routine before, and it surprised Nathan how often it worked. Ben strode straight for the door as Nathan approached from the side.

Ben looked at his uncle. Nathan nodded at the boy. It was *go time*.

The kid took a deep breath, exhaled, and rapped on the door three times.

A muffled voice came from behind the door. "What is it?"

"Pizza!" Ben declared, raising his voice so he could be heard. "Large pepperoni?"

"I didn't order a pizza!" the voice said.

Ben kept the bit going. "Yeah, I have the pizza you ordered! Large pepperoni!"

"I didn't order a pizza!" the man insisted, frustration in his voice.

Nathan nodded at Ben. The boy knocked on the door again. "Look, Mister, I've got other deliveries to make. Your pizza is getting cold."

"Son of a bitch!" the man behind the door snarled, followed by the sound of locks being undone. He pulled the door open quickly and looked down at Ben. It was Erik Landers, and he was in his underwear. "For fucks' sakes, kid, I said I didn't order a—"

Landers froze when Nathan stepped into view. The bounty hunter's bronze badge was hanging around his neck. In one hand, he had his service revolver, a .41 Magnum Ruger Sentinel with a flashlight mounted under the barrel. In the other, he held Shadow's short lead.

"Federal Recovery Agent!" Nathan announced. "Get your hands where I can see them!"

The bounty could have done things the easy way, but in Nathan's experience they seldom did. Instead of complying, he tried to slam the door in Nathan's face. He couldn't get the door latched, though, and Nathan turned Shadow loose. Landers futilely tried to scramble across the bed as the enhanced working dog shot after him like a fur-covered missile. He screamed as Shadow latched onto his arm and pulled him down.

Before Nathan could stop him, Ben ran in after the dog. Landers was struggling with Shadow, trying to hit him with his free hand in a vain attempt to let go. Ben didn't hesitate. He produced his can of pepper foam and sprayed Landers right in the eyes with it. The bounty's screams went high-pitched as he gasped for air.

"Shadow, out!" Nathan ordered. The dog let go of the mark, jumped off the bed, and sat, watching his prey warily. Ben backed up and moved behind his uncle. Erik Landers was curled up into a ball on the bed, blind, burning, and bleeding, struggling to catch his breath. Nathan kept his gun drawn and nodded at Ben, who went and checked the bathroom to make sure no one was hiding there.

"Erik Landers, *in compliance with the Extraterrestrial and Collaborator Recovery Act, and by virtue of the authority vested in me as a licensed and bonded Federal Recovery Agent, I am taking you into custody. You have the right to remain silent, and to be given proper and humane care while in my charge. If you attempt to resist or flee, I have the legal authority to use lethal force without further warning. You will be transferred to federal custody for processing and adjudication. Do you understand?*"

Landers didn't answer. He just kept gasping for air and cursing aloud.

"The rest of the room is clear, Uncle Nate!" Ben announced.

"Good job, boy. Go bring the truck around and get the first-aid kit. Keep your eyes open in case this asshole has friends." Ben did as he was told, leaving Nathan and Shadow alone with the wanted man. "It didn't have to be like this, man," Nathan said. The alleged gunrunner looked pitiful, bleeding from his left arm, snot dribbling down his face, his eyes watering, dressed in nothing but a pair of tighty-whities. "I would have let you get dressed, given you a bottle of water, and you'd have had a perfectly nice ride back to the office. Now you're going to be miserable for the rest of the day."

"I want a lawyer," Landers gasped.

"I look like a cop to you? You'll get a lawyer when Homeland Security comes to pick you up. Until then, I suggest you keep your mouth shut. We'll get you patched up before we haul you off."

Nathan was surprised when Ben's voice sounded over his radio. "Uncle Nate!" he said, excitedly. "Someone's pulling into the parking lot! They're coming in hot!"

"Coming in hot?" Nathan repeated. "What the hell does that mean?"

He got his answer seconds later. A white panel van screeched to
a stop in front of the motel room. Nathan grabbed Shadow's collar
and pulled the dog into the bathroom. Hugging the dirty tile floor,
he gritted his teeth as a gunman opened fire in full auto. Plaster and
tile exploded into dust as rifle rounds tore through the wall. The
mirror shattered. The lights blew out. Then it was over. There was
muffled shouting, but the loudest thing was the ringing in his ears.

You have to move, Nathan told himself, trying to will his body to
listen to him. *You have to move or you're going to die.* His muscles
finally obeyed. He rolled to his side, drew his revolver, and scrambled
to the bathroom door.

Nathan caught the gunman mid-reload. A masked man with a
short-barreled Zhukov assault rifle was fumbling for a spare
magazine, trying to get it out of his jacket pocket. Erik Landers was
behind him, clutching his wounded arm. His eyes went wide as
Nathan popped out of the bathroom, lying on his side, gun drawn.
BOOM! The shooter fell to the floor, and Landers was sprayed with
blood and bits of brain matter.

"Freeze!" Nathan shouted. "Don't you fucking do it!"

Erik Landers hesitated for just a second. Nathan had him in his
sights, but the door was so close. Two steps and he'd be out of sight.
A few more and he'd be in the van. His muscles tensed, telegraphing
his decision.

You dumb bastard, Nathan thought, squeezing his revolver's
trigger again. The gun roared. Landers didn't make it those two steps;
the slug hit him square between the shoulder blades, and he dropped
like a puppet with its strings cut.

Tires squealed again as the driver of the white van stomped on
the gas. He almost did a donut in the parking lot, he flipped around
so fast, and in seconds he was gone. Gun in hand, Nathan checked
Erik Landers. He was dead. Sighing, the bounty hunter called
Shadow, stepped over the dead men, and went outside.

Ben pulled up in the truck a second later and jumped out so fast
he almost forgot to put it in park. "Uncle Nate!" the boy said, eyes
wide. "Are you okay? What about Shadow?"

"I'm fine," Nathan said, pulling two spent cases from his revolver's
cylinder. Shadow trotted out of the motel room and approached Ben,
tail wagging. "So's he. Our bounty's not."

"Oh, shit! Is he dead?"

Nathan only nodded as he dropped two fresh cartridges into the revolver's chambers, then closed the cylinder. "This is gonna be a long day. The police will be here soon. Did you get a look at the van?"

"I just saw a white van," Ben said. "But I was pulling up in the truck. The dash camera should have recorded everything."

"Good," the bounty hunter said, holstering his revolver.

"I'm sorry I didn't help," his nephew said, looking suddenly dejected. "You could have died. It just happened so fast. I tried calling you on the radio but you didn't answer. I should have grabbed the shotgun. I should have—"

Nathan stepped forward and put a hand on his shoulder. The boy was rattled. "Ben, listen to me. You did the right thing. You couldn't see what was happening from your position. You didn't know how many shooters there were, or what weapons they had. You lost comms with me because my earbud fell out. For all you knew, I was already dead. Charging in blind would have been a stupid thing to do."

Ben took a deep breath and wiped his eyes. "I know. I just wanted to help."

"You do help, boy. You're my partner. When we get home, I'll show you how to use that revolver I picked up in Vegas, and I want you to start carrying it when we're working."

"Really?" Ben knew the basics of shooting, but he'd never expressed much interest in it before.

"Sure, why not? You'll be fifteen in a few months. If you're going to keep doing this, you need to be able to protect yourself." Nathan paused; sirens wailed in the distance, drawing closer. "Quick, get on the horn with Stella and tell her what happened. Get the video from the dash cam pulled up for the cops. I'm going to check the room and see if there's any intel we can grab before the cops get here. Get going now."

Ben did as he was told and got back in the truck. The boy was pretty tech savvy, and normally searching for intel was one of his jobs, but he'd been through enough today without seeing one dead man covered in another dead man's brains.

Jesus, Nathan thought. Jesse was right: this was no life for a kid.

"DID YOU DRIVE ALL THE WAY UP HERE just to make my life more difficult, Nate?" John Yazzie was a lieutenant in the Navajo

Nation Territorial Police. He looked around the grisly scene in the motel room, shaking his head. A pair of his officers was zipping the two dead men up into body bags. "The chief is going to be apoplectic. He didn't want to let you guys come on the Reservation. I talked him into it. I vouched for you."

Yazzie had served with Nathan in the war. They'd both been tank commanders in the same battalion, and they'd seen a lot together. "Please tell the chief I'm awful sorry about this," Nathan said. "No, I mean that. You know how I operate. I always try to de-escalate. This is going to create a lot of headaches for me, too. Unfortunately, he didn't give me a choice."

Yazzie kicked a piece of spent 5.45mm brass from the dead gunman's assault rifle. "No, he didn't. But what about the other guy, Erik Landers?"

"What about him? I told him not to run."

Yazzie sighed. "Nate, you shot an unarmed man, in his underwear, in the back. Don't get me wrong, I don't particularly give a damn. What these clowns did to you was attempted murder. But the Tribal Council Prosecutor, he's kind of a stickler for things like this. I know him. He might want to press charges."

Nathan frowned. He didn't like quoting the law to people, especially not to an old friend like Yazzie, but there were a lot of misconceptions about Federal Recovery Agents out there, and about the rules they were required to operate under. "I appreciate the warning, but he can't do that."

"Trust me, he can. He's a real hardass. Every time there's a use-of-force incident in the Department, he's on us like a mosquito. He—"

"No, I mean he *can't*. Legally. This was a Homeland Security tasking. I read him his Thirty-first Amendment rights. I warned him that trying to flee would result in the use of deadly force. He thought he could outrun a bullet, and he was wrong."

Yazzie raised his eyebrows. "Wait, he's a collaborator? Stella didn't say anything about that when she called me. He didn't have the mark on his arm."

"Don't take this the wrong way, but as a matter of course we don't divulge the specifics of bounties to cops."

"What about the tattoo? He didn't have one."

"Landers wasn't a direct collaborator. As far as we know, he was never involved with the UEA or the war. Allegedly he's been running weapons to pro-alien insurgent groups down in South America. That suspicion was enough to convince a judge to move this case from the DOJ to DHS, I guess."

"Wow. They can do that? That's kind of scary."

Nathan shrugged. "Supposedly there are legal requirements, and it all has to get signed off by a federal judge, but I'd be lying if I said I didn't think the system got abused sometimes. If not for the asshole with the Zhukov I wouldn't have fired. I didn't know if the guy in the van had a gun, though."

Yazzie nodded. "No, I follow you. No big loss, anyway. If you'd shot a Navajo citizen it'd be a different story, but some asshole from back east who's arming collaborator terrorists? I think the chief will understand. I'll need you to write up and sign a sworn statement before you go, though."

"No problem. I told Ben to give the video from my dash camera to your officers outside. He got a pretty good view of the whole thing."

"We already put out an APB for the van. We'll notify the police around the Four Corners in case he leaves the Rez."

"Oh, hey, before they get it loaded up into the meat wagon, I need the body."

"What?"

"I need Erik Landers's body. I'm required to turn my bounties over to DHS, dead or alive."

"Seriously?"

Nathan nodded. "We've got a big industrial refrigerator at the office that we use for this. The Feds do autopsies on every one of the DHS cases, looking for alien modifications and implants. I think they test them for diseases, too."

"Holy hell. Can you send me a copy of the regulations that state that? I didn't know that, and the chief probably doesn't, either."

"Sure. Some of this stuff is pretty obscure. You know, in the years I've been doing this, I've only ever had to kill a handful of men. It's my job to bring them back to stand trial, not to be an executioner. I'm going to have to fill out a shitload of paperwork over this."

Yazzie nodded knowingly. "I know how that is. Come out to my car, will you? You can type the statement into my computer. I'll print it out and witness you signing it, and then you're free to go. I'll call you if anything changes, but the situation being what it is, I'm going to recommend that they just drop the matter."

"You need one from Ben, too?"

"No," the police officer said, "he's a minor, and he wasn't in the room anyway. The video from your truck should suffice."

"Thank you, Yazzie." The two men shook hands. "It was good seeing you again."

"Next time, come visit without shooting somebody, yeah? We'll go fishing."

Nathan loved to fish, but he didn't get to do it very often. "That sounds like a plan. I'll bring Ben. It's about time I taught that boy to fish. He's more interested in video games and online chat boards."

"Come on, let's get that statement signed so you can go. It's getting dark."

Thirty minutes later, Nathan returned to his truck, were he found Ben looking at a laptop. A body bag with the corpse of Erik Landers was secured in the bed of the truck. Shadow had sniffed curiously at the dead man but was now curled up on his cushion. He'd been a good boy today, and he was going to get a raw steak when they got home.

Wait a second, Nathan thought. "Ben, that's not your laptop."

"It's the dead guy's," Ben said, casually, not taking his eyes off the screen. "He had it unlocked when we showed up. I've been looking through it for intel."

Nathan was so proud of Ben he could bust. He didn't gush, because that would embarrass the boy, but still. "Outstanding work. Find anything good?"

Ben looked up from the screen. "Not really. There's a second drive and it's encrypted. If we can unlock that, we might find something good."

"Can you, I don't know, hack into it or something?"

"No, Uncle Nate, I can't *hack* into it," Ben said, doing finger quotations. "Without the encryption key, there's nothing I can do. Except"—he reached into a bag, and pulled out a small plastic pad with a cord hanging from it—"he had this."

"What is it?"

"It's a biometric scanner. I'm willing to bet he used this to access the drive."

Nathan raised his eyebrows. "Well, there's only one way to find out. I'm sure he won't mind. And listen, you did good work today. Things went to shit and you held it together. I'm proud of you."

Ben's face flushed a little. "Thanks."

"Now, let's get going, hey? I'm hungry. You wanna stop and get some Navajo tacos on the way home?"

"With a dead guy in the back?"

Nathan shrugged. "Like I said, I'm sure he won't mind."

Federal Detention Facility
Gallup, New Mexico

AS WAS OFTEN THE CASE, Emmogene was the last one in the prison library when it closed down for the evening. The guard gave her a curt nod as she left, and he closed the steel door and locked it behind her. It would be lights out soon, and normally all the prisoners in the women's wing would be making their way to their cells right about now. Things seemed quieter than usual, though. Emmogene didn't think she'd lingered that long, but she picked up her pace. She didn't want to get in trouble for not being in her cell at 2100 hours on the dot.

Her cell was on the second level. Her cellmate, Gretchen, was in the high-risk bloc for an attempted suicide, so Emmogene had the place to herself for a while. She liked it, even if the circumstances weren't great.

The corridor to the main cellblock was wide and dimly lit. Emmogene didn't dawdle here; she didn't know if it was true, but there was a rumor that the cameras in this corridor didn't work, and she didn't want to be any place where they couldn't see her. The crew on cleaning detail for the week was gathered around the janitorial closest, putting their equipment away for the night. One of them, a tall woman with her hair shaved down to fuzz, glared at Emmogene in silence.

Her coverall sleeves were rolled up. She had the Internal Security tattoo on her arm.

Emmogene's heart dropped into her stomach and she got ready to sprint to the cellblock. As she took her first step, though, a hand clamped around her arm. She whipped her head around to see who had grabbed her—it was Red. Without another word, the woman slugged Emmogene right in the face. She hit her again in the stomach.

Emmogene gasped for air and tried to focus as at least two women dragged her into the cleaning closet. Her eyes were watering and swelling up, and she could barely see. She knocked over an empty mop bucket as they tossed her roughly to the floor. There were three women in the closet with her.

"Please!" Emmogene pleaded. "I'm sorry! I didn't—"

"Shut up!" Red snarled, cutting her off. She grabbed Emmogene's arm and showed her alien marking to the others. "She was Section 37, right?"

A woman to Red's left, a sullen-looking, bespectacled blonde who had tied the top half of her orange jumpsuit around her waist, pushed her glasses up, leaned in, and squinted at Emmogene's marking. "I think so." She looked Emmogene in the eye. "What's your name?"

"E-Emmogene. Emmogene Anderson."

The stout, muscular woman to Red's right spoke up. Her voice was so raspy it sounded like she ate cigarettes instead of smoking them. "I think I remember her from when I worked for Section 37. She was a program subject."

Section 37. Program subject. Emmogene struggled to remember, her mind filled with a torrent of incoherent, disconnected images and sounds. She remembered being strapped to a table, conscious but immobilized, while they drilled into her head. One of the Visitors themselves was personally supervising. It considered her coldly through oversized eyes. Emmogene remembered being run through a series of tests, where she was trying to do...something...to different people.

Looking up, Emmogene summoned the courage to speak. "Do you know who I am? I don't...I don't remember."

"No, you wouldn't," Red said. "You would have been memory-wiped at the end of the war."

"But...how do you know all this?"

The blonde pointed to the tattoo on her arm. *Of course. InSec.* They had been the United Earth Alliance's counterintelligence operatives. They were little more than a criminal gang now, but during the aliens' reign they had been omnipresent within the UEA, and had enjoyed almost unlimited power.

"What do you want from me?" Emmogene asked, unable to hide the fear in her voice. "Is this because I bumped into you? I'm sorry! I didn't mean to!"

"How did you get yourself captured?" Red asked, ignoring her question.

"I was with a group of refugees in southern Mexico. I'm not sure where, exactly. We moved around a lot. I was with an Earth Storm commando named Anthony Krieg at first, and he took me to a man named Suliman Alvarez."

The three ex-InSec looked at each other. They seemed to recognize that name.

"There were about twenty of us at first, right after the war ended. Then Anthony and some others left to fight, said they were going to build an insurgency against the Americans. After that it was just Suliman's people and me. In the end, it was just me."

"The end?" the blonde asked. "What happened?"

"The Mexican Army raided the farm we were staying on. I don't know how they knew we were there. Maybe somebody betrayed us. They sent in commandos. Everyone was killed except for me."

Red raised an eyebrow. "Why didn't they kill you?"

Emmogene's expression hardened. "Because Suliman had me locked in a little room in the basement—for my *safety*, he said. He was worried I'd try to run away. The soldiers probably thought I was a sex slave or something. I didn't try to fight. They figured out I was American and turned me over to the US government. That was four years ago. I don't know why they dragged me around and kept me locked up for years after the war ended. They said I was important, but they never told me why."

"Suliman Alvarez was InSec," Red said. "He kept you with him because you came from Section 37. A Section 37 asset is to be protected at all costs and never allowed to fall into enemy hands. He should have killed you instead of letting you get taken alive."

"There were plenty of times I wished he would have," Emmogene said, bitterly. "The Mexicans didn't give him a choice."

"Yeah, well, that puts me in kind of a bad spot, kid. Right now, the Americans don't know who you really are."

"*I* don't know who I really am!" Emmogene protested. "I barely remember anything from the war! Whatever it is you think I know, I don't know! They erased my memory!"

"It's not what you know," Red said. "It's what you carry. Sooner or later they'll figure out that you're not just another prisoner. When they do, they'll dissect you, and what you're carrying will fall into the hands of the US government. This can't be allowed to happen."

"What am I carrying?" Emmogene asked, pleading. They were going to kill her. She knew it. They were going to kill her and she had no idea why. "Why do you care? Don't you get it? The war is *over*! We *lost*! The Visitors aren't coming back! They abandoned us and they're *not coming back*!"

"We used to send people who talked like that in for re-education," Red answered, ice in her voice, "or liquidation, if they couldn't be re-educated." She pulled a screwdriver from inside her coverall. The point had been filed into a sharp tip.

"Are you sure about this?" the blonde asked, pushing her glasses up again. "They might hang you."

"Maybe," Red replied. "I'm going to die in here one way or another. This will be seen as just another act of violence from an unstable prisoner. They won't question it. They probably won't even bother with an autopsy. It needs to be done."

"Please don't do this," Emmogene begged. "Please. I won't tell anyone. I don't know anything. Please."

Red's expression softened, if only slightly. "Sorry, kid. It's nothing personal." The softness was gone in an instant. She looked at the other two. "Get out of here, go find the guards. Tell them I'm going crazy. Act like you were trying to stop me."

"Understood," the blonde said.

"For the Future," the raspy woman croaked. It's something the alien loyalists always used to say. Everything they did was to build a better future.

"For the Future," Red agreed. The other two women left the janitorial closet, leaving Emmogene alone with her murderer. "I'll be quick," the former InSec operative said. "It's best if you don't struggle."

Emmogene tried to say something, but lost the thought before the words got out of her mouth. She felt the oddest buzzing in the back of her head. Even in the face of her impending death, it was so strange as to be distracting. *What's happening to me?* Red stepped forward. *Stop it! Leave me alone!*

Red took another step forward, stopped, and stood up straight. Her eyes were wide but her pupils were pinpricks. In one smooth motion, she raised the improvised shiv and plunged it into her own left eye, burying it to the handle. She stood there for just a moment, twitching. Her other eye rolled back and she collapsed to the floor.

Emmogene screamed.

EMMOGENE WAS AFRAID. The riot alarm was blaring throughout the prison. Back against a concrete-block wall, she surveyed the carnage in front of her and tried to comprehend what she was seeing. Her other two assailants had come running back when they heard her scream. They saw their comrade dead on a floor, her shiv buried to the handle in her eye socket, and they immediately attacked Emmogene. At least, they tried to. The buzzing in the back of Emmogene's head got louder, and as she covered her face and head, about to be beaten to death, her attackers had stopped. It was like they were entranced, unaware of their surroundings. A few moments after that, a pair of guards came rushing in, batons drawn. They charged into the cleaning closet and saw the body. One of them raised her baton to strike Emmogene, but the blonde woman had thrown herself in the way.

Now? Now both of those guards were on the floor, having been savagely attacked. Red's two compatriots were down as well—one had been bludgeoned by the guards while the other had some sort of seizure and collapsed after the fight. A riot squad was stacked outside the door, bearing shields and shotguns. They were ordering Emmogene to come out or they would have to shoot her. She was pressed into the corner, and they couldn't see her from where they were, but it was only a matter of time before they came in, and then they would probably kill her.

Emmogene was struggling to hold back tears. How had this happened? Why did Red kill herself? Why did the other two ex-InSec prisoners suddenly attack the guards to protect her? Her head hurt. The buzzing in the back of her skull had subsided, leaving only a headache and some dizziness. Images flashed through her mind, pieces of memories long suppressed. She remembered standing in a room, wearing scrubs, with wires connected to her head. There were bright lights above; the glare from the lights obscured the men observing her. She could only see their silhouettes, black and ominous. A couple of the silhouettes weren't human; the features were too gaunt, the heads too large and oblong. Commands were issued to her over a loudspeaker, but she couldn't quite make the words out.

A man was let into the room. He was young and fit, and wore the black uniform of Internal Security. The voice blared over the speaker once more, but this time Emmogene could remember what it said: *"Now, you must kill her."* The man looked up at the people observing them, then back at Emmogene. He charged.

"Emmogene!"

Hearing her name snapped her out of the flashback. Emmogene was once again in the cleaning closet, backed into a corner, waiting to be shot. Her breath was ragged. She was confused. The alarm had ceased.

"Emmogene Anderson?" Someone from outside was calling her name. It was much calmer than the others had been. "I'm going to come to the door. I just want to talk to you."

"I didn't kill them!" Emmogene pleaded. "I don't know what's happening!"

"I believe you," the man said, appearing in the doorway. He held his hands up in a nonthreatening manner. "I'm just trying to figure out what transpired."

"Who are you?"

"I'm Doctor Grayson," he said, calmly. He was fifty or so, and was dressed in the same blue coverall that the guards wore, but had on a white coat over it. He didn't have any armor, weapons, or a helmet. Black-framed glasses adorned his face, and his hair was gray. "I'm the facility psychiatrist."

"I'm not crazy!" Emmogene insisted, in a manner that definitely sounded crazy. "I don't know what's happening!"

"Neither do I," Dr. Grayson said. "But, if you'll come with me, perhaps we can find out. I need to run a few tests."

"You're going to dissect me!"

"We don't dissect people at this facility, Emmogene," he answered.

His voice was calming. "I'm a doctor, not a butcher. No one is going to hurt you. However, wouldn't you agree that you seem to be a danger to others, and perhaps even yourself?"

That *did* sound reasonable.

"I can't help you if you try to stay backed into that corner like a spider," the doctor continued. "If you don't come with me, those men out there are going to come in here and get you, and nobody wants that." He stepped closer. "I read your file. I know you were in alien custody for quite some time, and that you were subjected to a memory wipe. We've seen this before in other people they have experimented on. Do you think they did something to you?"

The silhouettes of men and aliens observing her flashed before her eyes. She nodded, tears streaming down her face. "I'm scared."

Dr. Grayson leaned forward and extended a hand, reaching over the pile of bodies on the closet floor. "I know. Come with me, Emmogene. Please. I want to help you."

Emmogene looked at him, then down at the injured and dead, then back up at the doctor. She took his hand.

The Foster Residence
Prescott Valley, Arizona
Several days later ...

NATHAN FOSTER HAD RETURNED HOME to Arizona after the war. He wanted a quiet place of his own that was big enough for him and Ben, and with a little bit of land. Land had been available for cheap in Prescott Valley, so he'd settled there, fixing up an old, prewar farmhouse. It had its own well, came with a barn, and sat on twenty acres. It was close enough to town that he was still able to get good internet access, but far enough outside of town that he could shoot without the neighbors complaining.

In the morning sun, he stood on the back ten with Ben, watching closely as the boy fired his new revolver. The target, a life-size silhouette of one of the gaunt aliens, was only fifteen feet away, but that was enough for a start. Ben had shot rifles and shotguns before but had never been interested in handguns. He'd go plinking with a .22 pistol now and then, and Nathan had taught him the basics of using a handgun, but the Canadian revolver was the first handgun of his own.

"The trigger is heavy," the boy complained, "and long."

"It's a revolver trigger," Nathan explained. "It's like that because it has to cock the hammer and rotate the cylinder, all in one motion. Jesse polished it a little. It's smooth."

BANG. "I keep missing."

"You're just pulling to the right, is all," Nathan said. He bent down and adjusted Ben's grip. "Hold it firmly. Shift your grip up a little. There you go. Now concentrate on pulling the trigger straight back toward you. Don't worry about being fast. Be smooth instead."

Clad in earmuffs and shooting glasses, the boy had a look of concentration on his face as he fired again. *BANG. BANG. BANG. Click!*

"You're out," Nathan said. "Nice shooting, though." All three rounds had hit the silhouette center-of-mass. "That's three good shots. Now reload, like I showed you."

"Oh, right." Grasping the barrel with his left hand, Ben depressed the release lever with his thumb and broke the action open. Just as he'd been shown, he angled the cylinder back toward himself. All six cases ejected cleanly. Then, holding the weapon by the barrel and cylinder, he reached down with his right hand and retrieved a speedloader from his belt. He fumbled a little bit, trying to align the six cartridges with the chambers, but he got them in. He twisted the knob, dropping the cartridges into the chambers, and let the speedloader fall to the ground. Regaining his firing grip, he closed the weapon's action and pushed it back out in both hands, reacquiring his sight picture.

"Excellent!" Nathan said, pleased with how well he was doing. "Fire another string, clear your weapon, then re-holster."

The boy did as he was told, placing six more .38 wadcutters into the target's chest area. He unloaded and stuck the revolver into a surplus holster that Jesse had been able to scrounge up for it. It wasn't a speed rig, but it was secure, and Nathan was more worried about the boy losing the gun than he was about his draw speed.

"You really think I'm going to need all this stuff, Uncle Nate?" Ben asked. He was a skinny kid, and not particularly tall. He was energetic and surprisingly strong for his size, but he'd never been very athletic. He was more interested in video games and reading than sports. In a sane world, a young man like Ben would be in school or something, not bounty hunting.

Unfortunately, they didn't live in a sane world. "I hope not, but shit happens sometimes, like the other day. I don't plan on putting you in danger, but if the situation gets sideways you need to be able to protect yourself."

"What was it like?"

"What?"

"Killing those two guys. What was it like?"

Nathan paused. He didn't really know how to answer that. "That's a hell of a thing to ask a man," he said.

"No, for real, what's it like?"

"Fine, you really wanna know? I didn't feel anything except recoil. When it's going down like that you don't have time for feelings. You act on adrenaline, training, and experience. If you hesitate, you die. You can't afford to second-guess yourself when people are trying to kill you. There's time to moralize later."

"Can I tell you something?"

"What? Of course you can, boy. We're family."

"Promise you won't get mad?"

"I'm not gonna get mad, Ben. What's on your mind?"

Ben's eyes were downcast. "I know what happened to Mom. I remember."

"What?" He'd always said he didn't remember. The shrinks figured it was a result of the trauma. She'd been caught behind enemy lines when the UEA invaded California during their final offensive of the war. Ben had been found in a refugee camp after the war, but his mother had never been located.

"I'm sorry I lied," Ben said, struggling, and failing, to choke back tears. "It was easier to just lie and say I didn't remember, but it's not true. I remember. I just . . . after the shooting, I couldn't stop thinking about it. I remember. I saw Mom die."

Jesus. "Come have a sit-down," Nathan said, gesturing to a pair of faded lawn chairs under a raggedy old umbrella. Sitting down, he reached into the cooler and got a Dr. Pepper for the boy. "Talk to me. Tell me what happened." He never let it show, but it had been hard for Nathan, too, not knowing what had happened to his sister, Samantha.

He remembered, vividly, the day California was invaded. A combined Army, Marine Corps, and Air Force offensive had finally pushed the UEA out of Texas and back into Mexico. The damned Greys counterattacked by opening up a second front in the Continental United States. They were somehow able to jam NORAD's radars effectively enough to conceal hundreds of hypersonic transport aircraft. The planes dropped troops and weapons into Southern California before turning kamikaze and striking various targets throughout the region.

Having secured a beachhead, the UEA was able to bring up more assets from Mexico and South America by sea, reinforcing their toehold in California and allowing them to break out of the Greater

Los Angeles Perimeter. They were able to take the entire LA-to-San Francisco corridor before being stopped, and they held that territory for two years. The number of American citizens caught behind enemy lines (and being used as human shields) prevented the US from responding with nuclear weapons.

"I don't remember everything," Ben said, sipping his soda. "One day we left the old house. Mom put me in my car seat. I didn't know what was happening."

"If I had to guess, that was probably when the invasion happened. You would have been about four. I was fighting in Northern Mexico when that happened."

"We ended up in a big camp, like, a really big camp. They built these little houses for us to live in. There were a lot of families, a lot of kids, each given their own little house. Ours had the number 264 painted on it. We had food every day, we had beds, after a while it just seemed normal."

"That was the intention," Nathan said. "Eventually they would have put all the kids like you into their creches to be indoctrinated to love the Greys."

"I remember some of that," Ben said. "They started a school. Every day, we'd go to the schoolhouse, and this man and this woman would tell us about the Visitors. The Visitors love you, they would say, and they told us they were going to take care of us and our families from now on. We'd also do stuff like reading and counting and art like it was a regular kindergarten."

Nathan's eyes narrowed, but he didn't say anything.

Ben continued, "We'd watch these videos all the time, cartoons about how great the Visitors were. A lot of them were hosted by this blonde girl, I remember that part. She was older, like a teenager, and she was really pretty. She had like this catchphrase she'd say, 'Together, we're building a better world.' I remember because the teachers would have us recite that at the end of the video. You'd say your name and then say, 'Together, we're building a better world.'"

"I see. How long did this go on?"

"I don't know. It seemed like forever, but I was just a little kid. A year, maybe? One day they all just left us. The teachers, the people who ran the camp, they all just, like, were gone one day. Everybody was confused. Then soldiers found us."

"That was close to the end of the war," Nathan said. "When I got you from the Refugee Resettlement Administration, they said you'd been located in a refugee internment camp outside Bakersfield. The camps were all abandoned by UEA forces before the Army got to them. Was...was your mom still with you, then?"

Ben was quiet for a moment. "No. One night, she got me out of bed and said we were leaving. I guess a bunch of people had been working on a plan to get us out."

Nathan struggled to keep his composure and let Ben keep talking.

"There were a bunch of kids," the boy continued, "but the grown-ups didn't tell us anything except that we were going for a ride in a truck. They said it would be fun. We were loaded into the back of a truck, like a big moving truck. Mom was with me, and so were a few of the other parents. Not all the kids' parents were there, though. Some were crying."

"What happened?"

"I'm not sure. We were in the back of the truck. It was dark. They told us to be quiet. Something must have gone wrong. There was shouting, then they opened the doors and shined these bright lights in on all of us."

"Who did?"

"Policemen. UEA security, I guess, I don't know. We just thought they were police. The separated the kids from the adults. I was crying as they pulled me away from Mom. Then...then they shot them."

There was a knot in Nathan's stomach. "The adults?"

"Yeah. Mom and a couple others. They just shot them, right in front of us. The last thing Mom said was she screamed at me to close my eyes. I didn't listen." There were tears streaming down Ben's cheeks now. "I watched them shoot her. I watched her die. Just *boom*, one shot, right in the head," he said, touching his forehead with his index finger, "and down she went. It didn't seem real. I didn't realize what had happened. For a long time after that I kept asking where she was, when she was coming back. I didn't understand." He paused again, choking back tears. "I didn't understand that she was dead and she wasn't coming back."

Despite his best efforts, there were tears in Nathan's eyes, too. After all these years, to finally know...it was almost too much. He leaned forward and hugged Ben tightly. "She loved you. She loved you so much she died trying to bring you home." Ben was sobbing into Nathan's shoulder now. "I know this wasn't easy for you," Nathan said. "Thank you for telling me what happened to my sister. It's good to finally know."

"I'm sorry I didn't tell you sooner. I think I made myself forget it, but I don't want to forget anymore. I want to remember Mom."

"I'm proud of you, Ben," Nathan managed, "and I know your mom would be, too." He pulled back from embracing his nephew, wiped his eyes, and put a hand on the boy's shoulder. "Now, how's about we shoot a little more? You up for it?"

Ben nodded. "Let's do it."

NATHAN WATCHED with some satisfaction as a pair of Homeland Security agents, in their gray fatigues and black vests, loaded Carter Reid into the back of a prisoner transport van and secured him. The prisoner looked to be in shock, as if the gravity of his situation was finally sinking in. The bounty, minus taxes, had been deposited into Nathan's account, and the traitor would face justice at last.

It was tempting to gloat sometimes, to fire off a mean comment as the prisoners were being hauled away, but he always refrained. There was the possibility, however remote, that they were actually innocent. More than that, what was the point? Carter Reid would, in all likelihood, be found guilty; the aliens' human administrators kept detailed records, and the government had built a solid case against him before the bounty was ever issued. For his crimes, he would almost certainly be hanged, and he knew that. Taunting him would be childish; his comeuppance would arrive soon enough.

With his prisoner handed off to the authorities, Nathan went back into the office. Stella, at her desk, looked up when he came inside. "Stop brooding."

"I'm not brooding," he said, sitting as his desk. His desk was pushed up against hers, so that they faced each other when they were both seated.

"You're brooding," she insisted. "You're still pissed off about Erik Landers, aren't you?"

"Yeah, I guess," Nathan admitted. "Damned fool should have just come quietly. Hell, the case against him was weak. He might have gotten off. We'd have still gotten paid, and he'd be a free man."

"We *are* still getting paid," Stella reminded him. "It'll take longer to process, but we'll still get paid. This is the only deadly force incident you've had this year so far, so we're not in much danger of getting audited."

"Say, when are they coming to pick up the body, anyway?" The gunrunner's corpse was still chilling in the basement.

"DHS says they can't get a meat wagon out here until Monday, but they swore up and down they'd get him then. I reminded them we're charging them for every day we have to store the body." She took a sip of her coffee. "That's not all that's bothering you about this."

"It's not. I came real close to getting my ticket punched and I had to kill two men. The whole thing was sloppy. Ben could have been hurt. I did some stupid shit when I was his age, but I never had to worry about being gunned down."

"Don't be so hard on yourself," Stella said, gently. "We can't know what we can't know. When you told me what happened, I thought I must have missed something, so I went back over every bit of information we had on the case. There was nothing in the dossier we were given to indicate that he was working with accomplices. It makes a certain amount of sense, when you think about it, but there are guys like him who work solo, too. I'm just glad that you boys weren't hurt."

"Kind of you to say."

"The last thing I want to have to do is dust off my résumé and find a new job," she said, pausing to sip her coffee again, "so you watch yourself out there. Have you talked to Ben about what happened?"

"Yeah, this morning. He's a little shook up, but he's handling it."

"He's a tough kid."

"That he is. I can't imagine growing up the way he did." Nathan was quiet for a moment, then looked around to make sure Ben wasn't within earshot. "He told me last night that he knows what happened to his mother."

"Really? Oh my God. What did he say?"

"Well, you know he was in a UEA prison camp for a while? I guess his mom and some others tried to sneak the kids out, but they got caught."

Stella held a hand up to her mouth. "Oh, Jesus."

Nathan nodded. "Yeah. They got caught. The bastards shot them, right in front of the kids. Ben was so little, and one of his earliest memories is of his mother being murdered. It ain't right."

"It's not," Stella agreed, "but it is what it is. How are you doing? That was probably a lot to take in."

"I'd be lyin' if I said it wasn't. I mean, don't get me wrong, I figured Sam was dead, and accepted that. There was no way she'd have ever given up trying to find Ben if she was still alive. It's just, hearing how she died, knowing, after all these years . . . it's enough to make a grown man cry."

"And that's okay!" Stella assured him.

Nathan smiled at her. Nobody would accuse him of being the most sensitive man ever, but he wasn't made of stone. "You know what I really felt, though, learning all this? Pride. Samantha died with her boots on, resisting those traitor sons o' bitches to the very end. It was a relief to hear, in a way. You know what kind of manipulation and brainwashing the Greys were capable of. I guess, deep down, I was always a little worried that I'd learn that they got to Sam, that they were able to turn her. I feel ashamed of myself for even thinking it, now."

"Not all of the Greys' servants went willingly. Like you said, they had methods of manipulation and control that we're only beginning to understand."

"I know. Still, I shouldn't have doubted her."

"I never knew your sister, but I think she would understand, given everything you went through. I also think she'd be proud of the job you're doing raising her son."

"You think? I'm doing the best I can, but sometimes . . ." He trailed off for a moment. "There has to be a better life for him. It ain't right that a fourteen-year-old boy has to worry about getting shot."

Stella's expression softened. "Hon, you're all the family he has left. I think taking that away from him would be harder on him than the business."

"Harder on him than seeing his uncle almost get killed?"

"Harder than that. Think about it. He lost his whole world. He watched his mom die. Hell, did he ever even know his father?"

Nathan shook his head. "Ben's father was a fellow named Greg

Nelson. He was Sam's fiancé before the war. Decent enough fellow, sold insurance. He was going to San Diego to pick up his folks, wanted to get them out of the city after the Greys hit Phoenix."

"Oh my God." Stella knew how this story ended without Nathan having to explain it. The aliens destroyed San Diego with an asteroid strike ten days after the destruction of Phoenix.

"Yeah. Sam stayed home with Ben, since he was just a baby. The kid lost his father when he was barely a year old."

"See? That's what I was saying. You're all the family Ben has. This life may not be the best for him, but it's his life, and I think taking it away from him would devastate him."

"I don't think I could do it anyway," Nathan agreed. He looked up at Stella. "I can't imagine sending him away. He's all the family I got left, too. I'm his godfather. I promised Sam that if anything ever happened to her and Greg I'd take care of the boy. I gave her my word. A man's only as good as his word."

"So, unless you want to try making a living in town or as a ranch hand, we're going to have to press forward as best we can. Ben's becoming a man." She smiled. "He's even got a sad little mustache coming in. He's done with school. Leaving him at home isn't going to teach him a trade, and if you want to send him to college you're going to need money. It's not like the old days where you could get loans from the government for it."

Nathan didn't say anything. She was right. They made decent money doing what they did, but a lot of it went to business expenses. Paying for his nephew's education while also making sure he had retirement funds would be difficult, if not impossible, with a lower-paying job.

Stella continued, "What I'm getting at is, as screwed up as this whole situation is, you're doing the best you can, not just for the business but for Ben, too. He's a good kid. He's a hell of a lot more mature than I was when I was his age. Yeah, it's sad that a kid that young has to worry about adult problems, but that's the way the world is, now, and we can't change it."

"No, you're right," Nathan said, after a moment. He looked up at his partner. "Thank you."

"Everyone needs a pep talk sometimes, even a tough guy like you."

"Where is Ben, anyway?"

"He's upstairs, going through Erik Landers's laptop. He was right, the dead guy's thumbprint did the trick. I was going to look at it later, but he insisted, so I let him have at it. Maybe there'll be something useful on there. In fact," she said, standing up, "why don't we go check on him?"

Nathan stood up as well. "After you."

Stella shot him a smirk. "You just like watching me walk away." She walked past him, heels clicking on the concrete floor, a faint hint of perfume wafting in the air as she passed. The pencil skirt she wore *did* sit nicely on her hips.

Nathan grinned.

Ben had the dead man's laptop open, and was busily clicking and scrolling when Nathan and Stella entered the small office upstairs. An old, government-surplus desk and office chair had been shoved against the wall, in the same room as the cots, and there was a cable outlet for net access. The boy had his own laptop set up next to Landers's.

"How goes it?" Nathan asked.

"I'm almost done copying everything. It's going to take me a while to go through all this."

"What all is on there?" Stella asked. "Just documents?"

"No," Ben answered, without looking up. "He kept crazy detailed records, which . . ." He looked up. "That's weird for a criminal, right?"

"Depends," Nathan said. "A business is a business, even if it's illegal. If you don't keep track of things, you'll fail."

"Well, he took a lot of pictures. I mean, *tons* of pictures."

Stella raised an eyebrow. "Pictures of what?"

"His guns, for starters. People. Places. I haven't looked through them all, but some of them look like they were taken with a hidden camera."

"Blackmail material, maybe," Stella suggested.

"Or an insurance policy," Nathan said. "The weapons pictures are probably part of how he managed his inventory. We might be able to track down where he kept his merchandise."

"You think?" Stella asked.

"Might be worth looking into, at least," Nathan said.

Ben opened up a picture of a shopping cart. It was sitting in the empty parking lot of a collapsed building someplace. "He has a lot of pictures of shopping carts, like, over a hundred. Who takes pictures of shopping carts?"

Nathan shrugged. "Everyone needs a hobby, I guess. What else? Any sign that he was actually working with alien collaborators?"

"I've only looked at a few of the pictures on here, and I haven't really read any of the documents. It's going to take me a while."

"Ben," Stella began, putting her hand on the boy's shoulder, "if you find anything, um, *disturbing* on there, you come get one of us right away, okay?"

Ben paused and looked up at her. "Disturbing? You mean like this entire folder full of porn videos?"

"What? Yes, like that!" Stella looked over at Nathan, who was trying his best not to break out laughing.

"It's rude to go through another man's porn stash, boy, even if he's dead," Nathan said, chuckling. "You go ahead and move that folder to a separate drive and not onto your computer. Stella can go through it later."

She shot him an evil look.

"You guys are gross," Ben said. "I promise I won't look at his porn, okay? And I'll let you know if I find anything useful, or disturbing, or whatever. It's going to take me some time to read all these files."

"You know what you're looking for?"

"Of course I do," Ben insisted. "Addresses or locations. Names. Account numbers and passwords. Stuff like that."

"Good man," Nathan said. "Alright, we'll leave you to it." He and Stella turned to leave.

"Thank you," Ben said, not taking his eyes off the screens. There was a little hint of attitude in his voice.

Nathan paused. "And stay out of the porn! I mean it. I come back up here and catch you *roughing up the suspect* it's going to be awkward for everybody."

Ben wheeled around, eyes wide. His entire face turned a deep shade of red. "Gross! Get out!"

Nathan headed back down the stairs, laughing the whole way.

Federal Detention Facility
Gallup, New Mexico

EMMOGENE SAT ALONE in a solitary confinement cell, reading a book. Dr. Grayson had been true to his word. He'd run a battery of tests on her, but the most invasive procedures had been the taking of a blood sample and an MRI. Being in solitary was lonely, but hardly any lonelier than prison had been for her already. She missed being able to go to the library, but the doctor was nice. He brought her books to read. Having new reading material almost made up for never being able to leave her cell, except for when she was escorted to the shower.

Almost.

Still, it was necessary for her own safety. There were other ex-InSec people in the prison, and now that blood had been spilled Emmogene would never be safe. It seemed like she was going to have to remain in solitary for the rest of her sentence, for her own protection.

If we admit that human life can be ruled by reason, then all possibility of life is destroyed. She looked up from the leather-bound copy of *War and Peace* and contemplated Tolstoy's words. This book was very different from the pulp novels and nonfiction books that filled the prison's library, but Emmogene found herself enjoying the intellectual stimulation. With enough reading material, she thought, perhaps spending the rest of her time in solitary wouldn't be so bad.

Emmogene went back to reading her book, but looked up again when she heard footsteps coming down the hall. She didn't think anything of it at first; there were a lot of solitary confinement cells in this block, and it wasn't yet lights-out. She didn't become concerned until she heard Dr. Grayson's voice echoing in the corridor.

"Will you just listen to me?" he said, almost pleadingly. "She's in a traumatized state and is under my care."

"You sound pretty protective of her, Doc. Need I remind you she's a traitor?" The other man's voice was dismissive. He sounded like he had somewhere he'd rather be.

"She wasn't convicted of treason! Either way, she has rights, damn it! She's a victim of extraterrestrial experimentation. You can't just barge in here, waving your damned National Security Letter, and take my patient!"

"Open it," the other man said, ignoring the doctor.

"Officer, do not open that door," Dr. Grayson ordered.

"Listen to me," the other man said, his voice threatening. "You need to open the door. I have authority here."

"Sorry, Doc," the guard said, apologetically. The door beeped as an electronic key was inserted from the other side. A loud buzzer blared, the light turned from red to green, and the door slid open.

Emmogene stood and backed up against the wall as several people crowded the door of her cell. Dr. Grayson was there, wearing his white lab coat over his blue uniform. With him was the guard who had opened the door. She'd seen him several times before, but had never caught his name. He stepped aside as a man in a dark suit and tie entered the cell. Two uniformed Homeland Security agents followed him, clad in charcoal uniforms, tactical vests, and helmets with face shields. Unlike the prison guards, the DHS agents wore pistols on their hips.

"You can't do this!" Dr. Grayson protested, from out in the corridor.

"I can and I am, Doc," the man in the suit said, without looking at the exasperated psychiatrist. He kept his eyes on Emmogene. "Emmogene Anderson?"

"Y-yes?" Emmogene managed, hoping she didn't sound as mousy and afraid as she thought she did.

"I'm with the Department of Homeland Security. In accordance with the Extraterrestrial Technology Control Act, I am taking you into my custody. You will be transferred to a different facility for analysis and medical evaluation. Put your shoes on and let's go."

"What about Dr. Grayson?" Emmogene asked.

The facility psychiatrist managed to barge his way into the cell.

"Emmogene, I'm sorry. There's nothing I can do. I was required to send a report to DHS. I didn't think they would overreact like this!"

She was scared now. "Overreact to what? What's wrong with me?"

"I found something, something implanted inside you. I don't—"

"That's enough, Doctor!" the government man said, visibly annoyed. "If you want to keep your job I suggest you step back and let me do mine."

"I'm sorry, Emmogene," Dr. Grayson repeated. "I didn't intend for this to happen."

"You'll get over it," the suit said. Dr. Grayson abandoned the cell, leaving Emmogene alone with the man in the suit and his two armed escorts. There were two more DHS agents in the hall, one of whom was carrying a rifle.

Emmogene was in shock, almost numb, as she slipped on the Velcro sneakers that were part of her prison uniform. *Section 37. Alien technology. Implant.* The Visitors . . . those alien bastards . . . had done something to her. Before, when Red was about to kill her, she'd felt a buzzing in her head, and her would-be assailant immediately killed herself. Is that what it was? Did she have some control over people? Could she use it to get out of this situation? She knew what was going to happen. Red had been right, they were going to dissect her. Standing up, Emmogene closed her eyes and concentrated. If she had some ability to influence people, it was now or never.

She gasped as a sharp, pricking pain shot into her neck. Her eyes snapped open—the man in the suit was next to her now, with an auto-injector gun in his hand. "What did you stick me with?" she asked, recoiling, her hand covering the sore spot.

The agent watched as his two uniformed compatriots shackled Emmogene's hands and feet. "Just something to help you relax, Miss Anderson."

Whatever it was, it was acting quickly. Emmogene felt drunk. Her muscles relaxed and her head started to swim. Suddenly she was very tired, and the urge to lie down and sleep overtook her anxiety. She offered no resistance as the government agents hauled her away.

Federal Recovery Office
Prescott, Arizona

"WHAT DID YOU FIND, BEN?" Nathan asked. He and Stella were standing behind the boy. He was still seated at the old desk, with Erik Landers's laptop open in front of him. The sun was low in the sky and they had been getting ready to go home when Ben called them upstairs.

The boy looked over his shoulder at his uncle. "I thought you'd really want to see this," he said. He tapped the keyboard, and a digital image opened on the laptop's screen.

"Well ho-lee *shit*," Nathan said, bemused.

"Is that what I think it is?" Stella asked.

Ben nodded slowly. The image was poor quality, taken in low light without a flash, but there was no mistaking the subject of the photograph. The slender body, the large, hairless head, the grayish skin, and the large, dark, eyes. It was one of *them*.

"When was this taken?" Nathan asked.

"The image is date- and time-stamped and geo-tagged," Ben said. He brought up the image's properties on the screen. "It's only about six months old."

"Those are coordinates," Stella said. "Lat-longs."

"They are," Ben confirmed. "I ran them through the map program. It's in Brazil. As near as I can tell, the coordinates are close to the location of a prewar resort town. It's been officially closed since the Amazon is overrun with alien wildlife."

"If you were a bunch of UEA holdouts on the run from the US government," Stella said, "that would be a good place to go." Brazil didn't have a collaborator extradition treaty with the United States the way other countries did. The country had never really recovered, having been subjected to both orbital bombardment and occupation during the war. "They could be Sagittarius Faction."

"Could be," Nathan agreed, rubbing his chin. The Sagittarius Faction was a terrorist group made up of fanatical alien loyalists, convinced that their extraterrestrial benefactors would return from Mars and *liberate* the world. "There's a pretty good standing bounty if you can bring in a living extraterrestrial, isn't there?"

"Mm, depends on the classification," Stella said. "The more common they are, the less money we'd get." The Sagittarian civilization was a complex hierarchy, with a small number of elites on top, and several subservient classes below that. Each class was engineered for its role in their society, and they all had been programmed to instinctively comply with the will of their masters for the good of their species.

"That's definitely not a *Brute*," Nathan observed. "They're more muscly than that. Bigger, too. All of 'em were over six feet, some over seven." The hulking *Brutes* occupied the bottom of the aliens' civilizational hierarchy. They had limited cognition and no free will. Essentially meat robots, they were used to carry heavy weapons and do labor-intensive tasks.

Ben nodded. "Look at the doorway it's standing next to. It's pretty short."

"The head, too," Nathan said. "The *Brutes* have thicker skulls with a ridge that goes down the middle. This one doesn't have that." He looked at his nephew. "What else can you tell from the picture?"

"Look at the shape of the head," Ben said. "Look how big it is compared to the rest of its body. It's hard to tell from this picture, but . . ." He trailed off for a few seconds before looking up at Stella. "You don't think that's a *Bright*, do you?"

"I think it is," Stella said. "Nate?"

Nathan nodded his head. "I think so, too, for the reasons Ben suggested. It's hard to be certain from the photo, but I'd say the odds are good." The *Brights* were the alien ruling class, the product of countless generations of genetic engineering. These beings had seemingly absolute power over the rest of the Sagittarians. They were exceedingly intelligent and the lower classes were conditioned to unquestioningly obey them.

"Look at this marking," Ben said, zooming in the picture. There was a line in the alien's flesh that went down the side of its face. "What is that?"

Nathan and Stella both leaned in. "Looks like a scar," she said. She looked at Nathan. "That's strange. *Brights* don't make a habit of doing anything that would risk giving them a scar like that. From what we understand, they live like royalty."

"Who knows?" Nathan asked. "Maybe it slipped in the shower." He patted Ben on the shoulder. "Either way, damned good work, boy."

Stella furled her brow. "The question is, what do we do with this information? The aliens that got left behind on Earth are supposed to remain in the Demilitarized Zone in Africa. That was part of the terms of the surrender of the United Earth Alliance and the Treaty of Khartoum. According to the regulations, we're supposed to report this to Homeland Security."

"Homeland Security can eat our asses," Ben said.

Stella's eyes went wide. "Benjamin Foster!"

"No, he's right," Nathan said. "We hand this information over, we won't ever be able to try and use it ourselves."

"You're not thinking of going down there," Stella said. "There's no way that thing is alone or unguarded. If Erik Landers was doing business with this group, that means its people are armed and ready to fight."

She wasn't wrong, Nathan thought. Assuming the alien was even still there, trying to infiltrate its hiding place alone to capture it would likely be suicide. Even getting down there would require paying some hefty bribes to the local authorities.

Nathan sighed. "You're probably right. Good work all the same, Ben. We probably won't be able to do anything about it ourselves, but maybe we can sell the information to someone with more resources than us. For right now, though, I say we head home. It's getting late, and I'm hungry. Nothing will change between now and tomorrow."

Federal Prisoner Transport Bus
Somewhere in New Mexico

LOST IN HER OWN THOUGHTS and the constant drone of the bus's engine, Emmogene shifted in her seat and tried to get comfortable. It was difficult to accomplish when you were shackled at the wrists and ankles, though. She couldn't even look out the window; they were deeply tinted, and it was dark out. There was nothing to see.

There wasn't much to see inside the bus, either. Emmogene was the only prisoner being transported. It was strange, she thought, to get a whole bus to yourself, but she guessed that there weren't all that many cases involving alien technology. She didn't know where they were going, and didn't bother asking the guards. They looked at her with contempt and wouldn't tell her anything. They treated her with the same aloof attitude that most of the prison guards always had. She was relaxed, but groggy, and it was hard to focus. Whatever they had injected her with hadn't worn off yet.

She'd had strange dreams while unconscious, vivid and surreal. Maybe it was a side effect of the drugs, maybe it was just her troubled psyche, but they had felt real. Some of it had felt so real that she wondered if maybe it was more than a dream, if maybe it was a memory.

"Remorse is an emotion that I am unaccustomed to." In the dream, one of the Visitors had told her that. Had that actually happened? It was a matter of some debate as to whether the Sagittarian aliens even had emotions comparable to human ones. Their psychology was, well, *alien*. If it had happened, when did it occur? What situation would she have been in where one of the Visitors would sound apologetic to her?

Emmogene had no answers. Shaking her head, she looked up and tried to focus on her surroundings. The interior of the bus was dimly lit with red lights. Two guards sat near the front, in rear-facing seats that allowed them to watch the prisoners, but they weren't watching her closely. One, a short man, was having a conversation about football with the driver, or so Emmogene thought. It was hard to hear from way back where she was. The second, a woman named Greta, was reading a book. She'd look up occasionally to frown at Emmogene. She was the one responsible for searching Emmogene and escorting her to the restroom. Greta's contempt for Emmogene was almost palpable.

A third guard, an older, heavyset man, alternated between sitting in one of the forward seats and pacing up and down the aisle. He made his way toward the back of the bus, shotgun in hand. Unlike the other two, he hadn't removed his helmet, but he had the visor lifted up. His armor was bulky and looked uncomfortable. He paused by Emmogene's seat.

"You okay, kid?" There wasn't any resentment behind his words. He was nice.

"M . . . may I have a drink of water?" Emmogene asked. The desert air was dry, and so was her throat.

"Sure," he said, giving her a brief smile. He handed her a plastic canteen, one that was nearly full. "Drink up. There's more if you need it."

Emmogene had enough range of motion in her shackled wrists to lift the canteen to her lips. The water was cold; they had a cooler up front, with ice in it. She drank quickly and deeply, only then realizing just how thirsty she was. Come to think of it, she hadn't had a drink in many hours.

At the front of the bus, Greta put down her book and glared at Emmogene. "What are you doing, Griggs?" Her voice was bitter, like always.

"I'm just giving her some water," Griggs said, not turning his back to Emmogene. "Relax."

Greta shook her head. "She's just going to have to piss again, and I'm the one who has to take her." She picked her novel back up. "You're too soft."

"Thank you," Emmogene said, handing him back the canteen. It was empty.

"Don't sweat it," he answered, screwing the cap back on. "We should be there in a couple of hours."

"What's going to happen to me?"

Griggs didn't answer. He either didn't know or wouldn't say. "Try to get some sleep." He turned around and headed for the front of the bus.

The driver of the bus looked up into the mirror that allowed him to see his comrades. He said something about a truck coming at them, but he was too far away for Emmogene to hear clearly. What she could hear was the roar of an engine as another vehicle overtook the bus on her side. The guards were alert now, reaching for their weapons. The driver was trying to raise someone on the radio and was shouting that he couldn't get through. Griggs went tumbling as the bus swerved hard to the right while the driver stepped on the brakes. Something slammed into the bus from the side. The driver yelled for everyone to hang on as the bus left the road, slid down an embankment, and rolled. Emmogene clamped her eyes shut.

When she opened them again, the bus had come to a stop, and was at least right side up. The guards were all down. The driver was either unconscious or dead. The red interior lights flickered intermittently, and the sounds of static from the radio filled the bus.

CLANK! CLANK! The noise came from the front of the bus, by the door, and it was followed by an awful metallic groan.

"They're prying open the doors!" Greta yelled. The bus was armored, but it wasn't impenetrable. She drew her pistol. She got two shots off before she was cut down by a burst of automatic weapons fire. Emmogene screamed and covered her ears but couldn't tear her eyes away. The other guard, the short one who had been talking football, brought his shotgun to bear when a big, masked man, clad in a long coat and a hat, coldly marched onto the bus. The weapon roared, and the intruder was hit, but he didn't fall. The big man reached out with a long arm, grabbed the guard's shotgun by the muzzle, and yanked it toward him. The guard, desperately trying to hold onto his weapon, was pulled closer to the big man. A huge hand clamped around the guard's throat; the big man lifted him off the floor with his right hand while taking the shotgun away with his left. The big man backed out of the bus, dragging the kicking and struggling guard with him into the night.

A lone figure appeared through the breach in the doors then, tall and fit. He had golden hair and a stubbly beard, and was dressed in camouflage pants and a body armor vest. He gave the driver, who still hadn't moved, a passing glance as he stepped onto the bus. The big man in the hat and coat followed him in, his face concealed behind a mask and goggles. The blond man nodded at the bus driver, who was starting to stir. The hulking brute grabbed the driver by the collar, released his seat belt, and dragged him off of the bus.

Emmogene recognized him then. Anthony. *My God.* Her heart dropped into her stomach and her head started to spin. She hadn't seen him in years but knew it was him. Anthony. *Oh no. What have you done?*

Many of Emmogene's fragmented memories revolved around Anthony. He was tall, blond, and had been ruggedly handsome. Passionate, strong, and brave, he'd been one of the Visitors' human soldiers, one out of countless millions they had recruited. He was an elite commando, one of their best, and he'd been assigned to be her guardian. Supposedly he was the perfect biological and psychological match for her; they had been meant for each other. She'd been just a girl then, a teenager. Anthony had been older. He had promised to wait for her until she was a woman, until she was ready.

As the war had raged on, the kind and gentle man she'd fallen in love with as a girl was slowly replaced by a heartless killing machine. That's the Anthony who stood before her now, looking bored with the death all around him. He turned his attention to Emmogene. Her face flushed as he locked eyes with her, and for just a moment, the world seemed to drop away. Somehow, someway, after all this time, he'd found her. Why now? Why here? What did he want?

Anthony stepped over Greta's body and approached. The huge man in the hat and coat stayed outside, but two others with masks and guns appeared behind him. He strode down the aisle toward Griggs, looking him dead in the eyes as he moved. Emmogene had seen that look before, and it frightened her. He stopped right in front of Griggs, who had just managed to get to his feet. A trickle of blood leaked from the guard's nose while he shakily held his hands over his head. The assault had been over before he even knew what was going on.

"I give up," Griggs said, weakly. "You can take her, just let me go! Please!" Emmogene could feel the anguish and shame in his voice.

Anthony inhaled through his nose. "No." He raised a gun.

"Anthony, no!" Emmogene screamed. BLAM!

It was over in an instant. Griggs was dead on the floor, and Anthony's eyes were locked onto Emmogene again. Without lowering his gaze, he holstered his pistol, stepped past Griggs's body, and knelt down beside her.

"Are you injured?" he asked, eyes wide, concern in his voice. "Were you hurt?"

Emmogene clenched her eyes shut and shook her head.

"I'm sorry you had to see that." He was so close she could feel his body heat on her face. "It's over now, my beloved. We're getting you out of here."

Emmogene opened her eyes, and tears rolled down her face. "You killed all those people."

"It was necessary," he said coldly. She winced as he ever-so-gently wiped a tear from her cheek with a gloved finger. His touch was gentle; loving, even. "I'm sorry. They were a liability." He turned and looked over his shoulder. "Find the keys! Get the bolt cutters! Hurry!" He turned back to Emmogene. "I promised you I'd find you, my love. It took me years, but I never gave up, and I've come for you." The two camouflage-clad assailants reappeared, one carrying bolt cutters. Despite their masks and body armor, Emmogene could tell that one was a man and the other was a woman.

"Where are you taking me?"

There were tears in Anthony's eyes now, too. "Home."

The Foster Residence
Prescott Valley, Arizona

NATHAN AWOKE to a horrendous electronic screeching. It took him a couple seconds to realize that it was his phone, ringing and rumbling on the nightstand next to his bed. Groggily, he reached over, grasping for the device, wondering who the hell would be calling him at 2:38 in the morning. Phone in hand, he looked at the small external display: Stella was calling. She wouldn't call at such an ungodly hour if it weren't important.

He unfolded the boxy device and squinted as the screen illuminated his face. Stella appeared on his display, looking like she had also just woken up, but she was sitting in her car. "Good morning, sleepyhead," she said with a weak smile. "Sorry to wake you."

"No, it's fine," Nathan managed. "What's the matter? Are you okay?"

"I'm fine," she answered, "but it was sweet of you to ask. We got a critical tasking from Homeland Security."

"Critical? Really?" That was rare. Even a wanted murderer didn't rate a critical priority level.

"Really. It's also classified."

"Classified? What?"

"I'm not kidding, Nate," Stella said. "I just arrived at the office. Please come in right away. We've got a secure briefing scheduled for as soon as you can get here. Leave Ben at home. I'll have a pot of coffee made."

"This is nuts," Nathan said, sitting up in bed. "What happened?"

"You know as much as I do at this point. I'll see you at the office."

"I'm on my way," Nathan said. "I'll see you there." He ended the call and closed his phone. There was no point in even waking Ben, and he'd taken a shower before going to bed. All he needed to do was get dressed, leave a note for the boy, and be on his way.

Forty-five minutes later, Nathan was sitting in the office's little-used conference room while Stella finished setting up the secure video link. The doors to the building were locked and this room had no windows. There was a small table in the middle of the room, surrounded by several chairs, all of which had been hastily dusted. There was a camera turret with a directional microphone mounted on the table, and a big, seventy-two-inch screen mounted to the back wall. Boxes were stacked against the wall and in the corners, as they mostly used this space for storage.

"That should do it," Stella said, sitting next to Nathan at the table. She hadn't bothered with makeup, but had still thrown a professional-looking blouse on. Sitting at the table concealed the fact that she was wearing jeans. Nathan, for his part, was wearing a tan work shirt and jeans, but this is how he always dressed.

"Who are we talking to?" Nathan asked. There was nothing on the screen but the logo of the Department of Homeland Security.

Stella leaned over to answer, but didn't take her eyes off the big screen. "They didn't tell me who, exactly, just that we were getting a briefing from DHS."

"I hope to hell this is worth it," Nathan said.

"Have I ever steered you wrong?"

Before Nathan could answer, the screen changed. On it were now two men in suits, sitting at a desk, in a very similar, if tidier, setup to the one they had in the office. Both wore identification badges on lanyards around their necks.

"Good morning, gentlemen," Stella said, professionally. "I'm Stella Rickles. This is my partner, Nathan Foster."

"Yes, good morning," the Federal agent on the left said, sounding as if he didn't really mean it. He was a bald man with a fair complexion and the older of the two, maybe fifty years old by Nathan's guess. "I'm Special Agent Delaney, and this is Special Agent Frampton." Frampton, on the right side of the screen, was much younger than his partner. He had to have been in his early thirties at most. He had a bored look on his face, as if this meeting was a waste of his time. "We're with counterintelligence operations. Ms. Rickles, I understand you come from our section?"

"Uh, yes," Stella responded, as if surprised. "Though it's been a few years."

"I know," Special Agent Delaney said. "This is the reason your office was selected for this matter. Your security clearance is still active, and I have been instructed by my superiors to seek your assistance with an incident."

"Assistance?" Nathan asked.

"Yes, assistance," Special Agent Frampton explained, as if this wholly unique situation was normal. "This is not a routine 'bounty hunting' assignment per se," he added, using air quotes when he said *bounty hunting.* "We will be leading a team of DHS agents in the pursuit of two individuals, both escaped fugitives."

Before the war, this sort of thing would have been a job for the US Marshals. In its aftermath, US Marshals were in short supply and there was no love lost between the Departments of Justice and Homeland Security. Stella knew a lot more about that world than Nathan did, but he'd come to understand that the two arms of the federal government were loath to work with each other. Homeland Security was generally more willing to employ licensed and bonded Recovery Agents, mainly because they were required to by statue. The Justice Department had standing bounties on wanted fugitives, as required by law, but almost never actively sought the assistance of a Recovery Agent, preferring to keep things in-house as much as they could. Homeland Security, on the other hand, never sent its own people out on something as mundane as an escaped collaborator. This was odd. "What's so special about this one that you boys are willing to leave the office over it?"

Nathan hid a wince as Stella kicked him under the table before speaking up herself. "What my partner is trying to say," she said, smiling at the screen, "is that this is an unusual situation. We have never been tasked with providing advisory assistance before and I'm not sure what regulations and pay scales would cover that."

"Ah, right, your fees," Delaney said. "We will have our legal department draw up a contract later. This meeting is primarily intended to give you two a basic rundown of the situation and see if you are willing to take the job."

Stella sounded skeptical. "I see. How can we help you?"

Special Agent Frampton piped up then. "Before we begin, we are required to inform you that by agreeing to receive this briefing, you are also agreeing to a standard government nondisclosure agreement. Under no circumstances is anything we discuss with you to be repeated to anyone else or discussed with the media. Furthermore, if you decline to accept the NDA, you will be expressly prohibited from attempting to capture the individuals involved. If you ignore this prohibition and somehow do capture them, not only will you not be paid, but your Federal Recovery Agent license will be suspended for review. Do you understand?"

"Yes, I understand," Stella said.

"Yeah, got it," Nathan answered.

"That's verbal confirmation from them both," Frampton said to Delaney.

"Confirmed," Delaney agreed. He tapped a few keys on a pad in front of him, and the screen split. The image of the two DHS agents was pushed to the left side of the screen. On the right side was what appeared to be a prison intake photo of a young woman. She was pretty, with blonde hair and blue eyes, and looked like she was in her late twenties at most. The markings on the wall behind her indicated that she was five foot five.

"This is Emmogene Anderson," Frampton began. "Twenty-nine years old, hundred and fifteen pounds, slight build. Two days ago she escaped Federal custody."

Nathan was incredulous. "That girl escaped? How?"

Frampton frowned. "I'll get to that in a moment. It is critically important that Ms. Anderson be recovered alive and unharmed. Mr. Foster, you've had some issues with this recently, it seems. You will not be paid if the fugitive is killed or harmed in any way."

Nathan was about ready to tell the uppity Fed to go fuck himself, but Stella spoke up before he could shoot his mouth off. "If I may," she interjected, "what did she do?"

"Miss Anderson was captured in Mexico several years ago. Mexican authorities turned her over to the United States Government. The forearm marking and record analysis indicated that she was an alien collaborator, and she was tried as such. She was found not guilty of treason by reason of her age, as her defense was able to establish that she was only fourteen when her mother, now deceased, defected to the UEA. She was, however, found guilty of providing material support to the enemy in wartime and was sentenced to five years in prison, with a possibility of early release for good behavior."

Material support to the enemy was a government catchall crime, used to charge people who had sided with the collaborators but hadn't fought on their behalf. It didn't entail being stripped of citizenship if one was found guilty, and the punishments were often much more lenient. "How does a fourteen-year-old girl provide *material support* to invading aliens?" Nathan asked.

Agent Delaney spoke up. "She was a willing participant in several enemy propaganda efforts after her eighteenth birthday, but that's not the issue here. The issue is what we believe she is carrying."

"We believe that Miss Anderson has been implanted with an advanced technology of alien origin," Frampton said. The image of Emmogene Anderson disappeared, replaced with a photo of a tiny device. It was an amorphous, fleshy blob, looking like nothing so much as a tumor, about the size of a dime. It was surrounded by series of metallic spheres, each the size of a ball bearing, connected with strands of wire so thin they might have been hairs. The wire was tangled, and the tumor at the center appeared to have been burned. The image was labeled TOP SECRET//NOFORN.

"What is that?" Stella asked.

"We call it the Persuader," Delaney continued. "Photographed here is one that was recovered from a deceased individual. It is, effectively, a mind-control device."

Frampton looked down at some papers in front of him. "According to laboratory analysis, it is designed to broadcast signals that affect the human brain. It utilizes specifically targeted radio frequencies and magnetic fields to disrupt and alter neurological function. The magnetic fields are generated by a series of microscopic magnetic monopoles. The device is powered by the natural energy produced by the human body. While dormant, there is no way of detecting the device short of an MRI, which is how it was discovered in Miss Anderson."

"Wait, wait, wait," Nathan said. "Back up a second. *Mind control?*"

"Yes," Frampton said. "In effect. According to what we know, those radio broadcasts and magnetic fields influence the natural neural activity of the human brain without having any direct physical connection. They call it ephaptic coupling. Theoretically, the effects could be widely varied, depending on how the device was calibrated."

"What kind of effects are we talking about?" Stella asked.

"It can render the victim extremely susceptible to suggestion, for one thing," Frampton said, "not unlike hypnosis. Our scientists speculate that it could, in theory, be used to artificially create hallucinations, panic attacks, seizures, memory loss, religious experiences, a variety of neurological disorders, even suicidal impulses."

Delaney spoke up. "We say they speculate because one of these devices has never been captured intact, and they've been unable to restore one to functioning condition to test it. What little we know of them comes from captured enemy records."

"We knew the Greys were using technology like this on their people," Frampton said, "but until we found one of these we had no idea that they had been able to micronize it."

"The war ended before they got it past the prototype stage," Delaney explained. "Like we said, we have not yet been able to recover one intact. That is why it is paramount that you bring Miss Anderson in alive and unharmed."

"This device..." Stella said began, trailing off for a moment as she collected her thoughts. "Can we counteract it? Did she use it to escape?"

"Yes and no," Frampton answered. "The device is very short ranged, no more than a few meters. Our scientists tell us that simply being aware of the device should reduce its ability to influence the intended target. So, if you feel strange, back away and take control of the situation."

"That's it? Back away? You don't seem very sure."

Frampton shrugged. "We're not. This is all an educated guess. This thing is far beyond our current technical capabilities, Ms. Rickles. We do know that sedating Miss Anderson is effective. As for the device itself, it has proven to be quite potent. She apparently used it to compel another inmate to kill herself, as well as to get other inmates to fight prison guards on her behalf."

"So is *that* how she escaped?" Nathan asked.

"No," Special Agent Delaney said, grimly. "She had help. She was being transported on a federal prison bus when was intercepted by another vehicle, rammed off the road, and then breached. We have the security footage." He tapped the keypad in front of him. "Watch."

The image on the right side of the screen changed again. Now it was footage from a security camera mounted inside a prison transport bus, centered above the aisle, at the very back. There was only one prisoner on the bus, a blonde woman Nathan presumed was Emmogene Anderson, three guards, and a driver. Two of the guards sat near the front while one moved to the rear, and spoke to the prisoner. There was no sound.

Nathan's brow furled as the guards were suddenly tossed around like the proverbial ragdolls. The bus apparently rolled. The camera shook violently until the bus came to a stop. Emmogene, restrained, was still in her seat, but the four officers were all down.

After a few moments, mechanical jaws pried the doors open. The first guard, a woman, was shot several times and dropped to the floor. Another guard leveled a shotgun at the door and fired as a big man in a coat and hat stomped onto the bus, but the weapon seemed to have no effect. The huge person disarmed the guard, hoisted him up with one hand, and choked him out.

"Damn," Nathan said, quietly, as the video continued to play. He had suspicions about what the big man really was, but he didn't say anything yet.

A few moments later, a tall, athletic-looking man with blond hair sulked onto the bus, moving down the aisle until he was facing the last guard. The guard had his hands up, and seemed to be pleading with him, but the intruder was unmoved.

Nathan grimaced as the blond man shot the last guard in the face, point blank. "That's an ice-cold son of a bitch right there. He didn't even blink. He's brazen, too, didn't bother covering his face. Who is he?"

"Anthony Krieg," Agent Delaney said. "He's a Swiss national, thirty-eight years old, known to be an active agent of the Sagittarius Faction. As a university student he went on a trip to Africa, into UEA territory, and decided he wasn't coming back. By the time the war started, he was an officer in one of their commando units, Earth Storm."

That explained the cold-blooded killing, Nathan thought. The Earth Storm had been fanatically loyal and seemingly without regard for their own lives. It had been used in daring operations all throughout the war. Their modus operandi was that none who saw them in action should live to tell of it. They took no prisoners and never willingly left survivors. It made perfect sense that a man like that would end up in the Sagittarius Faction—these sorts of men believed in their cause to the point of fanaticism.

Agent Frampton spoke up. "We only know who he is because of records the military captured at the end of the war. He's been sighted in the US and Mexico a few times over the last few years, but we've never had a good lead on him until this incident."

"Came out of hiding to spring her, huh? They must have some connection. Lovers, maybe?"

"We can only speculate," Frampton said.

"Could you replay the last part of the video?" Stella asked. The Feds did as she requested. As the footage played again, she pointed at the screen. "Look at her reaction when she recognizes him."

"I can't see her reaction from the back of her head," Nathan said.

"Watch," Stella insisted. One of Anthony Krieg's men retrieved keys from a dead guard and released Emmogene from her shackles. Despite being visibly groggy from the sedation, she seemed to tense up when he touched her, and hung her head as he led her away. "You catch that?"

"Yeah. She don't look too happy to see him."

"She's terrified."

"Maybe, maybe not, but it wasn't an enthusiastic hello." Nathan looked back up at the two federal agents on the screen, running his fingers through his hair. "Who are those two?" They were both built like weight lifters, but one had a distinctly feminine physique: more of a curve in the hips and what looked like a bust behind the body armor. A woman, he thought, but a big woman, probably enhanced.

"We have not yet identified the accomplices," Agent Delaney answered. "All we have is this footage." Earth Storm commandos had recruited from all over the world by the tens of thousands, and the UEA purged a lot of its records at the end of the war. There simply wasn't reliable information on a lot of the people who would later join the Sagittarius Faction.

"How in the hell did they find that bus? How did he know where she would be?"

"That hasn't yet been ascertained," Delaney said.

"An inside job, maybe?" Nathan speculated.

"It's possible," Stella said. "Maybe he had informants on the inside, and knew they were moving her."

"That aspect of the investigation is not your concern," Delaney said, tersely. The video footage ended, and the two agents took up the entire screen once again.

"Alright," Nathan said, "so what's the deal? You want him brought in, too?"

"No," Frampton answered, coldly. "Anthony Krieg is to be neutralized on sight. Shoot to kill."

"That's . . . unusual," Stella said, hesitating.

"Mr. Krieg is not a US citizen and is a known enemy combatant. His being on US soil at all is a violation of the Treaty of Khartoum. The DOD and CIA have a standing kill order for him should he be located overseas. That hasn't changed just because he's been located in CONUS."

"If you say so," Nathan said. "No skin off my ass. Now, you said that we were going to be advising you?"

"Yes," Delaney said. "We will be en route to New Mexico shortly. You will coordinate with us, but you're going to be our bloodhound. The Southwest Sector is your turf, I'm told, and you have the best record of any of the Recovery Agents in the region. We need you to shake the bushes and smoke these two out."

Stella raised an eyebrow. Nathan could tell the mixed metaphor annoyed her. "And what's in it for us?"

"You're helping your government apprehend an escaped fugitive and put down a dangerous terrorist," Delaney said, as if her question was stupid.

"Uh-huh," Nathan answered. "Helping the government don't pay the rent, Agent Delaney."

"You will be financially compensated for your time and expenses per federal regulations, in accordance with standard DHS contractor fee schedules. As I said, we're going to have our legal department draw up a contract."

"This seems like a lot of risk for standard contractor fee schedules," Nathan said.

Stella interjected. "Gentlemen, how about I send you a contract? It'll save you the trouble of drawing one up yourselves."

"We don't have a lot of time here," Agent Frampton said, visibly annoyed. "Every minute we waste gives Anthony Krieg that much more of a head start. If he gets Emmogene Anderson out of the country, we'll lose her forever."

"Well then," Stella said, "I suggest you read quickly."

Nathan smiled.

"WHAT DO YOU THINK?" Nathan asked, sipping his coffee.

Stella frowned at her computer screen as she reread the contract offer she had written. "I think this whole thing stinks a little."

"Yeah, it does seem weird," Nathan agreed.

"It's not just that it's unorthodox," Stella said. "I think it's illegal. I'd have to talk with our lawyer about the details to be sure, but I can't because of the NDA they made us agree to. That's a warning sign right there. As near as I can tell from the text of the Extraterrestrial and Collaborator Recovery Act and its associated body of federal regulations, they can't bring us in and then not pay us a standard, agreed-upon bounty for recovering a fugitive. The law is pretty clear about that, and it was reinforced in *United States v. Haskell* three years ago. They also can't order us to just kill somebody, even if he is an enemy combatant. We're not contract killers. That's against the law."

"I thought so," Nathan agreed. "You think we should tell them to go pound sand, then?"

"Normally I'd say yes, but I looked up their contractor fee schedules. The money isn't bad, and it's guaranteed income, regardless of whether we succeed or fail, but it's nothing like we'd get for bringing in a fugitive under normal circumstances."

"But?"

"I have an idea. The contract I've written up states that we will work with the Feds on this one, and that if we merely assist them in apprehension of the fugitives, then we are not entitled to a bounty. But, buried in the fine print, there are clauses that say that if we happen to capture the fugitives without their direct assistance at the time of capture, then they are relegated to our custody, and they are required to pay us standard bounties for them."

"But they want Anthony Krieg dead."

"They do, but there's been a reward for him for years." She tapped a few keys, and brought up an old wanted poster. "See?"

Nathan whistled. "Two hundred and fifty thousand. Damn."

"Yeah, he's dangerous and elusive. We bring him in, dead or alive, and we get a quarter-million dollars. The trick is, we have to not be with the Feds when this happens, otherwise they'll claim we merely assisted and we don't get paid."

"I see. You think they'll actually accept this contract? Seems like they want credit for this one."

Stella paused to drink some coffee. "If they don't accept it, I say we decline the offer. This whole thing is sketchy enough as is. But, I got a whiff of desperation off those boys. I think they'll agree and then try to keep us on a short leash. It's going to be up to you to find an opportunity to get away if you can. Don't let one of them ride in the truck with you, for starters."

Nathan chuckled. "I'll put Shadow in the back seat and feed him jerky. Between the dog farts and not wanting to get hair on their nice, pressed suits, I'm sure they'll want to take their own car."

Stella laughed. Shadow's jerky farts could clear a room.

"You know that big fella in the video, the guy in the coat?" Nathan asked. "I bet you money that's a *Brute*."

His partner looked up at him. "You think so?"

"I'd bet on it," Nathan said. "Sure, it could just be a big, muscly fella, or maybe a guy on drugs, but the way it moved, the way it didn't flinch, even when shot . . . I saw a lot of that in the war. UEA infantry units had squads of them as assault elements, or to carry heavy weapons."

Stella frowned. "It would make sense that a former Earth Storm commando would be able to get his hands on one. Does this change the situation? Should we tell them no?"

"Eh," Nathan said, with a half shrug. "They're tough, and I mean they are *tough*, but it's not a deal-breaker, just a complication."

"There," Stella said, after a few moments of typing. "I added a clause where we get an operational bonus of ten thousand dollars if we encounter and eliminate an alien *Brute*-class, just to be on the safe side."

"That's my girl," Nathan said, grinning again. Stella was clever like that.

"That's the standing bounty on *Brutes*," she explained. "I'm just worried that if you kill that thing, they'll try to say that it was part of your agreed-upon duties and not pay the bounty. This clause should cover that. Anyway, I'll print this off. We'll just need to sign it and send it to them on the secure FAX. They think we're a couple of yokels who they can pull one over on. We'll see about that."

Somewhere in New Mexico

"REMORSE IS AN EMOTION that I am unaccustomed to. I regret what we have done to you. I regret taking part in this." Somewhere in the background, "Clair de Lune" played on a piano.

Emmogene's eyes snapped open. There was sunshine on her face. The image of the apologetic Visitor was gone. The light was warm, leaking in through a dirty, boarded-up window on the wall above her. She sat up, trying to remember where she was. She had been sleeping in a bedroll, a sleeping bag and a padded camping mattress, on the floor. She was still wearing her prison jumpsuit. The room she was in looked like it had been a bedroom once, but all the furniture was gone.

She remembered, then: Anthony. The image of him murdering Griggs came back to her in a flash, and her stomach lurched. How had he found her? What did he want with her after all this time? How many more people was he going to kill? She was still in shock over the whole thing.

She was startled when someone gently knocked on the door. It was him. She always seemed to be able to feel his presence, like a tingling at the base of her skull. The knob turned, and he opened the door just a little.

"May I come in?"

Emmogene looked around the room, but what was she going to do? She had nowhere to go. She didn't even know where she was. "Yes," she said, trying to sound brave. "You may come in."

The door creaked loudly as Anthony pushed it opened. His combat boots clomped on the bare hardwood floor as he stepped inside. He was still wearing the black shirt and camouflage pants from when he'd taken her off the bus, but he didn't have his gear on. He did have his pistol, though, in a holster strapped to his leg.

Neither one of them said anything for a several moments. Anthony seemed hesitant to even make eye contact with her, like an awkward schoolboy. He was hard to read, but he looked nervous.

"Th-there's food," he said, stammering a little. He was so different when he was acting normal. Quiet, shy even, and polite to a fault. It was just a disguise, though. Beneath that mask of a shy intellectual and artist was a cold-blooded killer. "You must be hungry. You've been asleep for over twenty-four hours now."

Emmogene was starving, in fact, but she didn't want to seem too eager. She sat up on her bedroll. Her eyes locked onto his when they met. "Why are you doing this, Anthony?"

"Why? What . . . what kind of question is that? I rescued you! Aren't you happy? Did you want to stay in prison, or be experimented on?"

"No!"

"Then you should be happy!"

"You killed all those people, Anthony!"

"They would have done the same to you!" he insisted, his raised voice amplified by the emptiness of the room. Emmogene looked down at the floor. "I'm sorry," Anthony said, almost pleading. "I . . . this is hard for me."

"Anthony, what's happening to you?"

He ran his fingers through his hair. "I'm sorry. I get . . . I get a little crazy sometimes."

He'd always been that way, of course, and some of it was by design. The Visitors had enhanced his strength and his stamina, but also his aggression. They hadn't let just anyone command their elite commando units, after all.

Emmogene's tone was softer now. "Have you been taking your pills?"

"No. No pills. Not anymore. I have to keep my mind sharp," he said, tapping the side of his head. "The pills slowed me down and I needed to find you. I never gave up."

Emmogene slowly shook her head, unable to stop a tear from rolling down her cheek. He was still in love with her. He always had been, ever since he'd been assigned to her by the Visitors. He'd done all this for her. He'd killed people for her. In a way, their blood was on her hands, even though she'd had no say in what he had done. She still benefitted from his murderous insanity.

"I haven't seen you in almost six years. Where have you been all this time?" Emmogene's earliest post-mind-wipe memories were of Anthony and Suliman Alvarez secreting her out of Africa before the Americans and Russians destroyed the cities and infrastructure of the United Earth Alliance in nuclear retaliation. They spent years on the run, moving from place to place, trying to avoid the wrath of a vengeful world. "One day, Suliman told me you'd left and wouldn't tell me anything else." She didn't mention what a relief his departure had been to her at the time. "Where did you go?"

"Suliman and I had a . . . disagreement . . . over how best to proceed. I became aware of the existence of the Faction. It needed people with experience to help it continue the effort." The poor fool always had been a true believer. She didn't know how much of that was of his own volition or how much it was due to the things the Visitors had done to him, but even after the war, even after they'd abandoned the human allies who had fought, suffered, and died for them, he was still loyal to them. "Suliman insisted that our mission was to keep you alive and protected until such a time as the Visitors saw fit to return. I told him he just wanted to protect his own skin. InSec was full of men like him, deceitful worms whose primary concern was their own comfort and safety."

"Let me guess—you told him that, too?"

"I am a solider, not a diplomat. I told him the truth, that it was our duty to continue the fight. He told me that his primary concern was you. A Section 37 asset needs to be protected, cannot be allowed to fall into enemy hands. He had the gall to quote protocol to me."

"You went off to join the Sagittarius Faction and left me with Suliman."

"Yes. I hated to do it. I'm sorry I left you, I truly am, but my duty was clear. Suliman would not be persuaded and I did not have the means to force the issue. His InSec lackeys would have killed me if I had tried to take you, and he kept you under constant surveillance."

Emmogene remembered that part very well. She lived as little more than a prisoner.

"I made the best decision I could given the circumstances," Anthony continued. "You would be as safe with him as you'd be anywhere. The Faction needed me. In time, I intended to come back to you, to find you and take you home, but by the time I had the means it was too late." He cast his eyes downward for a moment. "I know you think I'm a monster."

"Anthony..."

"I *am* a monster," he insisted. "I'm under no illusions about what I am, Emmogene, or what you think of me. You must understand, though, that everything I did, everything I have ever done, it was because it was necessary. I left you with Suliman because it was necessary. I fought because it was necessary. I took no pleasure in killing the guards on that bus, but it was necessary, and I do not regret it. Do you know what was going to happen to you? Where you were going?"

"Does it matter? Haven't enough people died already? The war's been over for years. Can't the killing finally end? My life isn't worth four other lives, no matter what was going to happen to me!"

Anthony took her hand. "It's worth it to me, Emmogene," he said, resolutely. "I will do anything to keep you safe, to keep you from... from being dissected. That's what was going to happen to you, you know. They were going to cut you open to see if they could figure out what the Visitors gifted you with."

Emmogene was scared now. "What did they do to me? Why am I so important? What is Section 37? There were other prisoners, former InSec, and they were going to kill me because they said I was a Section 37 asset. What does that mean? They could tell from the marking on my arm."

Anthony's face darkened. Internal Security and the UEA's military forces had never had much love for each other, but for Anthony it was personal. Emmogene didn't know why, but he had always hated InSec, loathed them. He'd nearly come to blows with Suliman's people on several occasions. "Section 37 was an independent scientific research organization. Under the guidance of the Visitors, they worked with, and on, humans, mostly volunteers, to develop new technologies to help us in our cause. It is they who created the physiological boosters that give us all better health and longer life, for example."

"What was I doing there? I don't remember any of that." That wasn't exactly true, but Emmogene felt it best if Anthony thought it was.

"That is a long story, and you have been through a lot."

"Just the short version, then. Anthony, please, help me understand what's happening."

Anthony was quiet for a few moments, his eyes studying Emmogene's face. "There is a device in your head which gives you the ability to manipulate the wills of others. It was a gift from the Visitors, a product of their incredible technological capabilities. It broadcasts a range of electromagnetic waves, varying in frequency and intensity, to temporarily alter the neurological function of nearby targets. It can make them extremely susceptible to suggestion, cause memory loss, and alter behavior patterns."

It all made sense now. The buzzing at the back of her skull. Red suddenly killing herself. The other inmates turning on the guards to protect her. She shook her head slowly, unable to keep back the tears. "How? How is this possible?"

"As I said, it is a product of their advanced technology. I have only been briefed on what it does, not how it does it. I should also explain to you that it may not work correctly. Our benefactors were unable to perfect it before the war ended."

"Is that why it had never activated before? All that time after the war, when I was with you and Suliman, and I never even knew it was there."

"I have contacts at the prison in which you were kept. I heard of the incident only after it happened. I'm sorry that I was unable to prevent it."

"You . . . you knew where I was?"

"Yes, my dear. There is a network of those still loyal to the cause in the American prison system. It is through them that I was able to keep track of you. I had hoped that your identity would remain secret from those InSec fools, and that was why. I knew that if they learned who you are, they would try to kill you to protect the secrets you carry. That is how InSec has always operated—there was never a problem that couldn't be solved by killing someone on your own bloody side."

Even during the war, there was no love lost between the United Earth Alliance's military forces and Internal Security. After the war, Anthony would frequently complain about Suliman Alvarez and his ex-InSec followers. "I'm sorry," Anthony continued. "I'm sorry I wasn't there for you. We were waiting for an opportunity to get you out, but such things take time and careful planning. What I feared most, that you would be injured or killed in prison, nearly came true, and I'm so sorry."

He is so sweet, Emmogene thought, sadly. It brought back fragments of memories she had of him from before and during the war. The Visitors had matched him with her, told them both that they were a perfect biological and psychological pairing. She was only a girl then, a teenager. Anthony was older, strong and handsome. Young and naïve, she would have jumped into bed with him right then if he'd asked, but he didn't. He'd said he'd wait for her until she was ready, until she was of age, and he had. She was nineteen years old when she had finally convinced him that she was ready. One of the few memories she had from that time was the night he took her virginity. She had been so nervous, so self-conscious, but Anthony was gentle, kind, and understanding. It had been sweet and wonderful, and he held her in his arms the entire night afterward.

But as she looked into Anthony's eyes, Emmogene saw something else. The war changed him. He had seen terrible things, done terrible things, and had terrible things done to him. The Visitors inflicted multiple batteries of enhancements and conditioning upon their soldiers, especially elite Earth Storm commandos like Anthony. He lost the gleam in his eye, some part of his soul, and he never got it back.

"I don't know what I would do if something happened to you," Anthony said, distantly. "I do know that I would burn the world to prevent it."

Emmogene repressed a shiver. She forced herself to smile and tried to change the subject. "You know, I *am* hungry," she said. "May I join you for breakfast?"

Anthony's demeanor changed in an instant. "I would love that," he said. "We brought up some water if you want to wash up first. The plumbing doesn't work, I'm afraid. This town has been abandoned for years."

"It's okay. Show me where the washroom is, then I'll come eat with you."

Anthony smiled. Emmogene kept a smile on her face for him. She had to keep him placated until she could figure out what to do.

✪ ✪ ✪

THE TOWN THEY WERE IN was called El Blanco. Before the war, Emmogene had learned, it had been a small ranching community, with fewer than two hundred residents, and had been abandoned since the plague outbreak. It was remote, accessible only by a no-longer-maintained county road, and the electricity had long since been cut. There were dozens of such ghost towns across the Southwest, created when the residents fled or died off.

Half of El Blanco had burned down in a fire at some point, but this house was still intact. The windows had been boarded up, and there was a barn in which they could hide their vehicles. Anthony said that the nearest functioning gas station was far enough away that few ever came through El Blanco anymore. They couldn't stay there for too long, but it was a safe place for them to hole up for a couple of days.

"Is the food to your liking?" Anthony asked. There were five people seated at the table, all eating in awkward silence. An old wood-burning stove had allowed them to heat up some rations to eat.

"It's good," Emmogene answered, managing a smile. In truth, it was. Anthony's lieutenant, Henry, had prepared the food for them. He'd added some seasoning to the otherwise bland, military-issue rations, and she was very hungry. "May I have some more?"

"Certainly," Henry answered. He was a muscular man, tall and broad-shouldered, with brown hair and a beard. He was quiet but he seemed nice. Emmogene didn't get the intense, angry vibes off of him that she got from the others, and he was pleased that she liked his cooking. "We have plenty." He stood up and made his way back to the stove.

The rest of Anthony's team continued to eat, not having wolfed down their food as eagerly as Emmogene had. The Vlodov Twins, Olga and Ivan, were Russian. They were both tall and muscular, with short-cropped blond hair. Their English was rough, and they quietly spoke to each other in Russian.

The hulking combat automaton they called Rook had given Emmogene quite a start when she came down the stairs. It was one of the Visitors' biomechanical, heavy soldier units, a seven-foot-tall alien killing machine. It stood silently in the front room and kept watch out the window as it fed. Its "meal" consisted of a thick, blue-gray nutrient paste being pumped from a pressurized canister directly into a port in its abdomen. Its voice encoder attachment was in place, but like all such units it didn't speak unless there was a reason to.

Rook looked similar to the Sagittarian aliens themselves but was enhanced for combat and difficult physical labor. Its skin was a muddled gray-green. It would have towered over the Visitors, the tallest of which were barely as tall as Emmogene. It shared the large eyes, dual nose-holes, and small mouth of the Sagittarians, but proportionally was closer to a man than the race that created it. Instead of a slender frame, small abdomen, and comparatively short legs, Rook was built for cross-country endurance. Its arms and legs rippled with gray sinews, and its sleeveless, one-piece coverall bulged with muscle.

Rook hadn't so much as acknowledged Emmogene when she was led past it, but its black eyes followed her silently. It was eerie. These automatons were alive and capable of complex tasks, but supposedly they were nonsentient. All she knew was that, if it decided it needed to, it would crush her throat just as easily as it had the guard's. She'd hurried past it and into the kitchen.

Then there was Carmen. She, like the others, was lean and fit, a by-product of the Visitors' physiological boosters. Where Olga Vlodov was built like a weight lifter, Carmen had a more feminine physique. Her hair was long and black, her skin tanned, and her muscles toned. She ate in silence and seemed to be deliberately avoiding looking at Emmogene.

She doesn't like me, Emmogene thought. She could feel it intuitively. It wasn't obvious; Carmen was disciplined and held her feelings in check. But somewhere, below the surface, she was angry. The hints were subtle, but they were there. She wasn't happy about the situation. The way she looked at Anthony . . . there was some chemistry there, Emmogene thought. Had they been something once, only for Anthony to bring her along on a mission to rescue another woman?

"Where . . . where are you taking me?" Emmogene asked, meekly. Her voice seemed loud in the uncomfortable quiet of the room.

"You sound unhappy that we rescued you," Carmen said, coldly.

"Carmen," Anthony warned. He turned to Emmogene. "You have

a right to ask. We're going to a safe place, a refuge where no one bothers us. We call it Bolthole."

"Bolthole?"

Anthony smiled. "That's just what we call it. It's home for people like us, a last redoubt where we are hidden and safe from the outside world."

"It sounds nice," Emmogene managed. It sounded like just another prison to her.

"I admit," Anthony continued, "this is not the world we hoped for. Human governments consider us to be terrorists. Life can be hard at times. There are luxuries that we have to do without, but Bolthole is a safe place....at least, as safe as any place can be for us. There, you won't be pursued, you won't be experimented on, and you won't have to live in fear. Someday, when the Visitors return to reclaim the Earth, we will be waiting."

"*If*," Carmen corrected. There was bitterness in her voice. "If they return."

Anthony was unphased. "They will. Do not doubt me. They will be back. I have been promised."

Emmogene had large gaps in her memory. She knew she'd gone through an indoctrination process, but she couldn't remember most of it. Anthony's faith in the aliens had always been sincere, though, even after the war. He truly believed that they would return, journey from Mars to the Earth in force, to the salvation of all those who had fought for them. She wasn't sure who had promised him this, or why he believed that person; the Visitors' machinations had been difficult for humans to understand under the best of circumstances.

It was sad. Pathetic, even.

Emmogene didn't want the Visitors to come back. She didn't believe the narrative that they had been told, that the aliens came in peace and were driven to war by violent, militant humans. She knew the truth: the Visitors would suffer no rivals, would abide no challenges to their dominion over the Earth. When they couldn't subjugate humanity through subversion and manipulation they tried to conquer them by force of arms. When the conquest didn't go as planned, they attempted genocide. When that didn't work, they fled, having learned that humanity would destroy the world before letting them have it. The story that the humans had forced the benevolent aliens into war was a fairy tale that collaborators told themselves to assuage their guilt.

Some part of her wanted to make Anthony understand, make him see. He would never accept the truth, though, not even if it came from the woman he loved. Even now, after the war had been over for years, and after the aliens had abandoned their human compatriots, Anthony still had unwavering faith. That, Emmogene suspected, was another side effect of the conditioning they had imposed upon him.

It was monstrous. She hated the aliens all the more for what they had done to him.

"Getting there will be the difficult part, of course," he continued. "The border is heavily patrolled on both sides, and much of Mexico is still under martial law."

"We need to go east," Ivan Vlodov grunted. "They will be looking for us even in remote areas. We can go to safehouse in El Paso, cross into Mexico there."

Anthony furled his brow. "You are correct about our chances here in New Mexico, but I'm not sure how reliable things are in El Paso right now. I plan to go farther east than that."

"Laredo?" Carmen asked.

"Yes. I have arranged passage on a ship. If we can get to Altamira in time, the captain is willing to take us to Tangier. Command will send us a plane from there."

"Tangier?" Emmogene asked. "Are we going to Africa?" The table got quiet. Carmen glared at her. "I . . . I'm sorry."

Anthony managed a smile for her. "Yes. This homeland we've made for ourselves is in Africa. It's deep inside the Exclusion Zone, where few outsiders dare to venture."

Exclusion Zone, Emmogene thought. It was the polite name for the portion of Central Africa that the Visitors had spent twenty years terraforming before the war. Before the Visitors ever arrived, a terrible plague had ravaged much of Africa, killing millions. She'd read that it was now believed that this was the doing of the aliens, a softening of the target before their arrival. When they did land, the Visitors claimed the Congo region as their own. The rest of the world debated and argued, but no country tried to directly counter them, for fear of starting a war or losing favor with the newly arrived aliens. As the Visitors expanded their territory, the remaining human populations were forcibly resettled to the Human Sectors, a vast territory under direct Visitor control.

It was here that what would become the United Earth Alliance was founded. The Visitors managed their human populations as a vast farm. Previously existing cultural and ethnic conflicts were stamped out by use of overwhelming force. Children were raised in collective creches, indoctrinated by the Visitors. People were raised out of poverty. The poorest nations in the world became the richest and most advanced. Every aspect of life was micromanaged by the Visitors and their human proxies. Many more flocked there from the outside world, and the Visitors welcomed all who came. In exchange for a safe, peaceful life in their comfortable utopia, all they asked in return was absolute, unquestioning obedience. "Trust Our Benefactors" was the slogan.

In the Exclusion Zone, the native ecosystem was slowly superseded by one from the Visitors' homeworld, modified to thrive in Earth soil, water, and air. The native plant and animal species either adapted or died out.

Emmogene hesitated. "Is . . . is it really safe to live there? I heard it got, you know . . ."

"Yes," Anthony answered, not letting her finish. "It's quite safe. Outdoor radiological contamination is well within acceptable margins, and Bolthole is protected from such hazards." For most of the war, sophisticated defenses protected the Exclusion Zone from direct attack. Those defenses, degraded by years of war, went down completely when the Visitors retreated into space. The Americans and the Russians subjected the region to a sustained nuclear bombardment in an unsuccessful attempt to kill off the alien flora and fauna.

Emmogene took a deep breath. She knew that what she was going to say next wouldn't be received well, but she had to try. "Anthony," she began, hesitantly, "I don't want to go to Africa."

The room suddenly got even more quiet. Carmen's fork clinked loudly on her plate. The Vlodov Twins stopped speaking to each other. Even Henry had looked up from his cooking. All eyes were on Anthony.

He seemed nonplussed. He continued to eat, looking down at his plate.

Seconds ticked by. "Anthony," Emmogene repeated.

"I heard you," he said, coldly. He looked up at her. He was gripping his fork so tightly that his knuckles were turning white. "We risked a lot to get you out of there. I took lives. Paid bribes. I spent years watching over you, convincing my superiors to let me stay when they thought my efforts would be better spent elsewhere." He pointed his fork angrily at her, accentuating each statement. "And now you don't want to go with me?"

Emmogene was scared. She could see the anger surging in Anthony, bubbling just beneath the surface. "I'm sorry, I—"

He cut her off. "Sorry? Don't be sorry, Emmogene. Don't apologize for telling the truth."

Her mind racing, Emmogene tried to think of something to say that would defuse his anger, but she couldn't think of anything. "Can . . . can I go, then?"

"Go?" Carmen asked, angrily. "Go where, *puta*? You walk out that door, you'll be food for the coyotes before anyone finds you, and if they do find you, they're gonna take you to Area 51 and dissect you. Is that what you want?"

"No!"

"Then I suggest you shut your mouth and eat your food, *guera*."

"Carmen!" Anthony said, his tone a sharper than before. "That's enough." He turned back to Emmogene. "You'll have to forgive Carmen. She has sacrificed more than most of us for the cause, and you do seem rather ungrateful."

"I'm not ungrateful," Emmogene said, trying to fight back tears. "Anthony, I'm scared, don't you see? I don't know what to do!" She could see his anger subsiding. Like the old fable, beauty had soothed the savage beast.

Anthony stood up, came around the table, and knelt next to Emmogene. "I know. You poor thing, you've been through so much." Carmen rolled her eyes, pushed herself away from the table, and left the room without another word. The twins quietly followed her. Henry set his cooking aside and also left the kitchen. Once they were alone, Anthony took Emmogene's hand. "This has been difficult for me as well, but I need you to trust me. I need . . . I need you. We were meant to be together. Without you, I'm not my best. I can't . . ." He paused, looking down at the floor. "It's harder for me to control the conditioning without you. Without a mission, without purpose, I'm lost. I don't always know what to do, either."

"You scare me sometimes."

"I know. I'm sorry. I'm trying. That's why I need you. You help me stay in control. You give me purpose." He looked into her eyes, intently. "We were meant to be together, Emmogene."

She didn't say anything. She was trying to get a read on his emotions, to see if he was being sincere, but it was difficult. He was unpredictable. He'd tell you one thing, being completely sincere, only to change his mind later. On top of that, he was a masterful liar.

"Besides," he continued, "you're too important. Those InSec morons were going to kill you, but they didn't know how important you are. We have such plans for you."

"What?" Her eyes were wide. "What plans?"

Anthony caressed the side of Emmogene's face. She was nearly shaking. "You and I are going to build the future together. It is our purpose." He was much, much colder now. Distant. The sweet, tender part of Anthony had retreated. All that was left was the weapon.

"What are you talking about? I don't understand. Is this about the device in my head?"

"You will, in time." He let go of her hand, stood up, and turned to leave.

"Anthony . . ."

He looked over his shoulder. "If you try to run, my team will bring you back. If we have to tie you up, we will. I'm sorry, Emmogene. You're too important." Without another word, he strode from the room, leaving Emmogene alone at the table.

South Valley, New Mexico
Several days later . . .

SOMEHOW, SPECIAL AGENTS Frampton and Delaney managed to be bigger dicks in person than they were over the telecom. They had Nathan meet them in their mobile command center, a glorified RV, which was parked at the scene of the bus crash. Federal forensics investigators had gone over the bus with a microscope while recovery teams had taken the bodies away. They had refused to brief the New Mexico State Police on exactly what had transpired, just as DHS had failed to brief them on the prison bus move. They wanted it kept secret. So much for coordinating with law enforcement. The NMSP had predictably told them to go pound sand, leaving them with very little in the way of support. Agent Delaney had called the governor of New Mexico and told him about the bus. He blamed the State Police for the lack of cooperation, told the governor that multiple dangerous war criminals were on the loose, and had tried to strong-arm him into deploying the National Guard.

The Feds had been appalled when they met Nathan's team, a fourteen-year-old boy and a dog. He told them simply that this was his team, take it or leave it, and in desperation they relented. They needed him more than ever now that they'd burned their bridge with the State Police. Even if they got their National Guard deployment, the New Mexico National Guard didn't have investigative abilities.

Nathan told them that he was going to head out to shake the bushes. As Stella had predicted, Agent Frampton had wanted to go with them. Nathan had flatly refused him.

"I insist!" he'd demanded. "We're running this investigation!"

"Running doesn't mean micromanaging, Agent Frampton,"

Nathan had said. "I'm going to go talk to one of my contacts. The last thing I need is you federal boys poking around, scaring the locals. They know me. They don't know you."

"Don't think I don't know what you're trying to do," the federal agent had sneered. "We know what you money-grubbing bounty hunters put into the contract."

"You signed it anyway," Nathan had said, with a grin. "Look, it isn't like the two fugitives are going to be with my contact. I'm just going to ask around. There's a network people like that use to get in and out of the country, and my friends have an ear to the ground on it, that's all. I'll let you know if I find out anything useful. Like as not it'll be a bust anyway, so don't get your shorts in a bunch."

Frampton hadn't liked that, but he didn't really have a choice. He gave Nathan a government-issue satellite phone, a blocky, heavy, ruggedized and shielded monstrosity with a four-inch screen and fold-down keyboard. That was how he was to stay in touch, he was told.

Ben insisted that they turn it off, take the battery out, and put it in the shielded storage box they had for transporting things that may be sensitive to stray electromagnetic emissions. "I guarantee they'll be able to track us with it if we don't," he'd said. "GPS." Ben was a smart kid like that.

The next afternoon, Nathan and Ben were parked up the street from a weathered storefront in South Valley, New Mexico. The sign on the establishment's storefront read, FLETCHER'S BOOKS, NEW * USED * MOVIES * GAMES. Other signs indicated that the shop also sold cigars, tobacco, and smoking accoutrements. It was open, though the street was all but deserted, despite it being a weekday afternoon. South Valley had once been a suburb of Albuquerque, and had survived mostly intact when New Mexico's largest city had been destroyed by an alien orbital strike.

Nathan had been here before, but not with Ben. He looked at his young partner. "Alright, listen. I'm gonna head inside and talk to our informant. You keep a lookout out here."

"I can help!" Ben protested.

"Boy, I don't need help talking to this guy. I do need you to watch the street. Use the binoculars. Keep tabs on anyone coming and going. If, you know, a bunch of guys come in after me, call me on the radio so I don't get jumped." Nathan had a throat microphone and a small earpiece, both of which were hard to spot if you weren't specifically looking for them. It allowed him to use a radio discretely. He wasn't expecting trouble here, but trouble had a way of showing up when you least expected it.

"Okay," Ben said. "I'll watch your back." The truck's windows were tinted, so it wouldn't be obvious that someone was in the vehicle.

As Nathan stepped out of the truck, a dry gust of wind blew his sweater's hood off his head. He was dressed inconspicuously, in an old hoodie and worn jeans. He walked with a slouch, hands in his pockets, eyes downward, like the former collaborators often did. It was the stride of defeated, betrayed, and broken people, and he'd seen it enough times to emulate it. He'd also made it a point to not shave since leaving home, making him look scruffy and unkempt.

Most of the storefronts were boarded up, the buildings vacant. The wind carried trash and tumbleweeds with it. Even though it was broad daylight, if someone stepped out of an alley and gunned him down, there'd be no witnesses. It might be an hour before sheriff's deputies showed up, assuming they ever did.

South Valley was home to thousands of former collaborators: those who had been paroled, those who had served their sentences, and those who had yet evaded justice. Many of those who had been granted their freedom had not regained their US citizenship, but this was still America, and they were free to live their lives. The trouble was, many communities wanted nothing to do with them, so they were left to build their own. Between the former collaborators and the refugees from Mexico and Central America, the government didn't have a good accounting of who lived in the run-down city. This made it a good place for people on the lam to try and lay low for a while, if not disappear outright.

To Nathan, it seemed only fitting that they lived in the ruins of a city that their benefactors had destroyed.

A bell over the door jingled as he stepped inside. The bookstore was dimly lit and cluttered, with rows of old books packed so closely together that two people couldn't walk abreast down the aisle. Cigarette and cigar smoke hung in the air, despite the best efforts of a rattling old ventilation system and some rickety ceiling fans. In one corner, several patrons sat smoking and reading. In another, several big-screened computers were set up, with hourly rates for internet access posted, but no one was using them. Against the back wall was the counter and cash register; behind it, a heavyset Latina woman in a brightly colored dress.

Nathan made his way to the counter. "I'm looking for George," he said, quietly. No one else in the store paid him any mind, but the woman behind the counter didn't seem to understand. She looked at him apologetically. Nathan repeated his request, in Spanish, and that she understood. Nervously, she asked him if he was in some kind of trouble. Nathan assured her that he was just visiting a friend. She did a decent job of pretending to believe him before disappearing into the back room, leaving the bounty hunter alone at the counter.

Nathan scanned the room as he waited. The trio of men in the smoking corner murmured to themselves, but none of them were giving him the evil eye. Sliding a hand into his pocket, he clicked his radio transmit button twice, signaling Ben to give him an update from the outside. They'd done this sort of thing before.

"Street's quiet," Ben said, speaking very softly into Nathan's earpiece. "A hobo pushed a shopping cart by, and a couple cars went past, but that's it."

Another click acknowledged as Jorge "George" Vargas appeared from the back room. A balding, mustachioed, affable man, George looked like he'd gained a few pounds since Nathan had seen him last, not unusual for a guy pushing fifty. He came to the register, leaned on the counter, and greeted Nathan quietly.

"Been a while," he said. "I've got just what you need, my friend, if you've got the cash: genuine, prewar Cuban cigars."

"You know it," Nathan said. "You're the only guy I know who can find them."

"An experienced businessman such as myself has ways," he said with a grin. "Ways I will not divulge, but I think I do have what you're looking for." He looked over his shoulder, to the door leading to the back room. "Mira!" In Spanish, he asked the woman to watch the counter while he took his customer to see the good stuff in the back. She smiled at him as they passed and giggled like a schoolgirl when he smacked her on the butt.

The door behind the counter led to a large back room, one corner of which was set up as an office space. George motioned for Nathan to sit and took his own seat across from him. The desk was cluttered with papers and a dirty ashtray that served as a paperweight. A computer with one main screen and two smaller ones took up the other end, next to a desktop video phone. His chair was an antique, ornately carved and covered in red velvet padding. Nathan had to make do with a metal folding chair.

"It's been what, a year, since you've visited?" George asked.

"Something like that. You look like you're living comfortably."

"Mira is an amazing cook. I am but a humble merchant, yet I eat like a king!"

Nathan chuckled. "Does she know about all your side action? Women have a way of finding out."

George made a big show of looking offended. "You insult me! I'll have you know I'm reformed! I'm a new man, happily married and settled down."

"For real? Damn, George, I never thought I'd see the day."

George gave a wide smile. "As I said, she's an amazing cook. It's true, the path to a man's heart is through his stomach. Besides, the older you get, the more appealing the idea of settling down is. You will find out when you get to be my age."

"Well, I'm happy for you."

"And yet I doubt you drove all the way here to simply catch up. In fact, I'm certain you didn't."

"I think you know why I'm here, and why I didn't just call you. This one is sensitive."

"Of course. The bus, yes?"

"Yes."

"That was bad business. Four federal officers killed and a busload of escaped prisoners. There are rumors that the National Guard is being deployed. Many of my customers fear that they'll come here, and that it'll be like the old days."

Word travels fast, Nathan thought. "I don't have any inside information about that, George, but I doubt it. For now, I think I'm the only one who'll be visiting South Valley over this, but I do have the Feds breathing down my neck."

"Of course. I do have inside information, my friend, and you are correct. This attack wasn't conducted by any residents of our fair city, and they know that. The soldiers will just be security theater . . .

except for the checkpoints on the highways. Those have the potential to put a damper on things. I will have to pay bribes in addition to my usual operating expenses, or find ways around those who can't be bribed. As such, I'm saddened to inform you that my rates have gone up."

"I expected as much and came prepared. Genuine prewar Cubans don't come cheap."

George, a genuine, prewar Cuban himself, chuckled at that. "You can't say I haven't embraced the capitalist ethos, my friend."

Nathan grinned. George had been running a smuggling operation in and out of Cuba years before the Sagittarians showed up. He despised the Communists and was initially (understandably) thrilled when the aliens swept aside the decrepit old regime in his homeland. "So . . . what can you tell me about the bus?"

"Most of what I know, I think you already know. The Swiss man was responsible for it. He used to be an Earth Storm commando. The men of the United Earth Alliance Army called that unit the *Sombra de la Muerta*. Even those on the same side were afraid of them. Any regular-forces unit they fought with suffered heavy casualties, and if they tried to retreat, they'd be slaughtered by the commandos. These are dangerous men . . . and a woman, too, I've heard."

"There is. A big, blonde woman. Not sure who she is."

"I know of her, but she's not the one I was talking about. There's another. She's beautiful, a Latina, with black hair and brown eyes. Tall and dangerous."

"I see. How do you know all this?"

"I have eyes everywhere, my friend. A woman like that comes across the border, people talk. It's rare to see the Enhanced any-more . . . even rarer to see one break the neck of some drunk young fool who tried to be amorous with her."

"Jesus. I bet."

"He was a young man, too young to have fought in the war, too full of swagger to know any better. Her temper got them noticed, though. This was in Mexicali. The Federales got wind of it. They had to leave. They crossed the border into Arizona from there."

"Who brought them in?"

George shook his head. "No one brought them in. They crossed themselves. They are some of the deadliest warriors ever to have lived. They don't need the help of some dusty coyote to evade complacent Border Guard patrols."

"No, I suppose they wouldn't." Nathan's battalion had been attacked by commandos from the Immortals, a sister unit to the Earth Storm with an equally deadly reputation. They weren't immortal at all; he'd shot two of them dead with his rifle and wounded a third with his 10mm pistol. They were dangerous, though, brazen and fearless. "How long ago was this?"

"Six months."

"Six months? You didn't think I might want to know that information?"

George shrugged. "I am not a mind reader, my friend. I assumed that if you wanted to know you'd ask."

"If they came across that long ago, how did you know they pulled off the attack on the bus?"

George smiled but said nothing.

Nathan chuckled. His job was knowing things, and he was good at it. "Do you know what they've been up to since then?"

"No. They disappeared until the attack on the bus. They had some equipment with them when they crossed the border, but not vehicles. Whatever transportation they had they must have acquired up north. They did not use any of the common smuggling networks. I do not know if they had help this side of the border, but my gut tells me they didn't."

Nathan wasn't a cop. He wasn't interested in whatever illegal businesses George had his fingers in, and this allowed the two men to have a working relationship. In any case, Mexico had been destroyed in the war, its capital city obliterated the way Washington, Phoenix, and Albuquerque were. Cuba had been hit with dozens of American and Russian nuclear weapons when the fighting started. The aliens were still out there, having colonized Mars, and most thought that it was only a matter of time before they returned. Illicit cross-border commerce was pretty far down on the list of things the US government was presently worried about. "I think you're right about that. I'm willing to bet they spent that time planning the attack, watching the prison, waiting for a chance to make their move. I don't suppose you know where they're at now? That information would be extremely valuable to me."

"A less honest man would bullshit you, but you know I am always straight with you: I don't. I have not gotten word of them being seen in any of the towns around where the bus was hit. I have people keeping an eye out, in the towns, on the highways, at the border. I pay good money for information and knew as soon as I heard of this that they would be looking for these people. They have not been seen."

"Well, shit."

"But I do have an offer that will make this visit worth your while. For a very reasonable down payment, I will make sure you are kept in the know if the people you are looking for are seen."

"Fair enough. Anything else?"

"Yes. You must be careful, my friend." George's tone was more serious now. "These people are dangerous, as I've said, but there's more than that. They are from the Bolthole. You've heard of it?"

"I have. Supposedly it's a secret holdout of the Sagittarius Faction in Africa somewhere. I figured it was just a story. If it was real, we'd have bombed it."

"There are many stories about it, most of which are bullshit, but it's very real. Some of the traitors are still loyal to the aliens. Not many, not after this long, but some. The true believers will do anything to help the Enhanced. 'For the future,' as they say. The Faction has more of a presence in this country than the government knows."

"Is that so? Can you confirm this?"

"If I had any solid information I would have given it to the government myself. I am a patriot, you know. All I have is a hunch based on rumors I've heard and patterns I've seen. If I hear of anything actionable, I will contact you."

"That's good to know, George. I appreciate your help. Thank you." He reached into his pocket, retrieved his billfold, and began to count out hundred-dollar bills. "Please let me know ASAP if you hear anything. The longer they go without being caught, the more heat the government will bring. It could be bad for business."

"Tell me something, Nathan . . . I have heard a rumor, but I don't know if it is true. The rumor is, there was only one person on that bus, a skinny little white girl. They say she killed someone at the Gallup Federal Detention Facility, but it was very mysterious."

Nathan stood up. "If you are talking to people who were there, then you know more than I do. I'm just trying to find them and get paid. Like I said, I will make it very worth your while if you get me a good lead, especially if you get it to me and not anyone else who comes asking."

George smiled widely. "Of course, of course." He reached into his desk. "Here. Take a couple of cigars. Real prewar Cubans, hand-rolled. Only the best for my business partners."

Nodding, Nathan took the cigars and turned to leave. "I'll be in touch."

Quemado, New Mexico

FOR ALL OF HER APPREHENSION at the circumstances, Emmogene was quietly happy to be back out in the real world. She'd been in federal detention for years, eating the same food, wearing the same jumpsuits, doing the same things every day. The small taste of freedom she was experiencing was exhilarating—intoxicating, even.

It was also an illusion. She was every bit as much a prisoner now as when she was in prison.

She studied her face in a small mirror mounted to the side of a rack of sunglasses. Anthony had given her some money and told her to get whatever she wanted from the little general store and gas station. Quemado wasn't much of a town, and the establishment wasn't much of a store, but after spending all morning in the van, it was nice to just be able to stretch her legs and use the bathroom.

"Those look good on you." It was Carmen.

Emmogene looked up, surprised. "Oh! Thank you. I think I'm going to get these." Most of the pairs of cheap sunglasses were either gaudy or ugly or both. "They're cute without being too flashy."

Carmen actually smiled. Emmogene couldn't read her very well, even as perceptive as she was. She didn't sense anger in Carmen, not at the moment. She was trying to be nice, and Emmogene could tell it was difficult for her. "Are you almost ready? Henry should be done gassing up the van now."

Emmogene and Carmen were the only ones still in the store. Anthony remained in the van, while Henry pumped gas. Behind them was a pickup truck driven by the Twins. Rook was hidden in the back of the truck, concealed under tarps, lying motionless until needed.

"I'm ready," Emmogene said. She had a big bottle of water in one hand and some chocolate, snacks, and the sunglasses in the other.

Carmen nodded toward the register. "Let's go, then." The clerk, a squat, middle-aged man, had barely paid his patrons any mind. His attention was mostly focused on a small screen, on which played a baseball game.

A bell jingled loudly as the door swung open. Emmogene and Carmen froze as a police officer walked into the little store.

"Morning, Enrique," the cop said. He was dressed in tan fatigues, combat boots, and a black body armor vest. On his shoulder was a patch, shaped like a slice of pizza, which read STATE POLICE N. MEX. A revolver hung from his belt in a low-slung holster. "What's the score?"

"The Isotopes are up by two," the clerk said. The cop leaned on the counter and the two men continued to chat about baseball.

"Give me your things," Carmen said, very quietly. "I'll pay for them. You go get in the van."

"But . . ."

"No buts, *chica*. They will be looking for you, not me. You go. I'll go pay and flirt with the cop. It'll distract him so you can get to the van."

"Will that work?"

Carmen smiled, adjusting her tank top so as to show a little more cleavage. "It always does. Wait until I've got his attention and go."

Emmogene nodded and stayed back as Carmen sauntered off to the register. She gave the police officer, a handsome man with jet-black hair, a big smile as she set her things down on the counter. As Carmen chatted up the two men, Emmogene cast her eyes downward and made for the door. As she got close, the police officer noticed her, and looked her right in the eye. She froze. Her heart was racing. Carmen fell silent.

"Allow me," the cop said, pulling the door open for Emmogene. The bell jingled.

"Oh, thank you!" she said, hurrying out the door.

Once outside, Emmogene had to take a moment to breathe. Her heart was still pounding. She looked up and to her right. There, under the fuel pump canopy, was their big white van. Henry was still standing outside. He motioned for her to come over.

To her left, parked in the shade of a big tree, was a New Mexico

State Police truck. It was a large, heavy vehicle, and looked like it was armored. Leaning against it was another police officer, this one smoking a cigarette. His eyes were hidden behind sunglasses, but he was definitely watching Emmogene.

She looked back over at the van. The driver's window was lowered about halfway. Concealed in shadow, Anthony was watching her. She could almost feel his eyes on her, and his intense anxiety. Her eyes moved back over to the police officer, and before she realized it, Emmogene had made her decision. This was the only chance she was going to get. She started off toward him, walking quickly. He noticed her approaching and dropped his cigarette, grinding it out with his boot.

An instant later a hand clamped around Emmogene's arm like a vise. "Where are you going, *guera*?" It was Carmen. Her anger was palpable, threatening to boil over at any second. "Our ride is over here." Not letting go, she pulled Emmogene toward the van, roughly.

Emmogene stumbled, but Carmen was holding her too tightly for her to fall. "You're hurting me!"

"Oh, honey," Carmen said through a forced smile, "you haven't begun to hurt. Come along now."

"Excuse me." It was a man's voice, deep and authoritative. Both women froze. It was the police officer. He'd come over. He was a tall man with mirrored sunglasses and a big mustache. His hand was on the butt of his revolver. He looked right at Emmogene. "Miss, are you alright?" He could tell something was wrong. "Miss?" He looked at Carmen. "Ma'am, I need you to let go of her and step back."

"This is my friend, Officer," Carmen said, trying to sound pleasant. "She just got released from the hospital. She gets confused sometimes, is all." Her hand squeezed Emmogene's arm so tightly that it was bruising. "Isn't that right?"

Emmogene looked up into the police officer's eyes. The look of fear on her face had to be plain as day. In a flash, he drew his revolver and leveled it at Carmen. "Let go of her and step away, now! Do it now!" Carmen did as she was ordered, releasing Emmogene and raising her hands. "You, miss, come to me." He stayed focused on Carmen. "You, get down on the ground, facedown, right now!" She was carrying a gun, but the police officer had her dead to rights. Very slowly, she did as she was told. Once she was on the ground, the police officer kept his gun trained on her with one hand while he squeezed his radio microphone with the other. He started to speak rapidly into the radio.

Emmogene screamed as a burst of weapons fire ripped open the police officer's chest in a spray of blood, tearing right through his vest. He dropped his gun and collapsed to the dirt. She looked over at the van. Anthony was standing outside now, his eyes wide and full of hate. Rook loomed behind him, once again concealed in its hat, coat, mask, and goggles. In its hands was an oversized alien weapon, a high-velocity flechette gun. Henry moved toward Emmogene and Carmen, pistol in hand. Two bullets struck him as the other policeman opened fire from inside the store. Henry fell, Anthony took cover behind the van, and Rook turned and returned fire. The little town of Quemado echoed with the terrifying, electro-mechanical roar of its weapon.

Emmogene ran. She ran as hard as she could, making for the still-idling police truck, not knowing what she would do if she got to it. Her heart pounded in her ears with every step. It was so close, just a few more feet, and—*wham!* The wind was knocked out of Emmogene as Carmen tackled her from behind, knocking her to the rocky ground.

Pain shot through Emmogene's body as she gasped for breath. Carmen was on top of her. Shots rang out as the former commando fired her pistol, at something or someone. Hot brass hit the dirt near Emmogene's head as she tried to cover her ears.

Just like that, it was over. "Clear!" Carmen shouted.

"Clear!" Anthony replied. "Man down!"

"What?" Carmen asked, still holding Emmogene down. "Henry?"

"He's dead," Anthony confirmed. "Ivan is hit. Get Emmogene over here. We need to go."

"You heard him, *puta*," Carmen snarled. Taking her knee off of Emmogene's back, she stood up. Emmogene, still gasping for breath, was able to turn over onto her back. "Get up!" Carmen kicked her in the side so hard Emmogene thought she might throw up. "I said get up!" She didn't wait for Emmogene to get to her feet. She grabbed her by the hair and lifted her off the ground, her enhanced muscles rippling at the exertion. Once Emmogene was on her feet, Carmen shoved her forward, toward the van.

Anthony was kneeling by Ivan's side, trying to get the bleeding under control. Ivan had been shot in the stomach somehow, despite Rook laying down so much suppressing fire. Henry was nearby, on his back, in a puddle of blood. He'd been hit in the head. The other police officer was nowhere to be seen but was undoubtedly dead. Anthony looked up at Olga, still applying pressure to Ivan's wound. "No witnesses. Go." Olga nodded. She jerked her head at Rook, and the pair made their way into the store without a word.

"Anthony, no!" Emmogene screamed. She tried to, anyway. It came out as little more than a squeak. She tried to run to him but Carmen had her by the arm. Muffled gunfire erupted from inside the store. First a deep roar from Rook's weapon, then, a few moments later, a couple of regular gunshots. After that the town was quiet once more.

Olga stepped out into the sunlight a few moments later. "The building is clear."

"Good," Anthony replied. "I've got the bleeding stopped. Take Ivan and put him in the back of the van where he can lay down. I've stabilized him but if he doesn't get proper medical attention, he'll die. Carmen," he said, looking up at her, "I want you to stay with him. Monitor his vitals. Olga and Rook will take the truck."

"What about Henry?" Carmen asked. She was upset. She'd been fond of him. "We can't just leave him here."

"Put his body in the back of the truck. Wrap it in the tarp next to Rook. Go!"

Carmen snarled. "This wouldn't have happened if this little bitch hadn't tried to run!" she said, angrily. "I told you this would happen!"

Anthony slowly stood up, looking Carmen dead in the eye. "Carmen, do as I say!" His tone was a warning. "We don't have time for this. We need to go."

"You're the boss," Carmen spat, bitterly. She let go of Emmogene's arm and went with Olga as they moved their wounded comrade to the vehicle. Rook, acting on instructions, roughly picked up Henry's limp body and brought it to the truck.

Anthony and Emmogene were alone now. A dry wind blew through Quemado, and Emmogene shivered. Anthony approached until he was standing over her, looking down at her through his sunglasses.

"You shouldn't have done that, Emmogene."

Emmogene didn't answer. She just looked down at the ground. Anthony was seething with barely contained rage. The only reason he was holding it together right now was his programmed reaction to combat.

"Look at me, Emmogene." He took off his sunglasses. "Look at me."

Trembling, she looked up into his eyes. They were distant and hungry, like the eyes of jackal. "A . . . Anthony, I—"

The words were choked off as he wrapped a hand around her throat. He only squeezed a little, as if to let her know how easily he could kill her if he wanted to. "Listen to me, Emmogene. Those two cops, the people in the store, Henry . . . they're dead because of you. Do you understand me? Every time you try to do something stupid, like run, or get the police involved, you're going to get more people killed. I trusted you," he said, grimacing, squeezing her throat just a little tighter. "You betrayed that trust. I love you, Emmogene, but you were foolish. Your foolishness got these people killed."

Emmogene tried to speak but could only gasp for air. Anthony relaxed his grip just enough to allow her to talk. "Just let me go," she pleaded, tears streaming down her face. "Anthony, I'm sorry! I don't love you! I can't be what you want me to be, can't you see that?"

Anthony's expression softened, if only a little, and he released her. That had hurt him. It didn't take him long to push the hurt away, though, to bury it and regain his composure. He loomed over her, as if contemplating what to say next. "I know you don't love me. It doesn't matter. You and I were meant to be together. What we want, or what we think we want, that doesn't matter. All that matters is the mission, our destiny."

"What mission?" Exasperated, Emmogene flung her arms wide and managed to shout at Anthony. "Look around you! The Visitors are the ones who betrayed you, Anthony! They used you—they used us! When they couldn't win, they just abandoned you. They don't care about you and they never did. We were just livestock to them, don't you see?"

Anthony was quiet for a long moment. Emmogene could tell he was mulling over what she'd said. She was hoping, praying to the God she increasingly hoped was real that she could get through to him.

He sighed, and shook his head. "I'm sorry you see things this way.

I know what kind of propaganda they subjected you to in captivity. In time, you'll see the truth."

Emmogene was crying now, weak in the knees, wanting to throw up. "Anthony, please, please stop this. Just go. Leave me here. Please. I don't love you."

He put a hand on her shoulder. "You'll learn to love me, if you just let yourself. We were meant to be together. We were selected as a mating pair, and we will fulfill that destiny. Our children will be the first of a new, better human race. The Visitors will return when we are worthy. They will return and take our descendants to the stars." Emmogene stood there, shaking, tears rolling down her cheeks, as Anthony leaned down and very gently kissed her on the forehead. "Now get in the van or I'll put you in it. We have to leave."

Afraid, defeated, and numb, Emmogene did as she was told.

BY THE TIME NATHAN AND BEN ARRIVED in the town of Quemado, the New Mexico State Police had cordoned off the trading post. The NMSP didn't have a lot of officers to spare, though, and many were undoubtedly being tasked for the manhunt. Two of their own had been killed, according to the police scanner. Nathan suspected that Anthony Krieg was behind this.

Nathan parked on the other side of the highway, out of the way, and told Ben to let Shadow out as they got out of the truck. Putting on his hat, he crossed the road toward the site of the incident. There was a gaggle of locals standing around, but none of them were close to the perimeter the cops had formed. Several of the people were crying and holding each other, trying to comfort one another. It was a bad day for this little town. Nathan bypassed them and approached the nearest police officer.

"Uh, sir, this is a crime scene," the cop said. His hand was on his grip of his revolver, and he was eyeing the gun that Nathan openly wore. "You need to move along."

Very slowly, so as not to give the cop the wrong idea, Nathan retrieved his bronze badge and held it up for him to see. "Nathan Foster, Federal Recovery Agent. I have reason to believe that XT-collaborators were involved in this crime. May I speak with the officer in charge?"

The cop relaxed, but only a little. He turned and yelled for his captain. The other man approached and shook hands with Nathan. "Captain Jose Garcia, New Mexico State Police." He told the young officer to go take a break. "What can I do for you, Bronze?"

"Name's Foster, Nathan Foster. Captain, if you don't mind, I'd like to take a look at your crime scene."

"Does this have to do with the attack on the prison bus?"

"I believe it does. I'm on the trail of the people who perpetrated that attack."

"I see. The fucking Feds wouldn't tell us anything about that, and now two of my men are dead." There was bitterness in his voice. "What do you need?"

"I just want to bring my dog in," Nathan said, nodding toward Ben and Shadow. "He's a military-grade enhanced working dog. He should be able to tell me if persons modified by the aliens have been here."

"Sure, bring him in." He indicated Ben, who was still over by the truck. "Hey, who's the kid?"

"That's Ben. He's my partner. Also my nephew."

"He's a little young for this, don't you think?"

Nathan shrugged. "He is, but . . . he lost his parents, you know, in the war. I'm all he's got."

Captain Garcia nodded solemnly. "I ended up raising my brother's kids after the bastards hit Albuquerque. I understand, believe me. Still, would you mind at least leaving him here at the cordon? It's a mess in there. Kid probably shouldn't oughta see that."

Nathan agreed. He waved Ben over. Captain Garcia called his officer back to his post.

"I brought the camera and test kit," Ben said, handing Shadow's lead to Nathan.

"Good job. Let me have them." Ben looked for a moment like he was going to argue; usually, taking the pictures and running the test kit were his jobs. "I guess it's pretty bad in there. The police asked me to have you wait here."

The boy looked disappointed, but he didn't argue. "Okay. I'll wait here."

"Please, follow me," Captain Garcia said to Nathan. He turned to Ben. "Young man, Patrolman Bartlett here will give you a rundown on what we think happened. Do you have a notebook?"

Ben's face lit up. "I do!" he said, retrieving a pad of paper and a pen from his pocket.

"I'm doing what, sir?" the patrolman asked. He seemed confused.

"You heard me. This kid is working with the Bronze. Fill him in. I'm taking Mr. Foster here to examine the scene." With that, the two men and dog turned and left, leaving the bewildered state trooper to answer Ben's questions.

Nathan chuckled as they walked away. "Thank you for that, Captain. You made that boy's day."

"It's an ugly world we live in now. Kids have to grow up too fast. My niece is sixteen and she already works as a receptionist in a doctor's office. It does no good to treat them like children when they're trying to help earn a living. Speaking of ugly . . ." They came to a halt by the gas pumps. The pavement was stained with blood and littered with spent brass.

Nathan took in the scene. There was one large pool of blood by the gas pumps, along with some small bits of bloody tissue, but there was no body. Spent brass casings, each circled with chalk, were scattered around the area in front of the store. The bodies of the two fallen officers had been recovered; chalk outlines of where they had been found lingered like ghosts. "What happened?"

"We got a partial call by Corporal Higgins," he said, pointing to one of the outlines, "something about a suspected kidnapping. He was cut off and dispatch was unable to raise him again. His partner, Patrolman Brown, was inside when the firefight broke out. He was able to radio in during the exchange before he . . . before he was killed. Higgins died without having fired a shot. He was tore up pretty badly. I haven't seen wounds like that since the war, you know?"

"You're a veteran?"

The police officer rolled up his sleeve and showed Nathan an Eagle, Globe, and Anchor tattoo on his forearm. "Third Marine Division out of Okinawa. Fought the bastards in the Philippines. You?"

"1st Armored Division. I was a tanker. Fought in the Mexico and California campaigns."

Garcia nodded. Nathan got the conversation back on topic. "So you think it might be an alien weapon?"

"Seems like it. One of their automatic flechette guns, maybe.

Forensics is still inside, trying to recover a projectile for analysis, but from the damage the thing caused, that would be my guess."

"That would explain why there are so many bullet holes and not very much brass on the ground: they had a goddamn Ripper gun. What happened after that?"

"Patrolman Brown, from inside the store, put up a hell of a fight. He got off fifteen shots from his service revolver before they got him. He reported that he killed one of the sons of bitches and wounded another before his transmissions stopped. After he died, the perps went inside and cleaned house. They killed the owner of the store, his wife, and their son. The owner was ripped apart by the flechette gun. The wife and the kid were each shot once, in the head. We found 9mm brass."

"Christ Almighty. Did your men have body cameras?"

"No. We don't really have the budget for that these days. There was a dash camera in their vehicle, but it's missing. Camera, hard drive, all of it."

They were thorough, Nathan thought. "Captain, I am sorry for the loss of your men, and for the deaths of these people."

"Yeah. I told their families this afternoon. This hit the town hard. Quemado only has a couple hundred people in it. Everybody knows everybody, you know?" He paused to light a cigarette. "What do you think? Sagittarius Faction, maybe?"

"There's a strong possibility." The alien weapon was strong evidence, but it wasn't conclusive. Such things did turn up in the hands of criminals from time to time, even if they were big and unwieldy for humans to use. "Shadow here should be able to tell me for sure. Is it alright if I let him sniff the blood?"

Captain Garcia nodded. "Do what you need to do. I had to tell a nine-year-old boy his papa isn't coming home today."

Nathan understood. "C'mon, boy," he said, and led Shadow over to the bloodstains and bloody bits of meat. "Shadow, check it out."

On command, the dog moved in and began sniffing the blood eagerly. He had been trained to be very delicate about it, not disturbing the scene, just getting the scent of the blood. After a few seconds of this, Shadow sat and looked up at his master.

"What does that mean?" Captain Garcia asked.

"It means that whoever this blood came from has, in all

likelihood, been enhanced by alien means. Shadow is pretty good at his job. He's never given me a false positive."

"How can a dog tell?"

"You know all those boosters and enhancements the Greys gave to their minions?" Nathan took a picture of the bloodstain as he spoke. "They alter human body chemistry enough that they smell a little differently, at least to dogs. The only more accurate way to tell is a blood test." He lowered the camera. "I have a field test kit that's fairly accurate, but I'm already certain that whoever this was, he was a collaborator."

"Good work, Mr. Foster."

Nathan nodded. "If you don't mind, I'm going to get blood samples. Can you show me where the other bloodstain was, the one you think came from a different individual? I can send these in to get analyzed and compared to the national database, see if it's anybody we know of."

"Yeah, right over here. Lots of blood. Sample away. We're just waiting for forensics to finish up so we can bring in the cleanup crew."

"I appreciate your help, Captain. It . . . shit."

Captain Garcia turned around to see what Nathan was looking at. The Feds' big, black, mobile command center, red and blue lights flashing, came to a stop on the road in front of the old trading post. It was trailed by two unmarked, matte-black SUVs, with lights flashing in the windows.

"Friends of yours?" the police captain asked.

"Not exactly," Nathan said, grimly. "Feds. They're pricks, but technically I'm working with them on this one. I had to tell them I was responding to this. I didn't think they were close enough to get here before y'all were done. I'm real sorry about this."

Nathan, Ben, Shadow, and the New Mexico state troopers were waiting at the cordon line when Special Agents Frampton and Delaney approached. Delaney was wearing a charcoal suit and tie, his eyes hidden behind aviator sunglasses. Frampton, the younger man, sported tan cargo pants and a black, long-sleeved polo with the Department of Homeland Security logo embroidered on the left breast. His ID hung from a lanyard around his neck, and he wore tinted shooting glasses. A .40-caliber automatic was strapped to his right thigh in a tactical holster.

"Special Agent Delaney, Department of Homeland Security," the older agent said, flashing his ID as he approached the cordon. "Mr. Foster answers to me. Who's in charge here?"

"Nice of you Feds to stop by," Captain Garcia said, before introducing himself. "This is my crime scene."

"Not anymore it's not," Agent Delaney said. He looked at Nathan. "Were you able to confirm that XT-enhanced individuals have been here?"

"I got confirmation from the dog," Nathan answered, "but I haven't had time to run the blood tests yet."

"Hand those blood samples over to us," Delaney said. "We'll run them. The dog's confirmation is enough for the moment. Captain Garcia, the Department of Homeland Security is handling this investigation. Your cooperation is appreciated, but we'll take it from here."

"The hell you say," Captain Garcia snarled. "We offered you assistance with this from the start. You told us to get bent. You didn't fill us in on any details, or even tell us who you were looking for. Had my officers known that, this"—he pointed to the bloody crime scene—"might not have happened. Now, two of my men are dead, and you think you're going to roll up and send me on my way? Fuck you, Fed! You step over that cordon line and I'll arrest you."

One of the young patrolmen got between his captain and the federal agents, trying to defuse the heated situation. Shadow was getting visibly upset from the arguing. "Ben," Nathan said, looking at his nephew, "take Shadow and put him in the truck. This is getting stupid."

Ben didn't argue. He was a shy kid and he hated conflict. He tugged Shadow's leash and quickly led the dog away.

Agent Frampton spoke up. If he was trying to not sound condescending it wasn't working. "Captain, I'm sorry for your loss, but we are in authority here." He raised a laminated document with DHS letterhead.

Captain Garcia snatched the National Security Letter out of Frampton's hands and threw it away like a Frisbee. "Kid, I was pushing a patrol car when you were in junior high. You step across that cordon and you're going to jail, do you hear me?"

Visibly agitated, Frampton stepped forward and jabbed a finger into Captain Garcia's chest. "Impeding a federal investigation is a felony, Captain," he said, the last word coming out as a sneer. "If you want to keep your job I suggest you stand aside!"

Garcia wasn't impressed. "Listen here, you little shit—"

"Fellas, hey!" Nathan said, raising his voice. He held his hands up and moved in between Captain Garcia and Agent Frampton before a fistfight broke out. "Everybody just calm down, alright?" He turned to Agent Delaney. "Two of Captain Garcia's men were murdered and so were the owners of this store." He looked at Captain Garcia. "Four DHS agents were killed on that bus." He stepped back and addressed the entire group. "We have nine people murdered in the last few days, and we're no closer to catching these bastards than we were when it started. Delaney, I know there are national security considerations, and I'm sure you're under a lot of pressure from on high, but the longer you wait to bring state and local law enforcement in, the worse our odds of catching our fugitives get."

Delaney looked at him but didn't say anything. Frampton had something to say, though. He always had something to say. "You're just a civilian advisor, Mr. Foster."

Nathan took a breath. He wasn't going to let this cocky little shit get to him. "I am, and I am advising you to stop getting into pissing contests with everyone who can help you accomplish the mission and actually get the job done." He turned and walked away, putting his hat back on as he left.

"Where are you going?" Agent Frampton sneered.

Nathan paused. "I'm doing what you hired me to do, Agent Frampton. They're still out there. The longer we take to catch them, the more innocent people are gonna die." He walked away without another word.

Alpine, Arizona
The next day...

HIGH IN THE MOUNTAINS and deep in the Apache-Sitgreaves National Forest, the village of Alpine had once been a destination for outdoorsmen and hunters. With fewer than two hundred year-round residents, it had been remote, even before the war. Now it was a ghost town, nothing but empty houses weathering away from neglect. Emmogene had heard Anthony say that this stretch of US 180 wasn't even plowed in the winter anymore. It was remote enough, he'd reasoned, that it would be a good place to lay low for a few days. The incident in Quemado would have consequences, and they needed to be careful. The houses at the edge of town were surrounded by trees, giving them some cover from aerial surveillance. Carmen, Olga, and Rook had done a quick sweep of the town, scanning for signs of life, but hadn't seen anything.

Emmogene sat alone in a bedroom as darkness fell. The only light came from an electric lantern next to her bedroll. It was cold at this altitude, and she sat huddled in her sleeping bag for warmth. The house she found herself in had been abandoned some years before and most of the furniture was gone. The windows were so covered with grime that you could barely see out of them, and they'd hung up blankets over them to keep the light in.

In her hands she held an old photograph, one she'd found on the floor, covered in dust. The glass was broken but the frame was intact. In it, a young girl, probably nine or ten, sat smiling with a big Saint Bernard. She found herself wondering who that little girl was. Was she still alive? The wind howled outside, and another wisp of chilled air leaked in from the window. Emmogene put the picture down and zipped her sleeping bag up a little further.

She heard footsteps approaching the door to the room and Emmogene cringed. It was Anthony. She could tell from the way he walked, from the sound of his footsteps. He swung the door open without announcing himself and came into the room.

"It is cold," he said. "This will help." He carried an item in each hand. One was an electric space heater, which he set down on the floor. The other was a metal and plastic cylinder, perhaps eight inches tall, with strips of translucent material around its body. He set it on the floor, turned a knob on top, and pushed a button. The device started to hum, quietly, and the translucent strips glowed blue. It was a high-density fuel cell, one of the kind adapted from Visitor exo-technology. Anthony plugged the space heater into it, and warm air began to flow into the room.

"Th-thank you," Emmogene said, not looking at Anthony.

Anthony didn't say anything for a few moments. He loomed over Emmogene. His presence felt oppressive to her.

"You're afraid of me," he said.

Emmogene looked up at him. "Yes. Does that surprise you?"

Anthony averted his eyes and looked at the floor. His face was ashen. He looked genuinely ashamed of himself. He took a deep breath and slowly lowered himself to the floor, sitting a few feet from Emmogene. "No," he answered at length. "No, I don't suppose it does." He looked up at her, into her eyes. "I am sorry about that."

He hadn't always been like this. He had been warm. Kind. *Sweet,* even, and all of that seemed gone. "Anthony," Emmogene said, "what did they do to you? I never asked. You're different."

He lowered his eyes again. "You don't remember. You wouldn't. Things were desperate at the end of the war. They ... were desperate. They sent Earth Storm to do terrible things. Things they said were necessary. Some of it ... some of it seemed wrong, at first, but they gifted us with more enhancements." He looked back up at her. "They gave us more conditioning. I ... I only remember parts of it. It removed the weakness from us, cut it out like a cancer. We were stronger. We were better. We sacrificed our humanity for the future."

Emmogene could hear the conviction in his voice and it broke her heart. Could she get through to him? "Anthony," she said, delicately, "you were a lab rat." He didn't react. After a pause, she pressed on. "Listen to me. You know I'm telling you the truth. They were desperate because they were losing the war. They tried to take your humanity . . . all of our humanity . . . because they needed our world. They needed a home."

"I thought that, too," he admitted, staring off into space. "But I know this not to be the case. They could have wiped us out, you see, remade the Earth in their own image. That would have been easier for them. They . . . they're not monsters, even if we don't understand them always. They wanted to preserve us. Nurture us. They wanted to show us a better way."

"They wanted us as their *slaves*," Emmogene said, harshly.

Again, Anthony didn't react. "Some see it that way." He looked at her again. "Do you blame them? Look at how they found us, Emmogene. The Earth was being ravaged by our pollution. Species were going extinct. They had been watching us, you know, studying us, and our history was full of violence and conquest. They timed their arrival to prevent a nuclear exchange between the United States and the Soviet Union, did you know that? They saved us from ourselves."

Emmogene thought about the orbital bombardment the aliens had unleashed upon the world, the biological weapons, the tsunami-causing ocean strikes, but didn't say anything.

"We're not fit to rule ourselves," Anthony said. "It's hard to accept but it's true. We are a savage and destructive species, unable to focus our collective efforts on a common goal. Instead we squabble amongst ourselves. We cling to superstition and fairy tales, and invent false moralities based on them. We consume every available resource and multiply out of control. In the grand scheme of things, we're no better than locusts. Had the Visitors not arrived, we'd have destroyed the Earth or otherwise wiped ourselves out in time. It was inevitable." He sighed. There was sadness in his voice. "They were going to take us to the stars, Emmogene. They would have guided us into the cosmos. They would have given us the universe, and we rejected them. It's a tragedy. A waste. The fate we deserve, I suppose."

"You said . . . before, I mean, you said that they were coming back. What did you mean?"

"They are still out there, you know. Even though we have forsaken them, they have not given up on us."

"They're on Mars," Emmogene said. "Everyone knows that. Everyone thinks they'll come back someday."

"I don't *think*," Anthony replied, "I *know*. I have been told."

"Are there still Visitors on Earth?" Emmogene asked. "Not . . . not like Rook. You know what I mean: the Bright Ones. Are they at Bolthole?"

Anthony was quiet for so long that Emmogene wondered if he'd heard her. She was about to repeat her question when he looked up at her again. "Yes. It is they who sent me on my current mission. I am to bring you to them."

Emmogene's heart fell into her stomach. It was everything she could do not to shake. "What do they want from me?"

"They want what you carry," he said.

"The device in my head? Is it really so important? It doesn't even work. I can't—"

"No," he said, gently cutting her off. "That's why the Americans want you. They want to take it and copy it and use it for themselves. They cry that the Visitors oppressed them but they wish to use the same techniques on their own people. No, you carry something far more important inside you."

"What is it?" Emmogene couldn't keep the fear from her voice. "Anthony, what did they do to me?"

"I wasn't supposed to tell you yet," he said, staring off into space again, "but I think you need to know. I think you need to understand why you're so important. Perhaps then you will cooperate with us." He paused for a few seconds, as if lost in thought, before looking her in the eyes again. "You have inside you an egg."

Emmogene's eyes went wide. "What?"

"An egg," Anthony repeated, "designed by the Visitors. After many years and many unsuccessful attempts, you are the first to carry such a thing. You may not be the last. I know they took some humans to Mars with them, but you are the only one on Earth with such a treasure inside you."

"What kind of egg?" Emmogene demanded, on the verge of panic. "What did they put inside me? Is . . . is an alien going to hatch out of me?" Images from gory old sci-fi horror films filled her mind.

"No, no, nothing like that," Anthony said, raising a hand to try and calm her. "It is like one of the eggs human females normally carry, but enhanced. Made better."

"Made better *how*?"

"You know that when the Visitors immigrated to Earth, they had to adapt the life from their homeworld to be compatible with our ecosystem. The atmospheres of our two worlds were similar but not the same. The chemical composition of the oceans is different. Their life-forms couldn't digest or process many Earth nutrients and proteins without being modified to do so. Without such adaptation, they would not have been able to survive on our planet, not without completely terraforming it, and that would have left it uninhabitable for us. They changed *themselves* to suit *us*, Emmogene. At least, at first. What you carry is the first effort at asking us to adapt to suit *them*."

Emmogene put her hands on her belly and tried to breathe. She felt light-headed. The shock and the altitude combined were almost too much.

"You're not pregnant," Anthony said, "but you were intended to become so." He paused again. "I was to be your mate. That is what I mean when I say we were meant to be together. You . . . you used to know this, but you forgot in the mind-wipe. You loved me once." Another long pause. "I, too, have been adapted. We were selected as a breeding pair. Our child is to be the first of a new hybrid species, one that takes the best of humanity and the best of the Visitors and combines them. All of the enhancements we've been given, those will be innate to our child. He'll be smarter, stronger, less prone to panic and superstition. Better cooperative survival skills will be bred into his very genes. He will be immune to many common diseases and more resilient all around. His bones and muscles will have been enhanced so that even long durations in zero gravity will not result in deterioration. He will be designed to lead humanity to the stars, don't you see? They believe in us. They want us to join them. They are willing to become one with us. We will be symbiotic life-forms, each contributing to and benefitting from the other, and in this manner we will become infinite. Don't you see?"

Emmogene didn't say anything. She was in shock.

"The implantation process was minimally invasive. If the pairing works, if our child is healthy and meets expectations, they intend to start implanting such eggs in millions of human women. It wouldn't be successful in every instance, but the egg is designed to sterilize all normal human eggs. Women who couldn't produce the improved hybrid children would be left infertile, and the eggs could only be fertilized by men with suitable genetics. It would keep the human population at sustainable levels while ensuring the superiority of the subsequent generations."

Emmogene felt sick. Anthony didn't seem to notice. "The device you carry in your skull, that, too, was supposed to have been passed on, grown organically in all the new generation. Each would have been able to influence lesser minds, and, in turn, would have been susceptible to direct influence from the Visitors themselves. But, as you say, it doesn't work. They were not able to perfect it. The neural interface is unreliable. They were also unable to engineer an organic magnetic monopole, which I'm given to understand is critical to its function. The device would have to be manufactured externally, then implanted."

Emmogene was shaking now. She couldn't hide it any more than she could hold back the tears. "So that's what this is about," she said, bitterness dripping from her voice. "You talk about the future of humanity, you talk about the stars and this grand purpose, and this is what it boils down to? They promised to let you *fuck* me?"

Anthony visibly winced when she uttered the obscenity. Emmogene rarely swore. "That's . . . that's not how . . ."

She cut him off. "That absolutely is how it is, Anthony Krieg," she said. "Don't you sit here and lie to me. This whole thing, from the day they assigned you to me, this whole thing has been a setup. Don't you get it? They used us, both, so that they could *breed* us like . . . like livestock! Like *animals*, Anthony! How old was I when they promised me to you, huh? Fifteen?"

Anthony said nothing. He couldn't even look at Emmogene. He stared into his lap while she unleashed his anger on him.

"All this talk of love, of the future, and you just want me as your . . . as your *concubine*! Were the other women not enough for you? Was Carmen not enough? She's prettier than me. She's just like you. Wasn't she good enough?"

"I don't love her!" Anthony barked. "I *never* loved her. It was just *sex,* do you understand? I know they've done things to me but I'm still a man, don't you understand that? I love *you.* I did all of this, I risked my life, for *you!*"

Emmogene couldn't contain her anger anymore. She raised her

hand and slapped him across the face, so hard it stung her hand. He barely reacted. "You don't *rape* people you love, Anthony! Don't you look away from me. You listen to me. I am not an animal! I am not some brood mare that you get to breed with on demand, do you hear me? I'm not your *whore*! I don't *belong* to the Visitors! I'm not their piece of meat to give to you as a prize!" Emmogene felt the buzzing in the back of her skull, then, steady and strong. Was the device active? Was it working? Would it work on Anthony?

She lowered her voice but continued to press him. "You don't do this to people you love, and I know you love me. You always said so. I know somewhere under all that conditioning is a good man. This isn't you. This is what they did to you. Please, Anthony, this isn't right." The buzzing in the back of her head grew more perceptible. The inside of her face felt slightly warmed, as if she were having a hot beverage. "I don't want to go to Africa. I don't want to be impregnated against my will. If you really love me, if you mean what you've said all along, you won't do this to me. You're a better person than that. I know you are."

He didn't say anything. He just stared into space again, glassy-eyed, as if in contemplation.

"Look at what they've done to us," Emmogene said, more quietly still. "Look at what they made you give. I'm carrying some alien hybrid mutant egg and you've been conditioned to be their bloodhound, their breeding stud. Does that sound like the bright future for humanity they've promised you?"

"No," Anthony said, after a long pause. "It doesn't."

"And you said they took humans with them. Why do they need me, then? They can make all the hybrid babies they want on Mars, can't they?"

"I never thought of that before."

"You were conditioned not to question them, Anthony. Think about it, though. How does any of this make sense? If we're so damned important to them, why didn't they take *us* to Mars, too?"

"I don't know. I don't . . ." He trailed off and looked up at her. "I don't understand."

"I think they're lying to you, Anthony. They lied to us all."

"Then why? Why send me to do all this?"

"Who knows? Does it matter?"

"No . . . no, I guess it doesn't." He shook his head, as if struggling to concentrate. "My God," he said, invoking the name of the Creator for the first time that Emmogene could ever recall. "I came here planning to . . . to . . . mate . . . with you. It was what . . . it was what they wanted me to do." He looked at her with tears forming in his eyes. "I'm sorry, Emmogene. It's not me. It's the . . . the . . . it's not me. It's like . . . it's like I'm thinking clearly for the first time in . . ." He trailed off. "I'm sorry. Please forgive me."

"Of course I forgive you," Emmogene said. Her face felt hot now, and the buzzing in her skull was so loud she wondered if Anthony would be able to hear it. "You haven't gone so far that you can't come back. We should go."

"Go where?"

"Anywhere we want. You and me. We can figure out what to do once we get clear of all this."

"Yeah . . . yeah," Anthony said, nodding slowly.

The door to the room swung open then, loudly, startling Emmogene. The buzzing in her head abruptly stopped. Carmen was there, glaring at them with murder in her eyes. How much had she heard? A few seconds later, Olga appeared behind her, and the two women came into the room.

"Is there problem?" Olga asked, curtly.

"I heard shouting," Carmen added. She looked at Emmogene. "I heard a *lot* of things."

"No, no problem," Anthony said, standing up. "I'm fine." He shook his head. "Everything . . . everything is fine. I just have a headache."

"Did she try to use the device on you?" Carmen asked, still staring at Emmogene. "I told you we can't trust her."

"Carmen, that's *enough*!" Anthony snapped. "I said it's fine." He looked back at Emmogene for a long moment, and his eyes narrowed. "We were just talking. She didn't do anything." He turned to his compatriots. "How is Ivan?"

"His condition is deteriorating," Olga grunted. "He has persistent infection, I think. Our antibiotics are not effective. He needs doctor or he will die."

"Yes, of course," Anthony said. "I think I know of a place we can go to get him treated. We will proceed there as soon as it is safe to do so."

"And then what?" Carmen asked.

"And then," Anthony said, looking back at Emmogene, "we proceed to Bolthole as planned." Without another word, he turned and left the room. Olga followed behind him.

Carmen lingered for a moment, staring daggers at Emmogene. "Sleep tight, *puta*," she snarled before pulling the doors closed.

Emmogene was shaking uncontrollably now. She felt like she was going to throw up. She curled up in her sleeping bag and wept like a child.

THUMP!

Emmogene's eyes snapped open. Her heart racing, she looked frantically around the darkened room, trying to get her bearings. It took her a couple seconds but she remembered where she was: in an abandoned house in the remote mountains of Arizona, dimly lit by the blue glow of the fuel cell. She'd been having a strange nightmare, one in which she was in a mindless rage and physically attacked one of the Visitors. It felt more real than a dream, it felt like a memory, but how could it be? She never would have done such a thing when she served them. To do anything of the sort would have been unthinkable, and even if she had, it would have resulted in her liquidation.

The image persisted in her mind nonetheless. She'd gotten ahold of an instrument of some kind, a sharp tool, and slashed at the being's face. She cut it, down the side of its head, between its left eye and the aural membrane. The image of the glowing blue blood trickling out of the wound, of this enlightened, superior being recoiling in fear and pain, stuck with her. There was piano music, too, "Clair de Lune," she thought. It felt real. It seemed too vivid, too detailed, to just be a dream. How could it be, though?

THUMP! There it is again, she thought. *What is that?*

She got her answer when muffled shouts resonated through the wall. "I fought with you!" Carmen said, anger and hurt in her voice. "I believed in you! Even after we lost, I never gave up!"

"Have you lost all faith in me?" Anthony answered, his voice calm and cold. "When have I led you astray?"

"Henry is dead! Ivan is dying! And for what? All this so you could spring your whore from prison?"

"That's not it!" Anthony said, sounding more defensive now.

Carmen's voice was venomous. "Don't lie, Anthony Krieg. I know you. I see the way you look at her. I know what you want. Why can't you just admit it?"

There was another loud thump, and a rattling of dishes. It sounded like Anthony had slammed a fist down on the table. "That's not what this is about!" he roared. "You don't understand!"

Emmogene crept across the room, putting her ear to the door so she could hear better.

"Then help me understand," Carmen said, almost pleading. "Since we left home, you've barely told me anything. You only say, 'Trust me, Carmen, trust me,' but you don't tell me why we are doing this. Why her? Why now? Is it because of that thing in her head?"

She doesn't know about the egg inside me, Emmogene thought. *Why didn't Anthony tell her?*

"No, and you've been told everything you've been authorized to know."

"Authorized by who, Anthony? Who sent us on this mission? I asked around before we left. These orders didn't come from the Plenipotentiary Council. Tell me the truth: this is a just a personal errand for you, isn't it?"

My God, Emmogene thought. *She doesn't know any of what he told me.* Did the device work on him? If it did, why didn't he tell her when she asked? Did he not want her to think he'd been compromised? Could it really be so subtle that even a person who's aware of it and its capabilities can fall under its influence and not realize it?

"It's *not* a personal errand!" Anthony boomed. "Do not question my authority, Carmen! We are taking her to Bolthole. You will be told what you need to know, when you need to know it. Am I making myself clear?"

"Fuck you!" Carmen snarled. She was every bit as volatile as Anthony.

There was more thumping then, and shouting, as Carmen apparently stormed off. Anthony roared as a muffled crash resonated through the wall. It sounded like he had flipped a table or something. Emmogene pulled away from the door and moved back to her bedroll. Her hands were starting to shake. Memories flashed through her mind, some clearer than others, but she'd seen him like this before. Without the medication, sometimes he lost control. Sometimes the beast that the Visitors had turned him into took over. Without the enforced discipline of their alien overlords, the conditioning grew unstable.

She couldn't place exactly where it had happened, but Emmogene distinctly remembered Anthony killing a UEA security guard over some perceived slight. It had been after the orders to surrender had come down, when it had become apparent that the Visitors were abandoning their human allies. Things were panicked then; United Earth Alliance person expressed shock, disbelief, fear, even outright denial. The man had grabbed Emmogene's arm for some reason. She closed her eyes and tried to remember why, but she couldn't. She did remember what happened next, though: Anthony slammed the man's head into the wall, fracturing his skull, then let him drop to the ground. He then stomped on the hapless guard's neck, audibly snapping it.

She remembered the look on his face after he killed that man. It wasn't the normal calm Earth Storm commandos displayed while carrying out their grim duties. It wasn't even a look of shock or surprise, as one might expect from a person who suddenly found himself in a violent situation. Anthony had let his mask slip for just a moment while brutally killing a man over a misunderstanding, but Emmogene saw, and despite the attempted mind-wipe she hadn't forgotten that moment.

He'd had a smile on his face. A cruel smile, as if from a school bully, or a child pulling the wings off of a fly.

Emmogene's heart was pounding as the realization overtook her. She hadn't wanted to believe it before, but maybe . . . maybe Anthony was too far gone to ever come back. Whoever he was working for now, whoever he answered to at this so-called Bolthole, they clearly didn't have the means to effectively control him the way they had before. He was getting worse. She had been able to stave off his violent impulses tonight, but what about the next time, or the time after that? Sooner or later, he would come for her, and he would try to take her.

Her thoughts coalesced as another loud crash almost shook the house. Olga was trying to get Anthony to calm down now. Olga, Carmen, and Anthony were all distracted. Rook would likely be consuming its nutrient sludge, unconcerned with and incapable of understanding its human masters' arguing.

Emmogene moved to the window. She flipped the lock and pulled it upward, ever so slightly. It was stuck, but with a little more effort, it opened a few inches. If there had ever been a screen there, it was gone now. It was dark outside, the moon concealed behind clouds. She was on the first floor.

In that moment, Emmogene knew she had to run.

STRUGGLING TO BREATHE in the thin mountain air, Emmogene pushed on into the forest. Her breath was visible in the dim night as she exhaled. Legs burning, she forced herself to continue onward, though her initial dash had slowed to a hurried walk. She hadn't gone for a run in a long time, and she didn't think she'd ever been at such a high altitude.

Emmogene paused, leaning against a tall pine tree. Her breathing was strained as she rested, trying to catch her breath. The clouds had parted, allowing pale moonlight to trickle down to the forest floor though the canopy of pine boughs. It was quiet, save for the sounds of her labored breathing and the wind sighing through the pines like a loud whisper. She realized, then, that she was truly alone for the first time that she could recall. Her breathing slowed, and she took a long swig from the bottle of water she had taken with her.

She was cold. Emmogene was wearing only a hooded sweatshirt and jeans. She realized she would have to keep moving in order to stay warm. She'd been out of the house for an hour now. They had to have realized she was gone. She didn't know where she was, didn't know where she was going, but she had to keep moving. It would have been easiest to follow the highway, but that's what they would have expected. She reasoned that her safest bet was to keep going across country, even if navigating the rugged terrain was difficult.

This is insane, she thought. *You're going to die out here.* She didn't know if her captors had any kind of sensors or alarms set up, or if they had any inkling of which way she had gone. Angrily shaking her head, Emmogene pushed herself off the tree and pressed on. It didn't matter if she died out here. It was better to end up as food for the coyotes than it was to let Anthony rape and impregnate her. She'd rather die on her own terms than be his forced concubine.

After a few more minutes of walking, she came to a dirt road, little more than a Jeep trail, cutting through the forest. Beyond it, the terrain leveled out and opened up into a vast clearing, probably half a mile or more across. It was tempting to just push on, but she hesitated. The moon was behind the clouds now, but it could reappear at any time and illuminate the clearing. A person crossing the field would be exposed, easy to spot from a long way off. No, Emmogene thought, it was better to follow the woodline and go around.

Emmogene followed the trail for a while. She was tired now, and had run out of water. It was much easier to manage than stumbling through the forest in the dark had been. Perhaps it was riskier, but her odds of escape would not be improved if she sprained an ankle. Every so often she paused to listen, but the only thing she could hear was the wind blowing through the trees. She wrapped her arms around herself as she walked, trying to retain some of her body heat as she shivered.

After a some time, maybe ten minutes, she happened upon a small camper trailer. It had been abandoned in the middle of the trail and looked like it had been there for years. Both tires were flat. The door was closed but unlocked. Cautiously stepping inside, she felt around in the darkness in case there was anything worth taking. The only thing worthwhile she found was an old, musty-smelling wool blanket.

Wrapped in the blanket, she sat in the trailer's doorway and tried to take stock of her situation. She contemplated climbing into the trailer and holing up there for the night. It would get her out of the wind, at least, and maybe she could sleep for a little while. *No, she thought. It's too obvious. If they come down this trail this trailer will be the first place they look.* If not there, though, then where? Emmogene didn't know where the next town was, or how far she would have to travel before she could find shelter. She was exhausted. She didn't know how much farther she would be able to go. Leaning against the doorframe, she closed her eyes for a just a moment.

Her eyes snapped open when she heard the throaty rumble of a diesel engine. The telltale glow of headlights could be seen down the trail. She jumped to her feet and ran into the trees, just as the approaching vehicle rounded a bend and came into sight. She pushed as hard as she could manage, getting as much distance between herself and the road before the oncoming vehicle got to where the trailer was. Just as it pulled to a stop in front of the abandoned camper, Emmogene dropped to the ground behind a tall pine tree, put her hands over her mouth, and tried to muffle the sounds of her ragged breathing.

She waited. Maybe the vehicle would just go around the trailer and keep on going. Maybe it wasn't Anthony at all. Maybe it was a policeman, or someone she could ask for help. The engine cut. A door slammed as someone got out. Daring a look, Emmogene peeked around the rough trunk of the Ponderosa Pine and tried to see what was going on.

Oh no. It was the truck. A feminine figure, illuminated by the truck's headlights, shined a flashlight into the trailer for a few seconds. Finding nothing, the woman knelt down and examined the ground. It was Carmen. *They're tracking me*, Emmogene thought, trying to stave off panic. As the deadly commando inspected the trail, Emmogene noticed a hulking black figure, weapon in hand, in the bed of the truck; it was Rook. The alien killing machine had one hand on the roll bar, bracing itself, and seemed to be scanning the trees.

Emmogene pulled herself back behind the trunk of the towering pine and clenched her eyes shut. Her heart was pounding so hard it seemed like they might hear it. *Brutes* like Rook had thermal vision capabilities. The only way it wouldn't detect her is if she kept the tree between it and herself, didn't move, and didn't make a sound. Seeing Carmen inspecting the ground had Emmogene on the verge of panic, though. *They're tracking me. I left footprints. Of course they can follow your footprints, you stupid idiot!*

Emmogene's eyes opened when she heard a branch snap loudly in front of her. As far as she knew, Carmen and Rook were still down on the trail. Peering into the darkened forest ahead of her, she couldn't see anything, but she strained her ears to listen. The breeze had ceased and with it the sighing of the pines, but there was another sound now: breathing. It was followed by a heavy, earthy shuffling sound, as if something large was moving, just out of sight.

She wanted to run, to move, to do *anything*, but her body wouldn't cooperate. Wide-eyed, she stared helplessly into the darkness, trying to see the source of the heavy breathing sound, terrified of what it might be. It wasn't Carmen. It wasn't even Rook. Whatever it was, it was *big*. Above her, the clouds began to part. Shafts of dim light pierced the forest now, revealing two pairs of eyes, one above the other, glinting at her through the gloom. The heavy shuffling sound, footsteps on a soft forest floor, returned, and the eyes raised up higher as a loud, hollow, rattling sound echoed through the trees. The eyes had to be ten feet off the ground. The clouds opened up then, revealing the beast. It was huge—a scaly, four-eyed, reptilian creature with four legs, an elongated neck, and a spade-shaped head. It opened its gaping maw, four feet wide from left to right, and emitted a deep hissing sound. Its rows of teeth caught the moonlight, flanked by sharp mandibles on either side of the creature's mouth. Its body was long and serpentine, almost like an oversized Komodo dragon. The rattling sounded again, accompanied now by an ear-piercing screech. Emmogene scrambled to her feet, turned, and ran.

In the throes of panic, she ran back toward the road, not daring to look behind her. She dimly remembered learning about these creatures, carnivorous apex predators from the Visitors' homeworld, adapted and engineered to be able to survive in Earth's ecosystem. Terror rattlers they were called, on account of the rattlesnake-like structure running the length of its tail. She couldn't outrun it, but maybe she could make it to Carmen and Rook before it ripped her apart.

Rook's digital voice encoder uttered a warning tone as Emmogene sprinted toward the truck. "TARGET ACQUIRED," the alien soldier said, its synthesized voice deep and flat. Carmen jumped to her feet, pistol drawn, but Emmogene was almost on top of her.

"*Run!*" Emmogene screamed, her voice gasping and broken. Carmen tackled her, slamming her onto the ground so hard it knocked the wind out of her. Rook put itself between the two women and the charging monster, but the terror rattler pounced before the *Brute* could bring its weapon to bear. It raked Rook with its foreclaws, slashing through its coverall and knocking it to the ground. As Rook tried to sit up, the creature bit down on it, picking it up and tossing it into the side of the truck. The parked vehicle was rocked at the impact, its windows shattering, but the terror rattler didn't let up. It placed a claw onto Rook's chest, pinning it down, and moved in for the kill.

Before it could rip Rook apart, Carmen drew her pistol and opened fire on the creature. It screamed as the bullets struck its thick hide. She dropped to the ground just in time to avoid a whip of its tail. She fired again and the rattler leapt backward, faster than something that big should have been able to move, and landed right on top of the truck. Glass shattered and metal groaned as it tried to place the vehicle between itself and the firearm.

Carmen's gun was empty. She dropped the magazine out, her left hand trying to grasp a reload. As if it sensed her vulnerability, the terror rattler scrambled over the top of the truck, flowing like water, rushing toward its attacker with a vengeance. Emmogene, in that instant, realized that at least she would get to watch Carmen die before being killed herself.

Rook's alien weapon roared. A stream of high-velocity flechettes tore into the rattler's long neck and body. The creature was cut off mid-scream and dropped to the ground. Thick, bluish blood, naturally bioluminescent, poured out of a hundred wounds along its body. Its back legs and tail twitched for a few seconds, and then it was over.

"THREAT ELIMINATED," Rook synthesized, the report of its weapon still echoing through the hills. It was awkwardly holding its weapon in its right hand. Its left arm hung limp at its side, glowing blue blood oozing from multiple wounds. "THIS UNIT HAS SUSTAINED DAMAGE."

Emmogene was on her back, gasping for air, trying to catch her breath. Carmen was sitting on the ground next to her doing the same thing. Neither of the women spoke. The truck Carmen had arrived in was smashed and one of its headlights had been broken. Before she could sit up, the commando slammed her back down to the dirt and stuck a pistol in her face.

"You fucking *bitch*," Carmen snarled through gritted teeth. Her eyes were wide, her hair hung in her face. "This is all your fault! This is..." She trailed off. To Emmogene's shock, the deadly operative was fighting back tears. "Henry's dead. Ivan might die. Rook is damaged," she said, accentuating each point with her gun, "and here you are, not a scratch on you. You're going to get us all killed." She shook her head angrily. "I should cut you open and bleed you, real quiet, leave you for the vultures."

Rook sounded a warning tone again and angled its weapon toward Carmen. "THREAT DETECTED."

Defeated, Carmen slowly holstered her pistol and got off of Emmogene. She stood up and grudgingly helped Emmogene to her feet.

"I'm sorry," Emmogene managed, trying not to cry herself. She was shaking from the cold and from the adrenaline. "I didn't ask for any of this. I don't want it. Did he tell you what this is about? Did Anthony tell you?"

"He said the Higher Beings want you for something. We have our orders. That's all that matters."

"I have an egg inside me," Emmogene said softly. "An alien hybrid egg. Anthony is supposed to impregnate me, and I'm supposed to carry his baby, and that baby will be the first of a new generation of humans."

"What?" Carmen asked. The edge was gone from her voice now. "What are you talking about?"

"He told me. We were meant to be together, the Visitors arranged it. At some point he's going to . . . to . . . *take me*, and then . . . I don't know. Our baby will be an *improved* human being, according to the Visitors."

"Is this a trick? Are you using that device on me?"

"The device doesn't work!" Emmogene pleaded. "At least not the way it's supposed to. I can't control it. I'm just telling you what Anthony told me tonight. It's all true, you can ask him."

Carmen seemed unsure of herself for the first time that Emmogene could remember. "Your baby . . . you said it's going to be *improved*. Improved how? What did they do to it?"

"It's supposed to be more resilient," Emmogene answered. "Better suited for space travel or something, but mostly it's going to be more compliant. It'll be faithful and obedient to the Visitors, like a . . . like a house pet. Domesticated." She shook her head. "All those promises they made to us, do you remember? They said we would be their equals, and that together, we would overcome all the problems that have held us back and go to the stars. Do you remember?"

"I remember," Carmen said, bitterly.

"It was a lie. They want slaves. They're going to take what makes us human and cut it out, and that'll be the end of us." Emmogene looked up at Carmen. "I'm sorry you have to hear this from me. I'm sorry about Henry. I don't want to go back. I don't want to have Anthony's baby." She looked back down at the ground. "I wish you would have just killed me."

Carmen sighed. "I can't, *chica*," she said, nodding at the *Brute*. "I can't let you go, either. We're being watched. Rook will have contacted Anthony by now. They'll be along to pick us up." She looked down at the ground, briefly, then back up at Emmogene. "We all have our orders."

EXHAUSTED AND NUMB, Emmogene stared listlessly into space, trying and failing to withdraw into her own mind. She sat on an inward-facing bench seat, just behind the passenger's seat, with her hands and feet bound. She had also been buckled into the seat. Olga was in the driver's seat, visible through a narrow opening in the heavy curtain that separated the cab from the cargo area of the van.

Rook was crammed into the back of the van as well. The hulking soldier unit sat on the floor across from Emmogene, staring at her. The biomechanical warrior sat so still that one could almost mistake it for a statue. If you looked closely, though, you could see it gently breathing. It was dressed in its hat and oversized coat again, its face wrapped in a mask. Its flechette gun, a bulky weapon almost four feet long, was cradled in its lap. Olga had patched it up, but it hadn't regained the use of its left arm.

Emmogene turned her head a little when Ivan groaned. They took an old mattress from the house in Alpine and had placed it on the floor of the van's cargo compartment. The Russian commando lay there, fading in and out of consciousness. He had taken a fever, probably due to an infection that even his enhanced immune system wasn't impervious to. She remembered reading somewhere that, with the widespread adoption of immuno-enhancements developed from Visitor technology, particularly resilient strains of bacteria had emerged. People who weren't up to date on the latest vaccinations were especially vulnerable.

The van's rear cargo doors were open. The sky was lightening as dawn approached. Anthony and Carmen stood behind the van, their breath smoldering in the cold air as they had a heated conversation. The engine wasn't running so Emmogene was able to overhear.

"We were *this close* to losing her!" Anthony said, holding his ·thumb and finger a couple inches apart. "This close! She could have been captured or killed."

Carmen stared daggers at her former lover. "It was your turn to be on watch," she said, icily. "I can't be held responsible when you were too busy throwing a tantrum to make sure she didn't run off."

Anthony angrily pointed a finger in Carmen's face. "I have had enough of your defiance. This has been difficult for all of us, but your lack of discipline is threatening to compromise the entire mission. We very nearly failed. I trusted you, Carmen, and you've let me down."

Carmen looked like she was ready to explode. "*You* trusted *me*?" she snapped. "You know, your little baby doll there, she and I had a chat out in the woods. She told me everything. I know what this is about. We've risked all this, we lost Henry, and we're probably going to lose Ivan because you want to *fuck* her!"

"For the last time, that's not what this is about!"

"Oh it's *exactly* what this is about. You're supposed to breed with her and produce the perfect hybrid baby." She shook her head slowly. "She doesn't want to have your baby, Anthony. There was a time when I would have, gladly."

"You can't have children," Anthony said, coldly.

"I can't," Carmen agreed. "They took that from me."

"You accepted the enhancements willingly. After everything we've done, you don't get to play the victim now."

"I suppose I don't." She looked back up at him. "I have done terrible things, things I can't forget, because they said it was necessary." She pointed at Emmogene. "Is *this* necessary? Is it necessary for you to rape that girl so they can have your hybrid baby? With all of their technology, you honestly think there's no other way?"

Anthony's demeanor changed in an instant. The emotion was gone; all that was left was the conditioned killer. "I've heard enough, Carmen. I was willing to tolerate your insubordination, your questioning of my authority, because of everything we've been through together. This? This is treason."

Carmen laughed, bitterly. "Treason. Rational thinking is treason, now? Did the Visitors not promise us a sane, rational, orderly world?

Listen to yourself. You sound like a religious fanatic, blindly obeying the will of your gods. It's pathetic."

Anthony's voice was cold. "This is why the baby that Emmogene will mother is so important. We are not ready for the rationality they offered us. We're animals, governed by instinct, emotion, and superstition. Even you and I can't escape this evolutionary baggage, and we're the best they have. The baby will be different. The baby will be the first of a superior species. If the project is successful, the Visitors won't have to risk another destructive war to save this world. Don't you see? All they'll have to do is wait. Our descendants will welcome them with open arms."

"This is insanity," Carmen said, stepping toward the van. "When we get back I'm taking this to the Command, and—"

Anthony put up a hand and blocked her from getting in.

"What are you doing?" Carmen asked. A pit formed in Emmogene's stomach. She saw that look on Anthony's face, the same look he had when he executed Grimes on the bus.

"You crossed a line tonight," Anthony said coldly. In one smooth motion he drew his pistol and leveled it at his former lover. "I'm sorry, Carmen."

"Anthony, *no!*" Emmogene screamed. In a flash her face was hot, and the buzzing seemed to resonate throughout her brain. Rook, who had been paying the human drama no mind, looked up at her and tilted its head, but didn't move. Anthony hesitated and looked at Emmogene. "Please," she continued, pleading. "You don't have to do this. Nobody else has to die on my account. Please." Anthony hesitated. Emmogene didn't know why the device was working now, or if she had any control over it, but she tried to channel her will through it and gain his compliance. "Anthony, look at me. Nobody else has to die. I'll do what you want. I'll go with you. Just, please, put the gun down."

Anthony closed his eyes, grimacing for a moment before opening them again. He took a deep breath and holstered his pistol.

"Thank you," Emmogene said, tears streaming down her cheeks. "Thank you."

Anthony turned back to Carmen. "Go."

"What?" she asked.

"You heard me. Just go."

"Go where?"

"Wherever you want. There's no place for you in Bolthole anymore. I will tell them you died protecting Emmogene from the terror rattler. They won't question it so long as I successfully bring her to them. I would advise you to never return to the Exclusion Zone or the Free Territories."

Without another word, he closed the van's rear doors, leaving Emmogene in the dark. A few seconds later, the buzzing in her skull ceased. Sweat trickled down her face, in spite of the cold, and she felt dizzy. As she tried to get her breathing under control, she thought about what Carmen had said to her, about how Rook was monitoring them. Was Carmen *really* free to go, or would they come after her? Why had she said anything?

A few moments later, the passenger's side door of the van opened, and Anthony climbed in. Without warning he yanked the curtain back, leaning around his seat to look Emmogene in the eyes. Did he know the device had been activated? Did it have any effect, or had that been entirely his decision?

"I did that for you," he said, coldly. "She'll be fine. She's a survivor. She knows how to disappear. The Americans will hang her if they catch her, and she knows that, too. She won't be a problem for us anymore."

"Anthony, I—" Before Emmogene could finish that sentence, Anthony reached back and jabbed something into her neck. "Ahhh! What did you stick me with?"

"Something to help you rest," he said, studying her. He tapped the side of his head. "And something to keep you out of my mind."

Emmogene felt groggy and sleepy, like being drunk but more intense. She struggled to keep her eyes open.

"Even before they put that thing in your head," Anthony continued, "you always had a way of getting me to do what you wanted. Do you remember?"

"No," she answered slowly.

Anthony smiled.

Several miles southwest of Alpine, Arizona
Several days later . . .

NATHAN FOSTER WATCHED, disinterestedly, as the Feds' forensic team went over the wrecked pickup truck. The vehicle had been found abandoned on a little-used 4x4 trail, spotted by a reconnaissance drone. That in and of itself wouldn't have warranted a response. What caught the interest of the Homeland Security agents was the dead terror rattler nearby. It appeared that the huge creature had attacked the truck before being shredded by an alien weapon.

"You really think it was them?" Ben asked, sipping a Dr. Pepper from the cooler. Shadow was nearby, idly sniffing around the woods, looking for bunnies to chase.

"Oh, I'm sure of it," Nathan answered. He was leaning against his truck, arms folded across his chest. Shadow had found splashes of blue alien blood on the trail, even though it lost its natural luminescence after a few hours of exposure to ultraviolet radiation. "I'm also sure they've got an alien *Brute*-class soldier unit with them."

"You said before you thought the big guy from the bus might have been one."

Nathan nodded. "I was pretty sure then, but I'm positive now. Some of their human soldiers were so jacked up with enhancements and modifications that they could be big and strong enough to hoist a guy up with one hand, especially if they were on synthesized drugs at the same time. Hell, I've seen what a big man on PCP can do, even without alien involvement."

Ben looked at his uncle. "But?"

"But now we've found the blood. The Feds say they still need to run ballistics on that terror rattler, but I'd bet my hat that was a Ripper gun."

"A what?"

"It's an automatic flechette gun that the alien soldiers used in the war."

"Wow, really? How can you be sure?"

"I've seen enough guys tore up by the damned things to know what it looks like, boy. The wounds are distinctive. They fire a dart made out of some kind of hardened metal alloy. They've got three barrels and a rate of fire of, like, thirty rounds a second. They'll cut into light-armored vehicle at close range, but the guns are so heavy and have so much recoil that a man can't use one by himself. The guns weigh something like forty pounds, and it takes great strength to control them while firing."

"Is that why we didn't use them in the war? You know, reverse-engineer them?"

Nathan shrugged. "I guess. I've seen them adapted as crew-served weapons, but in that role they won't do anything a regular fifty-cal won't, not really. They're also really, really complicated. Lots of moving parts, and every little thing has to be machined precisely. They also need a power source in addition to ammunition. They weren't practical for the way we fought."

"The Visitors didn't really know how to fight wars," Ben said, returning his attention to the federal agents swarming over the wrecked truck and dead alien apex predator. "That's what I read, anyway. They think they've been unified into one civilization for thousands of years, and that they didn't have any experience in fighting wars. They think that's part of the reason they lost."

"Maybe so," Nathan said, images of armored alien mechs vomiting missiles invading his mind, "but if that's the case, they learned fast."

"I'm sorry," Ben said. "I didn't mean to . . . you know."

Nathan shook his head. "No, you're fine. I actually think that book you read might have been onto something. The Greys made a lot of mistakes during the war, mistakes that cost them. Especially early on, their tactics were very basic. They were predictable."

"They underestimated us," Ben said. "They thought we'd all join them, or that we'd give up when we realized how advanced they were."

"They did indeed," Nathan agreed. "They didn't read history like you do, I guess. If they had, they'd have known better."

"Some people think their minds are just too different," Ben suggested. "I read that, too. They think differently than we do. Some things that make sense for us are crazy to them, and vice-versa. That's part of the reason they relied on humans so much."

"There weren't enough of them, either," Nathan said. "Sure, there were millions of them in the colonization fleet, but what are their millions compared to our billions? So yeah, they relied on their humans, too much so. They thought they could control us the way they control their own species. It never worked, not completely. We had problems with defectors and infiltrators, but their problems with them were a hundred times worse. Hell, even some of the Greys themselves, worker classes, surrendered so they wouldn't have to fight. I guess they thought the humans would do all the fighting and the dying for them, and they were wrong."

Before Nathan could say anything else, his phone in the truck rang. He climbed in, rolling up the windows as he did so, and answered the call. His phone was docked with the truck's receiver, but he didn't bring the video up on the dashboard screen. He answered in audio-only mode.

"Nathan? Are you there?" It was George.

"I'm here," Nathan answered. "I've just got Feds all around me."

"I see," George said. "Can you talk?"

"It's fine. I'm in my truck with the windows up. What's going on?"

"I think I have something for you, but you may have to move quickly. You know the woman I told you about, the pretty one who killed a man in Mexicali?"

"I remember." Nathan hadn't actually seen this woman and didn't know for certain if she was even with Anthony Krieg.

"I have a cousin in Nogales. A woman matching the description of the one I told you about has been frequenting his establishment, trying to secure passage across the border. I told him to stall her until I could talk to you. He is an entrepreneur like myself, and we always put the family business first."

"I understand," Nathan said. He retrieved a pen and a pad of paper from the glove box. "Where is this? Is Anthony Krieg or Emmogene Anderson with her?"

"That's the thing," George said. "She's alone. The other people you are looking for aren't with her."

Interesting, Nathan thought. "How certain was your source, that this woman was with Anthony Krieg?"

"He was confident," George answered. "Not many tall Swiss men in Mexicali, my friend."

"I suppose there ain't," Nathan agreed. "I'll look into it. What sort of establishment does your cousin run, exactly?"

"His name is Alejandro. He's in the import-export business, and it would be appreciated if you'd use discretion."

"I understand," Nathan said. In other words, George didn't want the Feds to know about his cousin's *import-export* business, which undoubtedly consisted of cross-border smuggling. While he was technically supposed to report all such criminal activity, Nathan was able to maintain his network of contacts by earning the trust of people like George. Betraying that trust would ruin his reputation and make his job a lot harder. "How are we doing this? Am I going to contact your cousin directly or are we using you as an intermediary?"

"He suggested that you make your way to Nogales as soon as possible. He can arrange for you to meet this woman. She will think she is being taken across the border. I will find out exactly where you need to be, and when, and call you back. Can you do this?"

"I think so. We're not doing much out here anyway. I can tell them I've got a lead."

"If they try and follow you, will you let me know? The meeting can be rescheduled if they don't respect your professional privacy. If they do follow you, the meeting won't happen at all. I have told him to expect you, a boy, and the big dog. No one else."

That was a subtle warning. Nathan's working relationship with George and his network depended on him upholding his end of the deal. "I understand. Just us. Anything else?"

"That is all for now, I think."

"Okay. I'll be waiting for your call." With that, Nathan disconnected the call and got out of the truck.

"What was that all about?" Ben asked. Shadow was next to him, lying in the grass, scanning the treeline for critters to chase.

"We might have just gotten the break we need. Load Shadow into the truck and get ready to roll out. I've got to go talk to the Feds."

Nathan found Special Agent Delaney sitting in the passenger's seat of his car. He had a computer in his lap and was writing a report. He typed slowly, using only his two index fingers, pausing occasionally to sip coffee from a Styrofoam cup.

"I can't talk right now," the Homeland Security Agent said, tersely. "I've got to get this report sent out." He looked up at Nathan, frustration apparent on his face. "When I submit it, it gets encrypted before being uplinked to the satellite. It's slow. It can take more than five minutes just to transmit."

"Five minutes? To send an e-mail?"

Delaney shook his head and sighed. "I wish it was that simple. No, Mr. Foster, this is the government. There's a form to fill out on the SIPRNet"—the separate internet the government used for classified data—"and all of these transmissions are encrypted. Every so often, attempting to send the report form through the satellite uplink will cause the system to freeze up. When that happens, you have to restart the computer, log back in, and start the whole thing from scratch. It's maddening."

"Sounds like it. Listen, I'm going to take off. I might have a lead."

That got Delaney's attention. "Oh? I don't suppose you want to tell me where?"

"Look," Nathan said, trying to sound reasonable, "I have a network of contacts. It took me years to build it up, and they're willing to talk to me because they trust me. They trust me because I'm not a cop."

"I see. Dare I ask how much criminal activity you willingly overlook?"

"Like I said," Nathan answered with a shrug, "I'm not a cop. It ain't like it was in the old days."

"I suppose it isn't," Delaney admitted. "So what's the plan?"

"I've got to go meet some people who may have some info on our fugitives. Face-to-face, just me. They know me. Anybody else shows up, they might get nervous and bolt. Time is a factor, here, too, so I've got to get going. This contact is trying to leave the country, and if they get across the border they're as good as gone."

"I understand," Delaney said. "Do what you need to do. We're running into delay after delay on our end. It practically took an act of God to get that aerial drone assigned to this operation."

Nathan was glad he didn't have to navigate the federal bureaucracy as part of his job. "I'll call you when I know something either way. This might be a good lead, it might be nothing, but it's all we've got right now."

"No, you're right, any lead is worth following up. Before you go, though, what do you make of all this?"

"They've got a *Brute*-class with them, that's for sure. I suspected it based on the video from the bus, but now I'm positive. Looks like the terror rattler wounded it in the scuffle."

"We've only encountered a few *Brutes* in the United States in the past few years," Delaney said. "They require maintenance, and you need exo-tech to do that. They degrade in effectiveness over time without proper care. Eventually it renders them combat-ineffective."

"Yeah, this ain't no everyday bunch of ex-UEA we're dealing with," Nathan agreed. "They've got to be Sagittarius Faction. They're getting logistical support from somewhere. You might want to make sure your boys have armor-piercing ammo, maybe a fifty-cal with API if you can get one."

"Because of the *Brute*?"

Nathan nodded. "If they've got their armor they can be tough to kill. The joints are the weak points, especially at the neck and under the arm. Even without the armor, you wanna aim for the head. They're basically meat robots. They don't feel pain or fear. They don't go into shock. If you wound one, it'll keep going until it's either incapacitated or killed. They have a way of rapidly sealing wounds to prevent them from bleeding out. Even if you take an arm off, they'll keep fighting with the other one. You drill one through the brain, though, and it's lights out."

"Mm," Delaney said, mulling that over. "We'll keep it in mind. Keep me updated, will you?"

Nathan turned to leave. "I'll let you know as soon as I know," he said, walking away.

Nogales, Arizona
That evening . . .

DARKNESS WAS OVERTAKING NOGALES by the time Nathan got there. With a fuel stop it had taken him six hours to make the drive from the mountains near Alpine. He'd pulled off of Interstate 19 north of the city, well before the checkpoint, to call George. While Ben let Shadow out to pee, Nathan received instructions on where to meet Alejandro. He was assured that the woman, the one spotted with Anthony Krieg, would be there.

Since the end of the war, everything within ten miles of the Mexican border was a federal exclusion zone, with fortified checkpoints at every border crossing, patrols, and physical barriers along the length of the border. The US Border Guards, a paramilitary successor organization to the old Border Patrol, were one of the few federal agencies still operational during America's reconstruction and rearmament. They served as a land-based equivalent to the Coast Guard and had taken over policing the border from the US Army.

"What's the point of all this?" Ben asked, as they made their way through Nogales.

"All what?"

"This," he said, indicating a trio of armored trucks as they rumbled past. "The soldiers and checkpoints and stuff. The war's over."

"It is. You gotta understand, though," Nathan said, pausing to check his mirrors before making a turn. "America hadn't actually been invaded since the War of 1812. We thought we were almost invincible. Sure, there were big wars and little wars, and for a long time we were worried about the Russians and their nukes, but there was never really any danger of foreign soldiers on American soil.

Then the war with the Greys and the UEA started, and all that changed." He remembered, vividly, the news footage of quadrupedal alien war mechs marching into Texas, followed by a seemingly endless stream of human-made tanks, trucks, and armored vehicles, all flying the flag of the United Earth Alliance. "It changed this country. All this? Mostly it makes people feel safer. We've still got the Army forward-deployed down in Mexico, helping the Mexicans provide security while they rebuild their country."

"Who are they trying to keep out? The UEA is gone."

"People, mostly. Wildlife, too, specifically critters like that terror rattler. Parts of Central America are so overrun with alien wildlife that they're almost uninhabitable. But it's not like it used to be. Immigration and migration were driven mostly by economics. The war changed all that. A lot of people fled north during the war, and a lot of them went home, after, to rebuild. Mexico lost a third of its people. They need all the manpower they can get. Anyway, we're almost there," he said, indicating the GPS. "I need you to stay in the truck again." Ben started to protest, but Nathan spoke up before he could say anything. "It's not because I don't want you around. I need to you keep an eye out for me, and if this goes sideways I don't want our target to be able to grab you as a hostage. If she was with Anthony Krieg, that probably means she was Earth Storm. That means she's enhanced and dangerous."

"Are you worried about this being some kind of a trap?"

"Not particularly. I can't see how it would benefit George or his cousin to double-cross me. Besides that, I sort of trust him, as much as you can trust a man in his business."

"Then what am I looking for?"

"All because I *don't* think it will be a trap doesn't mean it *won't* be a trap, boy. You need to take every possible precaution in situations like this. I want you to be in the driver's seat, with the engine running, monitoring me on the radio. We're going to park so you don't have to back up or turn around to get out of there. You're my escape plan."

"Got it," Ben said. "You can count on me."

"I know I can. Now, you remember what to do if you lose contact with me completely?"

"Run. Take the truck and go to the nearest checkpoint or police station. Call for help, then call Stella."

"Outstanding. Okay, I think that's it up ahead. You ready?"

Ben looked over at his uncle. "Are you?"

THE DUSTY INTERIOR of the warehouse was dimly lit. It was a large structure, with rows of steel shelves stacked almost to the ceiling. A pair of forklifts was parked against one wall, plugged into their charging stations. Nathan carried his Olin-Winchester Model 1500 lever-action combat shotgun in his hands, the tube loaded with 12-gauge buckshot. Shadow trotted along next to him, quiet but alert, his claws clicking on the concrete floor.

Alejandro led the way. He looked a lot like his cousin, except he was a few years older and a few pounds heavier. "The *malinchista* is at the loading dock," said, quietly. That particular pejorative for the collaborators had originated in Mexico but eventually spread throughout Latin America. The two men and dog entered a hallway that ran along the warehouse's outer wall. "A truck is backed up to the one of the doors. It is headed to Mexico, and she intends to be on it. I told her that we are waiting for one more person before the truck leaves."

"I suppose that's true."

"I suppose it is," Alejandro agreed. "I have people watching her who can prevent her from leaving. Do you intend to use that?" He indicated the shotgun in Nathan's hands.

"Only if I need to. If this woman is who I think she is, she's dangerous. Enhanced. Former Earth Storm."

"Earth Storm," Alejandro repeated. "Yes, I think you are correct. She has the look, you know?"

Nathan nodded. "I'm not an executioner. I'm just taking precautions."

"And the dog?"

"He can tell if someone was a collaborator."

Alejandro smiled. "He can smell the stench of the traitors? That's fitting." They came to a personnel door. "This leads to the loading dock. She is on the other side."

Nathan took a deep breath and pulled out his bronze badge, so that it hung around his neck on top of his armor. He took a moment to click his radio and tell Ben he was going in. "Okay, let's do this."

Through the doorway was a row of metal roll-up doors, the kind that trucks back into. All of them were closed except one, and that one had a box truck backed up to it with its rear door open. A trio of nervous-looking toughs, each wearing pistols in shoulder holsters, looked up at Nathan as he approached. Alejandro nodded at them and they all quietly stepped back.

"What is taking so long?" a woman's voice said. It had come from inside the truck, and she sounded irritated. She stepped out of the truck and into the light of the loading dock, only to realize that the men guarding the truck had backed away into the shadows. Then, she saw Nathan, his badge dully glinting in the light, and she froze. Her eyes went wide as Nathan shouldered the shotgun, racking a round into the chamber as he raised it, and leveled it at her.

"Freeze!" Nathan ordered. The woman complied but stared him down. She was tall, probably six feet, and like most Enhanced was built like a professional martial artist. Her lovely face was marred only by a scar that ran down her left cheek. Long black hair hung down past her shoulders. Her feminine features belied the physical strength and speed she undoubtedly possessed. Like Alejandro had said, she had *the look*. "Federal Recovery Agent!"

"You've got to be fucking kidding me," the woman said, bitterly, slowly raising her hands over her head. She stared daggers at Alejandro but didn't say anything to him. Her eyes darted to Shadow as the dog bristled and growled. That reaction from the dog was enough to tell Nathan that she was, in fact, an Enhanced.

"Listen to me very carefully," Nathan said. Enhanced or not, she wasn't wearing armor and a load of buckshot would put her down. "I think you're former Earth Storm. You being on American soil at all is a violation of the Treaty of Khartoum, and that gives me the legal authority to take you into custody and kill you if you resist. I'm going to ask you some questions. You're going to answer them truthfully. That is the only way this doesn't end badly for you. Do you understand?" The woman didn't respond. Nathan continued, "My associates here tell me you were seen crossing into the United States with Anthony Krieg about six months ago. Is that true?"

"If you're going to shoot me, shoot me," she said, defiantly. "I'm not telling you anything."

"You sure about that?" Nathan asked. "See, I'm not actually

looking for you, specifically. I'm looking for Anthony Krieg and Emmogene Anderson. The United States Government very badly wants to know where they are. So does the New Mexico State Police on account of a couple of dead officers and a family that was murdered in cold blood."

The woman's eyes narrowed but she didn't say anything.

"Your legal status notwithstanding, if you can tell me where they are, I would be grateful enough to let you get on that truck, and that'll be the end of it. If you don't cooperate I'm bringing you in, dead or alive. It's up to you."

The expression on the woman's face softened ever so slightly. She was thinking it over. "Maybe I do know something," she said after a long pause.

Nathan lowered his shotgun just a bit. "Okay, that's good. How many of them are there?"

"Four, now, not including the girl. She makes five. One of them is injured."

"What about the *Brute*-class? Was it damaged by that terror rattler?"

Her eyes widened a little at the realization of how much Nathan knew. "Yes," she said. "Its shoulder and arm were injured, but it will heal."

"Who else was injured?"

"Ivan," she said. "His name is Ivan. One of the policemen shot him. They killed another of our group."

"What about the girl, Emmogene?"

"She was alive and unharmed when I last saw her."

"What happened? Why did you get separated from the group?"

The ex-commando didn't answer at first. "That . . . that is complicated."

Nathan lowered his shotgun to hip level. It was still pointed at her, but this position made conversing easier. "I'm listening."

The woman let out a resigned sigh. "My name is Carmen," she said, "and I do know where they're going."

"WHAT HAPPENED?" Ben asked, as Nathan returned to the truck. "Was it her?"

"It was." Nathan had the back door open and was taking his gear off. He shoved the shotgun back into its case behind the seat, then stripped off his vest. "Her name is Carmen, and boy, did she tell me a story."

"Where is she?" Ben asked, getting out of the truck.

"On a truck to Mexico, I expect," Nathan answered, putting his hat back on. "Up!" he commanded, and Shadow jumped up into the back seat. He then closed the door. "She gave me information so I let her go. She wasn't responsible for the killings in Quemado, either. She told me the *Brute* and a big Russian woman named Olga did that, along with Anthony Krieg."

"What if she was lying?"

"I think she was telling the truth. Hell hath no fury like a woman scorned, so they say."

"I don't understand."

"Hop back in the truck and put in a call to Stella. I'll fill you both in at the same time."

"Okay!" Ben reached for the driver's door handle.

"Hold on there, buddy," Nathan said, grinning. "Nice try. I'm driving."

The video call with Stella lasted almost half an hour. Nathan relayed Carmen's story to both her and Ben, detailing the strange tale of Emmogene Anderson.

"That poor girl," Stella said, shaking her head slowly. "She's at the mercy of a psychopath."

"An *enhanced* psychopath," Nathan added.

"This isn't right," Stella said. "Emmogene is a victim in all this."

"Assuming Carmen was telling the truth, yeah," Nathan agreed. "All we can do is explain that to Homeland Security and hope they believe us."

Stella frowned. It seemed like this was bothering her, too. "What are you thinking?" she asked. She knew him well enough to read the expressions on his face, even over a video call.

"This is a big deal, right? That thing in that girl's head, if they could get it, copy it, make it work, that could be a pretty powerful weapon. But, from what Frampton and Delaney told us, being aware of it means you have a better chance of resisting it. So it's only really good if it's secret, right?"

Stella nodded. "I follow you."

"If they want it so bad, then, why bring us into this? They gotta know we're a security risk."

"We did have to sign all those NDAs," Stella suggested. "They could prosecute us if we blabbed about it, just like anyone with a security clearance. If we tell the world about this, we could both end up in prison. Conveniently for them, we're the only ones who know about it right now, so if any word of this ever makes it out into the open, we'll be the first ones they suspect."

"You guys," Ben said, nervously. "I don't like this. Are we gonna be okay?"

"We're gonna be fine, boy," Nathan said, trying to sound reassuring. "Stella and I are just, you know, thinking out loud. I just don't know that I trust the government with a secret mind-control device. Too much temptation to use it."

"What are we gonna do?" Ben asked.

"The first thing we need to do is find Emmogene Anderson," Nathan said. "You know how I said one of their guys was injured in the shoot-out with the cops? Apparently he's in a bad way. Serious infection. He needs a doctor."

"Do we need to check with hospitals?" Ben asked.

"No, but that's good thinking," Nathan said, patting his nephew on the shoulder. "She gave me this." He reached into his jacket pocket and retrieved a folded-up map. Unfolding it, he showed it to Ben. "This is a map of southern Arizona, New Mexico, and California. They have it marked with locations they'd planned to use on their mission. She said they were planning to cross the border in Laredo, get to the coast in Mexico, and get on a ship."

"A ship? A ship to where?"

"I couldn't get that out of her, but probably Africa. Maybe even this Bolthole place we keep hearing about. Anyway, all that got a wrench thrown into it when the one fellow got shot. He needs a doctor, and they can't just take him to the ER. She said that there's an underground clinic in the vicinity of the Phoenix Crater. It's part of the Sagittarius Faction network in the American Southwest. She told me that's probably where they're going."

Stella looked thoughtful. "Assuming she was telling the truth, then we've got everything we need to head them off. We can get to them before the Feds do."

"What if she wasn't telling the truth?" Ben asked.

"Then we're back at square one," Nathan said. "This is really all we've got to go on right now. It's worth following up on even if it turns out to be a bad lead."

"Are you headed to Phoenix, then?" Stella asked.

"Not right this second. We don't have a lot of time, but I don't know that just kicking in the door by myself is a good strategy. I'm going to make some calls and come up with a plan."

"Understood," Stella said. "Keep me posted."

"You know it. I'll send you the info on the supposed safehouse. Run it down and see if you can find anything on it."

"Will do."

"Thank you. I'll call you later. Have a good night." Nathan terminated the call and looked at Ben.

"Now what?" Ben asked.

"Now we find get some dinner, then find a room for the night. It's not a good idea to rush into a situation hungry and overtired if you can avoid it."

"What about the Homeland Security guys? What are you going to tell them?"

"Nothing yet. Do me a favor, get Jesse on the horn. I have an idea."

The Ruins of Chandler, Arizona

EMMOGENE PEERED through the transparent viewport in an armored shutter covering a window, camouflaged on the outside with boards. Before the war, the building they were holed up in had been a veterinary hospital, located in the downtown commercial district. It had been surrounded by retail stores, boutiques, and restaurants. Now everything was quiet and still. The buildings were dark. Everything was covered in dust and bleached by the sun. Chandler had been far enough away from the asteroid impact that it survived the initial blast, but was subsumed by dust and debris in the aftermath.

The former vet clinic now served as a clandestine hospital on an underground railroad of ex-UEA loyalists, helping them get out of the United States. It wasn't directly controlled by the Sagittarius Faction. The building was battered on the outside but well maintained on the inside. It was mostly sealed and kept at above ambient air pressure, to keep the pervasive dust out. It was also sealed electromagnetically, to keep the signature of the exo-tech power cell that provided them with electricity from being detected.

The Phoenix Valley had never been repopulated after the war. Phoenix was the first American city the Visitors destroyed. It was an opening gambit, Emmogene had once read, intended to shock the American people and break their resolve. The asteroid they dropped on the city was dense, composed largely of heavy metals, and impacted with a force equivalent to fifty million tons of TNT. The blast didn't produce radiation like a nuclear weapon did, but heavy metal contamination in the dust would prove to be quite toxic. Prevailing winds carried it as far as Denver.

"Are you doing okay, Emmogene?"

The woman's voice had startled her. She turned to see one of the nurses, Nomusa, standing behind her. Emmogene managed a smile for the woman. "I'm fine. It just, you know, seems so sad. So much destruction out there. What was the point of it all?"

"That's how war always is," Nomusa said with a shrug. She was a fortyish woman from somewhere in Western Africa. "When I was a girl, a militia group came into my village. Dey took everyting dey wanted, including all da women an' girls. Anyone who resist, dey killed, or cut deir hands off wit' machetes." She made a chopping motion with her hand. "To dis day, I don' know who dey were, or what dey were fighting for."

"Oh my God," Emmogene said. "I'm so sorry. I didn't know."

Nomusa shrugged again. "Dat's da way war always is, girl. Big men decide to have a war, young men go an' fight an' kill an' die. Da world goes on. Sometimes it get better, sometimes it get worse, but it always goes on."

"How did you end up in Arizona? I don't mean to assume, but it just seems very far from home for you."

The nurse smiled, her perfect white teeth contrasting with her complexion. "When da Visitors come, dey recruited people to work for dem, even fight for dem. Dey say dey building a better world. I don' know if dat was true, but dey did rescue me from da militia camp and send me home to my family. Dey provided food, housing, an' school. As I grew older dey taught me to be a nurse, gave me shots so I don' get sick an' stay healty. I even learned English, even if my English is not so good."

Emmogene smiled. "You're doing better than me. I studied French at some point, but I barely remember any of it."

Nomusa's face lit up. "Really? I study French, too. My French is better den my English." Her expression changed, then, subtly. She seemed more distant. "When da war started, da Visitors say dey need doctors an' nurses to treat da wounded and da prisoners. I was sent. I di'n mind. I like to help people. I don' want to hurt anyone, so I'd be no good at fighting. I was down in Mexico when de Americans came an' told us to lay down arms. Dey said da war over, dat da Visitors left us, an' dat we all were gon' be sent home. My home was gone, dough, so I stayed wit' the people I knew."

"Your home was gone? What happened?"

"I lived in City Twelve wit' my parents an cousin," she said, quietly. "Da Americans an' da Russians destroyed it wit' deir atomic bombs."

"I . . . I'm so sorry. I don't even know what to say."

Nomusa shook her head sadly. "The Visitors destroy American an' Russian cities, too. Dey dropped da rock on Phoenix when da war started. Dey dropped da rocks in da ocean an' flooded China an' India. Dey . . . dey make da Red Deat' dat kill so many people. It don' matter now, who did what. We all jus' tryin' ta survive now. I come up here for a few monts at a time, helping people who need help. I'll be going back soon, I tink. Is dat where you all are going?"

"I . . . I think so," Emmogene said, looking down. She looked back up at Nomusa. "You've been there, right? To Bolthole?"

"Don' say dat name out loud," Nomusa warned. "Da Faction boys hear you, dey get mad. No, I neva been dere. I don' even know where it is. I live in da Free Territories where all da ex-UEA stay. I jus' work wit' da network. Dey pay me good for dis, an' I like helping people."

The Free Territories were what became of parts of Nigeria, Chad, and Cameroon, the former Human Sectors. A vast demilitarized zone created by the Treaty of Khartoum, millions of former UEA citizens lived there, since most of their native countries wouldn't take them back. An army of UN Peacekeepers, mostly from countries that had stayed neutral during the war, kept the ex-UEA separated from the rest of the population of Africa, lest that continent see more war and genocide.

"Are there people like Anthony there? You know, people still loyal to the Visitors?"

The nurse sighed. "Dere are, but dey not in charge anymore. So many kids raised by the Visitors, dey neva had real parents, dis was boun' to happen. Sometimes dey remind me of da militia boys from back home. You know, always shootin' an' plannin' an' talkin' about war. Dey tink da war isn't over, dat dey can still win. I tink dey crazy. We fought the whole world an' we lost, even wit' the Visitors' help. Wit'out it, what could we do? Why would we do it? I don' want to fight anybody. Too many people died already." She looked down. "Half da world burned. What was da point? Billions of stars in da galaxy an' da Visitors need to come here? Sometimes I tink maybe we were on da wrong side, even wit' all da good da Visitors did. Dere was a price for deir help, a terrible price."

"There was," Emmogene agreed. She changed the subject. "How is Ivan?"

"I tink he will recover, but it will take time. Da bullet missed his spine, but da wound is bad. If he weren't enhanced I tink he woulda died. He won't be ready to move soon. Will you stay here? It would be best for him to stay. Eart' Storm commandos are strong but dere still can be complications."

"I don't know," Emmogene answered. "That's up to Anthony." A bulky monitor bracelet was clamped around her right ankle. Anthony had put it on her as a condition of letting her out of his sight, or having Rook follow her around everywhere. The hospital was protected by armed guards, but he wanted the ability to know where she was at all times.

Nomusa looked at the device clamped around Emmogene's leg. She leaned in close, her voice a whisper. "Why are dey tracking you?"

"I'm a prisoner," Emmogene said, flatly. "I tried to run."

Nomusa leaned back and said something in her native language. "Why are you a prisoner?"

"I'm not supposed to talk about it. Anthony will get angry with me if I do."

A look of understanding appeared on the nurse's face. "I will talk to da boss."

"That won't be necessary," Anthony said, stepping around a corner, startling the two women. "Emmogene is in my care."

"I-I didn't mean—" Nomusa stammered, but Anthony cut her off.

"I don't care what you meant," he said, looming over the nurse, backing her against the wall. "Emmogene is a high-value asset, and she's in Faction custody. I, and I alone, decide where she goes, and how. Am I making myself clear?"

"Y-yes sir."

"Good. Now get back to whatever it is you are supposed to be doing. Stay away from Emmogene."

Nomusa, eyes wide with anger and fear, hurried off without another word.

Emmogene couldn't muster the emotional energy to be frightened anymore. Anthony's emotional state was deteriorating.

She had seen him like this before, after the war. Without either recurring conditioning or his medication, he became unstable, even to the point where he acted like a high school bully. Before, she felt pity for Anthony; he was, after all, a victim of sorts. No longer, though. Now there was only revulsion, disgust, and resignation.

She wondered, darkly, if taking her own life would be the only way out.

"I'm sorry about that," Anthony said, "but—"

Emmogene interrupted him. "No you're not." She looked up into his eyes. "I'm not sure that you even understand what it means to be sorry anymore. I think they conditioned that out of you."

"You may be right about that," Anthony said, distantly. He didn't look at her. "It doesn't matter now. The only thing that matters is completing my mission. I need to get you to Bolthole."

"Nomusa said that Ivan needs to stay here to recover."

"Who?"

"Nomusa, the nurse you just frightened off."

"Oh. Yes, I'm aware. We will be leaving him here. He will only slow us down at this point."

Emmogene folded her arms across her chest. "Have you run that by Olga? She might not like it."

"Olga is my subordinate. I don't *run things by* her. She will do as I tell her to."

"Her brother might be dying, for God's sake! You expect her to just abandon him?"

"I do, and if she refuses, then I'll leave her here and take you in myself." He turned to walk away.

"This isn't going to end the way you think, Anthony," Emmogene said, coldly. "Whatever you've been promised, whatever it is you think you're owed, you're not going to get it."

Anthony paused. "You may be right about that, as well. We'll see. I've already spoken with Command and have secured us transport. They are sending extra personnel to ensure the mission is completed. We will be leaving in a couple of days." He left her without another word.

The Ruins of Chandler, Arizona

"YOU THINK THIS IS THE PLACE?" Jesse asked, his voice muffled by the respirator he wore. He peered through a pair of binoculars at the building in the distance. It had once been a veterinary hospital in downtown Chandler. Now, Carmen had alleged, it served as a clandestine base of operations for UEA loyalists.

"I do," Nathan answered. He was hunkered down behind an electronic spotting scope. "Those tracks are fresh."

"That doesn't mean anything," Jesse said. "Locals come through here sometimes, scavenging, taking pictures, or just exploring."

The two men were set up on the top floor of a nine-story building that had once been a hotel. The structure was tall enough that they were able to see the building of interest without getting too close. The floor-to-ceiling windows at the ends of the hallways had all shattered in the destruction of Phoenix. The darkened interior provided a good surveillance point and allowed the pair to set up in the prone, so as to not risk standing in the window. Dry winds occasionally gusted down the hallway, stirring up the dust that coated every surface. Both men wore respirators to avoid breathing the potentially toxic particulate. Nathan was dressed in desert camouflage fatigues, Jesse in his olive drab Arizona Ranger uniform.

"Look where the tracks lead, though. Here." Jesse's binoculars didn't have the high magnification that Nathan's spotting scope did, and it was more difficult for him to make out some details in the early morning twilight. Nathan pushed himself back from the optic so that Jesse could use the scope.

"Wow, this is some nice glass," Jesse said idly, settling behind the large, boxy device, which was set up on a short tripod.

"Steiner-Hensoldt twenty-to-sixty-power," Nathan said, "gyro-stabilized. It's night-vision compatible and has a built-in laser rangefinder. Would you believe I paid four hundred bucks for it? Euro-Fed military surplus, never issued. Buddy of mine managed to get a case of them into the country from Mexico."

"Holy crap. If he gets any more, let me know, hey? Okay, I see the tracks . . . looks like they turn into that parking garage next door."

"Yup. They went in the entrance that leads to the underground levels, too."

"Hmm," Jesse muttered, continuing to peer through the spotting scope. "That would make for a pretty discreet hideout, wouldn't it? Especially if you could close off the entrance somehow."

"Right, and if people come nosing around, it probably wouldn't be too hard to make them disappear."

"We still can't be sure, though," Jesse said. "We're either going to have to try to get closer and investigate, or wait for . . . Hang on. What's this?"

"What's what?" Nathan asked. He picked up Jesse's binoculars and trained them on the building of interest. "Hello . . ."

A group four vehicles, two 4x4 trucks and two vans, made their way down the street, driving in a tight column, kicking up a cloud of dust as they went. None of them had lights on. They came to a stop near the front of the supposedly abandoned veterinary hospital and waited.

"What are they doing?" Jesse asked.

"Let me see," Nathan said. His friend moved out of the way so that he could get behind the scope again. The vehicles were so coated in dirt that it was difficult to determine what color they were. The State of Arizona hadn't bothered to issue license plates since the war started, either. The windows were all tinted, making it difficult to tell how many people were in each vehicle.

"The van!" Jesse said, looking through his binoculars.

Nathan panned the scope to the right slightly, until the reticle was settled on the first of the two vans. The sliding side door was open and he could see inside. The sun had just crested the horizon, allowing him to make out some detail. "That van is full of dudes. They're armed. That one fella, looks like he's scanning this way with binos. Shit." He exhaled slowly. "Don't move."

Seconds ticked by. Nathan watched as the man in the van scanned his surroundings with binoculars. After a few moments of this, he pulled the door closed, and the vehicles in the convoy all started their engines again.

"They're rolling," Jesse said. "They're heading into the underground garage." Once the vehicles were out of sight, he put the binoculars down and looked over at Nathan. "What the hell do we do now?"

Nathan backed away from his scope and rested on his elbows. He sighed. "Son of a bitch. There ain't no way I can go in there myself. That one van was full of armed men, and for all we know the other was, too. On top of that, we don't know how many people are already in there, or if the person I'm after is even there." He wasn't supposed to, but Nathan had filled his friend in on the details of the case he was currently working. Jesse had gone to college at Arizona Tech before the war, and that university's main campus had been in Chandler. He'd lived in the area for a couple of years and knew his way around better than Nathan did. Using the abandoned hotel as a lookout spot had been his idea.

"So what now?"

Nathan shook his head. "I don't have a choice. I'm going to have to call the Feds."

"That means you don't get the bounty, right?"

"Right, but sometimes you gotta know when to call it. Trying to raid that place by ourselves is probably suicide. Better to let the Feds deal with it, they've got the manpower. Let's pack it in and head back to your truck. Then we can radio Ben and let him know what's going on." The boy had wanted to come along, of course, but Nathan had insisted on him staying behind to watch the truck. There was no cellular reception where they were, and having Ben on the radio was their only way of communicating with the rest of the world.

"You think they'll move on it?" Jesse asked.

"Oh, I expect they'll make a big show of it. I've got the feeling those Homeland Security boys got something to prove."

The Ruins of Chandler, Arizona
The next day . . .

EMMOGENE SAT UP ON HER COT, startled awake by the shouts of men. She didn't know what was going on, but something was obviously wrong. A pit formed in her stomach when she recognized the *thwup-thwupp*ing of a helicopter outside. Were they under attack? Had the government found them? She got up in bed and quickly got dressed. No matter what happened, she had a feeling she was going to want to be wearing pants and shoes. No sooner had she finished tying her shoes than the door to the little room she'd been locked in swung open. It was Anthony.

"What's happening?" she asked.

"We're being raided," he said, coldly. She backed away as he stepped into the room, looming over her. "The Americans are here. They have us surrounded."

"H-how did they find this place?"

Anthony's eyes narrowed. "Carmen. It has to be. The bitch sold us out."

"How can you be sure?"

"What else could it be? It can't be a coincidence." He looked down at Emmogene. "This is your fault. I should have killed her. You stopped me."

"Anthony, I didn't mean—" Emmogene's voice was cut off as Anthony backhanded her across the mouth. She stumbled backward, her face stinging, and tripped over her cot. She unceremoniously fell to the floor in front of the cot, holding her hands up to protect her face.

Anthony didn't give her a moment to breathe. He knelt down and grabbed her by the collar of her jacket. "It's ironic," he said, sounding distant. "You had so much to say about how the Visitors are using me, controlling me, and how I'm their victim. Such sanctimony. Yet, when you are able to use that device in your head, what do you do? You control me. You invade my mind. You manipulate me. You tell me lies."

Emmogene tried to speak, but Anthony twisted his grip on her collar, tightening it around her throat. "No, you be silent now," he said, his calmness standing in contrast to the commotion coming from outside the room. "With the Visitors, I had a *choice*. I *chose* their side, Emmogene. I gave myself to them willingly. They made me more than I was, stronger, better. They gave me a purpose. They give me purpose still." He looked down at the floor for a moment, relaxing his grip slightly. "You? Given the slightest bit of power, you have no qualms with using it to violate the free will of another person. You're every bit the monster that I am."

Tears were streaming down Emmogene's face now. She couldn't speak. She couldn't move. She was shaking.

Anthony let go of her and stood up. "No more games. Your stupidity got Ivan shot and Henry killed. Your meddling drove Carmen to distrust me, and now she's betrayed us. The only way we're getting out of here now is by force, and a lot more people are going to die." He turned to leave. "You will stay here until I come and get you. I have orders not to let them take you alive. If it comes to that, I promise it'll be quick and painless." He took a step out the door, but paused and looked back. "If I don't come back, I suggest you find a way to kill yourself. They will kill you, without a second thought, in order to extract the device intact." He stepped out, closing and locking the door behind him.

Emmogene sat on the floor, her face buried in her hands, and wept. Gunfire echoed from somewhere outside.

WHAT A CLUSTER-FUCK, Nathan thought. From the Feds' mobile command post, he watched the raid go down from a distance. They had gathered dozens of Homeland Security agents for the task, equipped with body armor, helmets, and assault rifles. They also had a trio of M31 Ruffners, eight-wheeled armored personnel carriers that the Army had used during the war, painted black and marked with the eagle logo of the Department of Homeland Security. Each was equipped with a remote-controlled .50-caliber machine gun turret and could hold an entire squad of troops. A helicopter circled overhead, complete with a door gunner.

Special Agent Delaney was in charge as the raid began. He stood in the command vehicle, watching video feeds from the Ruffners and the helicopter. His young, gung-ho partner, Frampton, was in the lead APC as they advanced toward the target building. Each agent's armor vest was equipped with a vitals monitor, allowing the command team to monitor their heart and breathing rates, as well as track their locations. They had been working on something like that toward the end of the war, Nathan recalled, but mercifully had never deployed it. It was the ultimate in remote micromanagement.

Delaney looked over at Nathan. "This is how you get things done, Foster," he said, confidently, indicating the bank of screens and radios, and the trio of technicians monitoring them, as he spoke. "We've got the whole block cordoned off. We've got air support and armored vehicles. We've even got a drone overhead, monitoring the situation."

"That's why I called you boys in," Nathan admitted. "This place is too fortified for me to take on by myself."

"You did good work," Delaney acknowledged. "Your government appreciates your contribution to this operation." He looked back at the monitors. "I have to be honest, though, I think your days may be numbered."

Nathan raised an eyebrow. "Is that right?"

"Bounty hunters, I mean," Delaney explained. "If you think about it, it's a ridiculous system. The United States of America should not have to rely on Wild West bullshit to enforce its laws. It's not like it was right after the war, you know, when we were struggling to keep the lights on. We have a functional government again. No offense, but it's time for men like you to hang up your spurs and leave this sort of thing to professionals."

So that's what this is really about, Nathan thought. He didn't say anything, though. He just folded his arms across his chest and watched the situation play out.

A voice crackled over the radio. It was from the helicopter. "Roof access hatch is opening. One individual." The chopper's gyro-stabilized camera zoomed in on the former veterinary clinic. A large man in a hat and coat climbed through the hatch and stepped onto the roof. "Moving in," the pilot said. "We've got a bead on him."

"Delaney," Nathan began, "that's the *Brute*-class."

"What?" Delaney asked. He leaned in closer to the monitor. "You might be right."

"Tell them to open fire, now!" Nathan pleaded. "Shoot it!"

"Steady, Foster," Delaney chided. "We expected this." He told one of his technicians to tell the pilot to engage the man on the roof.

The technician did as she was told, relaying the command to the helicopter, but there was no response from pilot.

"What's going on?" Delaney asked, concerned. "Tell them to open fire."

The technician tried again. After a few moments, she looked back at her boss, shaking her head. "It's like they can't hear us."

Another one of the technicians spoke up then. "Sir, I'm not getting anything from the lead vehicle anymore, either. There's a lot of interference."

"We're being jammed!" the third technician said, excitedly.

"How did we miss that?" Delaney demanded.

"I think it's targeted ECM, sir," the technician answered. "We'd have picked up a barrage jammer right away. This one is rapidly targeting our transmissions and interfering with them on the same frequencies!"

"Delaney, you need to pull that chopper out of there!" Nathan said.

The pilot's voice could be heard over the video feed, but not the radio. "Command, individual is armed, I repeat, individual is armed." The video showed the big man on the roof now holding a weapon in both hands. He'd pulled it from behind his back.

Delaney tried to raise the chopper again, to no avail. The pilot's voice could be heard over both the video feed and the aircraft's loudspeaker. "You on the roof!" he ordered. "Drop your weapon and place your hands on top of your head."

Nathan watched, helplessly, as the soldier-type raised its weapon, pointing it directly at the camera. A second later, the screen went black. NO SIGNAL, it read.

"We've lost the feed," the female technician said. "Do you think—" She fell silent as an explosion erupted from somewhere outside.

"Command! We've lost the chopper, I repeat, we've lost the chopper, please advise!" The voice on the radio, barely intelligible through the heavy static, was pleading for instructions, but Delaney couldn't get through to any of them.

BOOM!

"What was that?" one of the technicians asked.

Another excited voice crackled over the radio. "Command . . . lost . . . APC! I . . . gain . . . lead . . . down! . . . antitank weapons!"

"Did he say antitank weapons?" one of the technicians asked.

"Tell them to pull back!" Delaney roared.

"We're trying, sir!" the technician answered, on the verge of tears. "They can't hear us!"

"For fuck's sakes," Nathan snarled, turning toward the door.

"Where are you going?" Delaney demanded.

"I'm going get to those APCs and tell them to pull back!" he said. "Keep trying to raise them on the radio!" He left the command vehicle before the Homeland Security agent could answer, taking off toward his truck at a run.

EMMOGENE SAT ON HER COT and tried to keep her hands from shaking. Gunfire echoed throughout the building and there'd been several rumbling explosions from outside. She could no longer hear the sound of the helicopter. They must have shot it down somehow.

This is all my fault, she thought, shaking her head. *This is all my fault.* She buried her face in her trembling hands as the battle outside dragged on. Anthony was right. None of this would be happening if she had just cooperated. How could she be so selfish? She'd kept telling him that she wasn't worth other people losing their lives over, but every action she had taken since escaping custody had led to the deaths of innocent people.

I should end this, she thought, grimly. She looked down at her shoes. She could use the laces to hang herself, maybe. Would that do it? If they found her dead, would this insanity finally be over? Would the killing stop? Was death the only chance she had of being free from Anthony, once and for all?

Her head snapped up. Someone was unlocking the door. Maybe it was Anthony, here to make good on his promise to not let her be captured again. She stood up slowly. Her heart was racing. She clenched her shaking hands into fists. Emmogene was determined to face whatever came next head-on. She held her breath as the handle turned and the door quietly slid open.

Nomusa?

The African nurse put her finger to her lips and closed the door behind her. "Are you hurt?" she asked. "What happened to your face?"

"A-Anthony hit me," Emmogene answered, quietly.

Nomusa shook her head. "I knew he was a bastard. He remind me of da militia boys back home." She knelt down in front of Emmogene and began to lift up the cuff of her jeans. "I stole da key," she said, sticking something into Emmogene's ankle monitor. The device released with a loud click. "You are free now."

"Free?" Emmogene repeated. She didn't even know what that word meant anymore.

Nomusa stood up, and looked up into Emmogene's eyes. "Yes, girl, you free. Come on. We have to go. Dere is not much time."

Emmogene hesitated. "Go? Go where?"

"Dere's a way out," Nomusa said, pulling at Emmogene's arm. "A secret way, trew da old sewers."

"What about Anthony?" Emmogene asked, following Nomusa into the hallway. The nurse quietly closed and locked the door behind her, leaving the ankle monitor inside the room. "He'll come looking for me."

"Maybe," the nurse said, leading her down the hall. "Or maybe he die here. Dey all distracted wit' da fighting. You have a chance. Your ankle monitor is still on. He tink you still in da room. By da time he come check, you be gone. Now shush and follow me."

Nomusa quickly guided Emmogene through the clandestine hospital. The medical staff was all hunkered down or tending to the wounded, and all of the security people were up front or in the parking garage, fighting with the Feds. There was nobody in the hall, giving the two women the opportunity to get to the back room unseen. "Dis is it," the nurse said, unlocking the door. Once it was open, she pushed Emmogene through and followed her into the room, closing the door behind them.

Emmogene found herself in an old boiler room. The floor was bare concrete and the walls were painted brick. In the center was a black metallic cylinder, maybe five feet tall and three feet in diameter. It was an exo-tech power cell used to provide electricity to the facility. Translucent sections along its surface glowed blue, and several cables were connected to it, running through holes that had been drilled into the walls. There didn't seem to be any way out.

"Over here," Nomusa said, gesturing for Emmogene to follow. At the very back of the room there was a stack of large cardboard boxes. "Help me move dese," she said, picking one up. Emmogene did the same, discovering that the boxes were all empty. A couple of minutes of removing boxes revealed a manhole cover in the concrete floor.

"Dat's it," Nomusa said. She had retrieved from one of the boxes a pair of steel hooks with handles on one end. She handed one to Emmogene. "Please help me wit' da lid. It heavy." As quickly as they could, the two women used the hooks to lift the steel manhole cover from its resting place, setting it down on the floor nearby.

Emmogene peered in. A ladder led down into darkness. She didn't know how they were going to navigate their way out in a pitch-black tunnel. She looked up when Nomusa handed her the small knapsack she'd been wearing.

"What's this?"

"Tings you will need to make it out," the nurse said. "Dere is a flashlight wit' a UV lens. Use it to follow da path. There are arrows on da walls in UV paint, dey will lead you out. Dere is more dan one way. Dis is a utility tunnel dat connects to da sewer. In da pack is a canteen of water and some money, not much, maybe a hundred dollars. I'm sorry, dat's all I could get. Hurry now, you need to go."

Emmogene's eyes widened as she realized what Nomusa was saying. "You're . . . you're not coming with me?"

The nurse smiled. "No, girl, I can't. I need to help da wounded. Anyway, if I disappear too, dey get suspicious. Dis already a risk. Dere's no time to talk, you need to go before dey check on you. I will cover every-ting back up behind you."

Tears were in Emmogene's eyes now. "I can't just leave you here!"

Nomusa grabbed Emmogene's arm. "You have to! It's okay. I'm a nurse, da Americans won't shoot me if I surrender."

Emmogene didn't know what to do. Anthony would suspect Nomusa when he realized that she'd escaped, and God only knew the things he would do to her then. Unable to think of anything else, she reached forward and hugged Nomusa, squeezing the nurse as tears streamed down her face. "Thank you."

Nomusa nodded, wiping away tears of her own. "No more goodbyes. Get going. Good luck."

"Good luck," Emmogene repeated. She put on the knapsack she'd been given and, without another word, climbed down the ladder into the musty utility tunnel. As the lid closed above her, she retrieved the flashlight from the pack, and switched it on just as she was about to be plunged into utter darkness. As Nomusa had indicated, there was an arrow painted on the wall in UV-reflective paint.

As the battle raged above, Emmogene made her way down the dark tunnel, alone.

IT WAS LIKE BEING BACK IN THE WAR.

Nathan's heart pounded in his ears as he advanced, the sensation amplified by the earplugs he wore. In his hands was his Colt/AAI Saber, a commercial copy of the M91A2 semiautomatic battle rifle he'd carried for half the war. It was a big, heavy, powerful rifle chambered in .277 Fury (6.8x51mm NATO), with a magazine full of armor-piercing ammunition. He normally kept it loaded with commercial hunting ammunition, but for this job he had opted for armor penetration over terminal effectiveness.

He wasn't as young or as fit as he had been when he served in the Army. Moving through the deserted streets of Chandler, weighed down by an armor vest, load-bearing gear, a gunbelt, a medical kit, water, and ammunition was harder than it used to be. Tinted goggles and a high-filtration respirator protected him from the potentially toxic dust, but it made it harder to see and breathe. He had to keep going, though. The Feds' advance was stalled, one of their vehicles was apparently disabled, and they were caught out in the open. If they stayed there, they were all going to get killed.

The gunfire had only been sporadic before, but now it had died off completely. An eerie quiet settled over the ruined city as Nathan moved. There were other structures between him and the target building, but he was alert for movement. The enemy had an opportunity to press the advantage, to counterattack and wipe out the Homeland Security troops. He had to figure out what the hell was going on and tell them to pull back before it was too late.

The Ruffner APCs were only about half a mile from the mobile command center. All Nathan had to do was follow the plume of black smoke drifting up from the street. There was another, smaller one farther away, probably the wreck of the Feds' helicopter, but he wasn't going to go look for it by himself. The APCs had followed a doglegged path through the streets, keeping themselves out of view of the target building until the last possible moment. That had been smart, for all the good it had done them. It was likely, he thought, that the UEA insurgents had rigged the entire area with sensors and alarms. *Hell, they might be watching me right now*, he thought, moving up a dust-covered alleyway.

The alleyway ended at a wide, four-lane, divided street. A row of desiccated tree trunks ran down the center of the divider island. Either side of the boulevard was lined with abandoned cars, faded from years of sun and weather. To his left, just before the intersection, were two of the three Homeland Security APCs. They were idling, one right behind the other, too close together. The third one, presumably the one that had been hit, had already rounded the corner.

They got lucky, Nathan thought, running across the street. If the defenders had waited a few seconds, they might have gotten all three APCs into the kill zone. Breathing hard through the respirator mask, he paused for a moment to catch his breath and check his surroundings. No sign of any UEA insurgents. Keeping close to the empty storefronts, he jogged up the sidewalk, approaching the two stopped APCs from the rear. The vehicle commanders' hatches were open. Both men had their seats elevated so that they could see better, and saw Nathan coming. He kept his weapon slung and held his bronze badge up as he approached, lest he be shot. Breathing hard, he climbed up onto the lead vehicle.

"You're that Recovery Agent," the vehicle commander said. "What the hell are you doing here?" He was just a kid, in his late twenties at most. "This is no place for civilians."

Nathan didn't bother reminding the kid that he was a civilian, too. "Delaney sent me," he said, yelling so as to be heard over the noise of the vehicle's diesel engine. "He can't raise you on the radio."

"We can't hear anything from the command truck."

"They probably have ECM," Nathan suggested.

"What?"

"Electronic countermeasures. You know, radio jammers. Why are you just sitting here?"

"We were waiting for orders! We can't go back, we've got wounded men in the lead vehicle. But every time we try to send someone around to secure the casualties, they take fire."

"Well, no shit they take fire!" Nathan said, trying not to snarl at the kid. He realized, then, just how woefully inexperienced the Feds were. This vehicle commander was probably too young to have served in the war, and whatever training regimen Homeland Security had put together for them clearly wasn't enough. They didn't even have a contingency plan in the event they lost radio communications.

"We can't send the vehicles forward," the young commander insisted. "They might have more antitank weapons!"

"They probably do," Nathan agreed, "but you can't just sit here. The wounded will all be dead by the time you can get to them."

"You don't think I know that?" the commander shouted.

Nathan sighed in his mask, trying to not scream at the kid. "Listen, I was a tank commander in the war. I've been in situations like this before. I got an idea to recover the wounded, but it's your call. You don't have to do what I say, but I can tell you Delaney doesn't know what to do any more than you do. You up for it?"

The kid's brow furled with determination. "Let's do it."

"Okay. You know this thing has smoke launchers, right?" Nathan pointed at one of the clusters of tubes jutting out of the Ruffner's armored hull. "Are they loaded?"

"They should be. We've never used them, though. We were told that smoke would obscure the view of our air assets."

"It will, but right now your air asset is down. Here's what you boys do." Nathan got the commander of the other APC to leave his vehicle and climb up with them, so the three men could have a quick face-to-face-to-face planning session. Radio communications were still spotty at best; the damned Greys always did have the best ECM.

As quickly as he could, Nathan laid out an impromptu plan for the Homeland Security agents. He suggested that both APCs pull forward and get ready. They would angle the vehicles so that they could launch smoke into the street without exposing themselves to direct fire. Then, both vehicles would pull forward, using the concealment provided by the smoke. Each Ruffner was armed with a .50-caliber machine gun on a remotely controlled turret. The APCs would position themselves so they wouldn't be in each other's way. They would lay down suppressing fire as they rounded the corner. One vehicle would park itself between the target building and the destroyed APC to provide cover while the other transferred the wounded and the dead over. "Keep using your smoke," Nathan insisted, "and keep up the suppressing fire. Aim for the windows. You gotta keep their heads down while you evacuate the wounded."

"Then what?" the APC commander asked.

"Then we go back to the command post and regroup. Delaney needs to call in the damned National Guard for this."

"Where are you going to be?"

"Right behind you," Nathan said, resolutely. "I'll use you for cover, then I'll try to pull out the wounded while you boys set up. Just don't forget about me out there."

"We won't leave you behind."

"I appreciate that. Let's move out!"

JESUS, WHAT A MESS, Nathan thought, looking down at the row of bodybags. A dry wind blew through the streets of Chandler, kicking up more dust. Empty buildings cast long shadows as the sun hung low in the afternoon sky. The gunfire had ceased now, but helicopters still patrolled the skies.

The raid had been an abysmal failure. Homeland Security lost both its helicopter and the Ruffner armored personnel carrier. In total, eleven federal agents had been killed: eight in the APC and three in the helicopter. Special Agent Frampton was among the dead. Fearing that the UEA insurgents would counterattack and go for the mobile command post, Special Agent in Charge Delaney had pulled his men off the cordon of the target building so that they could provide security while they waited for reinforcements.

Reinforcements came, eventually. A military police company from the Arizona National Guard had rolled in, backed up by a couple AH-71 Crow compound attack helicopters. They had the man- and firepower to do the job, Nathan reckoned, but by the time the government forces regrouped it was too late. Most of the insurgents had fled. Some had escaped in vehicles while others apparently used the old city sewers.

Special Agent Delaney was dejected. He stood silently, looking at the bodybags, his face ashen behind his respirator. Nathan approached, respectfully, and gave him one brief pat on the shoulder. It was awkward, but Delaney nodded his appreciation. "Hell of a day, Foster," the Homeland Security man said, after a few moments. "I want to thank you for your assistance in this matter. I know we didn't exactly see eye to eye, but you risked your life to get my men out of harm's way. You saved lives today."

There was a lot that Nathan wanted to say. He wanted to scream at the man, ask him what in the hell he thought was going to happen, sending in a bunch of green kids who barely knew how to use their equipment. He also wanted to console him, tell him that in war, you can do everything right and still lose, and that you can't plan for every possible contingency. How was anyone supposed to know this place had military-grade electronic countermeasures? Nothing of the sort had been used by pro-alien militants in the United States before, not even by the Sagittarian Faction.

In the end, Nathan didn't know Delaney well enough to say much, so all he could do was change the subject. "Any word on the vehicles that escaped?"

"Hmm?" Delaney seemed surprised by the question. "Oh, yes. They scattered, but our overhead drone managed to track one of them as it fled east. They were caught in a pincer as they tried to cross into New Mexico, with the New Mexico State Police ahead of them and the Arizona Highway Patrol behind them. A gun battle ensued when the insurgents were stopped, and they were all killed. The cops didn't even let them get out of the vehicle, just opened up on them."

"That's not surprising after what happened today, and before in Quemado. Any sign of our two targets?"

Delaney shook his head. "Neither Anthony Krieg nor Emmogene Anderson were among the dead, either here or in the vehicle the police stopped. Neither was the *Brute*, for that matter, so that damned thing is still on the loose. The other vehicles that escaped haven't been located yet."

"Were you able to get anything out of the survivors?" A handful of medical personnel from the insurgent stronghold had stayed behind, treating the wounded, and eventually surrendered.

"I'm under orders to hold off on interrogating them. Higher-ups aren't happy with this, as you can imagine. They're sending in their own team to take the prisoners and do the questioning, and legal says we need to bring an attorney for them as well. They won't get here until tomorrow."

"Don't they know how dangerous that device you're looking for is? Do we really have that time to waste?"

Delaney sighed through his respirator. "This operation was heavily compartmentalized due to its sensitive nature. I'm not supposed to talk about the classified details with anyone who hasn't been briefed. My boss and his boss are doing some serious ass-covering right now, and I'm the one who's going to get left holding the bag for this. Shit rolls downhill, you know. It's already been suggested to me that I consider an early retirement."

Nathan had seen enough of that in the Army to know exactly how Delaney felt. "So what now?"

"I've got nothing else for you, Mr. Foster. Our finance department will be in contact with your office to ensure your fees are met per our contract." He paused. "You know, you might want to have a talk with the prisoners before you go."

"Say what?"

"It's only a suggestion. They told me that I'm not allowed to interrogate them. I'm not your supervisor, and you, being a private citizen, can ask them whatever questions you want."

"You sure? I don't want to cause you any trouble."

"Like it matters now," He said, humorlessly. He pulled a radio out of a pocket on his vest. "Harper, this is SAIC, do you copy?"

"This is Agent Harper," a voice replied.

"Are the prisoners still secure?"

"Yes, sir. We've got them locked up, ankle-cuffed, and under guard. They're not going anywhere."

"Alright. I want you to grab Hernandez and come meet me at the command trailer. I have something I need you two to do."

"Sir? You want us to leave the prisoners?"

"You said they're locked up and ankle-cuffed, correct?"

"Uh, yes sir."

"Then you and Hernandez get over here. It will only take a couple of minutes. Don't forget your masks, I don't want you boys inhaling this dust."

"Understood, sir. We'll be right there."

"Good. SAIC out." Delaney tossed Nathan a key. "This will get you into the prisoner transport vehicle. You have fifteen minutes. You'll be on camera in there, so keep it professional. Good luck."

"Thank you," Nathan said, offering his hand. Delaney shook it. As Nathan was walking away, he got on his own radio. "Ben, I need you up here. Meet me at the command trailer ASAP."

"What? Really?" Ben and Shadow had been safely secured in Nathan's truck, well away from the fighting. The boy hadn't gotten to do anything so far, and he sounded excited at the opportunity.

"Yeah. Leave Shadow in the truck. Keep the windows up and the engine running so the AC and the air filter keep working. Bring your notebook. We've got prisoners to question."

"Prisoners?"

"Yes. Get a move on, now. The clock is ticking."

"I'll be right there!"

The Homeland Security boys had brought a second RV with them aside from their mobile command center. It wasn't really a recreational vehicle, but to Nathan's eye it resembled one of the big campers that retirees used to tour the country in before the war. Like the command vehicle, this one was painted black and was adorned with the logo of Homeland Security. It also had the words PRISONER TRANSPORT painted on the sides.

"Are we supposed to be here?" Ben asked, looking around nervously. The area was crawling with National Guard troops in camouflage and a few Homeland Security agents in their dark gray fatigues, but no one was watching the prisoner transport. The vehicle was parked and locked up; a secondary generator provided power to the back, so that the engine didn't have to idle to keep the lights and air conditioner running.

"Not really," Nathan said, quietly. Ben looked uncertain. "Don't fret now, boy. You act like you're supposed to be doing something and people just assume you're supposed to be doing it. I got the go-ahead from Delaney, we just need to be quick."

The door to access the prisoner compartment was on the side. Climbing up the metal steps, Nathan tried the key Delaney had given him on the door, smiling when it unlocked. "We're in," he said to Ben. "Come on."

Nathan and Ben removed their masks as they stepped inside and closed the door behind them. The interior of the prisoner transport was cramped. Just inside the door was a small monitoring area, with a swivel chair bolted to the floor and a few screens displaying the feed from internal and external security cameras. The door to the prison compartment was to the rear. A lever on the wall unlatched it, like a hatch on a ship. Nathan pushed the heavy metal door inward and locked it in its open position. Inside, crammed into four tiny holding cells, were the prisoners.

There were five of them in total, three men and two women. All were dirty and looked like they'd had a rough time. Three of them had bandaged injuries. As Delaney had said, they were secured in the cells and were all wearing ankle cuffs. The prisoners all seemed to be eying Nathan's bronze badge as he strode in, his boots thumping on the metal floor plating, revolver slung low on his right hip.

Nathan asked Ben to hand him the pictures of his two targets. He held them up so that all the prisoners could see. "I'm looking for these two," he said levelly. "Emmogene Anderson and Anthony Krieg. Their bodies were not found at the site. Were they there? Did they escape? Where did they go?"

None of the prisoners said anything. Nathan turned, still holding the pictures up, looking each one of them in the eye. "You're all looking at long prison sentences. If you're not an American citizen, you're looking at a long prison sentence then deportation to your native country. Some of you may even be sentenced to die. A lot of men died here today. You people embarrassed the United States Government. I have no doubt that they will pursue the maximum sentencing available. The only chance any of you have for leniency now is to cooperate." He pointed up to a camera mounted on the ceiling. "Everything you say and do is being recorded. This recording is admissible in court as evidence on your behalf. You can either tell me what I want to know," he said, looking around the room again, "or you can refuse to cooperate and face life in prison with hard labor, or the gallows. Your call."

Ben was watching Nathan as he put on this performance. The boy had never seen him do this before. It was time. He was old enough. He needed to know what he was getting into. "No takers?" Nathan asked. "Seriously? You're going to swing to protect people who abandoned you to get captured?" He forced an evil grin onto his face. "Hell, why not? Here you are, still fighting for the damned Greys, and they abandoned you, too. How'd that work out for you?"

There was still no response, but several of the prisoners shifted uneasily. *Good*, Nathan thought. *Let them sweat.* He held up the picture of Emmogene Anderson. "This woman is an American citizen. She was taken off of a prisoner transport against her will by Anthony Krieg. Her sentence was almost up. She was going to be a free woman, and this man Krieg abducted her. He's former Earth Storm. I know you all know what that means, what kind of man he is. I can't help but notice that the brave, enhanced commando turned tail and ran, left you all behind. You all willing to spend the next fifty years breaking rocks so he can be free to stalk this woman?"

That got the attention of one of the prisoners. She was a short black woman, late thirties, early forties. Her right arm was in a sling and her shoulder was bandaged. Nathan zeroed in on her. "Anthony Krieg had a run-in with the law over in New Mexico. See Emmogene, she tried to run. She doesn't want to go with him. His men killed two police officers and a family of three in a little town called Quemado. I can guaran-goddamn-tee you that the prosecution will try to saddle you with accessory charges to that." Nathan didn't know if that was actually possible, but he figured these people would be even less familiar with the legal system than he was. "I know all this because one of his own team, a woman, told me so. He's obsessed with her. They were assigned as a mating pair or some such horseshit. He wants to make her his woman and never let her go. You people still believe in your cause so hard that you're willing to abet that? You," he said, looking the black woman in the eye. "What's your name?"

"N-Nomusa," she said.

"Listen to me, Nomusa. You help me, you're not only helping Emmogene, you're helping yourself. You are going to be put on trial for your part in this. Cooperating with me can mean the difference between a few years in prison or spending the rest of your life there. Emmogene, she's a victim in all this. She was kidnapped. She's in danger. If you know anything, anything at all, I am begging you, do the right thing and tell me."

The woman called Nomusa hesitated for a moment. "She was here," she said at last.

"Be quiet!" one of the other prisoners, a middle-aged man in a tattered coverall, shouted.

"Shut your goddamn mouth," Nathan snarled, "or you're going to be standing trial without any teeth." He turned back to Nomusa. "What happened to her?"

The woman continued. "She... she didn' wan' go wit' Ant'ony Krieg. She told me so herself. She was his prisoner, had an ankle monitor an' everyting. He hit her. She had a big bruise on her face."

"What happened to her?" Nomusa didn't say anything. Nathan leaned in closer and pressed her. "What happened to Emmogene Anderson?"

"She's dead," the woman said, flatly, not looking at him. "He killed her."

"Is that a fact?" Nathan looked around at the other prisoners. A couple of them stared blankly at him, but none of them said anything. Ben was watching him, wide-eyed. "Why did he do that?"

"I don' know!" Nomusa insisted. "He was crazy! He t'ought he own her! She didn' want to go wit' him!"

"Where's the body, then? I need to ID her remains."

"Dey took her," the woman replied, looking down. "Dey took her body wit' dem, loaded it into one of deir trucks."

"Why would they do that?"

"I don' know dat, eidder!" Nomusa said, looking up at him. "Ant'ony Krieg is Faction, dey don't tell people like me why dey do what dey do."

Nathan looked around the room. "Can any of you confirm this? Is Emmogene Anderson dead?"

The middle-aged man, the one who had mouthed off before, spoke up again. "We don't have to tell you anything, Bronze."

"Is that right?" Nathan asked, turning toward him. He stepped close to the steel bars of the cage.

"I'm an American citizen," the man insisted, "and I know our rights. We don't have to tell you anything, and we have a right to an attorney."

"American citizen," Nathan repeated, looking down at his arm. Like the others, he had the Sagittarian identifying tattoo on his forearm. "For now."

"Yeah, well, I know you're not trying to help anyone. You're a bounty hunter. All you want is to get paid." He looked at his comrades. "You don't have to tell this man anything. Anything you say will be used against you. Just be quiet and wait until they give us lawyers."

Nathan leaned in close to the bars, his voice lowered. "It's kind of ironic, don't you think? You preaching about lawyers and rights I mean. You people didn't have lawyers under your precious United Earth Alliance. You didn't have any rights. Whatever the fucking Greys told you to do, you did. If anybody squawked about it, Internal Security hauled them off for . . . what did you people call it? Re-education?"

The man didn't say anything. He stared Nathan down, defiantly.

"Okay then," Nathan said, backing away. "You think about that when they're putting the noose around your neck, you fucking traitor." He looked at Ben, who had been dutifully taking notes. "Come on, boy, it's time to go." Before leaving, he turned back to Nomusa. "Thank you for the information," he said, politely. He pointed to the cameras. "I'm sure your lawyer will use this to your defense."

"Tank you," the woman said, distantly. Nathan nodded at her. He and Ben turned and left the prisoner holding cell, securing it behind them as they went. They masked up and exited the vehicle. Once outside, he locked the door to the prisoner transport vehicle behind him and dropped the key into the dirt nearby.

"What now?" Ben asked as they walked away. The boy seemed a little shook up, but was holding it together.

"I don't know," Nathan answered.

"You really think she's dead?"

Nathan shook his head. "No, I'm pretty confident she was lying. It don't matter much, though."

"What do you mean?"

"Right now the National Guard is trying to lock down Chandler, but this one MP company doesn't have the manpower to do that by themselves. By the time they do get the city cordoned off, everyone who fled from this hideout will be long gone. Maybe they'll roll up some of them later, maybe not, but they missed the critical window. Hell, it'll probably take them days just to search and clear the old sewer tunnels."

"But if Emmogene's still alive, they'll want us to keep looking for her, right?"

Nathan let out a muffled sigh through his mask filters. "I wouldn't bet on it. This whole operation has been a colossal screwup. A lot of people died and the people they were after got away. Delaney told me they're probably going to force him to retire, if they don't fire him outright. Everyone up and down the chain is looking to cover their own asses now, and I suspect they're going to try to hang this all on Delaney, especially since Frampton is dead. I wouldn't be surprised if they just try and bury the whole thing. Having testimony that she's dead will only bolster that argument."

"Really? What will we do then?"

"Nothing. We'll get on with our business. We signed nondisclosure agreements. If we try and talk about this publicly, we'll get sued and I'll lose my license. They have the power to ruin us."

"So that's it? We're just giving up?"

Nathan paused and looked at his nephew. "As your Grandpa Foster would have said, them's the breaks, Ben. Sometimes you eat the bear, sometimes the bear eats you. Nature of the beast. He had a lot of sayings like that. The point is, sometimes, even after a lot of work, you come up empty-handed. Anthony Krieg may be crazy but he's not stupid. There's too much heat on for him to keep being as brazen as he was. He'll probably go to ground, maybe even leave the country. No way of telling when he'll show up again."

"Well, crap," the boy said, dejectedly.

"Cheer up. We still get paid for our time, at least. If this had been a regular bounty, we wouldn't even get that. Besides, who knows? Maybe we'll get a lead later. You never know."

"Yeah, I guess you're right. Can we go home, then?"

"Yes, we can."

Eloy, Arizona
Three days later...

"HERE'S YOUR WATER, SWEETIE," the waitress said, "and your check. Can I get you anything else?"

Emmogene had drunk no fewer than three glasses of water with her small meal. She was still hungry, but she needed to ration the little bit of money she had. "No, thank you." She paused, then looked up at the waitress. "Is it alright if I stay here for a little while? I just...I just need time to think."

The waitress was a heavyset woman, probably in her late forties. Her nametag said JOAN. The concern on her face was obvious. "Sure. You take all the time you need. We're open twenty-four hours a day. I'll be back to check on you in a little while, okay?"

"Thank you," Emmogene said, weakly. She took a sip from her glass of water and tried to process everything that had happened in the past two days. She'd escaped Anthony, but where was she going to go? She didn't know anybody in Arizona. The government was still looking for her. She'd been walking for two days, trying to avoid the main roads, trying to avoid people, but she was no survivalist. She didn't know how to live off the land, especially not in the middle of the Sonoran Desert.

Three days on the run and she'd made it something like forty miles. The physiological boosters the Visitors had given her helped her endurance, but she still needed food, water, and rest. She'd spent the first day and night in an empty house in an abandoned, prewar subdivision, southeast of the old Phoenix metro area. Helicopters were circling the ruins of Chandler, Arizona, but she didn't know if they were looking for her, more Sagittarian Faction to shoot, or both.

In any case, they hadn't come as far southeast as she'd gone. She took a chance and decided to hide instead of continuing to run.

Even after darkness fell, she'd been so terrified that Anthony would find her that she only fell asleep when exhaustion overcame her paranoia. To her great surprise, she found a few unopened bottles of decade-old drinking water and a couple cans of beans. The next day, she followed a lonely highway through the desert, heading mostly south, hiding whenever a vehicle went by. If a helicopter had come looking for her, she probably wouldn't have been able to hide from it in that open terrain, but none did. That afternoon, she found an old barn on an abandoned farm outside a town called Coolidge. She spent the night there, daring to start a small fire to stay warm and to heat her last can of beans with.

After a fitful night's sleep in musty old hay, she continued south, staying far enough away from the road that she'd have time to hide if a vehicle passed. It had been slow going, and Emmogene didn't feel well. When she saw the truck stop in the distance, her first thought was to avoid it and keep going. It was too obvious. Rusty's Truck & Travel Plaza, the place was called, just outside Eloy off Interstate 10. Anthony's people and the government both were looking for her. Surely there would be police posted at places like this, in case she came by?

She knew she needed to stop and rest, though. She needed to refill her canteen and eat, too, and she didn't know when she'd get another chance. Emmogene had approached the truck stop cautiously, through the truck parking lot, looking for police. There had been well over a hundred trucks parked there, engines idling, drivers coming and going, but there was no sign of law enforcement and nobody paid her any mind. After half an hour of trying, Emmogene finally spun up the courage to go inside and get something to eat, grateful that her shirtsleeve hid the alien tattoo on her forearm.

The problem was, now what? She could buy a little food and water here, enough to get her by for another couple of days, but where would she go? How would she survive when the little bit of money she had ran out? She didn't know. She just didn't know. Maybe it would have been more merciful to just let Anthony kill her.

It was all so unfair. She hadn't asked for any of this. She'd been in prison, serving her sentence, paying for the crime of having chosen the wrong side of the war. She hadn't wanted to break out. She didn't want to be on the run. Now she was alone, with nowhere to go, no way to survive, and whether Anthony or the government found her first, she'd end up as somebody's science project. It was all too much. Despite her best efforts to keep her composure, tears welled up in her eyes. A lump formed in her throat. Sitting along in a booth at a truck stop restaurant, Emmogene held her head in her hands and cried.

She looked up, startled, when she felt a hand on her shoulder. Eyes wide, she turned her head to see who it was, certain that Anthony had found her. It was the waitress, Joan.

"You alright, sweetie?" Joan asked, her voice lowered so that only Emmogene could hear her.

"I'm fine," Emmogene lied. "I've just had a bad couple of days."

Joan clearly didn't believe her. "Hon, I've seen this sort of thing before. Girl comes in here, scared and alone, obviously upset, with a bruise on her face. What's his name?"

"What? Who?"

"The guy who hit you. The one you're running from. What's his name?"

"Anthony," Emmogene admitted. It was so weird to be talking to a stranger like a normal person. She knew she shouldn't, she knew that interacting with people would only lead to her being caught, but she couldn't help herself. She needed this. "His name is Anthony, and he's a psycho."

Joan sat down across from Emmogene. "Do you want me to call somebody? Do you have any family, a safe place you can go?"

Emmogene shook her head. "N-no. I don't have any . . . any family. I don't know where I'm going to go. I-I slept in a barn last night."

"Jesus," Joan swore. "Okay. Listen, I know someone that might be able to help you. He's a friend of mine, and he has a place you can go."

"I couldn't," Emmogene said. "It's not safe. Anthony is . . . is . . . he's dangerous. Violent. He has people looking for me. I can't get anyone else involved."

Joan put her hand on top of Emmogene's. "Honey, helping people like you is what he does. He runs a rescue mission for people with nowhere to go. It's a safe place. You'll be protected."

"I'm sorry. I couldn't. I . . . it's complicated." Joan seemed nice. She seemed sincere, but Emmogene didn't know if she could trust her.

This whole thing could be a setup to sell her into prostitution or something. "I don't know."

Joan smiled. "Tell you what. Don't worry about the bill for your meal. Let me call my friend, and I'll bring you a piece of pie while you wait. Hear him out, and then you can decide if you want to go with him or not. Nobody is going to force you to do something you don't want to do."

Tears rolled down Emmogene's cheeks. "Why are you doing this? You don't even know me."

Joan squeezed her hand. "Twenty years ago, before the war, I was in the same place you are. I stayed with a guy who would beat me because I thought my only other option was to live on the street. I was messed up, addicted to drugs, trying to stay high to cope with my life. The Good Lord saw me through, though, and my heart tells me to pay it forward when I can. I know asking you to trust me is asking a lot. I understand if you want to say no, and if you do, I'll leave you be. But, honey, I'm begging you, let me call my friend. Hear him out. Maybe he can help you. What do you say?"

Emmogene wiped the tears from her eyes with her napkin. "Okay." There was always the chance that this was an elaborate setup, but it didn't feel like it. She'd been on the run for all of three days and she was exhausted. She wasn't going to make it on her own. Maybe this was the lucky break she desperately needed.

Joan smiled. "You won't regret it, hon. Stay here. I'll go call him, then come back with your pie. You want apple or cherry?"

HAVING FINISHED HER PIE, Emmogene sipped her water and listened, quietly, as Joan's friends introduced themselves to her. They were a married couple, probably in their forties, and they seemed earnest enough.

The man, fair-skinned and with dark blond hair, introduced himself, shaking Emmogene's hand as he sat down. "Thank you for agreeing to meet us," he said, "and I apologize for taking so long to get here. I'm Pastor David Hart. This is my wife, Maria. We represent the Second Chance Rescue Mission outside of Gila Bend. Joan called me and said that you're in trouble. I hope that we are able to help."

"My name is Arlene," she said. She hated to lie to him, but it was necessary.

"It's nice to meet you, Arlene," the pastor said, warmly. He paused, seemingly studying her face (or maybe the bruises on it). "Can you tell us what's going on?"

Emmogene hesitated. She desperately wanted this to be real. She wanted to be able to tell somebody, anybody, about what had happened to her, but she didn't know if she could trust anyone. "I have nowhere to go. People are looking for me, dangerous people."

"Who are these people?" the pastor's wife asked. She had a notable Spanish accent, as if English were a second language for her.

"A-Anthony. His name is Anthony. He is... was... a soldier. He found me. I don't know how but he found me. I hadn't seen him or heard from him in years, and then he just showed up. He took me."

The pastor raised his eyebrows. "Took you?"

"Kidnapped me, I guess," Emmogene said, matter-of-factly. "I tried to run a couple of times but he always found me. If anyone tried to help me he would hurt them."

"My God. Do you need us to contact the police? You said he's a soldier. We can report him to his chain of command."

"No! No, please, no police."

The pastor's wife leaned in a little. "My dear, are you in some kind of trouble?"

"Yes," Emmogene said, tears welling up in her eyes. "I'm in a lot of trouble."

"Can you tell us about it?" the pastor asked, softly.

"Some. There's a lot I'm not... I guess I'm not ready yet."

"And that's okay," Maria said. "We're not here to interrogate you. What about this Anthony? Is he still in the military now? Is he stationed in Arizona?"

"No. No, he isn't, not anymore. Also..." Emmogene hesitated. She didn't want to tell these people who she was or what she had done. They seemed so kind that she didn't want to disappoint them by revealing which side she had been on during the war. She had to, though. It wouldn't be right to lie, and sooner or later someone would see her tattoo. She rolled up her sleeve, revealing the long string of alien script on her forearm. "He wasn't in the US military. And... and I don't think calling the police would help."

"Oh," the pastor said. "Oh, I see." He was quiet for a few moments. Emmogene's heart was racing. She couldn't read his face, couldn't determine what he was thinking, but she was certain that he was politely trying to hide the contempt he now felt for her. He took a deep breath. "Arlene, Christ commanded us to help the poor. He didn't say, 'except for people who made bad choices.' We don't run background checks on our guests. Many of them were homeless and don't have any identification anyway. We also have a few who were with the UEA during the war, but the war has been over for years. We try to help people move on, better themselves, not punish them for the past."

Emmogene didn't say anything.

"You should know that occasionally deputies from the Maricopa County Sheriff's Office will stop by to see how we're doing. They don't come onto the property and look for people, unless they have a warrant, but we do have a good relationship with local law enforcement. It's necessary, given how many of our guests are in situations like yours, with people who might hurt them if they were found. We have armed security for the same reason."

"What about, you know, recovery agents?"

The pastor's smiled faded some. "Bounty hunters aren't allowed on our property at all. We've had some come through insisting that we were harboring a fugitive, even offering to pay us, but we don't deal with them. Now, if the police show up with an arrest warrant, we are legally obligated to cooperate, but enforcing the law is their business, not ours. We don't discriminate based on immigration, citizenship, or other legal statuses so long as you abide by the rules."

Emmogene felt hopeful for the first time that she could remember. Could this really be happening? There had to be a catch. "What are the rules?"

"Our facility is a working farm," Maria said. "We raise livestock and some crops, allowing us to be self-sufficient."

"Farming is hard work," the pastor said. "We ask that all of our guests pitch in as they are able."

"I don't know anything about farming," Emmogene admitted.

"That's okay, we'll teach you, if you choose to stay with us. There are ways for everyone to help, and we try to be as fair as possible with the work assignments. If there's something you're uncomfortable doing, or are unable to do for whatever reason, you can talk to us, and we'll find other ways you can contribute."

"We also ask that our guests refrain from using drugs and alcohol while they're staying on the property," Maria added.

"I don't do any drugs," Emmogene said. "I don't even drink, not really."

"Great!" the pastor said. "Some of our guests are recovering from addiction, and it's better for everyone if these things are left at the door."

"I understand," Emmogene said. "What else?"

The pastor smiled, warmly. "Those are the big ones. The rest we'll go over in orientation if you choose to stay with us. It's nothing too draconian. Our guests aren't prisoners and we don't treat them as such."

"I can . . . I mean, you'll give me a place to go? You'll have space for me?"

"Of course! I'm going to be honest with you, the work requirements and the no drugs or alcohol policy make a difference. We can only help those who are willing to help themselves, and farming is hard work. We're rarely full."

"So I can . . . I can just go with you? Right now?"

"Right now," Maria repeated. "You'll have three square meals and a roof over your head. We have church services on Sunday morning if you wish to join us, but it's not required. We mainly ask that everyone do their best, share the work, and be respectful of others."

"You're free if you decide it's not for you," the pastor added. "There are no contracts that require you to stay for a certain length of time, nothing like that."

Part of Emmogene had trouble accepting that this was real. It seemed too convenient, this smiling couple appearing by chance and offering her a place to go. She had doubts. Yet, in spite of them, she realized that she wasn't likely to get another chance like this. "Okay," she said, quietly.

"So you'll join us?" the pastor asked.

"Yes." Emmogene was fighting back tears now. "Thank you. Thank you."

Maria clasped Emmogene's hand. "Wonderful! You'll be glad you did."

Federal Recovery Office
Prescott, Arizona

"CARE FOR A DRINK?"

Nathan looked up from his computer. Stella was standing in the doorway that led from the break room to the main office. She had a bottle in one hand and two red plastic cups in the other. She looked good, he thought. Her hair was down, auburn curls hanging carelessly over her shoulders. She'd undone the top button of her blouse.

Nathan rubbed his eyes. "Don't we usually save the celebration for when we actually recover the fugitive?"

Stella sauntered over and set the bottle down on her desk. She set the cups down next and began to pour. "Usually, yeah, but you know what? This one was a nightmare and it's done. That's worth celebrating."

Nathan looked back down at his computer screen. He was working on a detailed report for Homeland Security. Stella had been busy going through receipts and making sure the financials were squared away. The paperwork was tedious, but if it every *I* wasn't dotted and every *T* wasn't crossed, it would only delay their getting paid. He'd dropped Ben and Shadow off at home hours before. "What the hell, why not?" he said, pushing back from his desk. "It's Friday anyway. Even if we sent this crap off tonight nobody would read it until Monday."

"It's settled, then," she said, setting a cup down in front of him. "Drink!" The partners clicked the plastic cups together in a toast before drinking.

The liquor went down smooth but was stronger than Nathan expected. "Damn! What is this?"

"Too much for you?" Stella asked, before taking another long sip. "I'll have you know this is premium West Virginia White Lightning, Boone County's finest. My family back home sends me a bottle now and again."

"Don't they sell moonshine in liquor stores now?"

"Oh sure, you can get *moonshine* in any liquor store, even in Arizona." She made air quotes as she said "moonshine." "If you want *real* West Virginia 'Shine, though, you gotta go to the source."

Nathan chuckled. Her Southern accent was always more pronounced when she'd had a few drinks. "This ain't your first cup tonight, is it? I wondered where you got off to."

Stella leaned on Nathan's desk. "Yeah, I'm a little drunk. It's been a long time. This job has been long, and it was all for nothing."

"We *are* getting paid for our time."

"Yeah, but that's time you could have spent tracking down a proper bounty, and we could have made a hell of a lot more than we did."

"True enough," Nathan agreed. "Where do we go from here?"

"I've got some leads I can follow up on. Nothing immediate, though."

"That's okay. I wouldn't mind some downtime after that shit-show in Chandler." Nathan looked up at his partner. "It was like being back in the war. Brought back a lot of bad memories, like the stench of a burning vehicle and the screams of the wounded. I helped pull one kid out of that Ruffner, the driver, and his legs were gone. Christ Almighty, I was hoping I'd never see that kind of thing again."

"I was so worried about you," Stella admitted. "I'm glad you're home now. I missed having you boys around." She paused, taking another sip of her moonshine. "I missed you."

Nathan took another sip of his drink, too. The 'shine was strong, and he wasn't much of a drinker anymore. He looked back at his computer. He saved his work on the report and closed the program. "That's enough of that."

"Hear hear," his partner said. "We spend half our lives staring at screens these days. I do, anyway. I've had enough of it for one night."

"I don't think either one of us are going to be in any shape to drive."

Stella lifted her cup and knocked back the remainder of her drink. "That's okay," she said, setting the empty cup down. To Nathan's surprise, she moved over to him and sat on his lap, throwing her arms around his neck. "I don't mind spending the night here with you."

Nathan carefully set his own cup down, while Stella, smiling, stared into his eyes. "You sure about this?" They'd kind of flirted now and again, but he didn't seriously think that she was interested in him like that.

"Shut up and kiss me."

"Yes, ma'am."

Gila Bend, Arizona
Six months later . . .

"COME AND GET IT, LADIES," Emmogene said, absentmindedly, as she was mobbed by hungry chickens. She held a metal bucket full of feed in one hand and used a plastic scoop to spread it around for the hens with the other. The Second Chance Rescue Mission farm had hundreds of chickens, some for meat, some for eggs, and Emmogene had learned the ins and outs of taking care of them.

Maria had been right; farm life was hard work. The Rescue Mission didn't have a lot of the automated implements of modern farming, so there was always plenty of work for everyone to do. Animals needed to be fed and cared for, eggs needed to be collected and stored, cows needed milking, fences needed mending, crops needed watering, on and on, every day. It was repetitive and tiresome.

Even still, Emmogene didn't recall ever feeling this free. It was ironic, she thought, because while she certainly wasn't a prisoner she really didn't have anywhere else to go. Yet, there was something refreshing about working the land. She felt like a frontierswoman in the Old West sometimes. The work was difficult, at times, but there was something satisfying about taking care of animals and the smell of freshly tilled earth. The nightmares were much less frequent now, and she had been sleeping more peacefully than she could ever recall.

The hard work had been good for her physique, too. When she had arrived at the ranch she'd been skinny, almost twiggy, and looked frail. Six months later, he was fit, healthy, even toned. She had to admit that she looked good, even with her usual attire of denim overalls, boots, a wide-brimmed sun hat, and a generous slathering of sun block.

She almost always wore long-sleeved shirts, too, not only to protect her fair skin from the harsh Arizona sun, but to hide the alien identifying marker on her arm. It wasn't so much that she was trying to keep it a secret from her fellow farmhands; she suspected most of them had seen it by now, and Pastor Hart had been right: there were a few guests at the Mission who bore a similar marking. No, Emmogene felt *ashamed* of the organic tattoo, ashamed that she had ever gotten involved with the Visitors in the first place.

The frustrating thing was, even after all this time, she still couldn't remember much about her past. Bits and pieces had come back to her from time to time, but everything between her early teen years and when she received the mind-wipe was still foggy. She hadn't had any more episodes from the device in her head, but she hadn't tried to use it, either. She preferred to not think about it, even if it had saved her life.

Her walkie-talkie crackled to life, interrupting her thoughts. "Arlene, this is Helen, are you there?" Helen was one of the Mission's work supervisors. She was a stout woman in her fifties, kind, funny, and possessed of a wicked sense of humor, but she was tough when she needed to be.

Emmogene sprinkled one last handful of chicken scratch and answered. "This is Arlene."

"Honey, this week's poultry feed delivery is here early. Can you swing by the front and pick it up?"

Emmogene hesitated. She normally avoided meeting strangers as a matter of course. She'd only been into town a couple times since arriving at the Rescue Mission. Still, it had been months. What were the odds that this was some kind of trick by Anthony? In any case she didn't want Helen to think she was trying to get out of work. "Yeah, no problem. I'll be right over there."

"Take the side-by-side. The keys are in it. They should have gotten the trailer emptied by now."

"Okay, I'm on it."

Emmogene found the side-by-side, a two-seat, diesel-powered off-road vehicle with a small trailer, parked by the big equipment shed. As Helen had said, the keys were in it and the trailer had been emptied. She started the vehicle up and puttered across the farm, following the gravel road that led to the main entrance. She went slowly, both to be cautious and to avoid kicking up too much dust. It was only spring but it was already hot and dry in southern Arizona. Only extensive irrigation works made this land suitable for farming.

A large pickup truck was waiting for her by the main entrance. A magnetic placard on the door read HARRISON BROS. HANDYMAN SERVICE. Under that, it advertised deliveries, repairs, towing, fencing, electrical, light mechanical, and roofing services. A man greeted her as she pulled to a stop in the side-by-side.

"Good morning," the man said. He stuck out a hand to Emmogene. "Dan Harrison." He was African American, a tall, muscular man with broad shoulders. He looked very much like a cowboy, from his jeans and boots to his wide-brimmed hat, to the leather gunbelt around his waist. Brass cartridges gleamed from loops on the belt, and a large revolver hung from his right hip.

"Arlene," Emmogene answered, shaking his hand. "Nice to meet you. What have you got for us today?"

"Feed for chickens and turkeys," Dan said, leading her to the back of his truck. He opened the tailgate. "Reggie! Let's get the lady loaded up!" The man he had called to was coming out of the Mission's small front office building, where the admin people signed for deliveries and such. Stepping around the truck, Emmogene got a good look at the man. In contrast to Dan, Reggie was shorter than Emmogene, albeit still muscular. His skin was fair and his face freckled. Red hair poked out from under a faded Arizona Diamondbacks baseball cap.

"That's my brother, Reggie," Dan explained. Emmogene looked up at him, then back over at the other man. A wide grin split Dan's face. "We're both adopted."

"Hi there," the short, red-haired man said as he approached. "You've got a dozen bags of feed, fifty pounds each." He opened the truck's tailgate and picked up one of the bags. "We'll get you loaded up in no time."

"I can help," Emmogene said. She reached into the bed of the truck, grasped a bag of feed herself, and pulled it to the edge of the tailgate. She hoisted the heavy bag up onto her shoulder and, holding it with only one hand, turned toward her little trailer.

Reggie Harrison looked surprised. Dan Harrison chuckled. "I see that," he said, still smiling.

As Emmogene was laying the sack of feed in the trailer, a gust of dry wind blew her hat off and got dust in her eye. She jogged off to retrieve her hat before it drifted away, trying to blink the dust out of her stinging eyes. A few moments later, she returned to the side-by-side, hat tucked under her arm. She had taken her sunglasses off and was gently rubbing her eyes.

"You okay, miss?" Dan asked.

"Oh yeah, I'm fine," she answered. "Just some dirt in my eye."

"We've got your order loaded into your trailer," Reggie said, closing the tailgate of the truck. He paused, glancing at her as if seeing her for the first time. "It was nice meeting you."

"It was nice meeting you, too," Emmogene said, smiling for the young man. With that, the Harrison Brothers climbed back in their truck and drove off in a cloud of dust, leaving her alone. Reggie's overlong glance gave her some pause. She had been noticing that the men at the Rescue Mission were stealing glances at her more often these days, too. This had made her uncomfortable at first, very uncomfortable. After everything she'd been through with Anthony, that kind of attention from men made her uneasy. Despite the occasional glance, though, no one made any advances on her, and everyone at the Mission was respectful. Eventually, Emmogene had been forced to admit that guys were noticing her because she was *pretty*, and that was taking some getting used to.

As she started up the side-by-side, Emmogene glanced at her watch. She needed to get this feed dropped off, then get cleaned up. She had about an hour until her biweekly counseling session and she didn't want to be late.

"ARLENE, IT'S GOOD TO SEE YOU."

"Good morning, Dr. Katz," Emmogene said as she entered the room. A balding man in his forties, Dr. Katz was a professional therapist who came to the Rescue Mission twice a month. He always seemed to be wearing the same pale yellow dress shirt and red tie. He was an affable man, easy to talk to and never overbearing.

"How have you been since our last session?"

"I'm doing well," Emmogene said, and that was the truth. She hadn't really wanted to speak with a counsellor, of course, but Pastor Hart had insisted. Dr. Katz, he had explained, volunteered to help people at the Mission, and he encouraged her to visit him. She'd been hesitant, especially at first, and even now she was careful about what she told him. She made no mention of the device in her head nor the alien egg she carried, but it felt good to be able to talk to someone about her past, even if she had to leave out some important details. "Things are going same as ever, I guess."

"I see. Anything on your mind? Have you been able to remember anything new since our last session?"

Emmogene was quiet for a few seconds. "Earlier this morning, I was picking up a grain delivery at the front gate. One of the deliverymen was looking at me."

"Oh? Did it make you uncomfortable?"

"It did, at first, but I don't think he was being creepy or anything. It was just a glance."

"Why do you think you're uncomfortable, then?"

"I'm not used to people noticing me like that, I guess. I'm used to trying to avoid being noticed, to always looking over my shoulder."

"I'm sure that was a survival tactic in prison."

"It was. Getting noticed was almost always a bad thing," she said. Memories of the woman gouging her own eye out with a shiv flashed into Emmogene's mind, and she winced.

"Something's bothering you," Dr. Katz said. "Did we touch upon a bad memory? Can you share?"

"I got . . . noticed . . . when I was in prison, once. By . . . by a gang. I thought they were going to kill me. I saw . . . I saw one prisoner get stabbed to death, get a screwdriver shoved right through her eye all the way to the handle. I've seen . . . other things . . . too. When I was with Anthony, I wasn't allowed to talk to anyone or go anywhere without him. He would hurt people, and worse." Emmogene realized that she was shaking.

Dr. Katz's calm, soothing demeanor didn't change. "You've mentioned this before, on the violence you were exposed to in prison and after. The story about the woman who was murdered was the most specific you've been. That you're able to talk about it is progress."

"I still don't want to, you know, get into a lot of the details. It's . . . I'm sorry, it's complicated."

"Is it an issue of trusting me?" Dr. Katz asked, pointedly, but not accusingly. "You know that our sessions are one hundred percent confidential. The only circumstance in which I would ever speak with outside authorities would be if I thought someone was in immediate or ongoing danger."

"I know. It's not that." It actually *was* that. Emmogene didn't want to put him in a position of being somehow legally obligated to report her. "I'm just . . . not ready to talk about all of this yet. I'm sorry."

"Don't be sorry, Arlene. That we're discussing this at all is progress. You've come a long way from our first session. I don't want you to feel like you have to tell me everything. This is therapy, not an interrogation. The important thing is that you are able to work through the things that are bothering you, and from what I can see, you're getting there. So, you were saying that you're not used to being noticed."

"Oh, right. I'm used to creeping around like a shy little mouse," Emmogene said, hunching down as if she were sneaking. "Now? I don't really, you know, have a lot of friends here, but I usually feel comfortable around everyone. Lately, people have been noticing me more, especially the men."

"I see. Well, Arlene, you *are* an attractive woman. It's only natural that this would get you some attention. You also seem a lot healthier than you did when we first started having these sessions."

"I am. I've gained weight, but it's good weight. I'm more fit now, and I feel a lot better."

"The Visitors would have given you a series of immuno-, caridio-, and metabolic boosters," Dr. Katz explained. "This is done in several iterations over the course of about eighteen months. Someone who has gotten the complete battery will see a lot of benefit from even modest amounts of exercise, and you certainly get enough exercise around here. It seems to me that you understand that this attention from the opposite sex is because you're attractive, but maybe you have a hard time internalizing that."

"I do," Emmogene admitted. "I still see myself as the skinny, timid girl, terrified that getting noticed will end in violence. When I look in the mirror, though, that's not what I see. I see a woman who is strong and healthy and pretty."

"The mirror is telling the truth," Dr. Katz said.

"Even still. I don't know that I'm ready for, you know, intimacy. Dating. Whatever."

"And that's okay! You are not obligated to do any of those things, Arlene. While being in a happy, healthy relationship is an overall positive for a person's emotional well-being, relationships are less likely to be happy and healthy if you're not in the right place for them. The hook-up culture can be even worse, psychologically, for women and men alike."

Emmogene's face flushed a little. "I don't sleep around."

Dr. Katz raised a hand apologetically. "I didn't mean to imply that you did, and I didn't mean it as a moral judgment. My point was, you shouldn't feel obligated or rushed to do any of these things. Dating, intimacy, all of that can wait until you're ready. It's okay to enjoy being noticed by people, and enjoying it doesn't obligate you to go any further than that. Move at your own pace."

"It's funny, you know," Emmogene said. "I used to be something of a star."

"Oh?"

"I mean, apparently. When I was with the . . . other side . . . I appeared in some propaganda videos, talking about how great living under the Visitors was. I didn't used to be so shy, it seems."

"I see. Have you regained any memories of this time?"

"Some. I had this stupid catchphrase I'd say in every video: My name is—" Emmogene paused. She had very nearly slipped and used her real name. If Dr. Katz noticed he didn't say anything. "My name is Arlene," she continued, "and together, we're building a better world. It was all bullshit. Even before I started regaining memories, though, I knew about that. It came up in my trial. It's one of the reasons I was convicted of aiding and abetting the enemy. My lawyer couldn't establish that my participation was coerced and, because of the documented effects of the mind-wipe, I couldn't even testify on my own behalf."

"Yes, the mind-wipe," Dr. Katz repeated. "You know, I've been reading up on this since we started having these sessions. It's a dreadful thing, absolutely unethical. There can also be many lasting side effects, including brain damage, in some cases. All things considered, you were lucky."

Emmogene wasn't lucky. They had been more careful with her, but Dr. Katz didn't need to know why. "Yeah. Anyway, I looked up the videos online, watched them all. It was bizarre. It's like, I know that's me talking, but I have almost no memory of any of it. I don't remember doing it and I'm ashamed of it."

"We all have to face up to our pasts. In your case, though, I think you should give yourself the benefit of the doubt. The Sagittarians didn't perform that procedure on just anyone. They only did it to a select few. The theory is, the procedure was meant to erase evidence of deep psychological conditioning or manipulation. I don't know that you were as willing a participant as those videos may have made it seem."

"Why would they cover it up? That stuff isn't a secret."

"That they did it isn't a secret, no, but how they did it has not yet been established. The Greys were very careful to not let that capability fall into human hands. But, that's not even really the point. The past is the past, regardless of why you did what you did. I've interviewed plenty of ex-UEA who had served their sentences and were struggling to reintegrate into society. They are all victims in a way, even if that doesn't absolve them of the choices they made. We are, all of us, the sum of our pasts, the good and the bad. It's important that you understand that having made bad choices in the past doesn't mean you deserve to be miserable now."

Emmogene didn't say anything. She was too busy trying to hold back tears.

"A lot of my ex-UEA patients struggle with this concept. Admittedly, I don't see many true believers who think the Greys are going to return for them someday. I mostly see people who have faced the consequences of their actions and are just trying to move on with their lives. I see a lot of guilt and self-loathing. It perpetuates a cycle of misery that often leads to substance abuse and further bad choices. The first step to avoiding this cycle is to tell yourself that, regardless of what you did before, it's okay for you to be happy now."

"I never thought anyone would tell me that," Emmogene said, with a sniffle. "Until I got here, everyone treated me with contempt. The guards hated us all. All of us inmates hated ourselves and each other. The only one who didn't hate me was Anthony, but . . . his love wasn't any better."

"That wasn't love, Arlene, no matter how much he may have insisted it was. He may even believe it's love, but it's not, it's obsession. It's the unhealthy infatuation of someone who is used to having power and being feared." Dr. Katz knew that Anthony had been Earth Storm. Emmogene had told him of his deteriorating emotional state.

"He's still out there," she said, quietly. "I'm always afraid that one day he'll show up here. I think that's the other reason being noticed bothers me so much. It reminds me of him. Or, worse, on some level I worry that the person noticing me will tell him that I'm here and that he'll find me."

"I understand, and I wish that I could tell you that your fears are completely unfounded. That's why Pastor Hart wanted me to remind you that you're welcome to stay here as long as you like. Normally, after six months or so, the Rescue Mission tries to help its guests find jobs and their own living accommodations, to move on from being destitute. Those options are still available to you, of course, but you're free to move at your own pace. I will say, though, that it's highly unlikely the deliveryman is an informant for ex-UEA fanatics."

Emmogene smiled. "I know that up here," she said, pointing at her head, "but in my gut I worry."

West Salt Lake City, Utah

UTAH HAD CHANGED, Nathan thought, and not necessarily for the better. With the destruction of Phoenix and several major cities on the west coast, the Salt Lake City area had seen a huge influx of people and capital, much like Denver had before the war. The population of Utah had exploded as over a million people, fleeing the war in California, resettled there. The Greater Salt Lake Metro Area, newly unified and taking up almost the entirety of Salt Lake County, had replaced San Francisco as America's tech hub. The Wasatch Front had been informally dubbed "the New Silicon Valley."

It wasn't all tech sector, finance, and the Mormon Church, however. Systemic poverty plagued many of those who had been resettled there during and after the war, with countless people having been put in hastily built public housing projects. With poverty came desperation, drugs, and crime. Even eight years after the war, some parts of the Salt Lake Valley were sketchy at the best of times. At the worst of times? Nathan recalled news of a street war between Tongan and Mexican gangs that had killed dozens, ending mostly because both sides had lost too many members to continue the fight.

And here I am, Nathan thought, looking over at Ben, *taking a fifteen-year-old into the middle of this*. He shook his head as he put the truck in park.

"This is the place," Ben said, looking up from the GPS at the trio of imposing, Brutalist apartment buildings in front of them. "Sunset Towers. It was originally built during the war as a public housing project, now it's run by a real estate conglomerate out of Las Vegas. Three buildings, ten floors each."

"Good," Nathan said, pleased with the boy's research. "Where are we headed?"

"We're looking for Apartment A-612 on the sixth floor of the north tower."

"What else?"

"That apartment is currently leased to Melissa Kent."

"And who's she?"

"She's the sister of our fugitive, Wallace Kent." He thumbed through his notebook. "Stella did a records search on her. She works in the office of an auto shop in the city and has a son in the third grade."

"Good job, Ben. When you're trying to find somebody, you need to figure out where they might go when they can't go home. In most cases, they'll shack up with a friend or a family member. That's why we do so much research on the family or associates of the people we're looking for."

"Stella is, like, scary good at cyber-stalking."

"That she is, boy, that she is. You listen to her, you'll get pretty good at it, too. Now listen, I'm going to go bang on her door, see if anybody's home."

"I know, I know," Ben said, "wait in the truck."

Nathan shook his head. "Not this time. You're coming up with me."

"What? Really?"

"Really. Leave the truck running, though. We're leaving Shadow here."

"How come?"

"Pets aren't allowed in this place and having a dog will draw attention. He might have friends watching the parking lot and I don't want to risk tipping anybody off."

"What if he's not there?"

"Then we get to wait and watch, see if we catch him coming or going. Now come on."

Ben paused to open the back door of the truck. He retrieved the net launcher that Jesse had given them and slung it over his shoulder. He'd gotten pretty good with it, practicing catching crows in midair from the roof of the office.

"You're bringing that thing again?"

"Sooner or later I'm going to get to use it," Ben declared. "You'll see."

"Okay then," Nathan said with a chuckle, "let's go." He closed the truck door behind him and headed across the parking lot with Ben. He was dressed to blend in, wearing clothes he'd picked up from a local thrift store: worn jeans, a T-shirt for some band called Sloshy, and a baseball cap. He wore an untucked button-down shirt over the T-shirt, allowing him to conceal his .41 Magnum snubby, handcuffs, and a pepper foam dispenser on his belt. The cap and his sunglasses would make him harder for people to recognize. He'd let his stubble grow out for over a week, too. He didn't stand out and, most importantly, he didn't look like a cop. Cops never bring kids with them to do an arrest. The boy might draw an eye or two carrying the net launcher, but it looked innocuous enough slung over his shoulder. Nobody would know what it is.

Ben was also carrying his Canadian .38 break-top, concealed on his belt under his shirt. Nathan had been ensuring the boy practiced regularly with the revolver. He'd gotten proficient enough that Nathan was comfortable letting him carry it when they were out on a job. It may not have been technically legal for a minor to carry a concealed handgun, at least not in the State of Utah, but there were few places that enforced such regulations anymore.

The apartment tower wasn't any more pleasant on the inside than it had been on the outside. The walls were painted cinder block, the interior hallways covered in an old, stained, green carpet. Fluorescent lights buzzed overhead, but many of them were burnt out, giving the interior a dank, gloomy feel.

"This place smells funny," Ben noted, quietly. There were two elevators in the lobby, but only one of them worked. They took it up to the sixth floor and headed for apartment A-612. Somebody was definitely home—music was playing inside the apartment and he could smell food cooking.

Nathan knocked on the door. It took a few moments, but a woman opened the door a crack. She had long brown hair and matched the photographs of the fugitive's sister. The chain lock was still latched. "Who are you?" she asked, suspiciously.

Nathan looked down at her. "Melissa Kent?"

"Who's asking?"

"Nobody asks *who's asking* if you're at the wrong door, ma'am." He held up his bronze badge. "I'm a Federal Recovery Agent. I'm looking for your brother, Wallace Kent."

The woman's eyes went wide. "He's not . . . I don't have to talk to you!" She moved to push the door closed, but Nathan had already stuck a steel-toed boot in the way.

"Hold on a second, will you? I just want to ask you if you've seen him."

"Go away or I'll call the police!" she said.

Nathan smiled humorlessly. "I think we both know you don't want the police here. Your brother has a federal warrant out for his arrest: money laundering and wire fraud. It's only a matter of time before the law catches up to him. The only difference, in the end, will be whether or not you get charged with knowingly harboring a fugitive from justice. That's illegal in Utah. Best-case scenario, you get charged with a Class-A misdemeanor and CPS takes your son away. Worst case, they slap you with a third-degree felony and you do time in the state prison, too."

"You can't stand here and threaten me! Wally's not here! I haven't seen him!"

"I'm not threatening you, I'm just explaining the reality of the situation. Now listen to me very carefully." As he spoke, Nathan reached into his pocket and retrieved a money clip. "This is seven hundred dollars in cash. You unlatch that chain for me, I hand this to you and you can go take a walk, check the mail, or whatever. When you get back, I'll be gone, and that's the last you'll see of me."

This gave the woman pause. She looked back into her apartment, as if to make sure no one was listening. "What? You'll just give it to me? Bullshit."

"No bullshit," Nathan replied. He took the billfold out of the clip and held it up so she could see the hundred-dollar bills. "Free money, no strings attached. You just let me in to have a look around real quick and that's it." Melissa Kent looked like she was mulling it over.

A man's voice could be heard from inside the apartment. "Is someone at the door?"

Nathan lowered his voice and leaned in. "You know, before they busted him, your brother was doing alright for himself. Laundering money for criminals paid well. He had a big house in Florida and drove a prewar Italian sports car. He ever send any of that your way? Seems like he left you out in the cold while he was living high on the hog. Let me guess, though . . . as soon as he was in trouble, needed a place to stay, he shows up and tries to play the *but we're family* card. Am I right?"

"Melissa?" the voice asked again. "What's going on?"

The woman looked down at the money and frowned. She quickly undid the chain lock, opened the door, and stepped into the hallway. "He's in my bedroom." She took the cash out of Nathan's hand and started down the hall at a brisk pace.

"Melissa, you fucking bitch!" the man shouted from inside the apartment.

Nathan paused to nod at Ben, drew his pepper foam dispenser, and headed inside. "Recovery Agent!" he declared. "Wallace Kent, I'm taking you into custody!" He pressed through the kitchen, pepper foam held at the read in his left hand, his right hand on the butt of his holstered gun. He paused in the living room. There were two bedrooms in the apartment, one to his left and another to his right. The shouting sounded like it had come from the one on the right. "Come out! Come quietly and this will be easier on you." There was no response. The door to the bedroom was partially open, but Nathan couldn't see very much from his angle. He approached, cautiously, calm despite his racing heart, and pushed the door the rest of the way open.

Wallace Kent was waiting for him with a baseball bat. He swung wildly at Nathan as the bounty hunter dodged, backing out of the bedroom, trying not to get bashed in the head. Kent swung again, smacking Nathan's hand with the very tip of his bat. The foam dispenser went flying across the room, leaving Nathan with an empty, stinging hand.

The wanted man saw an opening and bolted for the door. He still had the bat in his hands. "Ben!" Nathan shouted. "Weapon!" He got back to his feet and ran for the door, only to hear a loud *boom* before he crossed the threshold. He stepped into the hallway to see the fugitive on the floor, ensnared in a net, thrashing like a wild animal. Ben was farther down the hall, wide-eyed, breathing heavily. He had dropped to a knee to fire the net launcher and still had it aimed over his right shoulder. He looked like one of the little plastic army men that had the bazooka. A cloud of smoke hung in the air.

"You alright, boy?" Nathan asked. His revolver was extended in his hands, pointed down at Wallace Kent. The fugitive was down and struggling.

"I'm good," Ben answered. He stood up slowly, lowering the net launcher. "I heard you call me and I just, like, reacted. You said *weapon* and I got ready."

"You did good," Nathan said. He reached down and was able to yank the bat out of the net and away from the fugitive. "This asshole tried to whack me with this thing."

By this time, other residents were peering out of their apartments, curious at the commotion and what must have sounded like a gunshot. Curious, Nathan noted, but not overly concerned. He suspected that such incidents happened semi-regularly at the Sunset Towers Apartments. He held up his badge and raised his voice. "I'm a Federal Recovery Agent on official business. The situation is under control."

"This guy is kidnapping me!" Wallace Kent screamed. He was breathing hard and sweating from his futile struggle. He was hopelessly tangled in the net, and it was starting to dig into his skin. "Get me out of this thing! Help!"

"Please return to your apartments," Nathan urged, using his take-charge voice, but no one listened. They just watched, bemused, talking quietly to each other. At least one person appeared to be recording video. This was probably going to end up on the internet, so he needed to look professional. "Wallace Kent, *in accordance with Section Ninety-one of the Criminal Justice Reform Act, and by virtue of the authority vested in me as a licensed and bonded Federal Recovery Agent, I am taking you into custody. You have the right to remain silent, and to be given proper and humane care while in my charge. You will be transferred to federal custody for processing and adjudication. Do you understand?"*

"Fuck you!" the prisoner shouted. "You got the wrong guy!"

"Good enough." Nathan took a knee and paused, trying to figure out how to get the guy untangled from the net so he could get cuffs on him. He could hear police sirens approaching the building from somewhere outside. He sighed; it was going to be another long day.

"SOUNDS LIKE YOU BOYS HAD A LONG DAY," Stella said, smiling over a cup of tea. Her image on the screen of the motel videophone stuttered a little, but the audio was clear. "Where's Ben?"

"He's asleep now." The motel room had two queen-sized beds. Ben was fast asleep in one, with Shadow curled up next to him, snoring peacefully. "Kid was out like a light after we got in. Adrenaline dump, probably."

"Probably," Stella agreed. "How'd he do?"

"He did good," Nathan said, pride in his voice. "Kept cool under pressure. Took a knee and fired the netgun at our runner. Dropped him right there in the hallway."

Stella shook her head. "I still can't believe that thing actually worked."

"I'm a little surprised myself," Nathan agreed. "It's a little bit of a pain in the ass to reload, but it does what it's supposed to do."

"Will you be on your way home tomorrow?"

"I expect so. I'm just glad we didn't have to transport him all the way back to Prescott. It's about a six-hundred-mile drive." He had been able to turn Wallace Kent over to the US Marshals office in Salt Lake City.

Stella paused to sip her tea. "It's been too quiet here without you boys around. I miss you." Nathan and Ben had been up in Utah, on the trail of the fugitive, for almost three weeks.

"I . . . miss you too," Nathan said. She was at home, and wasn't done up the way she usually was, but even with her hair up in a messy bun and no makeup, she looked good. "We should be home tomorrow afternoon sometime. Maybe a little later, I don't see any reason to get up early."

"There is one more thing," Stella said. "Do you have signal on your PDA? Good enough to receive an encrypted message?"

"I think so. We're still in the Salt Lake Metro area. What's up?"

Stella frowned. "It might be nothing, it might be something. It's not urgent. Look it over when you get a chance. We can talk about it when you get in tomorrow night."

"You going to be in the office on a Sunday?"

"No. Come by my place. Just call first."

"Okay, I'll do that. Anything else?"

Stella shook her head. "I'm headed to bed. Be safe on the road."

"You have a good night, Stella."

She smiled. "You too." The screen went black, overlaid with text that read CONNECTION TERMINATED.

Nathan checked his PDA, which was plugged in and charging by the bed. The light was blinking red, indicating that it was downloading an encrypted message. After about a minute, the light changed to a steady green. He opened the device, flipping down the folding keyboard, and used the buttons to select the message from Stella. As an extra security measure, he had to enter a pass-code to get it to open the message. It was brief and to-the-point:

We may have found Emmogene Anderson. Informant thinks he saw her at a poor farm outside of Gila Bend. Let me know what you think.

PS: Clean yourself up before you come over. I'm making dinner. Leave Ben at home. OPSEC. We'll tell him if we decide to go forward on it.

Nathan was surprised. They hadn't heard a peep about Emmogene Anderson in the past six months. He had figured that she had either been recaptured by Anthony Krieg or was dead. "Well, I'll be damned."

Prescott, Arizona

"THAT WAS NICE," Stella said, laying an arm across Nathan's chest. "I missed you."

"I can tell!" Nathan said, with a chuckle. He put an arm over her and ran his fingers across her smooth, soft skin.

"I mean it," Stella insisted. "It's not the same without you here."

Nathan thought back to the first time he'd ended up in bed with his business partner. He'd been terrified that it would *get weird* after that, but Stella was her usual self afterward and they had gotten along fine. She didn't bring up that night, much, other than the occasional odd bit of innuendo, so neither did Nathan. After a couple weeks he figured she'd just wanted a onetime fling and wasn't interested in continuing that kind of relationship. Then, she'd invited him over for dinner, and they spent the night together again. It had been a regular occurrence after that, but they were always discreet about it. Nathan wasn't sure how Ben would react to this, and he wasn't entirely sure what Stella really wanted.

"Can I ask you something?" he said, softly, still holding her tightly.

"Uh-oh," Stella said. She sat up and propped her head up on her elbow. "That sounds serious."

Nathan looked over at her, into her big green eyes. Her auburn hair spilled over her shoulders. She wasn't built like a model, but Nathan thought she was beautiful. She had a curvy figure, including a gorgeous rack. But was that all this was? He didn't like ambiguity. "What are we doing? Is this a thing or are we just screwing around?"

"Oh. Wow." Stella sat up in bed. "I gotta be honest, the first time I was just, you know, pretty drunk and kinda horny, and you are a good-looking man, Nathan Foster."

Nathan grinned. "I happen to think so. But...look, I'm not trying to put you on the spot, I just want to know where we stand. I'm not good at the nuances of romance."

"I meant it when I said I missed you," Stella said. "I get lonely, and I happen to think you're a pretty good guy. I know you have Ben to look after, and I know it's weird because we've worked together for so long. If you want to break this off, keep it professional, I understand."

Nathan was quiet for a moment. It had been a long time since he'd had feelings for a woman. He hadn't allowed himself that since the war started. He'd lost too much. There was hurt enough to go around. Sure, he'd gotten laid often enough since, but he'd never allowed himself to get attached to anyone...at least, not until Stella came along. The older a man gets, the less fulfilling empty sex becomes. He gets to a point where he starts to think about what he wants out of life, and who he wants to spend it with.

He took a breath. "Stella, I...I don't know if I could go back to keeping it professional. I think you're pretty great, too. This makes me happy." He looked into her eyes again. "You make me happy. I just think if we're going to do this, we need to talk to Ben about it, stop sneaking around like we're having an affair."

Stella didn't say anything. She grabbed Nathan and kissed him again, deeply, before throwing back the covers and climbing on top of him. They made love again, and it was more intimate than it had been before. She kissed him more, she held him a little tighter, and he held her hand while they embraced.

Sometime later, Nathan was once again holding Stella in his arms. They were both still breathing a little hard.

"You hungry?" Stella asked.

"I could eat. I seem to recall you lured me here under the pretense of making me dinner."

"Yeah, well, you got dessert first. You mind if we order takeout? I'm too worn out to cook."

Damn right, Nathan thought with a smile. "Nah, takeout sounds good." He reached over to the nightstand and started fumbling for his phone. "You want Chinese or Mexican?"

"Chinese," Stella said. "So...have you thought about that message I sent you?"

"About Emmogene Anderson? Yeah. I don't know. Even if it is her, will the government still honor the contract?"

"I spoke with our attorney about it. The contract did not have a specified end date, and they have not sent us the required notice of contract termination. It probably got overlooked in the aftermath of the mess in Chandler. What that means, though, is legally, the contract is still valid, and they'll have to pay us."

"What if they refuse?"

"As bad as they wanted her? They won't. They'll probably pay us the bounty, make us sign another NDA, and claim credit for the whole thing. Otherwise, we can take them to court."

Nathan frowned. "Trying to sue the Department of Homeland Security don't seem like a strategy for success to me," he said, "but two hundred and fifty thousand?"

"That's a lot of money for what might be an easy capture," Stella said. "If my contact is right and it is her, that probably means Anthony Krieg isn't there."

"Shame we can't roll him up, too." It would mean another quarter-million dollars if they were able to track him down. "But, best not to get greedy. This contact of yours, how sure is he?"

"He didn't have an Identifier or anything like that, but he's pretty sure. He works for a local handyman business down there, one that does a lot of work for the Second Chance Rescue Mission."

"That's the poor farm in Gila Bend you mentioned, right?"

"The same. It's a good place to hide if you're on the run. They don't ask for ID, they don't let the cops search the place without a warrant, and they don't let Recovery Agents onto their property at all. The whole place is self-sufficient for food. It's run by a pastor named David Hart."

"I don't know," Nathan said. "I guess it can't hurt to check it out."

"You don't seem as excited as I thought you would at the prospect of earning a quarter-million dollars."

"It's not that. Look, if that thing in her head works the way Delaney said it did, do we really want to be the ones who hand that over to the government?"

"That bothers me, too. I don't know that any government, much less our government, can be trusted with that kind of technology. But, there's another aspect of this. Emmogene probably isn't carrying the only one of those devices in existence. What if other countries already have them? What if the damned Greys come back? Think of what they could do with a literal mind-control device, especially if they can mass-produce it. Maybe turning it over to the government is the best thing to do, not so they can abuse the power, hopefully, but so they can understand it and develop countermeasures."

"You make a good point," Nathan admitted. "Delaney said they'd recovered some already, but none intact. Might be doing that girl a favor to have that thing taken out of her."

"Yeah."

"You know, assuming they can remove it without killing her," he said.

"You think they'd kill her if it was the only way to get the device?"

"Hell, who knows?" Nathan said. "Maybe they want to keep her alive as a lab rat, test it, see what it can do."

"She *is* a traitor," Stella said.

"I know, but she's still a human being. She was in prison serving her sentence, and as near as we can tell, was taken against her will. It doesn't seem right for the government to turn around and say, *well, we convicted you of this, but now we're just going to kill you,* you know?"

"I'm pretty sure it would be illegal for them to do that," Stella said.

"You know that won't stop them."

"I *don't* know that!" Stella protested. "This is America, not the Soviet Union. The government doesn't just do medical tests on people against their will, not even prisoners."

"It's happened before," Nathan said. "That and worse."

"I know, and I know you don't like Homeland Security, but I don't think you're being fair. There are procedures and rules, checks and balances. They can't just abduct a prisoner and do whatever they want to her!"

"I know they're not supposed to," Nathan said. "I also don't know why I give a damn."

"Because you're a good man," Stella said, her tone softer now. "You're not in this business for revenge. You honestly care about justice and people's rights."

"It'd be real easy to say fuck it, they're all traitors, just shoot 'em. It can't be like that, though. We can't go back to how it was during the war. I don't want to live in a country that abides that. Even collaborators have the presumption of innocence and the right to a fair trial. They certainly have a right to not be cut open and experimented on."

"'The trouble with fighting for human freedom,'" Stella quoted, "'is that one spends most of one's time defending scoundrels.' H. L. Mencken said that."

Nathan grinned. "How about I just pretend I know who that is?"

"We don't have to follow up on this if you don't want to. It's just a possible lead. We're not obligated to follow it up. After everything you went through, nobody would blame you for wanting to just wash your hands of the whole thing."

Nathan was quiet for a few moments as he considered the situation. "Tell you what. I'll head down there and check it out. We might be getting ahead of ourselves here. If I establish that it is her, we'll go from there. Deal?"

"Deal," Stella answered, squeezing Nathan tightly. "Thank you."

Gila Bend, Arizona

EMMOGENE SAT UP IN BED, covered in sweat, her heart racing. On the verge of panic, she looked around the darkened room, trying to remember where she was. A sharp pain in the back of her head made it difficult to think, and it took a moment for her to remember that she was in her bed, in her room, at the Rescue Mission. The anxiety attack subsided but the pain lingered. It was concentrated at the base of her skull and seemed to radiate through her brain from there. Her face felt hot and flushed, much like when the alien device in her skull was functioning, but it was much more intense. She was dizzy and nauseated. The pain lingered for almost a minute before it suddenly stopped. The warmth she felt in her face and head dropped off as well. The dizziness and nausea faded soon after.

Turning the light on, Emmogene wiped the sweat from her face and took a drink of water from the bottle on her nightstand. *What was that? Did the device activate?* It didn't make any sense. The only times she'd been able to activate it had been when she was in close proximity to another person and was under stress. No amount of trying or concentrating had enabled her to activate the device at will. As Anthony had explained to her, it didn't work the way it had been intended to. Perhaps it was because they'd never perfected it, as he'd claimed, or perhaps it had deteriorated somehow. Either way, Emmogene hadn't felt a peep from the thing in months, and now, all of a sudden, it wakes up?

It's like it was screaming, she thought. Normally it whispered. It was subtle and the signal didn't transmit very far. When active, the device felt like a fever, a fever whispering through her brain. This? This time, it had felt like it was shouting. She'd been having strange

231

dreams again. Had that somehow triggered it? Did the device dream with her? Much of the Visitors' technology had been organic. The device was alive, in a sense. Was it also conscious? Was it tuned in to her emotions, or did simple physiological distress cause this?

She didn't know. That was what bothered Emmogene the most about all this—she barely understood the things that had been done to her. The device in her head, the alien hybrid egg, it was bad enough that these things had been implanted in her without her knowledge or consent; the fact that she didn't know how they worked or what they were doing to her both frightened her and made her angry. She hadn't been raped, that she knew of, but her body and mind had been violated all the same.

Sitting quietly for a few moments, Emmogene tried to relax and calm herself down. Dr. Katz had taught her some breathing and meditation techniques that helped with her anxiety attacks. Was it really a strange dream she'd been having, or a memory? She closed her eyes, focused on slow, deep breathing, and tried to concentrate. It was there, just beyond her grasp, like a chord from a song that you can't quite place.

"Remorse is an emotion that I am unaccustomed to."

There it was again, the image of the Visitor, looking down at Emmogene wearily. It was clearer this time.

"I regret what we have done to you. I regret taking part in this."

Emmogene's eyes snapped wide open, then. The memory came flooding back, all at once, overwhelming her. It had taken place years ago, before the war ended. She was in some sort of research facility, the kind the Visitors built, with its gleaming surfaces and non-Euclidian geometric architecture. She was alone with one of the Visitors themselves, in its private sanctum. She remembered being so overcome with awe that she was barely able to speak, like an old Bible story about a mortal man encountering an angel. That reaction was also part of the conditioning, and that was what the being was speaking to her about.

"We are building a better future," Emmogene had recited. The words weren't her own, not really. They had been drilled into her a thousand times, and she repeated it on command like a dog performing a trick for its master. *"I am grateful for the opportunity to contribute."*

She remembered the creature considering her through its large black eyes, unblinking in the soft blue light of the room. The Visitors *could* close their eyes, but they didn't do so as frequently as humans did. This one had a mark on its face, a scar. Had the dream where she had attacked one of them actually been a memory? The alien was seated in an elaborate chair, connected by a mechanical arm to a track on the ceiling. This allowed it to move effortlessly about the room and observe Emmogene from an elevated position *"I don't understand,"* she had said. *"Have I failed you somehow?"* She remembered being on the verge of tears, devastated at the thought that this being might be displeased with her.

"No," the alien had reassured her. It spoke through a voice encoder, much like the one that Rook had used, but the voice being broadcast was soft and pleasant. There was a faint, rapid humming and mumbling sound behind it, the natural sound of the Visitors' speech. Their mouths didn't move when they spoke, and in fact they lacked tongues. *"I am the one who has failed,"* the being said. *"You have done nothing wrong."*

Emmogene remembered that she had looked mostly at the floor. It was considered improper for a human to maintain prolonged eye contact with the Visitors. *"Please,"* she'd said, dejectedly, *"tell me how I can better serve."*

"Try to understand," the being had transmitted, its synthesized voice increasing slightly in pitch, *"you feel the way you do because you were conditioned to."*

"I am grateful!" Emmogene said again, this time in protest. *"Serving the future is an honor."*

The Visitor had tilted his head downward slightly. Their faces were not emotive and were difficult for humans to read. Yet, for all that, the being had looked *tired*. *"We are losing the war for your planet,"* it had continued. *"We cannot win without doing unacceptable levels of harm to this world, and this world is precious. There are few so perfect in the entire galaxy, so naturally, ideally suited for life. Even our home, at its zenith, paled in comparison. Yet, your species is willing to render it uninhabitable, even to yourselves, rather than submit to us. This cannot be allowed to happen."* It had paused for a few moments, actually closing its eyes. *"What has come to pass is not what we intended. Many of us doubted the wisdom of this course of action, of trying to forcefully subjugate your species, and our doubts have been vindicated. The decision has already been made to leave."*

Emmogene recalled feeling horrified at the notion. The Visitors were *leaving*? It was impossible! They were going to build a better future for all humanity! She was so confused and distraught by the notion that she couldn't even find words to reply with. It didn't make sense to her that the Visitors would *disagree* on something, that there would be dissent. Dissent was not tolerated!

The alien had continued to speak. *"We underestimated you. We thought controlling you would be easy—it is not. I knew it would not be, but others were more... optimistic. We had to resort to extraordinary measures in the pursuit of our goals, measures that previously would have been deemed unacceptable."*

She knew what the being was referring to, though she recalled being unable to contemplate criticizing the Visitors' actions. The orbital bombardments, the invasions, the biological weapons, all of it had taken its toll on the human race. Countless millions, possibly billions had died.

"Such senseless destruction is not unprecedented in our history, but it has been so long that many have forgotten it. I have not. I tried to warn my peers that this would not be an easy thing, that it might require more of us than we were willing to give. They did not listen, to the ruination of us all."

"Ruination?" Emmogene had asked. How could the Visitors be losing? Their technology was vastly superior, their intellects greater than any human minds.

The alien tilted its head, slightly, as a human might do when greeting a cute animal. *"Yes, young one, ruination. We are exhausted. We were few when we arrived, and those numbers have been depleted. We are all that is left of our kind and our resources are finite. Your species' rapid technological advancement is not something we foresaw. Your capacity for violence is not something we were able to imagine."*

Emmogene remembered looking down, unable to hold back tears. It was considered improper to display emotion in front of them, much less *cry*, but she couldn't help herself. She felt ashamed. Humans were ghastly things. *"You offered to bring us to the stars, to lead us into a brighter future, to free us from superstition, war, and want... and we threw it away. We lashed out like the frightened, wounded animals we are, and in doing so we had squandered a once-in-history opportunity. I'm sorry,"* she cried.

The Visitor had considered her kindly. *"You have nothing to apologize for, young one. The error was ours. We were . . . arrogant, too assured of our own superiority, and our error has led us to the brink of the abyss."* The being looked up as the room shook slightly. A deep *boom* had rumbled in the distance somewhere. Another missile attack, she thought. The being looked down at her again. *"I cannot undo what has been done, but I am not entirely powerless to correct my error."* To Emmogene's shock, the being lowered its chair until it was at floor level and stepped off. Standing up, the top of its head barely came up to her eye level. It seemed so small, then, so frail. *"Time is short,"* it had said. *"Follow me."*

Emmogene couldn't remember what happened next. It was strange, having a memory return to you so vividly but being unable to recall anything immediately after. That was normal for her, though. That was how many of her memories were: isolated incidents with no context or continuity. As more came back to her, though, she had been able to piece together a better understanding of her past. Since the incident in prison, she had been recovering more and more of her memories, more than she ever had in the years prior. She wondered if, somehow, the device activating, broadcasting through her brain, undid the mind-wipe.

She took another sip of her water. It was a few minutes past four in the morning. She decided to get up and start her day's chores. The earlier she started, the earlier she'd finish, and she knew that she wouldn't be getting back to sleep tonight.

Gila Bend, Arizona
Four days later . . .

"UNCLE NATE, are you asleep?"

Nathan had his seat reclined and his hat down over his eyes. "No." He lifted his hat slightly. "What's up?"

Ben was sitting in the passenger's seat, as usual. Nathan's electro-optical spotting scope was attached to a mount on the center console, with the arm swung over so that the device was in front of the boy. He was using it to surveil the entrance to the Second Chance Rescue Mission a couple hundred yards up the road. It was just past midnight, and the clear desert sky was full of stars. "How long are we going to keep doing this?"

"Couple more days, maybe," Nathan said, sitting up. "We'll try setting up during the day and see if we can spot her then. If that don't work, we'll have to figure out a way to get in there and have a look around. Anything happening at the front gate?"

"Not since they changed guards. Not a single vehicle has entered or left. This place is pretty quiet at night."

"That makes sense," Nathan mused. "This is a working farm, and farming's hard work. The residents bust their asses all day. Besides, the place is run by a preacher. The management probably frowns on wild parties."

"Oh," Ben said, and was quiet after that. Nathan relaxed in his seat again, pulling his hat back down over his eyes. He was just starting to drift off when the boy piped up again. "Uncle Nate?"

"Yeah?" Nathan asked, lifting his hat once again. The boy was quiet for a few moments. Nathan recognized this. There was something he wanted to say but for whatever reason was felt embarrassed to say it. "What's on your mind, Ben?"

The boy hesitated for a few more seconds. "Are you and Stella dating now?"

Nathan sat back up in his seat. "Yeah, we kind of are," he said. He'd been trying to find the right time to broach the topic with the boy, but apparently the right time was now.

"Oh," he said, simply.

Nathan sighed. "I was meaning to talk to you about it. I guess I was worried about how you'd react."

"I like Stella," Ben said.

"I like her, too. How did you figure it out?"

"Seriously? I'm not a little kid anymore. Sometimes you leave and you're gone all night, or you come back late. You two have been way more flirty than usual at the office, too. It was kinda obvious."

Nathan felt his face flush just a bit and grinned. "Well, damn. Not much gets past you."

"You've spent the last couple years teaching me to be observant," Ben pointed out. *Fair point.* "Does this mean she's moving in with us? Are you guys going to get married?"

"Slow your roll there, boy," Nathan chided. "You sounded like my mother for a second there. Right now, nothing's going to change. We're just seeing how it goes."

"If you guys break up but still work together it might get super awkward."

Nathan sighed again. Ben was never one for subtlety. "Yes, Ben, it might. Until then, we're just going to give it our best shot, okay?"

"I hope it does. She's a way better cook than you."

"She is, that's a fact." The truck fell silent for a while. Nathan reclined in his seat once again, while Ben continued to watch the gate through the spotting scope, occasionally sipping his Dr. Pepper. Nathan felt himself starting to drift off once again.

"So," Ben asked, "how would we get in there?"

Nathan lifted his hat once again. "What?"

"The compound," Ben said, nodding toward the gate. "If Emmogene Anderson doesn't leave, we'll have to go in and see if she's there, won't we?"

Ben was just bound and determined to not let Nathan get any sleep. *Fine*, he thought. If he couldn't sleep, he could use the moment to teach the boy some more about the business. "There's a few ways we could go about it," he said. "Sometimes you can pose as a city or county worker. Show up with an orange vest and a clipboard and act like you're supposed to be there. People usually fall for it, even at places with gate guards. I've even got some fake IDs I could use."

"That's kind of like when I pretend to be a pizza guy to get them to open a door."

"Exactly right. You'd have to stay behind for that tactic, though. Having a teenager with me would be too suspicious."

"Wouldn't the truck be suspicious, too?"

"Oh yeah," Nathan agreed. "You can't roll up in a big, black, armored diesel like this," he said, patting the dashboard. "We'd have to rent a white pickup or something, maybe one with a yellow light on top."

"Could we, I don't know, just *sneak* in?"

"Maybe," Nathan said. "Big property like this, it usually won't be fenced off to where you can't get over it. It costs way too much to put ten-foot chain link around dozens of acres of land. I'd have to go in at night, though, and then what? If she's there, she'd probably be asleep in a bed someplace. I can't check every room. Also, if I was to get caught doing that, I could get prosecuted for criminal trespassing. A Recovery Agent has a lot of leeway but he's not above the law."

Ben looked thoughtful for a moment. "Okay, so the best bet is to go in during the day, when everybody is up and about, right?"

"Right. That usually means convincing them to let you in. You still gotta be careful how you go about it, though. Posing as, say, a police officer is a crime. You can't threaten them, either."

"We can bribe them, can't we? You know, like you did in Salt Lake City?"

Nathan smiled with pride. "Hell yes, you can bribe them. Flashing a little bit of money can get you into a surprising number of places, especially these days, when times are so tough. You gotta be smart about it, though. People will still take your money even if they know the person you're looking for isn't there. They might also take your money and then tell you to get lost, and there's nothing you can do about it. Or, they might tip off the person you're looking for. You have to learn to read people and to be able to do risk assessments on the fly. One of the most important tools of the trade is a well-developed bullshit detector, and it's something you gain only through experience."

Ben looked thoughtful for a moment. "I think we need to figure out a way to get in there," he said. "Nobody comes or goes at night, hardly. If we try to stake it out during the day, they might spot us and call the cops."

Nathan nodded. "That's right."

"If she's there, and she learns a suspicious vehicle is watching the place, she can just wait us out. Heck, maybe she has friends that can sneak her out, then we lose her for good."

"That's a risk," Nathan agreed. "Stakeouts can be useful but they have limitations. I like to use them to get a feel for a place, even if I don't think it's likely I'll spot the target during. If you have to go in somewhere, it's best to collect as much information as you can about it ahead of time. They're also terrain-dependent. Sometimes you can't get close enough to see anything without being seen yourself."

His nephew looked thoughtful for a few moments. He unconsciously put his index finger to the tip of his nose as he contemplated something. Nathan was interested to hear what he came up with. Even if it wouldn't work, he liked to encourage the boy to think outside the box. "What if," Ben said, cautiously, "I show up at the Rescue Mission? You know, tell them I'm homeless and I need a place to stay?"

"That's . . . not a bad idea," Nathan said, after a moment. "If our target is there, she might be worried about bounty hunters, but she'd never suspect a teenager."

"I can show up and say I ran away from a bad home or something, tell them I need a place to stay. You know, maybe I was orphaned in the war and was staying with an abusive relative."

"That's a good story," Nathan said. "Shit like that happens all the time, especially these days. They might call police, though, since you're a minor."

"So what if they do? I don't have to talk to the police. I'm a minor, right? What are they going to do, arrest me?"

"Theoretically they could take you into custody. If you were younger, they definitely would, but a fifteen-year-old? Probably wouldn't bother." Nathan rubbed his chin. The war had devastated the United States. Even ten years after, a lot of people were still struggling with poverty and homelessness. Countless people lived as migrants or otherwise off the grid. Hell, the grid got blown to pieces and hadn't been put back together yet. People didn't even get Social Security numbers anymore, because Social Security was defunct. The cops didn't have the time or the funding to chase down every teen runaway who wasn't obviously in danger.

"I could bring a radio," Ben said. "I'd just have to keep it hidden, only use it when I'm alone. You think they'll search me?"

"You could have it hidden under your clothes. I doubt they'd pat down a kid, even if they checked your bag. Keep going, tell me how you'd run this."

"There aren't that many people living here. It's like a few dozen. It wouldn't take me long to spot her if she's there, unless she, like, stays holed up in her room."

"We know she doesn't do that," Nathan said, "because our informant spotted her at the gate."

"Right, so I could show up, tell them my sad story about how I need a place to stay, and snoop around for a couple of days. I can let you know if she's there or not, and if she is, we can figure out how to get to her."

"What's your exit strategy? You should never get into a situation without a plan on how to get out."

The boy thought for a few more moments, then looked back up at his uncle. "That's easy! I can just sneak out at night, and you can come pick me up. Like you said, property this big, they won't have a fence that I can't get over."

"What happens if you get caught?"

"So what? I tell them I want to leave. They can't hold me prisoner, can they?"

Nathan grinned again. "No, they can't. Well done, Ben. Just now, on the fly, you came up with a pretty good plan to investigate a lead." He patted his nephew on the shoulder. "I'm proud of you."

Ben looked up at him earnestly. "Does that mean I can do it?"

"I don't know. Don't get me wrong, it's a good plan, it's just . . . you'd be on your own in there, maybe for a couple of days. It's like going undercover. You'd have to keep your act up at all times, and not blow your cover. Do you think you're up for that? It's okay to say you're not. I'm not pressuring you one way or another."

"I can do it!" Ben insisted. "Can I try? Please?"

Nathan was being serious with the kid when he said it was a good plan—it was. As Ben's guardian, though, he worried about leaving the boy alone in a situation like that. There was always the chance that something could go wrong. Maybe one of the residents was a child molester or something. Being honest with himself, though, Nathan had to admit that this was probably putting the boy in less danger than a typical fugitive recovery job. More importantly, it would be a valuable learning experience for him. "Okay."

"Really? Holy crap, thank you!"

Nathan held up a hand. "Hold on, now. First thing we do is talk this over with Stella. She's our partner and she needs to know what the plan is. Also, as a general rule, it's a good idea to run your plans by someone else who can tell you if they're stupid or not."

"You think she'll say it's stupid?" Ben almost looked hurt.

"No, no I don't, but it's always good to get a second opinion." He fired up the truck's engine.

"Where are we going?"

"Back to the hotel so I can get some sleep. We'll call Stella in the morning and go from there."

"Thank you!" Ben repeated.

"Don't thank me yet. Odds are they'll have you shoveling cow shit in the hot sun."

"ARLENE, ARE YOU THERE? It's Helen."

Emmogene was taking her lunch. She sat in the shade of a tree and ate a sandwich while reading a cheesy romance novel. "This is Arlene," she answered, putting the novel away.

"We've got a young guest who will be staying with us for a little while. Pastor Hart asked if you would like to show him around, keep him company."

This was strange. Emmogene didn't know what to make of it. "Sure," she answered, standing up. "I'll be at the office in a few minutes."

"Thank you, sweetie!" Helen replied.

It took Emmogene a few minutes to walk across the property to the main house. What was once the living room of a large home now served as an administrative office for the Second Chance Rescue

Mission. Pastor and Mrs. Hart were there, as was Helen. With them was someone she didn't recognize, a young man, barely a teenager by the look of him. He had sandy brown hair and blue eyes, but his face was dirty. He looked bewildered, maybe even a little scared. His jeans and T-shirt had holes in them.

"Ah, Arlene," Pastor Hart said, welcoming her, "thank you for coming. I'd like you to meet Ben."

"Oh! Uh, hello, Ben," Emmogene said, leaning toward the boy. "My name is Arlene. It's nice to meet you."

"Hi," the boy said, shyly.

"Ben will be staying with us for a little while," Pastor Hart continued. "He showed up at the gate this morning."

"Where is his family?" Emmogene asked.

"We're working with the Sheriff's Office on that," Maria Hart answered. She put a hand on the boy's shoulder. "This brave young man has been on his own for some time, but he found his way to our doorstep. They asked us to take care of him until his family can be located, and of course we agreed. We're going to put him in a room in the south dormitory."

"I see," Emmogene said. She smiled at the young man. "Well, you came to a great place, Ben. Everyone here is super nice. You'll have your own room and three meals a day."

"It may take a little while, but we'll do everything we can to get you home," Mrs. Hart told him.

"Th-thank you," Ben said, quietly.

Pastor Hart looked at Emmogene. "Arlene, would you mind taking him over there and helping him get settled in?"

"Not at all," Emmogene answered.

"Thank you," the pastor said. "Do you feel up for a run to town later on?"

Emmogene hesitated. She had only rarely left the safety of the Rescue Mission since arriving there. "To town?"

"Yes. You can take the van. I need you to take him to the thrift store and get him some clothes. We have everything else he needs, but we're a little short on clothing donations this month, and we haven't found anything that'll fit him. I'm sorry to impose, but we're shorthanded at the moment. I'll be taking the other van to bring some of our guests to the dentist."

Emmogene didn't have a driver's license, but few did, anymore. The Arizona Department of Motor Vehicles ceased operations during the war and never resumed. "Okay, I can do that."

"Are you sure it's no trouble?" the pastor asked.

"No, no. I haven't gone into town in a while, is all."

"There's a map in the van with directions to all the places we frequent. The phone in it works, so if you have a problem don't hesitate to call. Here," he said, handing her an envelope and a set of keys. "This is some cash from the coffers. It should be enough to get everything you need. Please fill the van up with gas before you come back."

"Okay," Emmogene repeated, looking at the envelope of cash and the keys in her hands.

"Thank you for this," Pastor Hart said, apologetically. "It's a crazy day here."

"I'm happy to help," she said. Emmogene looked at Ben. "Come on, I'll show you around the farm, then we'll head into town."

"Okay," the young man said. He seemed on edge. Maybe he was running from an abusive situation, too? "Is it okay if I use the bathroom first?"

"Sure!" Emmogene said. "Right this way."

GILA BEND, ARIZONA, had proven to be a remarkably resilient town, Nathan mused. Where many such towns had withered and died in the aftermath of the war, Gila Bend had hung in there, carrying on as it always had. Pulling into the parking lot of a Salvation Army thrift store, he parked his truck in a spot where he could see the entrance and waited. Ben had successfully made contact with a woman he believed was Emmogene Anderson, and said that this is where she would be taking him. He was damned proud of the boy; the plan Ben had come up with on the fly was working better than he could have hoped. He not only could confirm that it was his target, but he could apprehend her without having to find a way inside the Second Chance Rescue Mission.

Something was bothering him about it all, though. Not once in seven years of service as a Recovery Agent had he contemplated simply letting a fugitive go, but he found himself considering it now. Sure, the money would be good, if the government actually paid the bounty, but somehow this didn't seem as simple as the others. Emmogene Anderson wasn't some war criminal trying to escape justice. She was convicted of a relatively low-level charge and had been serving her sentence when she was taken against her will. Now she was, apparently, living at a poor farm, minding her own business. She wasn't a threat to anyone. Or was she? What could that device in her head do if it fell into the wrong hands?

What if the US Government was also "the wrong hands"?

Nathan's thoughts began to wander. He thought of his last tank crew again, Cole Jackson, Greg Rasmussen, and Jake Guthrie. Jackson had walked away from a football scholarship at the University of Alabama to enlist in the Army when the Greys dropped the rock on Phoenix. He was a big, burly black guy, almost too big to be a tanker. He'd painted "ROLL TIDE!" on the sides of their tank in red letters, much to the chagrin of their platoon leader, who had gone through ROTC at Louisiana State. He'd been the best gunner Nathan ever had. The only reason he'd been sitting at Specialist-5 instead of being promoted to Sergeant was that there hadn't been enough of a lull in operations for admin to stay on top of everything. They had been pushing the UEA forces deeper and deeper into Mexico, not giving them room to breathe as they retreated from North America.

Jake Guthrie, the driver, was a skinny white kid from Tennessee, drafted two weeks after graduating high school. He liked fixing up and racing old beater cars, and had been happy to be a tank driver. He once confessed to having been worried that the war would end before he got a chance to go fight in it. It was the sort of attitude a lot of the soldiers Nathan served with had, a grim determination to see it through until the end. His mother had wept into Nathan's shoulder at his funeral, when he'd handed her a folded flag.

Greg Rasmussen, Nathan's loader, hailed from Brigham City, Utah. A Mormon, he was quiet and kind of shy, and had been drafted into the Army before he could go on the two-year mission his church expected of young men. He liked to read a lot, and usually carried some science fiction or fantasy novel in his pocket. He had dreams of being a writer himself. He had a manuscript that he'd been working on, insisting that he was going to submit it to publishers after he finished it. He died before he got the chance.

They'd all been so young and so selflessly, recklessly brave. Even until their final battle, they had fought furiously, and they died giving the enemy hell. They'd killed four human-manned tanks and two alien mechs in that battle, an achievement for which they'd all been posthumously awarded the Bronze Star. Serving with such courageous young men had been an honor for Nathan, and even now, years later, his chest swelled with pride thinking about it.

Yet sometimes, in his darker moments, Nathan regretted not dying with them. The guilt had been terrible, especially in the weeks and months after. He'd felt that he'd failed them somehow, as both an NCO and a brother-in-arms, by surviving. That feeling had been a big part of what had driven him to become a Recovery Agent. The best way to honor his fallen soldiers, he'd reasoned, was to dedicate his life to bringing to justice the traitors and collaborators who had contributed to their deaths.

Nathan's radio crackled to life, interrupting his thoughts. "Uncle Nate," Ben said, his voice little more than a whisper. "You copy?"

"Loud and clear, boy. What's your status?"

"We're stopped at a gas station. I think there's something wrong with her."

"Wrong? What do you mean?"

"When she was pumping gas she, like, had a seizure or something."

"A seizure?"

"No. I don't know. She grabbed her head like she had a bad headache and fell down. She could barely even talk. It passed after a couple minutes. She went inside to use the bathroom."

"Understood. Are you okay?"

"Yeah, I'm good. We should be there in a little while."

"Copy that. Good work, Ben. Out."

EMMOGENE'S HANDS were still shaking a little bit as she got back into the van. Ben, still buckled into the passenger's seat, seemed concerned, and asked if she was okay. She told him she was, that it was just the heat, and took a drink from the big bottle of water she'd purchased. Truth be told it was hot out, and the dry desert air certainly wasn't doing her any favors.

Heat stress wasn't what had caused the attack she'd just had, though. It was the device in her head. It had been just like the other

morning, when a similar attack woke her up from a dream. It felt like
the device was screaming, somehow, and experiencing it while awake
had been debilitating. It had hit her so hard she'd gotten dizzy and
fallen down, scaring the poor kid. He'd sat with her by the gas pump
for a few minutes while the pain and delirium subsided. Even now,
she could tell he was concerned. He was a sweet young man.

"You must be hungry," Emmogene said as she drove the van
across town. "You want to stop and get something to eat before we go
to the store?"

"I, uh, think we should go to the store first," Ben said.

"You sure?"

"Yeah," he insisted. "They gave me a sandwich when I arrived. I'm
okay for now."

"Where are your parents?" Emmogene asked. "If you don't mind
me asking."

Ben hesitated for a few seconds. "They're . . . gone. You know, in
the war."

It was all Emmogene could do not to wince. The boy's words hit
her like a knife to the heart. "I see," she said, quietly. "I'm so sorry. I
lost my parents, too. Do you . . . do you have any other family that
you know of?"

"I have an uncle," Ben said. "I might be able to go stay with him.
You know, if they can find him."

"I'm sure they will," Emmogene said, managing a smile for the
kid. She didn't want to press him too much. She was curious, but this
conversation was obviously making him uncomfortable. "They're
really good at helping people find family members."

"I hope so," he said.

"Anyway, we're here," Emmogene announced, hitting the turn
signal. "The Salvation Army Thrift Store. We should be able to find
you some clothes that fit here." She pulled the van into the parking
lot. "Ben?" She looked over at the kid. He was looking out the back
windows.

"I think that truck is following us," he said.

Emmogene's heart started to race at the words. She stopped the
Rescue Mission van in the parking lot and scanned her mirrors.
Right behind her, turning off the road, was a red SUV, its paint faded
from exposure to the sun. "How long has it been back there?"

"Since the gas station," Ben said.

"You noticed that?"

"Yeah. I was—" His eyes went wide. "Emmogene, look out!"

Emmogene's head snapped around just in time to see the red SUV pull up right next to the van on the driver's side. The passenger's side door opened—there was a man with a gun. She turned back to the boy. "Ben, *run!*" The kid was already out the door, leaving it open as he fled on foot. Emmogene stomped on the gas and turn the wheel, angling for the alley adjacent to the thrift store, clipping a dumpster as she went. The SUV was right behind her, so close she couldn't even see its bumper in her mirror. The alley opened up into the loading dock behind the thrift store. The lot was surrounded by concrete barriers. Her only chance of escape was to squeeze through a gap between two of the barriers, cross a dirt lot, and make it back to a street. The red SUV had other plans, though. It rammed into the Rescue Mission van, hitting it in the rear wheel on the driver's side. Emmogene lost control of the van as it spun out. With a crash, she came to a stop, the passenger's side crumpled against an unforgiving concrete barricade.

Shaking her head, Emmogene looked in her mirror. The driver's side back door of the SUV opened. The vehicle visibly lifted on its suspension as a big man got out. He must have been seven feet tall, and was dressed in a hat and coat. *Oh my God,* she thought. It was Rook. Soulless black eyes stared out from under the brim of the fedora as the alien drone approached. On the verge of panic, she fumbled with her seat-belt buckle, screaming at it until she could get it to release. Once free, she shoved the door open, jumped out of the van, and ran.

Rook wasn't alone in the SUV. Two men got out, shouting at her to stop. Shots rang out and gunfire echoed through the streets of Gila Bend. It was like Quemado all over again. *Oh God, oh God, oh God!* A huge hand clamped around her arm before she made it to the barriers. Pain shot through Emmogene's shoulder as she was yanked to an abrupt halt. Whipping around, she looked up into the emotionless face of the Sagittarian automaton.

"TARGET CONFIRMED," the *Brute* said, through its voice encoder. It was definitely Rook. It still had the scars on its neck from the battle with the terror rattler.

"Let me go!" Emmogene screamed. She punched at it as hard as she could with her free hand, knocking its hat off as she fought, but it wouldn't do any good. It didn't feel pain and it wouldn't let go.

"DO NOT STRUGGLE," Rook commanded. Behind it, by the wrecked vehicles, one of the men it had arrived with was attacked by a huge black dog. The man fell to the ground, screaming, as the dog viciously mauled him. The *Brute*, in its single-minded way, started to drag Emmogene back to the SUV, ignoring the man screaming for help as he fought with the dog. A man in a hat and a leather jacket came running up from the alley, gun in hand. He wasn't one of the men from the SUV. "THREAT DETECTED," it said.

Taking advantage of its distraction, Emmogene pulled out the knife she carried in her back pocket. She snapped open the blade and plunged it into Rook's arm. Its tissues were so dense that it was difficult to even stab a knife into it. The creature's head whipped back around, looking at the wound in its arm and then at Emmogene.

"Let me go!" Emmogene repeated, pulling the knife out. She thrust upward, hoping to plunge it into Rook's eye, but the *Brute* stopped her cold with its other hand. *Brutes* didn't have emotions, supposedly, but somehow it seemed angry all the same. Its grip on her arm tightened so much that it hurt. Its crushing grip on her other wrist made her drop the knife.

"DO NOT STRUGGLE," the creature repeated in its flat, digitized baritone. Then its forehead exploded in a splash of blood. A single gunshot echoed through the alley. For just a moment, Rook stood there, seemingly unsure of what happened. Blue luminescent blood poured from an exit wound a few inches above its eyes. Its mouth gaped open like a fish out of water, and its grip on Emmogene's arms relaxed. She managed to get out of the way just in time as the *Brute* collapsed to the pavement, dead.

Emmogene stood there in shock, alien blood splattered on her face. She was shaking and couldn't speak. The man in the hat and leather jacket stood before her, a gun in one hand, a bronze badge in the other. The big black dog approached the dead alien cautiously, bristling and baring its teeth. The two men Rook had arrived with were both down. It was suddenly very quiet in town, save the rustling of a dry Sonoran wind.

"Emmogene Anderson?" the man asked. Emmogene reflexively looked up but didn't answer. "Are you injured?"

"I . . . I don't think so," she managed, after a long pause. "There was a boy I was with, he got out of the van when we were attacked. Did you see him?"

"I'm here," Ben said, appearing from the alley. He approached carefully. "I'm okay, Emmogene."

She noticed then that the boy also had a gun in his hands. "What's happening?" Not only that, but he had addressed her as *Emmogene*, not *Arlene*. He knew her real name. "Who are you?"

"Shadow, check it out," the man commanded. Emmogene recoiled as the big black dog trotted up to her; after all, she'd just watched it maul a man. It didn't seem aggressive now, though. It sniffed at her for a few moments, then sat, looking at its master.

The man in the hat and leather jacket lowered his gun. "*In compliance with the Extraterrestrial and Collaborator Recovery Act, and by virtue of the authority vested in me as a licensed and bonded Federal Recovery Agent, I am taking you into custody. You have the right to remain silent, and to be given proper and humane care while in my charge. If you attempt to resist or flee, I have the legal authority to use lethal force without further warning. You will be transferred to federal custody for processing and adjudication. Do you understand?*"

Emmogene was numb. The boy, Ben, he had been in on this? It was all a trick by a bounty hunter? She didn't say anything.

"Do you understand?" the bounty hunter repeated.

"Yes, I understand," Emmogene said, distantly. She stood motionless as the Recovery Agent handcuffed her, and didn't resist as he led her away.

Federal Recovery Office
Prescott, Arizona
A few hours later . . .

"SO THIS IS HER, HUH?" Stella stood next to Nathan, arms folded across her chest, watching the video feed from the holding cell. Emmogene Anderson was sitting on her cot, arms wrapped around her, as if in shock.

"Seems so," Nathan said. The Identifier had given them a ninety-plus percent confidence indicator. She had responded to the name Emmogene, and seemed to match the pictures and video they had of her.

"She's pretty."

Nathan grunted in response.

Stella wrapped her arms around his. "I'm just glad you and Ben are safe."

"Yeah, it was pretty sporty. You file the report on the *Brute* yet?"

"I've compiled it but I haven't sent it in. They should pay us the ten thousand dollars for that without much fuss."

"Where's the body?"

"Maricopa County Sheriff's Office has it, along with the bodies of the two gunmen you killed."

"Anthony Krieg wasn't there. I don't know who those two were."

"MCSO says both of them have the standard collaborator markings on the arm, but that doesn't help much. They're trying to ID them. It might take a while."

Nathan looked at Stella. "What do you think?"

"Homeland Security will be here as soon as possible when I report that we have her. They'll know something is up as soon as they get the report of the *Brute* in Gila Bend. MCSO will report it even if we

251

don't. Whether or not they honor the contract and pay us remains to be seen, but my gut tells me they will. It's just easier that way. They refuse, we take them to court, then the litigation gets into the discovery process, and that might be embarrassing for them, given what a cluster that whole operation was."

"Maybe. Maybe they just cry *national security* and tell us to get bent. What do you think they'll do with her?"

"I don't know," Stella admitted. "Does that bother you?"

"No," Nathan said. He sighed. "Yes. Hell, I don't know. Something has been bothering me about this whole thing from the get-go."

"She's lucky," Stella said. "If we had decided to ignore the lead, or if you'd waited one more day, they would have taken her. God knows where she'd be now."

"I do have impeccable timing," Nathan agreed. "How do you suppose they found her?"

"Who knows? Maybe they have informants, too."

"Why don't we go ask her?"

"What?"

"Let's go talk to her. What's the harm?"

"Legally, we're not allowed to interrogate her," Stella said. "We never talk to them when they're in our custody."

"I know that. I'm not saying we interrogate her. I'm saying we just talk to her, see if she's willing to tell us anything."

Stella didn't seem comfortable with the prospect. Violating the rules was an easy way for a Recovery Agent to get his badge pulled. "I guess. Just make sure to explain to her that she's not obligated to tell us anything, and that we can't offer her anything in exchange for information."

Nathan looked back up at the video screen. "Maybe we should have told Ben that, first."

"Huh?" Stella asked, looking up. On the screen, Ben could be seen approaching the cell. He had a tray in his hands. "What is that boy doing? He's not supposed to be down there."

SITTING ON A COT, with her back against a concrete wall, Emmogene examined the small cell she found herself in. It was built into one corner of a windowless basement, its walls made of a thick steel bar grillage. There was a cot, bolted to the wall, and a combination toilet/drinking fountain like she'd had in her prison cell. The cell was open to the rest of the room, affording her no privacy, but the bounty hunters had put up an opaque modesty screen so she could use the toilet without being seen. Apparently they considered her to be a low-risk prisoner.

Emmogene was strangely okay with having been captured. She'd been waiting for it for the past six months, fearing the day when Anthony showed up to reclaim her. When she saw Rook, she knew immediately that he'd found her, somehow, and that if he got ahold of her again she'd never have another chance to escape. It was a relief to have been captured by a Recovery Agent, even if it meant getting sent to Area 51 to be a science project. Of all the awful things government scientists might do to her, she didn't fear that they would rape her, or impregnate her against her will. With Anthony it would be all but certain.

She wondered if the things he had told her were even true. They made sense, in a way. They explained the mind-wipe and the effort to recover her. The device in her head by itself might account for that, though. The rest of it, the alien egg inside her, the stuff about she and Anthony being a matched breeding pair . . . for all she knew, those were the delusions of a man whose mind had been corrupted by overt influence and deep psychological manipulation. Maybe the government scientists would be able to tell her, she mused. Anthony had said that they'd dissect her, but what if that was another one of his delusions, or just a lie to gain her compliance? After all, if the influence device was implanted without killing her, surely it could be removed nonlethally.

Or maybe you're just whistling past the graveyard, she thought bitterly. She always had been a terminal optimist.

"I brought you something to eat." Startled, Emmogene looked up. The boy, Ben, was standing just outside her cell, holding a tray in his hands. "It's a microwave burrito and an instant soup cup, if you're hungry."

"Oh." Emmogene was famished, but she didn't get up. She didn't want to seem too eager. "Okay."

Ben leaned down and put the tray on the floor. There was a gap at the bottom of the cage that was just big enough to slide it through. "Here you go," he said, pushing it into the cell.

Emmogene looked at the food for a moment, then back up at the boy. "Aren't you a little young to be a bounty hunter?"

"I'm fifteen," he protested, as if that were a perfectly reasonable age to be hunting people for money.

"I see," Emmogene said. Standing up, she moved across the cell to where the tray was. She picked it up, carried it back to her bunk, and sat down. Her stomach growled as the scent of the burrito and soup filled her nose. "Thank you for the food."

"We're legally required to feed you," Ben said.

"Oh." Emmogene picked up the burrito and took a bite.

The kid lingered outside the cell, awkwardly watching Emmogene eat. "Are you waiting for something?" she asked.

"I'm sorry I lied to you," he said, earnestly. "I had to."

"Don't be sorry," Emmogene said. "You're a good liar. You had me fooled." The boy's face flushed a little, and he looked down. Despite herself, Emmogene felt bad. Was this situation really his fault? She sighed. "How did you end up doing this, bounty hunting?"

"My Uncle Nate is the Recovery Agent," he explained. "I'm just an apprentice."

"I get that," Emmogene said, "but why are you doing this at all? Why aren't you in school? Where are your parents?"

"My parents?" The boy lowered his eyes again, looking down at the floor. "My mom and I were caught behind enemy lines when the UEA invaded California. We were put into a prison camp. My mom tried to escape, get me out." He looked back up at Emmogene. "They killed her."

The words hit her like an accusation. Emmogene's heart sank. "I . . . see," she said. It was all she could manage.

"Grandpa died from the hemorrhagic fever," Ben explained. "My dad died when they hit San Diego. Uncle Nate is all I have left." Emmogene couldn't bring herself to look at the boy. She stared at her tray, fighting to keep back the tears. "I said I was sorry I lied to you," the kid continued, "because you seem really nice. I'm not sorry for what I do. I didn't ask for this life. Nobody asked me if I wanted to hunt traitors. I didn't want the world to be this way, but this is how it is, and it's because of people like you."

"That's enough, Ben." That was a man's voice. Emmogene looked up to see the bounty hunter standing next to Ben with a hand on his shoulder. Behind him was a woman with auburn hair, dressed like a secretary in a skirt and heels. "You know you're not supposed to be down here by yourself. Now go on upstairs." The kid did as he was told and hurried out of the room without another word. The Recovery Agent stepped up to Emmogene's cell, hands on his hips. He was a tall man with brown hair, a tanned complexion, and a stubbly face. Dressed in jeans, a tan button-down shirt, and cowboy boots, he looked like he might have ridden a horse to work. His bronze badge hung from a lanyard around his neck. "I apologize if he was bothering you, Miss Anderson. He didn't tell me he was bringing you chow."

"It's fine," Emmogene said, tersely, as she choked back a sniffle. She took a sip of her soup cup. "Do you mind if I keep eating?"

"Not at all."

Emmogene took another sip of her soup, then looked back up at the man. "Neither of you said a word to me on the ride up here, now everybody wants to talk to me. Are you here to interrogate me? If so, you're wasting your time. I don't know anything."

"We're not here to interrogate you," the woman replied. "You have the right to remain silent if you want. Nothing you tell us here can legally be admitted into a court proceedings, and it's illegal for us to offer you anything in exchange for information."

"I see," Emmogene said, sipping her soup again. "I'm not sure what we have to talk about, then. What do you want from me?"

"You're lucky I found you when I did," the Recovery Agent said. *Nate.* His name was *Nate*, the boy had said. "It seems we weren't the only ones looking."

"It's Anthony," Emmogene said.

"Anthony Krieg?" the woman asked.

"Yes," Emmogene replied. "It has to be."

"Anthony Krieg wasn't at the scene when I caught up to you," Nate said. "How do you know he was involved?"

Emmogene was quiet for a moment. She was torn. On one hand, she had nothing to gain by answering the Recovery Agent's questions. On the other . . . Anthony was still out there, and he was still getting people killed. If nothing else, maybe her cooperation would help them track him down. He couldn't just leave her alone. As long as he was still out there, she'd never be safe, no matter where they put her. "Rook," she said, quietly.

"Rook?"

"The soldier-type drone," Emmogene explained. "You call them *Brutes*, I think? That was the same one he had with him when they kidnapped me."

"How can you tell?" the woman asked. "They all look the same."

"Not exactly," Emmogene said. "You spend enough time with one, you learn to tell them apart. They're all a little different. Besides, it still had the scars on its neck. It was damaged ... or, wounded, I guess, in a fight with a terror rattler."

"Up near Alpine," Nate said.

"Y-yes," Emmogene replied, taken somewhat aback. "How did you know about that?"

"I'm good at my job, Miss Anderson," Nate answered. "I tracked you for quite some time, from Quemado, to Alpine, all the way to Chandler. Unfortunately, I was always one step behind."

"How did you find the safe house?"

"In Chandler? A woman named Carmen told me."

"Carmen? She ... she helped you? Where is she?"

"Last I saw her she was on a truck to Mexico," the bounty hunter said. "I let her go in exchange for information."

"You said you can't legally offer me anything," Emmogene said.

"I can't, now that you're in my custody. She wasn't. She wasn't even on the wanted list. It gave me some leeway. Before that lucky break I was stuck following the trail of dead bodies you people were leaving across the Southwest."

"That wasn't me," Emmogene said. "It was Anthony and his people. I didn't ask for any of this. I tried to run away."

"I know you did," Nate said. "Three times at least. The third time you made it. I talked to the survivors of the safe house, including a nurse named Nomusa."

"Nomusa?" Emmogene's spirits lifted some upon realizing that the kind and courageous nurse was still alive. "What happened to her?"

"She's alive and well, if that's what you're wondering," the bounty hunter said. "She told me you were dead, though."

"She was just trying to protect me."

"I figured. I didn't believe her, in any case, but that's what went into my report. As far as I know, the government still thinks you're dead."

Emmogene was frustrated. "What? I don't understand. What is it you want from me?"

"Is Anthony Krieg still alive? He hasn't been seen since the incident in Chandler."

"I don't have any proof," Emmogene said, "but I know it was him. Rook was assigned to him. If they'd brought in anyone else they would have had a different soldier-type."

"All this because of that thing in your head," Nate said. He shook his own head. "Seems like it's more trouble than it's worth. It can't work that well, or else you'd have used it to make us let you go."

"It doesn't work," Emmogene admitted. Why was she telling him this? "Not like it's supposed to, anyway. I can't control it. If they ever taught me how, I don't remember."

"Your memory was wiped at some point," the woman said. "At least, that's what your attorney alleged at your trial."

"It's not an allegation, it's the truth. They provided the medical evidence."

The Recovery Agent leaned in a little closer to the cage. "Seems a little odd that they'd go through so much trouble for a little mind-control device that doesn't even work."

"That's not why he's after me," Emmogene said. She had to be careful here. They didn't seem to know about the alien hybrid egg that she supposedly carried. If they thought that all she had was a strange device that didn't even work, maybe they'd just let her go back to prison instead of being experimented upon.

The woman spoke up. "Then why? For legal reasons I need to emphasize that you are not obligated to tell us anything, but I'm curious. What's this really about?"

"He's obsessed with me," Emmogene explained. "When I was just a teenager, the Visitors . . . promised . . . me to him. They said that we were to be a perfect mating pair. It was like an arranged marriage."

The woman's eyes went a little wide. "Oh my God."

"It happened all the time," Emmogene said with a shrug. "The Visitors matched breeding pairs to produce healthy children. The parents didn't have to raise the children if they didn't want them, they'd be raised in a creche, but everyone was supposed to do their part if asked. If you weren't asked, you were given contraceptives."

"Jesus," Nate swore, quietly, to the woman next to him. "I heard about this shit, but it's different hearing it firsthand." He looked back up at Emmogene. "If they wiped your memory, how come you know all this?"

"The memory wipe isn't total," she said. "I remember bits and pieces. I never forgot, like, my name, or how to talk, or anything like that. It's like . . ." She paused, trying to come up with a way to explain it. "I have no memory of learning to play the piano, but I know how to play the piano."

"That makes sense, in as much as any of this makes sense," the Recovery Agent said.

Emmogene took a deep breath and exhaled slowly. She'd finished her soup. "Anthony . . . he's not well. He was Earth Storm. They did things to him, did things to his mind."

"He's enhanced," Nate said.

"He is, but they went further than that. I think they got desperate when they realized they were losing the war. He used to have to take medication to keep himself level, but he told me he hasn't been on it in a long time. His emotional state is deteriorating. I was promised to him and he thinks that still means something. He thinks that the Visitors are coming back. He thinks . . ." She trailed off, tears rolling down her cheeks. She wiped her eyes before looking back up at her captors. "Anthony is dangerous. If he didn't give up after all this, he never will. Whatever happens, please don't let him take me. I'd rather you just shoot me."

"We're not going to let him take you anywhere," the woman reassured.

"That bastard turns up here he'll get a bullet between his eyes," Nate said. "I won't let him get his hands on you, I promise you that." Emmogene didn't answer. The tears kept trickling down her face. "That's kind of why I came to talk to you," he continued. "In order to assure your safety, I need to know how he found you."

Emmogene could only shake her head. "I don't know. I hadn't seen or heard from him since . . . well, since Chandler. I began to let myself think he was gone." She smiled without humor and shook her head some more. "I was so stupid. I should have kept running."

"You could have turned yourself in," the woman insisted. "It's apparent that you were taken against your will. You would not be punished for returning to federal custody."

"Ha!" Emmogene said, laughing bitterly. "Sure. Don't kid yourself, lady, as soon as you turn me over they're going to dissect me to try and get this stupid thing out of my head. You know they want it for themselves."

"We're getting off track here," Nate said, gently. "Did anything usual happen during your stay at the Second Chance Rescue Mission? Could someone have talked? UEA loyalists, spies, something like that?"

"I don't know. I don't think so. I didn't even tell anyone my real name. The people I worked with had mostly been there from the start, but new people came in sometimes. You know, like your nephew."

The bounty hunter was unphased by her subtly accusatory tone. Like his nephew, he offered no apologies for what he did for a living. "Speaking of, he said you had some kind of seizure the day we picked you up. You collapsed by a gas pump? Do you think that might have had something to do with the device in your head?"

Emmogene was quiet for a moment. Did she have anything to gain by telling them? Did she have anything to lose?

"Miss Anderson?"

She tapped the side of her head. "It felt like it was screaming," she said, quietly. She looked up at him. "When it's active, I can feel it buzzing in the back of my skull, almost like a whisper. This was different. It made my ears ring. It made me nauseous and dizzy. I almost threw up. I was hot, like I had a fever, and started to sweat."

"Was this the first time this had happened to you?" the woman asked.

"No. It happened once before, when I was still at the Rescue Mission. It woke me up."

The bounty hunter and the woman looked at each other. "You don't suppose they put some kind of tracking device in you, do you?"

Emmogene's eyes went wide. She felt so stupid. She couldn't believe that she'd never thought of that before. "I . . . don't know," she said, slowly. "It makes sense, but . . . if that's caused by them tracking me, somehow, then they've never used it before. Not that I can remember, anyway. They didn't use it when I ran off into the woods."

The Recovery Agent was silent for a few moments. He rubbed his chin, as if contemplating the situation. "Alright. Thank you for the information." He turned to leave.

"Wait!" Emmogene said. "What's going to happen to me?"

"For the time being you're going to sit tight," he told her. "We will keep you safe for as long as you're in our custody."

Emmogene had more questions, but the bounty hunter made it clear that he wouldn't be answering them as he walked away. The woman, seemingly surprised, turned and hurried after him.

STELLA CAUGHT UP WITH NATHAN in the break room. "Nate!" she said, almost pleading. "What's going on? What are you thinking? We're a team, remember?"

Nathan was standing in front of the coffeemaker, getting ready to make a fresh pot. He sighed, set the coffee down, and turned to his partner. "I don't know."

Stella folded her arms across her chest and approached him. "It's not like you to be unsure."

"The easiest thing in the world would be to call Homeland Security and turn her over," he said. "That's what any sensible person would do. That's what *I* would do. It's what we're *supposed* to do!"

"But you don't want to do that."

"I don't know what I want. I don't know what the right thing to do is. What if she's right? What if we hand her over to the Feds and they dissect her, kill her trying to get that thing out of her head? It's not right."

"What makes you think they would do that?" Stella asked.

"What makes you think they wouldn't? You remember how it was, right after the war."

Stella's expression darkened and she looked down. "I do." She was quiet for a few moments. "But . . . what if she's manipulating us?"

"What? She said the device doesn't work." Stella glared at him over her glasses. "Right. You really think this might be that thing in her head? I didn't feel anything, did you?"

"No, but does that mean it's not working? It would defeat the purpose of it if you could tell it was influencing you, wouldn't it?"

"You're right, but we've talked about this before. This thing has been bothering me for a while."

"That's fair," Stella conceded. "Maybe it isn't some alien device working its magic on you. Maybe it's just a pretty girl trying to manipulate you with a sob story."

"What are you saying?" Nathan demanded. "We've been working together for years. She's not the first pretty little thing we've brought in here. I have never once, in seven years, let a fugitive go after getting them in custody. Never! Believe me, Stella, they tried. I've been begged, pleaded with, and threatened. I've been offered money, huge bribes. They've offered me drugs, guns, and yeah, every manner of sexual favor you can imagine. I've been nothing but professional, and I slapped the cuffs on every damned one of them."

"I know!" Stella insisted. "That's not what I meant!"

"Really? You wanna tell me what the hell you *did* mean, then?"

"This whole thing has been screwed up from the start," she said. "I hate that Homeland Security ever roped us into this. I know you don't trust them."

"Do you blame me?"

"It's not as bad as you think it is. Remember, I came from that world. There are a lot of good people there, patriotic Americans just trying to do their jobs. I also know that despite that gruff exterior, you're actually a very sweet, kind man, and yeah, this one isn't so black and white. I get that. She didn't ask to be broken out of prison, and she's terrified that the man who did it will find her. He undoubtedly filled her head with stories about how the government would dissect her to retrieve that thing in her head. Making the victim afraid to leave is a classic technique of an abuser. He was probably trying to convince her that she had nowhere else to go, and that it was either do what he wants or end up dead."

Nathan looked down at the floor and shook his head. "I just don't know what to do." He looked back up at his partner. "This one doesn't feel right. Maybe I'm going soft. Maybe I *am* being manipulated. I don't know. Something about this still doesn't sit well with me."

"We didn't have to go after her," Stella said. "I hope I didn't make you feel like you had to. I wasn't trying to pressure you."

"It wasn't anything you did, baby," Nathan replied, squeezing Stella's hand. "Hell, it was probably my own pride more than anything else. I'm the best in the Southwest, and the damned government thought that they could do it better than I did. I think maybe I wanted to show them up, remind them of why Recovery Agents do this stuff now and not Feds."

"Okay. If you ever feel like I'm pressuring you to do something you don't want to do, tell me, okay? We're a team. You can talk to me."

"I know. What do you think we should do?"

"Honestly? We can't keep her here if we're not going to turn her over. At a certain point it becomes kidnapping. We have to either call the Feds or release her. If we let her go, we can probably play it off as a case of mistaken identity, assuming we even report it. We're *supposed* to report it, of course, but it's not like Emmogene is going to call them up and file a complaint."

"If we let that girl go, it's only a matter of time before those Faction fanatics find her. God only knows what they'll do to her when they do, or how many people they'll kill in the process of trying to catch her."

"That only leaves us with one option, then," Stella said, quietly.

"Yeah. Yeah, you're right. Best thing to do is let the Feds take her, get paid, and have this whole thing not be our problem anymore."

"Okay. Then that's what we'll do." Stella stepped forward and hugged him. Nathan wrapped his arms around her and held her tightly. As he held her, he contemplated just how much he'd come to lean on her, emotionally. Her support and encouragement carried him through difficult times, and he couldn't imagine going back to not having her in his life.

Nathan realized that he loved her. He stepped back, keeping his hands on her shoulders, and looked down into her eyes. "Stella, I—"

"You guys!" It was Ben. Something was wrong. He sounded scared. "There's a problem!" Nathan and Stella hurried out of the break room and into the main office. The boy was there, looking up at the screens monitoring the prisoner's cell. "I think she's having a seizure!"

"Shit," Nathan cursed. On the screen, Emmogene could be seen lying on the floor of her cell, convulsing. He turned to Stella. "Call an ambulance. Ben, grab the first-aid kit and follow me downstairs."

"Is she going to be okay?" Ben's eyes were wide. He was genuinely worried about the girl.

"I don't know," Nathan said. "We'll do what we can. Hurry now."

Yavapai County Hospital
Prescott, Arizona
A few hours later . . .

"WHAT'S THE WORD, DOC?"

The night-shift doctor at the county hospital was rolling with the situation pretty well, Nathan thought, all things considered. He looked disheveled, with a five o'clock shadow and a rumpled lab coat. "She had multiple tonic-clonic seizures," he explained, looking at Nathan over the tops of reading glasses. "We have her heavily sedated for the time being and I've got her scheduled for an MRI. You mind telling me what's going on? Does she have a history of epilepsy? We don't get a lot of Recovery Agents or Sagittarian collaborators in here these days."

"I'm afraid I can't say much, but I can tell you that it involves exo-tech. This woman is a wanted fugitive and must remain in my custody until Homeland Security gets here to pick her up. Is she good to travel, or does she need to remain here?"

"I can't, in good conscience, release her in this condition. The paramedics reported that she was suffering from status epilepticus during the ambulance ride."

"What's that?"

"She had multiple seizures in a row without returning to normal in between them. It's not good. It could be indicative of a serious underlying condition. She needs to be seen by a specialist, and that won't happen until tomorrow at the earliest."

"I understand. I won't try to take her anywhere, but Homeland Security might. They've been looking for her for a while."

"Can you give us a day? I know what they'll do. They'll show up here with a National Security Letter and haul her off even if it might kill her. It's unethical. At least let me make sure she's not going to die."

"She could die from this?"

"Potentially," the doctor said, grimly. "Somewhere between one- and three-in-ten people who have status epilepticus die within thirty days."

"Jesus. Alright, I can buy you some time. I need to level with you, though, this is a high-risk case."

The doctor raised his eyebrows. "High-risk? What does that mean?"

"It means I'm going to make sure she has security on her twenty-four hours a day. If I can't be with her I need to be in the hall outside, for her own protection."

"Protection from who?" he asked, the concern obvious in his voice.

"I have reason to believe that Sagittarian Faction terrorists are looking for her. I don't know if they know where she is or not. If they realize she's here, they might try to take her by force."

That got his attention. "Terrorists? Are you serious?"

"Serious as a heart attack, Doc. I don't know that they know where she is, but I can't rule it out, either."

"Good God. She's so young. What did she do?"

"It ain't about what she did so much as it's about who she is. Look, it's complicated, and like I said, I can't get into it all. I'm going to get some people up here to help me keep an eye on her. If you can isolate her from the rest of the hospital, I suggest you do that, because we'll be armed and I don't want to upset the patients."

"Armed? The hospital has a no-weapons policy." Nathan just glared at him. "Ah. Right. I'll see what I can do. We've got plenty of room right now. I'll let everyone know that this needs to be expedited."

"Get her to where she can travel and let Homeland Security take it from there. I'll let them know she needs medical attention and they should send a medic when they come to collect her. Just do the best you can. I don't want to put anyone else at risk."

"I appreciate that."

"Look, I don't know how likely it is that they'll be able to track her down before she leaves here. I'm gonna call local law enforcement and let them know what's going on, too. Maybe they'll be able to send some backup over."

"I appreciate that, too," the doctor said, glumly.

"Thanks, Doc. If you'll excuse me, I got some calls to make."

EMMOGENE FOUND HERSELF gazing up at an alien sky.

It was twilight; there was a fading glow over the far horizon, but she had no way of knowing if the sun had not yet set or was about to rise. Dark clouds drifted steadily by overhead, blocking out portions of the sky as they passed. *Where am I?* she thought. *How did I get here?* She stood on a ridge, overlooking a vast and barren landscape bathed in the pale light of two moons. Before her lay a broken vista of rock and gray sands. Dry, powdery snow was on the wind and had accumulated on the ground, here and there, in scattered drifts. There was no sound save the constant wind, no movement except for the blowing dust and snow. Emmogene was utterly alone.

It was cold. It *looked* cold, in any case; she could see the snow, but she didn't *feel* cold. As she scanned the darkened terrain she felt as if she were lying down, even though she was standing with her arms folded across her chest. Being stranded in this desolate, surreal place should have been terrifying, but she was oddly calm about it, more curious than frightened. Turning around, Emmogene took in her surroundings as best she could in the dim light. One side of the ridge was nothing but a windswept wasteland, but what she saw on the other filled her with awe.

Jagged, angular towers, impossibly tall, dotted the valley on the other side. Each one, gray and black in color, stretched for what had to have been more than a mile up into the darkened sky, dotted by points of pale bluish light that may have been windows. They were scattered across the landscape before her, miles apart from one another, for as far as she could see. Their obsidian silhouettes stood stark and imposing against the failing light.

"Remorse is an emotion that I am unaccustomed to."

That voice! Emmogene whipped back around to find the source of the familiar, calming, synthesized voice. One of the Visitors had appeared, suddenly standing with her atop the rocky ridge. It looked up at her with its large, black eyes. Its eyelids were partially closed, indicating weariness or fatigue. Its smooth gray skin appeared dry and aged, and it bore a scar on the left side of its head. The one-piece coverall it wore bore no markings or ornamentation. It held up a three-digit hand in a sort-of wave that the Visitors used as a greeting. "Hello, young one," the being said, not discernably moving its mouth.

"It's you!" Emmogene said. "You're the one from my dreams." She knew which Visitor this was instantly.

"I was known to you as the Counselor," the Visitor said.

"Counselor," Emmogene repeated. "I remember now. You don't have names like we do. I'm sorry, I have forgotten so much."

"Your memories have not been erased, just suppressed. In time, they will return to you."

"Did I give you that scar?"

The alien was quiet for a few moments before answering. "Yes. You were initially chosen to test the limits of our psychological conditioning. You reacted violently to one of those tests." He paused again, looking out over the bleak landscape. "As I have indicated, I regret what we did to you."

"Is this a dream or a memory?" Emmogene asked. "It can't be a memory. I've never been to this place, have I?"

"This is not a dream, but it is similar to one." It gestured to the valley before them, "This is a rendition. Simulating a three-dimensional environment helps you maintain your orientation and allows you to focus and understand."

"I don't understand anything. I don't know what's happening."

The being's voice modulated at a slightly different pitch, causing it to sound gentler. "You are currently sedated, but the device you carry is active. It is both sending and receiving, allowing me to communicate with you in real time."

"The last thing I remember, I had been captured by bounty hunters, three of them . . . a man, a woman, and a boy. Then . . ." She closed her eyes, struggling to remember. "Then something happened. I had a headache. It got so bad it made me sick. I . . . I fell down. I was dizzy. The next thing I know, I'm here. What is this place?"

"This . . . was my home," the being said, sounding almost wistful. "What you see is not based on your memories, but mine. This," it said, raising a hand toward the towers again, "was the last time I saw it."

"This is your home planet? What happened here?"

"It would take too much time to explain in any detail," the Counselor said, "but this is not our homeworld. That had long since been lost to us. This was one of our last redoubts, as alien to us as it is to you, but this is where I was born. Long before, we were faced with a terrible and existential threat from space. When we should have resisted we instead allowed it to subvert us. We declined from our zenith to nothing but scattered remnants."

"I don't understand. Did you lose a war?"

"That would have been preferable. There is . . . what you would refer to as . . . dignity . . . in that course of action. It is the course your species chose. The will to survive is the basest and most powerful of evolutionary imperatives, and your kind has a stronger will than mine. No, young one, we were not defeated in conflict or exterminated by force of arms. We stagnated over the course of ages, then declined. In the end, we were not the sole authors of our own undoing, but we greatly contributed."

"I'm afraid I still don't understand," Emmogene said. "I'm sorry."

The Counselor looked up at Emmogene, studying her with its large eyes. "We chose the abyss," it explained. "We chose death. We ceased creating, we ceased exploring, we ceased imagining, and in time, we ceased everything else. The threat we faced did not have to defeat us in battle. Instead, it convinced us to lay down and die." As it said this, the lights on the towers started to go out, one after another. The ones nearest grew dark first. Slowly but steadily the darkness spread, until the last lights on the farthest towers that could be seen winked out.

Emmogene felt a chill. It wasn't from the cold, though, but was instead the chill one got when looking at a tomb. "That's horrible."

"It was the fate we chose for ourselves. Not all of us succumbed to that call, however. Some of us chose a different course. We went to the stars and scattered, putting a vast gulf of time and space between us and the threat. We fled as far as we could go, knowing that if those insidious forces caught up with us, we would be unable to prevail."

"Time and space?" Emmogene asked. "How long ago was this? How . . . how old is this memory?"

The Counselor was quiet for a moment. "The speed of light is the only constant in the universe. It binds together time and space, mandating that causes precede effects. Beyond it, linear time loses its meaning. Causality breaks down. It is impossible to say with any certainty when this happened in relation to now. It is sufficient to say that it happened, and that our species can never return home."

Emmogene was beginning to understand. "That's why you came to Earth."

"We brought with us not only the remnants of our civilization, but what remained of the other life-forms from our home. Your world is a jewel in the void, home to a greater breadth and diversity of life than any we had encountered. Adapting ourselves to suit this new environment was trivial compared to terraforming a less-suitable world or constructing habitats in space. It was the most logical course of action. Things did not go how we intended, however. In desperation we chose to try to do to you what was done to us. You know the rest."

"Why are you telling me this now? What's happening to me? You said I was sedated and the device was active. How come you never talked to me before?"

"The device was dormant until recently. Sending and receiving over long distances requires more energy, and that has the potential to cause irreparable damage to your brain."

"Is that why I was having seizures?"

"Yes. There is a location-tracking functionality to the device that was never activated for this reason. Those who are looking for you broadcast a query signal. Upon receiving it, the device responds, allowing you to be located. These emissions are beyond safe or acceptable levels for your physiology. This functionality was only intended to be used in an emergency."

"Who turned it on, then? Was it . . . was it Anthony?"

"Not him, but those who command him have the capability to activate it. He is but a tool for their machinations."

Emmogene was scared now. "Am I going to have brain damage? Am I going to die? If you can talk to me, can't you turn it off?"

"The only way to permanently disable this functionality is to destroy or remove the device itself. This cannot be done remotely."

The desolate alien vista behind the Counsellor began to fade into blackness. "What's happening now?" Emmogene pleaded. "Please don't leave me, I'm scared."

"We are coming to get you, Emmogene. Be strong."

Then the Counselor was gone, and Emmogene was alone. Everything dissolved to black as she drifted back into unconsciousness.

EMMOGENE SLOWLY OPENED HER EYES. At first, they wouldn't focus, and she couldn't tell where she was. She felt like she was moving, though, and was sitting up. *Am I in a car?* She raised her hands to her eyes to rub them and realized that her hands were shackled together. She *was* in a car, in the back seat of a large automobile or truck, and was buckled into her seat. Her mouth was dry and she coughed.

"Hey, Nate, I think she's coming around." The man in the front passenger seat said this, looking over his shoulder at her. Emmogene realized then that there was a transparent barrier, one of the kind with wire mesh embedded into it, between the front and rear seats. It had a little door in, which was opened, allowing her to hear the people in the front seat. The driver of the vehicle looked at Emmogene in his rearview mirror. She realized that it was Nathan, the bounty hunter who had captured her. She didn't recognize the other man.

"Can I have some water?" Emmogene croaked. Her throat was so dry she was barely able to speak, and her head hurt.

"Sure," the man in the passenger's seat said. He had curly hair and a goatee. The little door in the barrier between the front and back seats was just big enough for him to hand her a bottle of water through.

Emmogene unscrewed the cap and drank greedily, downing half the bottle before she was through. "What's happening?" she asked. "Where are we going? How long was I out?"

The Recovery Agent, from the driver's seat, glanced at her through the rearview mirror again. "You spent the last two nights in the hospital," he said, bluntly.

"Two nights?"

"You had multiple seizures on Saturday night. It's Monday morning now. The doctor wanted to keep you there, and I was inclined to let you stay, but the situation changed."

"I don't understand," Emmogene said. Her head hurt and it was hard to think.

"Anthony Krieg has my partner, Stella, and my nephew, Ben. You met them at our office."

Emmogene's stomach lurched. It was like waking up to a nightmare. "Oh, no," she said, quietly. "No, no, no."

"I was at the hospital protecting you. He tracked down our office and took them at gunpoint. If I don't hand you over, he'll kill them." He was quiet for a few moments, then looked at her in the mirror again. "I'm sorry."

"I'm sorry, too," Emmogene said, the reality of the situation setting in. "I didn't mean for any of this to happen. You should know that Anthony is vicious. Don't trust him. Don't trust any promises he makes."

"I don't," the bounty hunter said, slowing the truck down. They came to a stop on the side of the highway, and he shut the engine down. She watched, confused, as he got out, walked around the truck, and opened the rear passenger door. "Step out, please," he said. Doing as she was asked, Emmogene unbuckled her seat belt, clumsily due to the steel shackles on her wrists, and stepped out onto the gravel. They were in the desert somewhere in the predawn darkness, stopped alongside a two-lane highway. The eastern sky was just beginning to lighten. A million stars twinkled overhead. The air was cool and clear.

The bounty hunter was dressed like he was going to war. He had a vest, probably a bulletproof one, covered by web gear and pouches. "I told Anthony Krieg I'd bring you to him in exchange for the safety of my family. I also told him that if anything happened to Stella or Ben, I'd either kill you myself or turn you over to the government."

"That was smart," Emmogene admitted, her voice sullen. "He's obsessed with me." She felt stupid for thinking this could have possibly ended any other way. Anthony always got what he wanted in the end.

The Recovery Agent's friend exited the truck and stood next to him. Like the bounty hunter, he was dressed in tactical gear. A big pistol hung from his left hip in a leather holster. From his other hip hung a huge Bowie knife.

"Are you another bounty hunter?" Emmogene asked.

"Jesse Larimer," the man said, "Arizona Rangers. Nate and I go way back."

"You are a convicted collaborator," the bounty hunter said. "The easiest thing in the world would be to just hand you over, but I can't do that."

Emmogene looked the men, surprised by what the Recovery Agent had just said. "You can't?"

"Carmen told me about his obsession with you, the alien egg you carry, and how he thinks you two are going to be the Adam and Eve of some alien-hybrid-master-race. I have a pretty good idea of what will happen to you if he gets his hands on you. Just giving you to that psychopath would be . . . well, it'd be wrong, regardless of what you did during the war."

She didn't know what to say to that, so she didn't say anything.

He continued, "I called Homeland Security after your ex-boyfriend called me. I told them he had my family. They told me that the United States Government doesn't negotiate with terrorists. My instructions were to keep you in my custody until they arrived to pick you up. They assured me that they'd work with state and local law enforcement to try and get Stella and Ben back, but they couldn't give me any details as to when or how. You and I both know what that would mean, so I'm taking matters into my own hands. I'll probably lose my badge for this, assuming they don't try to prosecute me, but I honestly don't give a damn right now. That's where you come in."

"What is it you want from me?"

"I need you to help me get Stella and Ben back. By the time the Feds get their shit together they'll be dead, so I called some locals. We're on our way to meet up with a platoon of Arizona Rangers." He nodded toward his friend. "Jesse contacted his superiors and they were able to respond."

"You said you're not going to just give me to Anthony."

"I'm not. We have a plan, but for it to work we need you on board. I want to use you to make Anthony Krieg think we're doing the exchange. As soon as Stella and Ben are safe, the Rangers are going to light him and his Faction buddies up."

"That's not much of a plan," Emmogene said. Even she could think of a lot of ways in which it could fail.

"It's not, but it's the best we can do, not knowing how many men Anthony Krieg has. If I just show up with you by myself, I have no doubt he'll just kill me and then my family. A show of force is the only way I can think of to make him think twice. But, we still need your help to get the hostages to safety. These Rangers are willing to risk their lives to engage the Faction terrorists and make sure they don't leave with you. If you agree to help, no matter what, we won't abandon you."

"Rangers never leave a man behind," the man called Jesse said.

"I can't promise you it'll work," the Recovery Agent continued. "We could all still end up dead. But, if you're willing to help me do this, then when it's over I'll let you go."

"What?" Emmogene blinked a few times. Her head still hurt and it was hard to think. "You'll just . . . let me go? Before you said you couldn't give me anything in exchange for my cooperation."

"Legally I can't. That bastard has my family, though, and I don't give a good goddamn about the law right now. I'll tell Homeland Security you got away. Hell, I'll take you to the same guy who smuggled Carmen out of the country and put you on a truck to Mexico if you want."

Could this be real? Was he serious? He seemed sincere. "You would do that for me? Won't you get in trouble?"

He shrugged. "Probably. Like I said, I don't care about that right now. You help me, I'll help you, and to hell with what the law says."

Emmogene was quiet for a few moments. "And what if I say no? You said you wouldn't just give me to him."

"And I meant it. You don't have to do this if you don't want to. I'll leave you in the truck while we try and rescue them without your help. Assuming I live through it, when it's all over I'll turn you over to Homeland Security."

"That doesn't seem like much of a choice," Emmogene said. It was either risk her life to help this man, or sit it out and either end up captured by either Anthony or the US Government.

The Recovery Agent looked down at her. "It's not, but it's the choice you've got. What do you say? We don't have a lot of time."

Emmogene was quiet for a few moments before looking up at the bounty hunter again. "Your name is Nate, right?"

"It is."

"Your nephew . . . Ben . . . he's a good kid. I don't want anything to happen to him. I don't want anyone else to die for my sake. I will help you if I can."

Nate and Jesse looked at each other, then back at her. "Thank you," the Recovery Agent said. He leaned forward and unlocked the shackles on her wrists. Removing the restraints, he tossed them carelessly into the back seat of his truck.

Emmogene rubbed her wrists. "Now what?" She gasped as Nate drew a revolver from his jacket pocket. He broke it open, looked at it, then closed it again. It had a hinge in the frame.

"Watch," he said. He pulled the trigger and the gun clicked, loudly. "It has a long, heavy trigger pull. There's no safety or anything like that. Just pull the trigger and it'll fire." He broke the gun open again and began to drop bullets into its drum. "You've got six shots of .38 in the cylinder. It doesn't kick much." He flipped the gun around in his hand and offered it to Emmogene, grip-first.

"What?" She looked down at the revolver, then back up at Nate. "You're giving me a gun?"

"Yes. I'm not going to leave you defenseless. We may be able to make our move before they have a chance to search you. If you get the opportunity, use this on Anthony Krieg. Kill him. It's just a .38, it's not very powerful, so either shoot him in the face or empty the gun into him. Do you think you can do that?"

Emmogene looked down at the offered gun again. Narrowing her eyes, she took the weapon. She was done being afraid of Anthony.

"Good," the Nate said. "Be careful with that. Watch where you point it. Stick it in your waistband and keep it hidden, but make sure the trigger doesn't snag on anything when you're putting it in there. Oh, and in case you're getting any other ideas, the transparency between the front and back seats is bulletproof."

"We need to get going," Jesse said. "We're running out of time."

"I know," Nate replied. He looked back at Emmogene. "Do you think you'll be okay to walk? You shouldn't have to go far."

"I think so," she said. "Anthony . . . he scares me. He thinks he loves me but I don't think that'll stop him from . . . you know, from hurting me, if he has to."

"I don't think it will, either," Nate said, bluntly. "That's why I gave you the gun. It belongs to Ben. I guess he wasn't able to use it when Mr. Krieg showed up at my office, but maybe you'll get the chance." He took a resigned breath, then looked back up at her. "We don't have time to come up with anything clever. We're supposed to meet him at an abandoned tourist trap and exchange you for Stella and Ben. It'll just be us, the Rangers, and Shadow."

"Shadow?"

"Shadow, my working dog," Nate explained. "He's in the back of the truck."

"It's a good thing you had him with you instead of leaving him at the office," Jesse said. "They probably would have shot him."

"Probably," the Recovery Agent agreed. "As is, we don't know how many men he has or what kind of weapons they're packing. This could get ugly."

"I understand," Emmogene said. "I should have turned myself in when I got away. I was scared. I thought they'd dissect me. Maybe they will. But if I had done that, none of this would be happening."

"I'd like to get a look at that mind-control device," Jesse said. "I'm curious how it works." He was a strange one, thinking of that in a time like this.

"Speaking of, is there any chance you can use that thing to control Anthony Krieg?" Nate asked.

"I told you it doesn't work right," Emmogene said, looking down. "I don't have much control over it." She looked back up at him. "But . . . if I can use it, I will."

"Thank you. Now listen," Nate said. "We're going to meet him at the designated location. I'll walk you forward, and he'll have someone with Stella and Ben. If this goes down like he said, they'll walk toward us while we send you toward him. I'm going to have Jesse here with me, and the other Rangers will be backing us up. When the shooting starts, get down and try to find some cover. My goal will be to get Stella and Ben to my truck. After that, I'll come get you."

"You promise you won't let him take me? I'll kill myself before I let that happen," Emmogene said, determination in her voice. "I'm not going to be his concubine."

Much to her surprise, the bounty hunter reached over and patted her on the shoulder. "No matter what happens, I'm not going to just abandon you out there. You have my word."

Cactus Pete's Authentic Old West Boomtown
80 miles east of the Phoenix Crater

THERE WAS AN UNCOMFORTABLE SILENCE in the truck as Nathan drove. Neither he, nor Jesse, nor Emmogene Anderson in the back said much as they made their way down the highway. They were at the head of a column of almost a dozen privately owned vehicles, cars and trucks driven by Arizona Rangers. The sun was climbing over the eastern horizon now, casting long shadows behind them on the lonely desert highway. The Rangers had notified the Arizona Highway Patrol that things were going down and asked them to divert traffic away from the area, so they encountered few other vehicles. This was good; enough things might go wrong without innocent bystanders getting caught in the cross fire. They passed a sign for Cactus Pete's Authentic Old West Boomtown, and he began to slow the truck down.

"I remember this place," Jesse said. "I think my parents took me here when I was a kid. It's a replica of an Old West town. They used to have people in costumes working there in the summer, playing different roles in historical garb, like a Renaissance Faire. There were some creepy animatronic mannequins, too, that would play prerecorded messages when you pushed a button." He was quiet for a second. "You know, I don't think it's authentic in any sense of the word. They built this place in the nineteen-seventies, if I remember right. Anyway, it closed down years ago, long before the war, even. I'm kind of surprised it's still standing."

"This is where they wanted to meet," Nathan said.

"I can see why," Jesse acknowledged. "There are lots of trails and dirt roads in the hills behind it, some of which you can only get through with a four-by-four. Plenty of escape routes that don't involve the highway." He was, again, quiet for a moment. "How do you think they're going to react when all of us roll in there together? Didn't he tell you to come alone?"

"He did," Nathan said. "I doubt he actually expected me to. That would be stupid."

"Anthony will be expecting you to try something like this," Emmogene said. "It's what he would do."

Nathan turned the truck onto a poorly maintained gravel road, and the small convoy followed. He could see the entrance to the place in the distance, at the foot of the hills. Behind them, the cars and trucks in the caravan kicked up a huge cloud of dust. There would be no element of surprise.

Jesse realized that, too. "What's to stop them from just lighting us up right here on the road?"

"Me," Emmogene said.

"They wouldn't want to risk hurting the mother of the future, would they?"

"He's been conditioned to obey their orders," Emmogene said. "It's not just a matter of loyalty or even stubbornness, it's the product of years of deep psychological conditioning. I feel bad for him. Nobody should have that done to them."

"Hopefully we'll get the chance to put him out of his misery," Nathan said, coldly. The occupants of the truck fell silent again, to the point where the only sound was tires on gravel. They passed a faded sign with a cartoon cowboy on it. Beyond that was a large dirt parking lot and what had once been a welcome center and gift shop. There were tire tracks in the dirt, leading into the park, but no vehicles were visible. He brought the truck to a stop and scanned the area.

Past the welcome center, another gravel trail led up a hill toward the fake western town itself. The tire tracks led up that way. Anthony Krieg said he'd be waiting there. It was a good place to set up, Nathan thought: higher elevation and good visibility of the entrance. The trail was narrow so the vehicles would have to approach single file. Fortunately, they had no way of knowing which vehicle Emmogene was in.

There was nothing for it; they had no alternative but to drive up the trail and see this thing through. There hadn't been time to get any scouts into position ahead of time, and since it was already daylight, they wouldn't be able to sneak up on them now. Nathan picked up his radio microphone and transmitted his intentions to the convoy, but there was no response. His phone didn't have any signal, either. Neither did the GPS.

"What's going on?" Jesse asked, noticing the same thing.

"ECM," Nathan said. "We're being jammed. They did the same thing to the Feds in Chandler."

"Shit. What now?"

"Do me a favor, run back to the other vehicles and let them know we don't have comms. Tell them we're going to head up the hill. Tell them to follow my lead, and nobody shoot unless I say so, or they need to do so to save lives, okay?"

"Got it," Jesse said, unbuckling his seat belt. "I'll be right back." He opened the door and stepped out of the truck.

Nathan looked up at Emmogene in his rearview mirror. "You doing okay back there?"

"I'm scared," the girl said, matter-of-factly, fidgeting in her seat.

"I am, too," Nathan admitted. "Look, I'm . . . I'm sorry. I should have just let you be down there." He had never once, in his entire career as a Recovery Agent, apologized to one of the people he had captured before.

"Just promise me you won't leave me," Emmogene said, her voice trembling a little. He could see the fear in her eyes. "I'd rather you kill me than leave me with him."

"I gave you my word and I meant it," Nathan assured her. "I'm not leaving here without you." A moment later, Jesse returned to the truck, and informed him that the other Rangers had been filled in on the situation. Nathan took a deep breath and tightened his grip on the steering wheel. "Alright, then, let's do this."

EMMOGENE WAS QUIET as Nate came around and opened the door for her. She stood up, adjusting her shirt to ensure the revolver he had given her was still concealed, and took a breath. Her heart was racing. There were so many things that could go wrong and she figured that there was a better-than-even chance that she would die here today. Somehow, though, that didn't bother her as much as it should have. She had told the bounty hunter that she was scared and she'd meant it. Yet, as powerful as the fear was, it wasn't overwhelming. Whatever happened today, however this ended up playing out, it had been *her* choice. A choice made under duress, perhaps, but a choice all the same.

That thought was empowering, even liberating.

Nate had a heavy-looking rifle hanging from a sling across his chest now. His eyes were concealed behind tinted shooting glasses, hidden in the shade of his wide-brimmed hat. His bronze badge was stuck to the bulletproof vest he wore. His face was grim but his voice was calm. "He's here," he said, quietly. "We're going to walk forward now. I'm going to be behind you with my revolver at the back of your head. I'm just doing this for show. My finger will be off the trigger. No matter how much I have to bluster or threaten, please believe me when I say I'm not going to hurt you. I know it's hard to trust me, but I need you to trust me now."

"I trust you," Emmogene told him, and she meant it.

"Whatever happens, thank you for this."

Emmogene didn't answer, she just nodded quietly. She held her head high as the Recovery Agent placed his left hand on her shoulder and, with his right, jammed the barrel of a gun into the base of her skull. She took a deep breath and stayed quiet as he frog-marched her forward, carefully observing her surroundings. As she'd been told, Cactus Pete's was built to look like a stereotypical Wild West town. A row of weatherworn wooden buildings lined either side of a wide dirt street. The buildings, all one or two stories high, were set up to look like shops and businesses of the late nineteenth century. There was a general store, a post office, a sheriff's office, a doctor, a gunsmith, things like that, mostly connected by a wooden boardwalk. At the far end, casting a long shadow in the rising sun, was a church, the largest structure in the mock town.

There were armed men everywhere, all pointing guns at one another. Behind her, the Arizona Rangers had spread out, taking positions behind vehicles and buildings, aiming their guns up the street. They were all dressed in green uniforms, but they didn't look like any police or military Emmogene had ever seen. Their weapons and equipment were all different. Some of them were old and a couple of them were overweight. Like Nate's friend Jesse, a lot of them had goatees or beards, and some also had long hair. Their faces were determined, though.

On the opposite end of the mocked-up town, in the shadow of the church, was another cluster of vehicles and another group of armed men and women. Like their counterparts, they had spread out, taken cover, and were pointing their weapons down the street. Mostly clad in black, they had their faces covered in a mass and wore red armbands with black bow-and-arrow symbols on them. They were Sagittarian Faction. Anthony had gotten reinforcements from somewhere and things were tense. No one said anything as Nate walked Emmogene forward. There was scarcely any sound at all, save for the blowing of the wind and the crunch of boots on gravel. As the sun rose so did the temperature. A trickle of sweat rolled down the side of her head.

Nate stopped and held Emmogene in place. From around a large white van appeared a woman and a child—Stella and Ben! A hulking figure appeared behind them, probably eight feet tall and clad in composite armor of off-world design. It was another soldier-type, like Rook, except this one had its armor in addition to its heavy flechette gun. The Recovery Agent's hand tightened on Emmogene's shoulder as the biomechanical monstrosity marched forward, its weapon pointed at his girlfriend and nephew. "Shit," he whispered. He hadn't been expecting that.

Emmogene's eyes narrowed as another figure appeared from behind the van. He carefully stayed behind the soldier-type and his prisoners, but Emmogene recognized the blond hair and goatee. It was Anthony. As the alien soldier and the hostages stepped out from the receding shadow of the church, into the warm morning sun, they stopped. There was probably a hundred feet between them now, and it was all she could do to remember to breathe.

"Stella! Ben!" the bounty hunter shouted. "You alright?"

"We're okay!" Stella said. The boy stood next to her protectively but didn't say anything. The woman had a bruise on her face and her shirt was torn, but she seemed otherwise unhurt.

Anthony stepped forward, then, into the sunlight where Emmogene could see him. He, too, wore a bulletproof vest. His had the skull-and-planet logo of the Earth Storm Commandos emblazoned on the left breast. The left side of his face was scarred and had been badly burned at some point. His left eye socket was covered by a metal plate that had been affixed to his skull, and he walked with a slight limp. Her heart raced and there was a knot in her stomach, but Emmogene was determined to stay calm.

"Hello, Emmogene," Anthony said, an eerie smile forming on his scarred face. His voice was raised so that she could hear him but otherwise was almost blissfully calm. "I feared I wouldn't get to see you again." He looked up at the bounty hunter next. "I thought I told you to come alone."

Nate shouted back at him, "You didn't really think I'd be stupid enough to do that, did you?"

Anthony's face split in a cruel smile. "I had hoped you'd make this easy, but I didn't expect it. Send Emmogene forward and I will give you your family back."

"How about you send the woman and the boy forward, and as soon as they're in my truck, you get Miss Anderson?"

"You're trying my patience, Mr. Foster," Anthony said, coldly. "Do you want to watch these two die?"

Emmogene gasped as Nate made a big show of jamming his revolver into the back of her head. "So help me God, I'll kill this bitch right in front of you if you lay a hand on my family. I know what she means to you. If you want her to live so you can father your fucking hybrid master race, I suggest you keep calm and don't do anything stupid." Anthony's eyes went wide and he seethed with anger. "Yeah, that's right," the Recovery Agent continued. "I know about all of it. Your old girlfriend Carmen told me. You know what they say about a woman scorned."

Anthony's jaw clenched, but he otherwise made no outward sign of his rage. Emmogene could tell, though, she could tell he was barely containing it. That had caught him off guard. Carmen was still a sore spot for him. They'd been lovers for a long time. "Why don't we send them at the same time, then?"

"Fine," Nate said. "There's just one more thing. I told the government what's happening and where we were meeting. The longer you fuck around, the less likely it is you make it out of the country with her, regardless of what happens here this morning. If you want to survive long enough to be this girl's baby-daddy, I suggest you make the swap and be on your way. You don't have time to do much else."

Anthony's eyes narrowed and the tone of his voice changed. "I'll *make* time. I'll kill every last one of the people you brought." *Oh no*, Emmogene thought. Nate had pushed him too far. "You think you can dictate terms to me, you insolent ape?" He grabbed Stella by the hair and yanked her back toward him. In a flash, he had a combat knife to her throat. The woman's eyes were wide with panic but Anthony's arm was locked around her. "Try me. This brat of yours will get to watch me cut this woman's head off. I'll—"

"Anthony, that's *enough*!" Emmogene shouted. "That's enough. No one else needs to get hurt. I'm here. I'll go quietly. Please, just let his family go." He looked at her, eyes widened, but didn't let go. "Please, Anthony," Emmogene pleaded, taking a step forward. "I'll do what you want." She continued to approach, slowly. "I'll have your baby. I'll stay with you from now on. Just let her go. Nobody else has to die." From the back of Emmogene's skull there came a faint buzzing. *Really? Now?* Was the device active? Would it work on Anthony again, even after all this?

The enraged expression on Anthony's face relaxed, then faded. Without a word he let Stella go and shoved her forward. She grabbed Ben by the arm and walked forward, toward Emmogene, and toward Nathan, who was behind her. Emmogene kept her focus and concentration on Anthony as she approached him, only sparing a quick glance at the woman and boy as they passed her.

"Thank you," Stella whispered. Emmogene nodded at her and continued forward. The closer she got to Anthony, the harder she concentrated, the more intense the buzzing in her head got. The device was definitely active again, and she could feel the heat in her face as it broadcast its mind-altering signals.

Anthony's expression softened more as Emmogene drew near. She was only a few feet away from him now, and could clearly see the horrific burn scars on his face and neck. The device was putting out so much energy that she felt feverish. "I'm sorry you had to see me like that," he said, quietly, not looking at her. "I'm not . . . I haven't been well. I don't . . . do well . . . without you."

"I know," Emmogene said, gently. She slowly reached a hand up to Anthony's cheek. The hardened Earth Storm commando actually closed his remaining eye as she caressed the burned side of his face. The skin was leathery to the touch. "I'm here now. Everything will be okay. We can go, together."

Anthony's eye met Emmogene's. The world seemed to drop away. The morning sun, the heat, the dust, the armed standoff, the tacky fake western town, all of that faded into the background. Emmogene focused on Anthony as if she were taking his portrait, and everything else got blurry as she concentrated. Time seemed to slow down. For just a moment, between heartbeats, there was just the two of them. On his face, on the burned visage of a ruined human being, she briefly saw the face she remembered, the image of the man she used to love. He hadn't always been like this. He hadn't always been a monster. "I love you," he said, softly.

"I know." Continuing to gaze into his eye, concentrating as hard as she could, praying that the alien device would keep functioning as designed, Emmogene reached under her shirt and found the butt of the revolver. She felt dizzy, like she was about to pass out from overheating. Each heartbeat pounded between her temples and there was such pressure behind her eyes that it was physically painful. Without looking down, she pulled it out from under her shirt, moved her finger to the trigger, and raised the weapon toward Anthony's chin. She only needed to hold it for one more second.

"THREAT DETECTED." The synthesized baritone of the *Brute* startled Emmogene and cut through the induced fog. The device ceased functioning in an instant as her concentration was broken. Emmogene realized that the alien soldier was facing her now, pointing its huge flechette weapon at her.

Anthony blinked once, then twice, then his eye focused. He looked down at the revolver in Emmogene's hand and, for an instant, looked . . . hurt. Betrayed. Then it was gone. He clamped his hand around her wrist with an iron grip. Veins bulged in his forehead and neck and he clenched his jaw so hard that she could hear his teeth grinding. "You . . . lying . . . whore," he snarled, through gritted teeth. His hand crushed Emmogene's wrist so hard she thought he might break it. Her grip gave way and the gun fell to the dirt. His other hand clamped around her neck and squeezed, squeezed so tightly everything started to go dark. "You don't have to be conscious to have a baby," he hissed. "Your body just has to stay alive until it can be transferred to an artificial womb."

CLANG-BOOM!

Even as she struggled to breath, even as she began to black out,

Emmogene saw the bullet strike the *Brute*. She didn't know what kind of gun the Rangers had fired at it, but it must have been huge, because it punched through the side of its armor under the arm. It was just a grazing shot, but nonetheless it took a chunk out of its armor in a puff of smoke and a splash of luminescent blood. The soldier-type turned its weapon toward where the shot had come from, but it waited for orders.

"Open fire!" Anthony screamed. He yanked on Emmogene and started to drag her back behind the van. "Kill them! Kill them all!" The *Brute* opened fire, its weapon spewing flechettes with a deafening metallic roar. All around them the Sagittarian Faction militants started shooting, with the Arizona Rangers responding in kind.

Anthony was distracted long enough for Emmogene to take a gasping breath. The darkness faded and she began to thrash, kick, and bite. She clawed at his remaining eye. She screamed at him, an incoherent, furious primal shriek, and tried to get close enough to bite his face. Bullets snapped overhead like angry hornets. Gunfire had erupted all around them. He was trying to get her behind the van, get her to some cover, trying not to get shot, but Emmogene didn't let up. She knew it was all probably for nothing, but she wasn't going to go quietly. Not this time, not ever again.

Somehow, over the noise of the battle and her own physical struggle, she heard Nate's voice. Firm and commanding, the bounty hunter shouted a single order: "Shadow, *attack!*"

Anthony heard it, too. He looked up from the struggle at something behind Emmogene. A black blur flashed across her field of view a huge dog seemed to *fly* into them. Its jaws clamped down on Anthony's neck, its body whipping around under the force of its own momentum, and it pulled the enhanced commando and Emmogene both to the ground. He struggled and screamed as the dog furiously tried to rip his throat out.

Anthony let Emmogene go as he used both arms to try and keep the dog's jaws away from his face and neck. She scrambled away on her hands and knees, trying to keep her head down in the midst of the battle raging around her, and crawled toward the revolver she had dropped. She found the weapon, now covered in dust, and took it up in her hands. Anthony, with all of his enhanced strength, held the dog at bay with his left arm while he drew his knife with the right.

Before Emmogene could do anything, he plunged the blade into the dog's side, burying it to the hilt. Shadow yelped and let go, desperately trying to get away, bleeding as he went.

"Fucking animal!" Anthony snarled. Holding his left hand on his bleeding neck, he drew his pistol with his right and turned toward the wounded, whimpering dog.

"Anthony!" Emmogene screamed. She held the revolver in both hands and had it pointed at him. He froze, a look of realization appearing on his face. Emmogene fired. The gun made a loud *bang* and bucked in her hands. The bullet struck Anthony in the throat, right under his chin. He looked surprised for just a moment. He tried to say something, but blood gurgled from his mouth even as it poured from his neck. Dropping his pistol, Anthony put both hands on the wound. He took two steps toward Emmogene, faltered, and collapsed to the ground.

Emmogene stepped closer, keeping the weapon pointed down at Anthony's head. She let out another primal scream as she pulled the trigger again and again. The gun fired five more times, then clicked several times after that. She stopped, then, her arms going weak, and dropped the gun. Anthony was dead, his blood and brains oozing out of multiple holes in his skull. She couldn't pull her eyes away from the gruesome sight. Everything started to go dark again. She felt dizzy and nauseated.

She snapped back to reality when a deep, burning pain shot into her side. Instinctively covering the painful spot with a hand, Emmogene looked down to see what had happened. She lifted her hand only to find it was covered in blood. More blood poured from a hole in the side of her torso, a few inches above her hip. *Oh my God, I've been shot*, she thought, much more calmly than she had any right to be. Then she remembered Shadow. The injured dog was lying on its side, the handle of Anthony's knife still protruding from his body. He was breathing rapidly, whining, afraid and in pain. Her legs gave out and Emmogene fell to the dirt. It hurt too much to try and get back up. It hurt to breathe. It hurt to do anything, but she had to keep moving. She crawled toward Shadow, the brave dog that had saved her life, leaving a trail of blood on the ground behind her.

As the gun battle raged all around them, Shadow looked up into Emmogene's eyes. He was scared. He was dying. So was she. She collapsed next to the animal and put a hand on his side as everything faded to darkness.

"RANGERS, OPEN FIRE!"

Nathan wasn't sure who had shouted the command, but the Sagittarian Faction terrorists were already shooting at them. Taking cover behind his up-armored truck, he winced as the *Brute* fired its Ripper gun. That deafening, terrifying, mechanical, metallic roar was something you never forgot. He didn't see what had happened. He had sent Shadow to protect Emmogene then had hurried his family to cover. Ben and Stella clung to him now as a firefight erupted all around them.

He had hoped to get them in the truck so they could drive it away, but that wasn't an option now. Driving the point home, a burst from the *Brute*'s weapon tore into the rear of the truck, shredding the bed, the back wheels, and the fuel tanks all at once. Stella and Ben screamed and held their hands over their ears. "We have to move!" Nathan shouted. "Stella, look at me! You have to get the boy out of here!"

Stella's eyes were wide, but she was holding it together. "What about you?"

"I've got to get Emmogene and Shadow!" He pointed back to the west, toward the entrance of the faux–Old West town. "Take Ben and go that way. Stay low and put as much cover between you and the enemy as possible!" The wooden buildings wouldn't stop rifle bullets very well, much less the hypervelocity flechettes from the *Brute*'s weapon, but with enough wooden walls between them and the threat they'd be a lot safer.

"I want to stay with you!" Ben insisted.

"Don't argue with me, boy, you need to get to safety." Once they got down the hill and out of the line of sight, they'd be okay. He looked at Stella again. "Head back toward the old welcome center down the hill! Can you do that?" Stella nodded, jerkily, at him. He put a gloved hand on the side of her face. "Stella, I love you. Now go, go! I'll cover you!" Popping up over the hood of his truck, Nathan acquired a Faction terrorist in his sights and fired, twice for good measure. Both rounds hit the woman center of mass, and one or both of them defeated her armor. As she fell to the dirt, he desperately tried to spot Emmogene or Shadow. There! Near the big van. They were both down, and so was Anthony Krieg! He had to get to them. He'd made Emmogene a promise, and Shadow? That dog had saved his life more than once. He wasn't about to abandon his best friend, even if he was dead.

The *Brute*, moving surprisingly quickly, appeared from behind the van. Its armor, a dull gray in color, was pockmarked with impacts as the Rangers fired upon it, but nothing was getting through. Even Nathan's rifle, with its high-velocity, armor-piercing ammunition, wouldn't be able to defeat it head-on.

"Nate!" It was Jesse. He came skidding to a stop next to Nathan, huddling behind the truck's engine block with him, clutching a 6.5mm assault rifle. "Stella and Ben are down the hill. I saw you send them off so I went with them. They're clear." *Oh, thank you, Jesus,* Nathan thought. Jesse continued, "What the hell do we do now? The captain says we can't hold 'em, not with that Heavy laying down the fire like that."

"Emmogene and Shadow are still up there! I have to get to them!"

"I'm open to ideas, man!"

"We've got to take that fucking *Brute* out!" Nathan said. "Where's the guy with the fifty-cal?"

"He was up there!" Jesse said, pointing to one of the buildings. "He was up on the second floor. I think that thing fired at his position. He might be hit."

"We need that rifle," Nathan said. "Unless any of your guys have antitank weapons, it's the only thing that'll work on that *Brute*'s armor! We have to go, now! We can't give them time to regroup. They follow behind the Heavy and push into us they'll tear us up."

"Okay then," Jesse said, "Follow me!" Taking off at a run, utilizing what cover there was as best they could, Jesse led Nathan across the main street of the mock town, toward a two-story building that was supposed to represent a nineteenth-century hotel and saloon. The Rangers were, as Jesse had said, starting to fall back toward the west, away from their vehicles, as the Faction forces began to push forward. Several had been wounded and at least one was dead. Some of them would lay down suppressing fire while others would try to move the wounded. The Faction terrorists seemed to outnumber them two-to-one, and Nathan found himself wondering where in the hell Anthony Krieg had gotten this kind of manpower from.

Scrambling up onto the wooden boardwalk, Jesse and Nathan came to the front double doors of the hotel. They slammed the doors open and entered at the same time, guns up, and into the saloon. Just inside the doorway, to his left, silhouetted against the light coming in from a dust-covered window, was a man holding a gun. "Contact!" Nathan shouted, swinging his rifle over. He fired twice without even switching on his weapon-mounted flashlight. The man fell to the floor in a swirl of dust, and Nathan realized that his target was dressed like a cowboy.

"Nate!" Jesse shouted, putting a hand on his friend's shoulder. "That's one of the displays!"

"What?" He hit the thumb-pad that activated the flashlight bolted to his rifle, and sure enough, he'd put two rounds through an animatronic gunslinger. There were two exit holes in its back, surrounded by bits of broken plastic and rubber skin. "Fuck." Nathan was too amped up, too excited, too desperate to get to Emmogene and Shadow. That was sloppy. That could have easily been a friendly fire incident.

"You good, man?" Jesse asked.

"Yeah, let's go, we need that rifle." The two men went through a doorway off to the right of the bar and found the stairs. Weapons up and flashlights on, they moved quickly, but cautiously, up the steps and into the upstairs hallway. The walls were covered in graffiti and their boots crunched on bits of broken glass. At the far end was an open door, one that led to a room on the hotel's eastern side.

"He was probably in there," Jesse said. Nodding, Nathan led the way down the hall and, keeping his weapon at the ready, pushed the door open and entered the room. Everything in the room was covered in dust. On the floor by the window was a body, dressed in green fatigues. There was blood everywhere. The wall by the window, and the ceiling above and behind it, had been perforated with dozens of holes. The Ranger had been torn apart.

"Jesus Christ," Nathan said, quietly.

Jesse caught up with him a second later. "Hey man, did you—oh, shit. Oh shit." Jesse hadn't seen any combat during the war. This was probably his first time seeing what a Ripper gun could do to a man. "Jasper."

"What?"

"His name was Jasper. Older guy, went to high school with my dad."

"I'm sorry about your friend, but we need to get that rifle and get going," Nathan said.

"You're right, you're right," Jesse said. He stepped forward and, grimacing as he did so, pried the .50-caliber rifle out of the death grip of its previous owner. The rifle, a single-shot bolt-action four feet long, was stained with blood. "The scope is trashed," Jesse said. He flipped a couple of levers on the weapon's optics mount and removed the destroyed sight. "No irons." He opened the action, ejecting a single, spent case, which thumped on the wooden floor.

Nathan stepped forward and, turning the mangled corpse over, pulled a handful of .50 caliber rounds out of a pouch on his vest. He wiped the blood off on his pant leg and handed them to Jesse. "Raufoss rounds," he said. "These'll do the trick. You ready?"

Jesse took the ammunition and dropped all but one cartridge into his cargo pocket. He chambered the last round in the heavy rifle. "Yeah. Let's go kill that thing."

EMMOGENE WAS AFRAID. *She didn't know what was happening and nobody would tell her anything. She was locked in a large white room, illuminated so brightly that it almost hurt her eyes. Above her, through an observation window, she could see several figures looking down at her, watching in silence. One of them wasn't human. One of them was a Visitor, one of the Bright Ones known to her as the Counselor. In front of her was a young man from Internal Security, dressed in his black uniform. He was lean and muscular, and looked like he came from India or South Asia. He stood there, arms folded behind his back, seemingly as confused as Emmogene, and waited for someone to tell him what to do.*

A voice, a female, human voice, was broadcast over a loudspeaker. "Security Specialist Prabash," she said, "on the table next to you is a knife. Please pick it up."

"At once!" the young man said. He snapped to and, without hesitation, picked up the weapon on the table. It was a combat knife with a six-inch blade. He held the weapon in his hand and looked up at the observation window for further instructions.

"Now," the woman said, her voice cold and dispassionate, "you must kill her."

Emmogene's eyes went wide and she backed against the wall. What was happening? Why were they doing this? They told her they were doing an evaluation after performing surgery on her. Why would they go through all that just to have InSec liquidate her? What had she done wrong? How had she failed them? She had so many questions, yet she feared she would die without ever learning the answers.

The young man looked at her, then at the knife in his hand, then back at her. He hesitated for just a moment, then scowled. "At once!" he said. He tightened his grip on the weapon and started across the room toward Emmogene. In a smooth motion he roughly shoved her against the wall, brought the knife up, and moved to slit her throat with it. Emmogene screamed.

Then he stopped.

Emmogene realized that she could feel a buzzing in the back of her head, and warmth radiating outward from it. The security specialist held the knife to her throat but seemed unable to move. His eyes glazed over and, very slowly, he relaxed his grip on her, then let her go.

"What's happening to me?" Emmogene pleaded, raising her voice so that the observers might hear her. "What have I done?"

"Emmogene, you must concentrate," the woman said, her amplified voice echoing slightly in the large room. "We have given you the ability to manipulate the neurological functioning of other humans. One of its functions is to protect you, and so far, it is functioning as designed. We wanted to do a cold test to see if it would work even if you were unaware of it."

"Wh-what do I do now?"

There was no response for a few seconds. Emmogene was starting to sweat from the heat radiating through her skull. She felt feverish and dizzy. She feared that if she had to keep this up for too much longer, she would black out.

"Make him kill himself," the woman said, flatly.

"What? I don't understand?"

The next voice was that of the Counselor. There was no mistaking the pleasant, yet distinctive synthesized voice that enlightened being chose to make himself understood to humans. "Picture it in your mind, Emmogene," he said. "Picture him dying. Picture what you want him to do."

Emmogene didn't want to kill this man, but what she wanted even *less was to appear disobedient to the Visitors. Her mind raced even as the dizziness, now accompanied by nausea, got worse. He needs to die. How would he just die? Oh! He could take the knife and cut his own throat with it, she thought. That would kill him, wouldn't it?*

Security Specialist Prabash, with a surprised look on his face, raised the knife and slashed his own throat with it, almost from ear to ear. Blood poured from the hideous wound on his neck. He stumbled backward, dropped the knife, and fell down. He stayed there, unmoving, the white floor stained with an expanding pool of his blood.

Emmogene dropped to her hands and knees and vomited.

"Well done, Emmogene," the Counselor said.

Emmogene's eyes snapped open. The white room and Security Specialist Prabash were gone. She was facedown in the dirt with the morning sun beating down on the side of her head. Shadow was still with her. Despite the knife sticking out of his side, the big dog managed to raise his head to lick Emmogene's hand. Seeing that she was awake, he even gave a weak tail wag, then laid his head back down. His breathing was slower now, and ragged. All around them the sounds of battle raged. Gunfire from conventional weapons and the horrific alien weapon the *Brute* carried echoed across the Arizona desert.

Her side burned with pain, and she'd lost blood, but Emmogene was still alive. She was alive and she realized, in that moment, that she remembered *everything*.

HIS RIFLE SHOULDERED, Nathan led Jesse up a paved alley behind the row of wooden buildings. The mock western town sat in a narrow gulch between two rocky ridges. Behind the rows of buildings were access roads to allow for trash collection and maintenance, but they were just wide enough for that purpose. The whole thing was a damned fatal funnel, and that was undoubtedly why Anthony Krieg had picked it as the meeting place. Even showing up in force, there was limited room to maneuver, and a walking tank like the *Brute*, with its death-spewing flechette gun, put the Rangers at a disadvantage. Their best bet was to try to push up and flank the alien soldier while it was distracted by the Rangers.

Jesse had the huge rifle at the ready in case they got a shot at the heavy.His assault rifle was slung across the back. *At the ready* was a relative term, given that the .50-cal weighed thirty pounds and didn't have a sight. It wasn't designed to be fired while standing up and was too heavy to practically shoulder, especially if the shooter was already exhausted from the rigors of combat. They'd have to get close and they'd have to make the shots count. Nathan was on point, covering his friend as best he could.

A pair of black-clad Faction terrorists came into view, rounding the corner of one of the wooden buildings. They apparently had the same idea as Nathan, to try to push up the alley to flank the opposing force, but while they had their weapons up they didn't spot Nathan immediately. "Contact front!" he shouted, letting Jesse know to get down, while he cranked off a controlled pair at the closest of the enemy combatants. Even the .277 Fury round, with armor-piercing bullets, sometimes couldn't punch through the advanced composite armor Faction terrorists typically wore, at least not on the first shot. The man cried out in a language Nathan didn't recognize as he was struck, and stumbled to the dirt. His compatriot returned fire, forcing Nathan to dive for cover behind row of steel dumpsters.

Nathan waited for a few seconds, then popped up from behind the dumpsters with his rifle at the ready. The man he had shot was still where he had fallen and it looked like his friend had just left him there. He looked back at Jesse. "I'm gonna push up. Stay on me, and be ready—" He was cut off as the alien flechette gun roared, seemingly out of nowhere. A stream of hypersonic darts tore through the walls of the buildings like they were tissue paper. Nathan and Jesse dove for the dirt, both men desperately trying to make themselves one with the ground. The row of dumpsters offered slightly better cover from the onslaught, but only because the lightweight darts tended to destabilize, deflect, and fragment when penetrating multiple barriers.

The *Brute* didn't give them a chance to breathe. It smashed through the wooden wall of the closest building moments later, breaking 2x4s and splintering plywood as it stepped into the alley. Its armor was dented and scarred, and blue blood still oozed from the wound on the alien's side, but the biomechanical monstrosity was still very much a threat.

"Jesse, *shoot it!*" Nathan shouted. He pushed himself up off the ground and tried to bring his weapon to bear as the *Brute* kicked one of the dumpsters out of the way, giving itself room to swing its five-foot-long weapon around. There was no cover, nowhere to hide. The alien soldier had Nathan dead to rights as it brought its weapon down on him.

BOOM.

The concussion of the .50-cal firing in the alley would have been deafening, had Nathan not been wearing hearing protection. The *Brute*'s weapon exploded in a shower of sparks and debris as the armor-piercing, explosive, incendiary bullet tore through it and punched into the its chest armor plate. Nathan looked back at Jesse, who was crouched on the ground behind him. He had the stock of the oversized rifle tucked under his right arm and had fired from the hip. The *Brute* staggered for a moment but didn't fall as Jesse frantically began to reload the rifle.

Nathan got to his feet and opened fire on the alien, cranking off shot after shot, trying to hit the places where its armor had been penetrated. The *Brute* was fast, though, faster than it looked, and it swung the barrels of its weapon around again as it charged forward. It slammed the muzzles of the flechette gun into his chest with such force that, had he not been wearing an armor vest, it probably would have impaled him. It hit Nathan so hard he blacked out for a second. When he came to he was on his back on the ground, and his rifle was no longer in his hands.

The *Brute*, with an awful metallic groan, detached the disabled flechette gun from its left arm and dropped it to the ground. Jesse's bullet had punched clean through its left forearm and its weapon before striking it in the chest, and although it was wounded it was not down yet. It started toward Nathan, its armored boots clanking on the pavement, looking like it was preparing to stomp him to mush. He scrambled backward and drew his .41 Magnum. He fired again and again, striking the *Brute* in the chest- and faceplate, for all the good it did. In six shots he managed to damage the ocular lens system of the alien's helmet, but his rounds didn't have a chance of penetrating that armor, not even on the faceplate.

BOOM. The .50-cal roared again, this time so close that Nathan felt the muzzle blast on his face. This round hit home, punching through the *Brute*'s chest-plate and exploding out the back. The alien staggered for a moment, took a step back, then fell to the ground. Its armor hit the pavement with a clatter. It laid there, only feet from Nathan, slowly squirming as it bled out. Nathan gasped for air, trying to breathe, but each breath was painful.

"Nate!" It was Jesse. He'd dropped the rifle and rushed to his friend. "Holy shit, are you alright?"

"Yeah. Fuck. Help me up, will you? I think I broke a rib." Jesse did as he was asked, slinging Nathan's arm over his shoulder and hoisting him to his feet. "Gah!" Nathan cried, pain shooting throughout his body. "Easy, easy! Okay, yeah, I think I broke a few ribs." He looked over at the fallen *Brute*. "Nice shot."

"Sorry it took so long," Jesse said. "I dropped the first round I tried to load into it. Wait . . . is that thing still alive? Are you serious?"

Nathan nodded, still struggling to breathe. "Yeah, they're tough to kill. I saw one that had been ripped in half at the waist crawl for two hundred yards before it died." The *Brute* continued to writhe. It slowly reached up toward its face with its right hand. With a hiss of equalizing pressure, the creature removed its damaged armored faceplate and gasped for air. Nathan and Jesse approached cautiously. The *Brute* watched them, moving its mouth like a fish out of water, and Nathan wondered if they really didn't feel fear or pain, or if those responses were just heavily suppressed.

Jesse was less introspective. He stepped forward, drawing the big .45 Magnum automatic that he'd built, and leveled it at the dying alien's face. He fired once, then twice, turning the creature's head into pulp. The hand cannon echoed through the gulch, loud enough to be heard even over the ongoing gun battle.

Nathan put his hand on his friend's shoulder. "Nice work, man. I owe you." Jesse didn't take his eyes off the fallen alien, but slowly lowered and re-holstered his pistol. "Hey, look at me," Nathan said. "You need to go find your captain and tell him the *Brute* is down. They're still jamming the radios. I'm going to go ahead and try to get to Emmogene and Shadow."

"I'm not going to leave you like this," Jesse protested. "You're not in any shape to carry that dog to safety."

"Jesse, listen to me. Your fellow Rangers need your help. They need to know the Heavy is down so they can counterattack. I'll be fine. Anyway, I'm not going to ask you to risk your life to save my dog."

"I don't like this, man. Are you sure?"

Nathan winced with pain as he bent down to pick up his rifle. "Yeah, I'm sure," he grunted. "Get going. We've about won this thing. You boys need to regroup and mop up. I'll just be... right... over..." He trailed off as a warbling roar could be heard over the desert. It was a sound he hadn't heard since the war, and it got louder as its source drew near.

"What is that?" Jesse asked, looking up at the sky. "A jet?"

"I don't believe this," Nathan said. An alien aerospacecraft appeared over the town, its shape vaguely reminiscent of a metallic manta ray. It was in hover mode, held aloft by a cluster of downward-pointing thrusters. He looked at Jesse. "Get to your captain, tell him an alien ship is here! Go! I'm going to find Emmogene before they take her!"

"GET OFF OF ME!" Emmogene shouted, kicking and thrashing as two of the black-clad men tried to drag her to her feet. Each movement was painful, but she was so amped up from adrenaline and shock that she barely felt it. Anthony was dead and these people were still trying to take her. She didn't know how much longer she could resist before she passed out again, but she wasn't going to go without a fight. Around her, the Rangers seemed to have regrouped and were pushing back against the Sagittarian Faction forces. She had no idea where Nathan Foster was, or if the hostages had gotten to safety or not. Shadow was still holding on somehow, though his breathing had slowed and he wasn't moving much, and Emmogene didn't want to leave the courageous animal to die alone.

"We need to get her out of here!" one of the men said. His face was concealed behind a mask and sunglasses.

"What about him?" the other asked, nodding toward Anthony's body.

"We don't have time to collect the dead! We need to—" The Faction soldier was silenced as a bullet struck him in the head, splashing Emmogene's face with blood. She screamed and dropped back to the dirt, covering her ears as the surviving soldier desperately tried to return fire. He was cut down in a hail of gunfire. Bullets snapped over Emmogene's head and punched holes in the van that they'd been trying to drag her to. She got down in the dirt next to

Shadow, an arm protectively thrown over the wounded dog, and tried to stay as low as possible.

There was a new sound, then, a loud, reverberating roar, like a jet engine but different. The sound was familiar but she couldn't quite place it. She looked up in time to see the Visitor shuttle appear over the rooftops of the fake cowboy town. The craft deftly maneuvered over the gun battle, kicking up a huge cloud of dust as it went. It slid to a stop and hovered in place for a moment as bullets impacted its dull, metallic hull. Interposing itself between Emmogene and the Arizona Rangers, the craft unfolded its landing pads and descended, vertically. It disappeared in a blizzard of dust as it settled onto the ground.

"*I am here for you, Emmogene.*" The voice came from inside her head, broadcast from the device in her skull. It was the Counselor. He had arrived at last.

The Faction soldiers immediately stopped shooting as the ship touched down. A bright light appeared from the interior of the craft as it lowered a ramp that led up into its primary hull. The Rangers continued to shoot at it, but their weapons didn't seem to have much effect. Figures appeared from inside the craft. They were humanoid but did not have human proportions. *Visitors!* Actual Visitors, not their human proxies, had come to collect her. Perhaps it was a residual effect of years of deep psychological conditioning, but Emmogene felt flattered, even honored.

Those remnants of the Sagittarian Faction who hadn't fled, or been killed, watched in awe as a group of Visitors surrounded Emmogene. They weren't the enlightened Bright Ones like the Counselor, nor were they living war machines like the *Brutes*. These beings were of the utilitarian classes, the workers and soldiers that made up a majority of their civilization, but they were still held in high esteem by anyone who had been subjected to alien conditioning. Several of the beings, dressed in armor and holding weapons, provided security while another pair brought forth what looked like a gurney.

"I am a medical technician," one of the beings kneeling over Emmogene said, its synthesized voice resonating from its modulator. "You have been injured. We will transport you to safety and treat your wounds." She cried out in pain as they gently lifted her onto the gurney.

"The dog!" Emmogene said. "The you have to—" She was interrupted by a coughing fit, each convulsion causing burning pain in her chest and side. "Help the dog! He saved my life!" The two Visitor medics looked at each other as if unsure what to do. "Please!" Emmogene pleaded. The aliens said something to each other without using their voice encoders before unfolding another gurney from somewhere. As Emmogene was levitated off the ground on a magnetic field, the two alien beings gently loaded the wounded working dog onto the other gurney. If Shadow was bothered by being so close to two aliens, he didn't make it known.

"Emmogene!" A man appeared through the dust, rifle in his hands. It was the Recovery Agent, Nathan Foster. "Let her go, you bastards!"

Pain shot through Emmogene's body as she tried to sit up. He'd actually come back for her, just as he promised he would. He didn't know that the Counselor intended to take her to safety or that she wanted to go with him. He just saw several aliens trying to abduct a woman he said he'd protect. She had to intervene, to let everyone know what was happening before he killed the Visitors or they killed him. She didn't know why he hadn't fired already. He looked like he'd been hurt. "Don't shoot!" she shouted, trying to make herself heard over the roar of the craft's engine and the sporadic gunfire beyond. "Nate, please, it's okay!"

He must have heard her because he hesitated. It was only for a moment, but it was long enough for one of the security beings to level its weapon at him and shoot him right in the chest. The concussive force of the weapon knocked him back like he'd been kicked in the chest. He dropped his rifle and fell over backward, landing on top of a dead Faction soldier.

"No!" Emmogene cried, struggling to sit up. "He helped me, don't hurt him!"

The Counselor broadcast into Emmogene's head again. *"I do not understand. His badge indicates he is a Federal Recovery Agent. Is he not here to capture you?"*

"Yes, but he asked for my help!" Emmogene said aloud, looking for all the world like she was talking to herself. "Anthony had his family! He promised me he wouldn't let Anthony take me, and look! He came back to get me!"

"*So he did*," the Counselor acknowledged. "*Do not concern yourself. My security forces are using concussive disruption weapons. They incapacitate but are unlikely to kill.*"

"He was already hurt, though!" Emmogene said. "They could have killed him! The dog belongs to him, too. His dog saved me from Anthony!" Tears welled up in her eyes. She tried again to sit up on the hovering stretcher but had been restrained. "Please, don't leave him to die."

"*As you wish.*"

Unknown location
Some time later . . .

WHEN NATHAN OPENED HIS EYES, he didn't know where he was.
He was lying in bed in a brightly lit room. He sat up, wincing at the
pain in his midsection, and rubbed his eyes, trying to get them to focus
and adjust to the light. His last memory was of being shot by one of the
damned Greys, yet here he was, still alive. The sheets on his bed were
made of paper. His clothes had been replaced with something that
looked like pajamas, or maybe scrubs. They were lightweight and fit
loosely. He wasn't wearing any shoes. He still hurt, but not as badly as
he had before. Was he in a hospital? Had he been rescued? Where were
Stella and Ben? Where were Emmogene and Shadow?

Swinging his legs over the edge of the bed, he rubbed his eyes
again, blinked a few times, and looked up. He wasn't in a hospital
room, he was in a prison cell. Next to the bed was what he assumed
was a toilet. He was surrounded by three white walls and one that
looked like it was made of darkened glass. Shakily, he stood up and
made his way toward the glass wall. He cupped his hands around his
eyes and leaned up to it, trying to see through. He couldn't make
anything out through it. The material, whatever it was, was thick and
had no give to it.

Nathan was startled and stumbled back when the glassy wall
instantly turned transparent. The room on the other side was less
brightly lit, but there was light enough to see the woman standing
there watching him. "Emmogene?"

"Hello, Nate," Emmogene said. She, too, was wearing the pajama-
type clothes, except she also had shoes. She was bruised and
bandaged but was very much alive.

"What happened? Are we prisoners? Did they hurt you?"

She held up her hands as if to reassure him. "Everything is fine. Anthony is dead. I'm not a prisoner, but . . . I'm afraid you are, at least for now."

Nathan blinked a couple of times and shook his head. He was groggy and it was still difficult to think. If she wasn't a prisoner, but he was, did that mean she was still in league with the Greys? "I don't understand," he said, rubbing his temple. His head hurt. "Was this all a setup? Where are Stella and Ben? Where am I?"

"They are safe!" Emmogene said, stepping closer to the see-through cell wall. Nathan could hear her voice clearly despite the thick layer of material between them. "As far as I know, anyway. You got them to safety, remember?"

"Then what is this? What's going on?"

Before she could answer, the door behind her slid open. Nathan's eyes narrowed as a pair of Greys came in. They were grunts like the ones who had shot him, and they carried similar weapons. Behind them a third alien followed. This one looked more weathered than they did, and its head was slightly larger in proportion to its body. The two escorts posted on either side of the door as the senior Grey, a *Bright* by the look of him, approached the glass. Emmogene looked like she was going to bow to the alien, but stopped herself and simply nodded.

Nathan's blood ran cold. He was curious, to be sure, but seeing the aliens up close roused some old hatreds in him. If the *Bright* noticed his seething, however, it didn't give him any indication of it. Instead it approached Emmogene, looking up at her with its dark eyes. She wasn't a tall girl, and the top of the alien's head barely came up to her nose.

"They are waiting for you in the medical center," the Grey said to Emmogene. Its small mouth barely moved when it spoke. Its "voice" was synthesized by a linguistic translator. The alien's native speech, a rapid, warbling, mumbling sound, was barely audible.

Emmogene looked nervous. "Already?"

"Yes," the alien answered. "We sent word of your request ahead of our landing. Why do you hesitate?"

"I . . . I guess I'm scared," the woman said, looking at the floor.

"Do not be afraid, young one," the Grey said. "The procedure is safe. You will feel no pain."

"Okay," she said, sheepishly. She looked at Nathan. "What's going to happen to him?"

"He is safe as well," the alien assured her. "I wish to talk with him, nothing more." This made Nathan raise an eyebrow, but he didn't say anything. "Leave us, now."

Emmogene nodded at the alien, then turned to Nathan. "Thank you for coming back for me." Without another word, she disappeared through the automatic door. It hissed closed behind her as she left.

The Grey approached the transparent wall of Nathan's cell, looking up at him with its big, black eyes. The two armed aliens remained by the door but watched Nathan closely.

"What are you doing to her?" Nathan demanded.

The alien seemed surprised by this question, or perhaps by Nathan's demeanor. "You are concerned for her well-being."

"She was in my custody," Nathan said, trying to ignore the surreal nature of the encounter he was having. "Her safety is my responsibility."

"Yet you offered to let her go."

Emmogene must have told the alien that. What else did she tell it? "I did. Getting my family back from your fanatical worshippers was more important to me."

"Family," the alien said, as if pondering the word. "We do not reproduce in the same manner as you, but we do understand the concept of family. The base element of our civilization is what can be described as family, small groups of individuals who aged together. Amongst my kind, these group bonds, once formed, are maintained for the remainder of the individuals' lives."

Nathan wasn't interested in a lesson on alien sociology at the moment. "What are you doing to Emmogene?"

"She will not be harmed. We are doing what she asked of us: removing the implants she received."

"You mean the mind-control device in her head? You're taking it out?"

"Yes. She will not be harmed by the procedure."

"And the egg?"

The alien was quiet for a moment. It clearly hadn't expected Nathan to ask about that. "You know of this," it said, matter-of-factly. "Yes. It will be removed as well."

"Why did you go to all this trouble to get her back if you're just going to take the damned things out? Do you have any idea how many people have died because of this?" He shook his head. "I know that doesn't matter to you, but it matters to us. It matters to the families of the people who were killed."

"You misunderstand," the alien said, its synthesized voice level and calm. "Anthony Krieg was not working on my behalf. There are competing interests in this situation. I intervened as soon as I was able. I attempted to avoid harming anyone. The weapon you were incapacitated with was one designed to stun, not kill. If not for the injuries you had sustained, you would have recovered without lasting side effects. Emmogene insisted we provide you with medical attention, however. She was afraid that the effects of the concussive weapon combined with the injuries you sustained would result in your death. You have been treated for your wounds, but after examining you, we determined that you likely would have recovered even without our intervention."

Nathan rubbed his temple again. This was a lot to process and he still had a headache. "So if Anthony Krieg wasn't working for you, who was he working for?"

"You know them as the Sagittarius Faction," the alien said. "That is what their human arm calls itself. They are commanded by others of my kind, holdouts who would not accept our retreat from your planet."

The Greys had always been assumed to be a more-or-less monolithic group. There were some of their worker classes who surrendered during the war, but Nathan had never seen anything that would indicate that the aliens had internal factional conflicts. They apparently kept a tight lid on it. "Okay then . . . if you're not working with them, who are you? What do *you* want with Emmogene?"

The Grey was quiet for a few moments. It slowly blinked its big eyes as it seemingly contemplated what to say. "There is much I could say about that."

Nathan indicated the prison cell around him. "I don't know about you, but I ain't got anything better to do."

"Emmogene was brought to me as an adolescent, some thirteen solar cycles in age. She was not a willing subject. Her mother was; that human eagerly joined the interspecies society we were attempting to build, but Emmogene resented it. She resisted. My task was to gain her willing compliance through noncoercive means."

"What does that mean?"

"It is simple to gain compliance in humans by threatening them. You have a powerful survival instinct. This strategy is not successful in the long term, however. You quickly grow to resent the authority of the outsiders, even if your lives are made objectively better by their presence. Your species demonstrated this to violent effect in every part of this world that we occupied."

Nathan didn't say anything, but he felt a twinge of pride at that admission.

The alien continued. "This resulted in significant resources being expended just in maintaining control. Other solutions were sought. We initially had much success by offering your species great rewards for complying with our directives, but this, too, proved to be imperfect."

"You can only buy so much loyalty," Nathan said.

"You are correct. We had better results with the subsequent generation of humans who were raised entirely within our system, but all of our efforts were only partially successful in overcoming your natural impulses toward reproduction, pair-bonding, and out-group hostility. It was our intent to coexist with your species indefinitely. A long-term solution needed to be found."

"So you experimented on Emmogene until you were able to completely brainwash her."

Another long pause. "Yes. The conditioning regimen we devised was successful, but there was much trial and error." The alien raised a three-fingered hand and touched the scar on the side of its head. "Even adolescent human females can be dangerous if they are frightened and desperate. Despite this, our efforts with Emmogene proved very successful."

It hit Nathan then. This was the alien from the photograph, the one that Erik Landers had on his laptop. He was sure of it. Was he in Brazil, then? Best not to tip his hand on that just yet, he thought. "Is that what that thing in her head was for?"

"The device was the result of much experimentation and research. It could only influence the human brain for limited periods of time and at close proximity. It had promising tactical applications but was not sufficient for the task."

"She says it doesn't work."

"I discontinued my research before perfecting it. Implanting humans with such devices and broadcasting signals to control their behavior proved impractical, so we abandoned the project. We eventually discovered what we were looking for, the right mix of neurological modification and psychological conditioning, to gain a lifetime of willing, content subservience. Once performed, the modifications were persistent, and did not require further active measures on our part. Emmogene was my most successful subject. She did not suffer from the psychological deficiencies that our earlier conditioning efforts often produced."

"You mean like Anthony Krieg?"

"Yes. His emotional and psychological state deteriorated rapidly without frequent re-conditioning, as was the norm for humans who had been subjected to that indoctrination regimen. Some individuals would prove to be more stable, but would in turn be more prone to questioning authority. Emmogene was the solution to this conundrum. Moreover, I was able to manipulate the genetic code in her reproductive system so that her offspring would have these qualities innately."

"So Mr. Krieg was right. She really was intended to be the mother of a hybrid race."

"Anthony sincerely and deeply believed things that are not true. He was, at one point, assigned to be her mate, but this was only because they were a good genetic match with a high likelihood of producing healthy offspring. The egg Emmogene carries does not require Anthony's DNA. She can be impregnated by any fertile human male. They used his emotional fixation on her to manipulate him into accomplishing a difficult mission."

"She said he was a victim, too. I suppose she was right. Why are you telling me all this? What do you want from me?"

"As I said, we have our own concept of what you call family. I lost mine in the war, except for one. It is rare, anymore, that I get anyone new to talk to. I enjoy talking to new people."

Nathan didn't know that the Greys "enjoyed" anything. He had thought they were cold and emotionless. "I lost family in the war, too. The Red Death took my father. My sister was shot by your people for trying to get her son back. I had a lot of friends in Phoenix."

The alien slowly blinked its big eyes, as if contemplating Nathan. "I told Emmogene once that remorse is an emotion I am unused to. That is no longer the case. I have experienced little else but remorse since the war. Not all of us wanted to subjugate your species. Some tried to warn that attempting to do so would lead to unintended consequences, but it was seen as the better of two undesirable choices. The other option was to exterminate your species outright and terraform the planet."

Nathan folded his arms across his chest and stared the Grey down. "You'll have to forgive me if I don't thank you for your generosity."

"It was not generosity," the alien said, apparently oblivious to his sarcasm, "it was the choice we believed we were presented with. When we initially surveilled this planet, your species was much less numerous and was at a technological level that would have been easy for us to manage. By the time we actually arrived, however, you numbered in the billions and were capable of both spaceflight and the construction of atomic weapons."

Nathan wondered just how long these aliens had spent on their journey. "Did that surprise you?"

"Indeed. Even accounting for the chronological irregularities that result from faster-than-light travel, we did not anticipate that your species would go from developing agriculture to space travel in such a short period of time. This was very concerning, because even with our technological superiority, you were now a significant threat to us. It was believed that long-term, peaceful cohabitation with your species would be possible only if you were brought under our control. We believed that after a period of demonstrating our obvious technological and scientific superiority, those who would not submit willingly would do so out of fear. We did not fully understand your nature until it was too late. We did not have many options, however. Our journey here was long and arduous. Continuing on in search of another suitable planet was seen as too great a risk."

"Couldn't you have just, I don't know, built space stations or something? You were already living in space."

"Building space habitats suitable for the long-term preservation of our species is possible, but is both resource intensive and time consuming, and we had neither of those things in abundance when we arrived in this solar system. Adapting to living on your world was seen as the less risky option, and the survival of our species was at stake."

"Is that why they went to Mars, then?"

"Yes. I do not have any current contact with my species on the fourth planet, but I do not think they have the means to retake this world now. As we feared, your species was rapidly able to reverse-engineer much of our technology. Your space weaponry alone would make another landing difficult, if not impossible. That is why some sought to recover Emmogene and the others like her: if the genetic code in her eggs could be copied, and widely disbursed amongst the human population, their descendants would instinctively be deferential to my species."

"I don't understand. If they have the means to do this, why haven't they done it already? Why do they need Emmogene?"

"They do not have the means. I have the only remaining copies of my work. Everything else was erased. I was able to reverse most of the neural modifications I made to Emmogene's brain, and much of her psychological conditioning was lost in the memory wipe. I did not have time to have the device and the egg removed from her, though. I successfully did so on all of my other remaining test subjects, but Emmogene was taken from me before I could complete my task. As time went on and there was no sign of her, I began to hope that they would never find her. That changed when the device activated and your government became aware of her."

"Why do you care what happens to her?"

The alien was quiet, again, and blinked slowly as it seemed to decide how to answer that. "I told you that my species forms what you would consider to be familiar bonds with one another. This is . . . discouraged . . . in individuals of my status, but we are what we are. Emmogene was in my care for many solar cycles. I . . . grew fond of her. The more successful I was with her conditioning, the less there was of Emmogene. The price of gaining compliance from humans is destroying much of what makes you unique. The end result was little different from our own subordinate classes." He paused, and took what looked like a deep breath. "My superiors found that acceptable. I did not. They argued that it was better for us to be served by humans than to require members of our own species to continue to be bred for such menial tasks. Your kind is larger, stronger, and there are so many of you. You reproduce much faster than we can. Their arguments had logic to them, but I saw parallels to the decline of our own species so long ago."

"Decline of your species?"

"That is a lengthy story for another time. What is important for you to know is that there are others of my kind on Earth even now."

"You mean *Brights*, like you."

"Correct. They seek to pick up my work where I left off, to complete the project and plant the genetic seeds I designed into your species. Doing so will take considerably less time than suitably terraforming the fourth planet, and having humankind as a client species would be very beneficial to us."

"My country once had some pretty cavalier attitudes about slavery, too."

"This outcome is unacceptable to me. I have realized that I can no longer remain in seclusion, hoping my work will not be duplicated. The others, the ones behind the so-called Sagittarius Faction, they will either succeed in subjugating your species, or they will start another war in the attempt. These outcomes are also unacceptable to me. Something must be done while there is still time." The alien paused, blinked, and looked up at Nathan. "Your arrival is fortuitous. It made clear to me the best course of action."

"What do you mean? What do you want from me?"

"All will be explained to you. At this moment, though, here is something you are probably more concerned with." As the alien spoke, the door behind him slid open again. Two humans, both wearing matching coveralls, pushed in a hovering platform, like a gurney without wheels. On it was a black shape.

"Shadow!" Nathan exclaimed, pressing against the transparent wall. He looked back down at the alien, anger pulsing through him. "What did you do to him?"

"Your canine is merely sedated. It suffered a puncture wound while attacking Anthony Krieg. Emmogene insisted that we bring it with us and provide it with medical attention."

"She . . . she did that?"

"Yes. It will be placed in your cell with you so that you will be reunited when it regains consciousness. It should recover fully."

Nathan looked down and said something he never imagined he'd say to one of the aliens. "Thank you." He paused. "How long are you going to keep me here?"

"Your incarceration is temporary. I want to discuss a proposal with you."

"I'm listening."

Brazil
Deep in the Amazon Rain Forest

EMMOGENE AWOKE to the sound of Debussy's "Clair de Lune." The music was so familiar that she could almost feel her fingers on the piano keys. She'd been an avid pianist, once, and in the mind-wipe she'd forgotten it. She was still able to play the piano but had no recollection of the years of practice that had gone into it. This particular song had always been comforting to her, but she never knew why. Now it had all come back to her, every note and chord, and she knew it by heart. It was so moving that there were tears in her eyes when she opened them. She wiped her eyes and sat up.

"Gently, child," an unfamiliar voice said. It was synthesized soprano, feminine and soothing yet artificial. Emmogene was shocked at the realization that one of the Visitors was in the room with her, and it wasn't the Counselor. "You are still recovering," it said, approaching her bed. Like the Counselor, it was clad in an unadorned blue coverall. Its skin was a lighter shade, almost white, and its features were slightly softer. It took Emmogene a few moments to realize what she was looking at.

"Y-you're a female," she said, blurting the words out with less tact than she'd hoped for.

"Yes," the being said. It tilted its head sideways as it looked up at her. "You have never seen one of us before."

"No," Emmogene confessed. She'd lived for years under the United Earth Alliance and this was the first Sagittarian female she'd ever laid eyes on. She swung her legs over the edge of the bed but didn't get up. She was sitting in an undecorated but well-lit room. Surrounding her bed were monitoring instruments of both human an alien manufacture, though she wasn't connected to any of them. The walls were white, save the far wall, which was black like tinted glass.

"We are few in number," the being admitted, "no more than ten percent of our remaining population. We were kept in seclusion from our human allies, even before the war."

"Why are you here now? I mean, if you don't mind me asking, uh...how shall I address you?"

"You can call me Doctor, if you wish. I supervised your surgery. I oversaw the removal of the device from your head. There was symmetry in this; it was I who installed it."

"You did?"

"I did. I have been a colleague of the one you call the Counselor for a very long time. We collaborated on your modifications. Those modifications have now been reversed to the best of our ability. The device in your head is gone, as is the genetically modified egg you carried."

Emmogene looked at her arm. The alien tattoo, the length of script that had marked her since she was a teenager, was gone. There wasn't even a blemish from the removal like there was when human surgeons performed the procedure; it was as if it had never been there at all. The tears flowed freely then.

"Why do you weep?" the Doctor asked. "Is the music not to your liking?" The Visitors were not the emotionless monsters that they were often portrayed to be, but their emotional range was more limited than humans, muted. There was much about the human condition that they, for all of their knowledge and technology, struggled to understand.

Emmogene shook her head, slowly. "I never thought this would happen," she said, wiping away the tears. "All of my memories, everything I knew but had forgotten, it's all back. I'm not in prison anymore, I'm not living in fear of Anthony, I'm not..." She trailed off. It was not without cost, however. The Counselor had explained to her that with the removal of the modified egg she would be left infertile. She'd never be able to have children, now. There was an odd sense of loss that came with that realization. She never thought she'd actually get the chance, but now that she knew she couldn't, it was sad. Sad, and yet, she felt as if a burden had been lifted off her shoulders. It seemed that her ordeal was over. She almost didn't want to believe it. There was an irrational fear that it was all a dream, that she would wake up and find herself back in the Gallup Federal Detention Facility—or worse, locked in a room by Anthony.

"The procedure was a success," the Doctor continued, apparently oblivious to Emmogene's emotional roller coaster. "Aside from the reproductive issues you were informed of previously, there should be no long-term side effects. You seem to be recovering your memories at a better-than-average rate."

"I remember almost everything," Emmogene said. "Every time the device would activate, it seemed like I'd gain back a little more. This last time? Everything came flooding back all at once."

"The Counselor postulated that this might be the case. He was pleased to learn that you have recovered your memory, and even more pleased to be proven correct."

"Where is he now? The Counselor, I mean, if you don't mind me asking."

"He is preparing. He has decided upon a new course of action, and there is much to do before we proceed."

That was so vague as to be completely unhelpful, so Emmogene changed the subject. "Where's Nathan Foster? Is he okay?"

"You refer to the human that you insisted we bring with you. He is recovering from his injuries, as is his animal companion. They are incarcerated together, as a precaution, but they are both well."

"What's going to happen to them now?"

"They will be returned to the United States when the situation allows. For the time being, they will remain here with us."

"I see. What . . . what about me?"

"That is up to you, child," the Doctor said. She modulated the tone and inflection of her artificial voice so as to sound even more comforting. "You are not our prisoner. You may return with him, if you wish, or you can be taken to the Free Territories in Africa. That is where most of our former human companions live."

"Can . . . can I not stay here with you?" It was awkward even to ask, but she didn't know anybody in Africa, and as far as she knew, she was still a wanted fugitive in the United States. "I would like to go home but I don't know if I can."

The Doctor tilted her head and, much to Emmogene's shock, put a three-fingered hand on her knee. "We will not be staying here much longer. It has been decided."

"What do you mean?"

Before the alien could answer, the door to the room slid open. The Counselor made his way in, alone this time, with no guards to protect him. Emmogene had once considered it a great honor to be trusted enough to be alone with the Bright Ones. Few of their human servants were ever allowed to. For all of their incredible technological prowess and ancient wisdom, their bodies were small, almost like children. An adult human would have little trouble killing one with his bare hands.

The Counselor stopped in front of the wall that looked like smoked glass. He waved his hand and, to Emmogene's surprise, the darkness was lifted. Daylight filtered into the room as the window shifted to transparency. Beyond it lay a luscious green jungle, with trees so thick their canopies obscured the sky. There was a gap in the cover of the foliage where a river flowed through the rain forest. The alien stood in front of the window, looking out at the natural beauty beyond, and lowered his head slightly. "Join me, Emmogene," he said, his voice modulating calmly. He looked tired.

The Doctor stepped back as Emmogene cautiously stood up. The smooth white floor was cool on her bare feet, but not cold, and looked clean enough to eat off of. She walked across the room and joined him by the window, followed closely by the Doctor. "It's beautiful here," she said, gazing at the idyllic scene before her.

"Your world is beautiful," the Counselor agreed, his voice modulating downward a bit. "We do not share your sense of aesthetics, but even we appreciate the splendor of this planet. We journeyed across millions of light-years looking for a new home, trying to put enough time and space between us and our past that we might finally be safe. Never in our history had any traveled so far. There were some who thought it was impossible, that we were doomed, but we persevered. The fate of our race depended on it. When we discovered the Earth, we could not believe our good fortune. It brought to mind the ancient myths of our nearly forgotten past, of the primordial paradise that our ancestors believed life originated in."

"Like the Garden of Eden," Emmogene said.

"Your species has similar myths regarding your origin. We set those aside long ago, yet seeing such a world moved even us. Our homeworld was once like this, in places, according to our oldest records."

"What happened to it?"

"Progress. As we advanced, we abandoned sentimentality. Our world was merely a collection of resources to be exploited, and we exploited it. We remade it in our own image, time and time again, as our civilization advanced. We modified our own species, our own people, so that they might be more efficient components of the Great Machine. We, too, became nothing but a resource to be exploited. Everything that was not seen as advancing our civilization was cast aside and forgotten. Those who would not fall into place were coerced, exiled, or eliminated."

"You said before, in the dream, that there was an outside threat. What happened? Can you tell me?"

"We discovered an intelligence unlike anything we had previously encountered. It offered us great knowledge and great prosperity. We listened to its counsel and indeed we prospered. It guided our hand as we ordered our society, as we began to bind ourselves to the Great Machine. As we flourished and multiplied the Machine grew to encompass every aspect of our civilization. Every being was connected, every mind, biological and artificial alike, helped it grow. It fed us and we became more and more dependent upon it."

"Was this Great Machine like an artificial intelligence?"

"No. It was...is...a predator. We were its food. It cultivated us for ages and, when it was ready, it...*harvested* us. We were consumed from the inside. We succumbed without a fight and our civilization died."

"But not all of you," Emmogene said.

"No. This process took many lifetimes; this intelligence has infinite patience. Over time, those of us who rejected the Machine set out into space, hoping to find a home to rebuild our civilization. In every instance, the predator found us, and the cycle would begin anew. Under its malevolent influence we had genetically engineered away our ability to resist its call. Every time it found us, we would succumb. Those few who had the ability to resist were outnumbered by those who had been indoctrinated. Our only choice was to keep running, to travel so far and for so long that it would never again find us."

"Is that how you ended up on Earth?"

"It is. As far as we know, we are all that is left of our kind. Our homeworld, and every world we have set foot upon, has been consumed. Nothing survives the harvest. This is why we were so desperate, so willing to undertake extraordinary measures. We were barely holding onto survival when we arrived." He looked up at Emmogene. "Had the situation been reversed, you would have done the same."

Emmogene wanted to tell him that wasn't true, but she knew better. "What will become of your people now?"

"That remains to be seen. I do not know if the attempt to terraform the fourth planet will be successful. I do know that the odds of my species surviving only go down if we provoke a second war with yours. Should conflict begin again, it will end with one of our two species extinct. This cannot be allowed to happen. We cannot do to you what was done to us."

"The Doctor said you have come to a decision," Emmogene said, indicating the female alien next to her.

"Yes," the Counselor acknowledged. "I have spoken at length with Nathan Foster about this, and I believe I have devised a course of action that may lead to the best outcome."

"I am concerned," the Doctor said, the unease translating into the pitch of her synthetic voice. "There is much that we cannot foresee and a significant probability of failure."

"I am concerned as well," the Counselor replied, "but I cannot think of a better alternative."

"Nor can I," confessed the Doctor.

"What is this course of action?" Emmogene asked, exasperated at how the Visitors were talking past her. "Can you fill me in?"

The Counselor turned to Emmogene again and looked up into her eyes. "I will surrender myself to Nathan Foster. He will take me to your leaders. I will request asylum, *defect*, as you call it, and offer them my knowledge in exchange for my safety."

"And I will go with you," the Doctor said.

"This doubles our risk," the Counselor admonished. "My safety is not guaranteed."

"I am less concerned for my safety than I am with being separated again," the Doctor said. "You and I are all that is left of our Derivation. Where once there were twelve, now there are only two. Wherever you go, I will follow, irrespective of the consequences."

Emmogene was moved by their dogged loyalty to one another. It was sweet, in a surreal way. She wasn't convinced that their plan would end well for them, though. "Are you sure about this? They might just dissect you."

"I will provide them with detailed anatomical information if they require it," the Doctor said. "There should be no need for dissection."

"We represent an invaluable resource to your government, Emmogene," the Counselor said. "They have little to gain by harming us and much to gain from listening to our counsel."

"What counsel will you be offering them?"

"We will give them the information they need to eliminate the Sagittarius Faction and those beings who are controlling it. We will give them valuable intelligence and access to technologies that they have been unable to reverse-engineer. This will serve as a deterrent for my people on the fourth planet, and war will be avoided. When I chose to stay behind, I warned my peers that I would do this if they made it necessary. As before, they did not listen to me when they should have."

"Aren't you afraid the humans will take what you give them and go attack Mars?" Emmogene asked.

"That is a possibility," the Counselor. "To mitigate this we will also be informing our brethren on the fourth planet of what is transpiring, so that they may be prepared. My goal is to establish communication between our civilizations. Communication and cooperation is the only way we can coexist in one solar system together. If your species learns our history, perhaps you can learn *from* it. You are the only human to have ever been told the story of our fall, of being exiled from our own galaxy."

"We're not too good at learning from our own history, to be honest."

"It is still worth attempting."

"I just don't know if people will be ready for this. There's still a lot of bad blood from the war. Believe me, I've seen it firsthand."

"That is true, but the malevolent intelligence is still out there, somewhere in the universe. It may yet find us, given enough time. My species cannot resist it alone. If your species is not prepared, you will succumb just as we did. Our best hope of long-term survival lies in cooperation, not hostility. Reconciliation may not come quickly, but it will not come at all if we do not begin the process."

It was enough to make Emmogene's head spin. "Oh my gosh. What did Nate Foster say about all this?"

"He is eager to return to his family," the Counselor replied, "and expects substantial compensation for bringing us to his government. He is with us."

"I suppose he would be."

"The question remains, what will you do?" the Doctor asked. "As I indicated previously, we will be leaving here. You can come with us or we can bring you to the Free Territories."

"I would like to go with you," Emmogene said. She didn't even need to think it over—her heart told her it was the right thing to do. "Perhaps I can serve as a liaison."

"Are you sure?" the Counselor asked. "They still think of you as a criminal, do they not?"

"Maybe, but maybe I can get that overturned if you tell them what you told me about my own indoctrination. Besides, I'm tired of running and hiding. I just want to go home. Whatever happens, at least it was my decision."

"So be it," the Counselor said.

Prescott Regional Airport
Prescott, Arizona
A few days later...

NATHAN FOSTER LOOKED NERVOUS, Emmogene thought, as the Visitors' shuttle craft touched down. He was doing his best to project confidence, but she'd come to learn that he highly distrusted the government he worked for, and was worried that he would somehow end up in prison or dead for what he had done.

In any case, the Recovery Agent had, with the help of the Counselor and the Doctor, taken some precautions to ensure things worked out for them. Specifically, he didn't notify the government that he was bringing the aliens, or their ship, in. The Counselor had assured him that his shuttle was equipped with their most cutting-edge active stealth systems, whatever that meant, and would not be detected until they were about to land. This was good, as it ensured they'd be able to get where they wanted to go without the risk of being shot down by the Air Force.

Of all the places in the world he could have gone, Nate had suggested they return to his hometown of Prescott, Arizona. He'd been able to contact his partner and his nephew, who had been ecstatic to learn he was alive and healthy, and made some arrangements. Their arrival, he said, would be very public, and he reasoned that this was the best defense against the government trying to do anything untoward.

"This is it," the bounty hunter said, standing up as the shuttle settled onto its landing pads. He was wearing his tactical gear again. A holstered revolver hung from his hip and a rifle was slung across his back. His bronze badge was stuck to the left breast of his body armor. "You ready, Emmogene?"

Emmogene's stomach was full of butterflies. She was so nervous that she feared she might throw up. "I'm ready," she insisted, trying to project confidence. Her safety was not guaranteed. She had no way of knowing if anyone would listen to her stories of being manipulated and coerced by the Visitors, or if they'd just throw her right back into prison. It was worth the risk, however. She was tired of being at the mercy of other people's whims, of being fought over and sought after like a prize.

"Whatever happens out there," he said, "thank you for helping get my family back, and for getting them to save Shadow." The dog was at his side on a short lead, nervously panting. Travel in a hypersonic shuttle seemed to disagree with him.

"Thank you for coming back for me," she told Nathan. She knelt down in front of Shadow and scratched him behind his ears. "And thank you for saving my life." The dog wagged his tail and licked her on the face. The wagging stopped and he went into alert mode, bristling slightly but remaining still. The Visitors had come down to the cargo deck. Shadow had learned to tolerate the aliens but remained uneasy around them.

"I hope this works out for all of us," the Recovery Agent said, nodding at the aliens as they approached. "I did everything I could."

"What exactly did you do?" Emmogene asked.

"I told Stella to notify Homeland Security that I was arriving by air with suspected captured exo-tech in my possession. That should have gotten them to send a recovery team, but they won't be expecting anything like this. She also said she was going to call Jesse and ask the Arizona Rangers to deploy to pull security." He grinned. "I told her to call the *Daily Courier*, which is the city paper, and the local TV news station, too. Promised them the story of the decade. We should make quite a scene. Our best bet for getting clear of this is to make it as public as possible, I reckon."

"Your reasoning is sound," the Counselor said. "It is my hope that you are correct."

"Mine too. If everything you said is true... maybe it's time to try and put the past behind us. I don't know if it'll work. A lot of people hate you and would like nothing more for you to be wiped out."

"There were similar calls to eliminate your species from my peers," the Counselor said. "The biological weapon you call the Red

Death was a test run. Nonetheless, it is my hope that all of us can learn to coexist."

"That's my hope, too," Nate said. He then stuck a hand out to the Counselor. The alien reached up with his own hand and shook the Recovery Agent's. Nate then produced two pairs of handcuffs. They had discussed this ahead of time. It was for show, to demonstrate that he was in control of the situation, to reduce the likelihood of panic upon their arrival. Very gently he placed the handcuffs on the Counselor's and the Doctor's wrists. He turned around, facing the ramp, which was still closed, and reined Shadow in. "Look sharp, everybody, we're about to be on TV."

Emmogene stood behind them and took a deep breath. With a muffled mechanical *whirr*, the ramp on the front of the craft slowly began to open and lower itself down to the tarmac. Sunlight and warm desert air poured into the darkened craft. Squinting in the bright light, Emmogene followed the group as they made their way down the ramp and into the open.

We're making history, she thought idly, looking at the scene around her. The shuttle had landed in a parking area reserved for the Civil Air Patrol's propeller planes. A crowd had formed around the ship, held at bay by a cordon of Arizona Rangers and police. Dumbfounded locals watched in awe as Nathan Foster and his dog led two handcuffed aliens down the ramp from their ship. A TV news crew had pushed as close to the craft as the police would allow them to get. A reporter shouted questions at Nathan and the Visitors as they stepped onto the tarmac.

Nathan raised his voice so that he could be heard over the crowd. "I'm a Federal Recovery Agent on official business!" he shouted. "These two extraterrestrials surrendered to me and are in my custody. I'm here to turn them over to Homeland Security."

To Emmogene's surprise, the TV reporter, a pretty woman in stylish yellow dress, shouted her questions directly at the Counselor and the Doctor. "Why have you surrendered? What is it you want?"

The Counselor, himself squinting in the bright sunlight, increased the volume of his voice modulator so that he might be heard. "We come in peace," he said. "We have surrendered to this Recovery Agent and request political asylum in the United States." Nathan had told him to say that.

Emmogene noticed a group of people pushing their way through the crowd. As they got to the cordon the police let them through. She teared up as Stella and Ben ran across the tarmac and wrapped their arms around Nathan. He kissed her and hugged his family. Behind them a bewildered-looking team from the Department of Homeland Security looked at the aliens, looked at the ship, looked at the crowd, then looked at Emmogene. She smiled. This surely was going to create some headaches for them.

Prescott, Arizona
26 days later . . .

IT WAS A LOVELY SUMMER EVENING in Prescott, Nathan thought, as he looked over the city from the roof of his office. They'd set up a table with an umbrella and some lawn chairs up there, along with a grill. Shadow was lying nearby, happily tearing apart a big rawhide he had propped up in between his front paws. There were steaks on the grill, a cooler full of ice-cold beer and soda, and the weather was about perfect. After the mind-boggling whirlwind of the last month, it was nice to enjoy some peace and quiet and normalcy.

As he'd intended, his arrival at the local airport had made quite a splash. It was the number one story in the news, as a matter of fact, and Nathan was now world famous. This had made some folks in the government very unhappy. They held him for over three weeks for quarantine and debriefing, and they'd threatened him with prison and worse. In the end, though, his gambit had paid off. A veteran of the war, serving as a Recovery Agent, managed to bring in two alien *Brights* and an advanced exo-tech spacecraft. He was a popular celebrity now and that bought him a form of insurance. Besides that, he hadn't done anything wrong, not really. Oh sure, he may have bent the rules here and there, but in the end, he brought the government two alien defectors and their ship. It had been a win-win for everybody.

Emmogene Anderson had been taken into custody, too, but Nathan told the media that she had been integral to the operation. Much to his chagrin, Homeland Security had belligerently refused to pay him for either Emmogene or for Anthony Krieg, citing some legal loophole that they claimed nullified the contract. Stella had wanted to take them to court over it, but he didn't think it was worth the trouble, especially considering the very substantial bounty he'd gotten for bringing in not one but *two* Sagittarian *Brights* and their ship.

His days as a Recovery Agent were done, though. Homeland Security, mostly out of spite, had suspended his badge while they sorted through everything that had happened regarding Emmogene Anderson, the aliens, Anthony Krieg, and the incident in Chandler. Even if not for that, he wouldn't be able to continue the work. The entire country knew who he was, now, and where he lived. Krieg and his terrorists had managed to get to his office and take his family hostage once, and even though Krieg was dead, the Sagittarian Faction was still out there. Word was they had a standing kill order on Nathan, Stella, and Ben, and US Marshals had been deployed to protect them. Stella was looking into selling their office, contact list, and assets. It seemed like the only real option they had was to take the money and retire somewhere.

That was okay with him. Between the war, seven years as a Recovery Agent, and the events of the past year, retiring to a quiet life was appealing. He'd gotten offers from a few different publishers to write his memoirs, and that might prove to be pretty profitable, too. Ben was getting scholarship offers from colleges, and Stella was being approached by the intelligence community for information and analysis. Basically, if they were smart, they could be set for life.

Nathan pulled a beer out of the cooler, popped off the bottlecap, and took a swig. Looking back out over the town, he thought about the day he lost his tank crew. Since the war ended, he'd undertaken about the most dangerous profession he could, tempting fate with another chance to kill him. Somehow he'd survived it all, and that used to bother him. Not so much anymore, he realized. He'd made the most of the time he had, and had tried to never take life for granted. Hell, maybe he'd actually accomplished something that would make the world a better place. Time would tell.

"This one's for you, fellas," he said, saluting the setting sun with his beer. He took a long drink, thinking of the good times and bad he'd had with his comrades, and hoped he'd done right by them.

"Hey you." He turned around to see Stella. She'd come up to join him on the roof. She was dressed casually, in a blouse and jeans, but

Nathan thought she looked beautiful. "Ben said dinner was almost ready."

"Yeah. Medium rare, just the way you like it. The potatoes should be cooked, too."

"Perfect. Where's Ben?"

"Oh, I sent him downstairs to grab something. He should be back up in a minute."

"Oh, okay." Stella gave Nathan a quick kiss, then reached into the cooler and grabbed herself a beer. "I heard a rumor today."

"Really? About what?"

"The aliens you brought home, the Counselor and the Doctor." They'd been sequestered at some secret government facility, and Nathan had no idea what would become of them. "Word is, what they're saying is making some waves."

"You think anything will come of it?"

"It's too early to tell. Some people won't want to believe anything they're saying. They will claim it's all an elaborate trick."

"It didn't seem like a trick to me."

"Me either, but I can't blame people for being paranoid. Even still . . . what if we were able to cooperate with them instead of this interplanetary cold war we've got going on now?"

"Seems like that's what they promised when they first arrived. We all know how that worked out."

"You're right, but now we're on different planets, and from what they told you, that's the way it will stay. Good fences make good neighbors, as they say. I'm just glad they are at least willing to listen. A few years ago, that wouldn't have happened."

"You're not wrong," Nathan agreed. "Say, you hear from Emmogene?"

"I got a message from her this afternoon, as a matter of fact. Some pretty powerful law firms offered to take up her case, so she's got good legal representation now. According to her lawyer, they have a good chance to get her conviction overturned based on new evidence. She might not be the only one, either, now that we're learning more about the psychological conditioning methods the aliens used."

"I hope it works out for her. She's a good kid."

"My gut tells me she'll be fine. She said that she's already getting approached by book publishers. Once she gets clear of this she might do alright for herself." Stella sipped her beer. "You know, I was thinking about what the aliens told you—you know, about their history?"

"Yeah?"

"I wonder what exactly it was that destroyed their civilization."

"I wonder, too. They were so vague about everything that I couldn't make heads or tails of it. Whatever it was, it convinced them to just give up and die somehow, their whole damn race."

Stella looked up at the darkening sky. "You think it's still out there, somewhere?"

Nathan put an arm around her. "Maybe. The universe is a big place."

"Can you imagine if they give us their faster-than-light technology? We might see, in our lifetimes, people setting out for the stars."

"You know, it might be nice if, after the war, the death, the destruction, and all this suffering, something good came of all of it. Maybe in a hundred years we'll be living on other planets instead of struggling to rebuild here on Earth."

"Uncle Nate!" It was Ben. Nathan let go of Stella and turned around to face his nephew, who had just come up the stairs onto the roof. "I got that thing you sent me to get."

"About time, boy," Nathan said, taking a small box from Ben's hand.

"What did you have him get?" Stella asked. "I could have brought it up."

"I think that might have ruined it," Nathan said, holding the box in his hand.

"What?"

Nathan dropped to one knee, held the box out in his hands, and opened it. Inside was a diamond ring. "Stella, will you marry me?"

Stella's eyes opened wide. Her mouth fell open and she reflexively covered it with her hand. She looked at the ring, then at Nathan, then over at Ben, then back at the ring. Setting her beer down, she gently lifted it out of the box and slid it onto her finger. "Yes!" she said, looking back down at Nathan.

Standing up, Nathan took Stella in his arms and kissed her, deeply.

After a long moment, he pulled away, and she wrapped his arms around him and squeezed.

"I didn't think you were ready for this," she said with a sniffle.

"I wasn't ready for anything that happened in the last few months, but we got through it together. I can't think of anyone I'd rather spend the rest of my life with."

"I love you, Nathan Foster." She squeezed him even tighter.

"I love you, too, Stella."

Ben piped up. "You guys?"

"Good job, Ben," Nathan said. "The boy was in on it from the start," he told Stella. "He borrowed that sapphire ring you wear sometimes to get your size after you left it at our house."

"Clever boys," Stella said, smiling ear to ear.

"Guys?" Ben said again.

"What is it, Ben?" Stella asked, still smiling.

"Can we eat now?"